I0577432

Lucky Girl

KIMBERLY WENZLER

BY
KIMBERLY WENZLER

Both Sides of Love

Letting Go
Love Story for Sammy

The Fabric of Us

Seasons Out of Time

Lucky Girl
Shelf-Life of a Single Woman

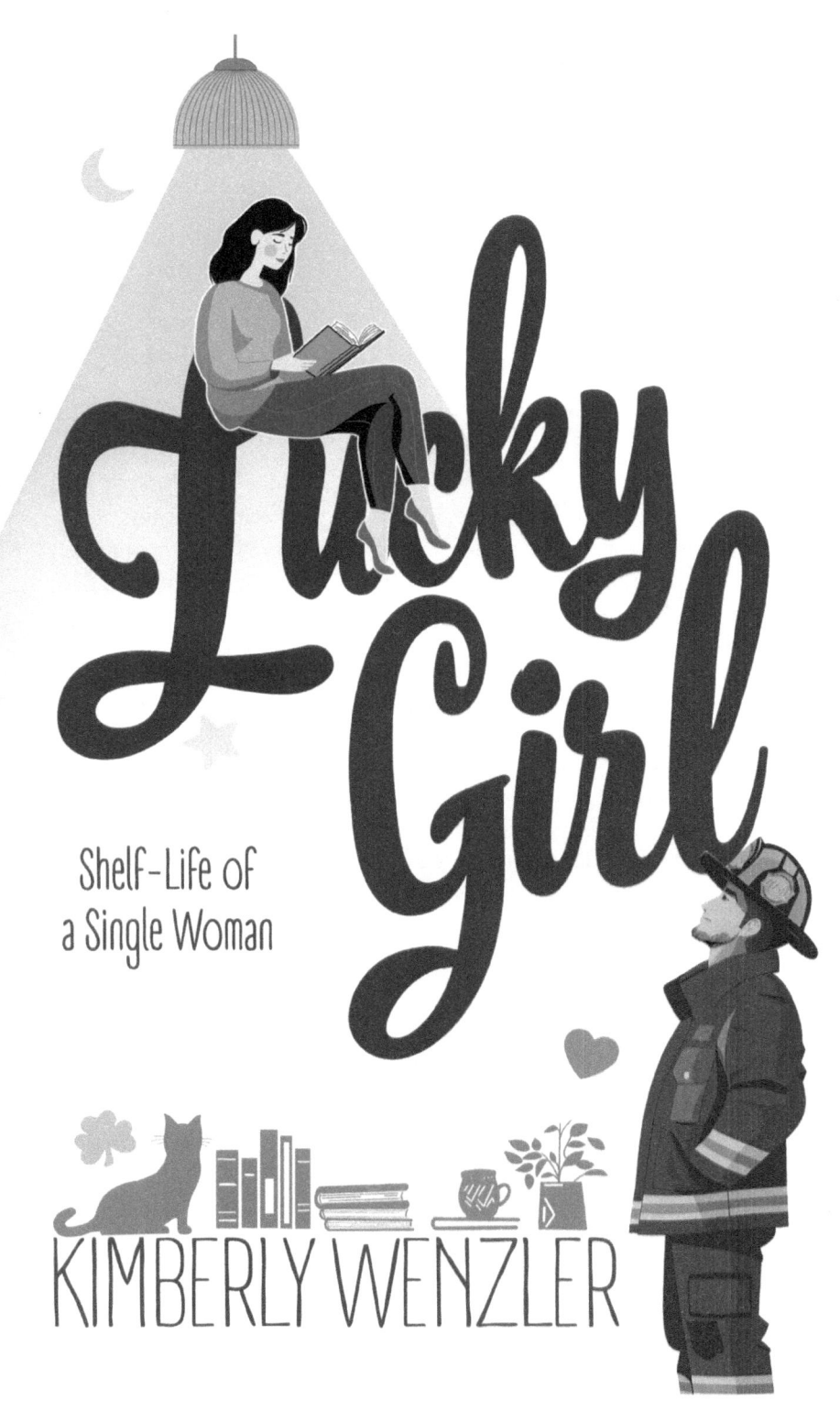

Lucky Girl

Shelf-Life of a Single Woman

KIMBERLY WENZLER

LUCKY GIRL, *Shelf-life of a Single Woman*
by Kimberly Wenzler

Copyright © 2025 by Kimberly Wenzler
All rights reserved.

First Edition Sept 2025
ISBN 979-8-9930448-0-4 (pbk)
ISBN 979-8-9930448-1-1 (epub)

No part of this book may be reproduced in any form or by any electronic or mechanical means, including information storage and retrieval system, without permission in writing from the author except in the case of brief quotations embodied in critical articles and reviews.

This is a work of fiction. The events and characters described herein are imaginary and not intended to refer to specific places or living persons. The opinions expressed in this manuscript are solely the opinions of the author.

Cover image © 2025 Kimberly Wenzler
Book formatting, Cover design by Suzanne Fyhrie Parrott
Cover illustration, "Lucky Girl" by Suzanne Parrott

Seaplace Publishing
Northport, New York

For Rico Suave Salsa–

the Titan of Tango,
the Sultan of Swing,
the Master of Merengue,
and the Wizard of the Waltz—

who taught me to dance,
and so much more.

CHAPTER 1

The wind whipped my scarf, making me feel and probably look like Amelia Earhart crossing the Atlantic solo in a twin-propeller airplane, instead of what I was doing, which was crossing a market parking lot. Solo.

The rising sun did little to combat the January chill in my bones, so when my cell phone buzzed a text alert from somewhere in the depths of my coat pocket, I ignored it, not wanting to expose my fingers to the air. It was my sister, Charlie. She was the one who texted me the most. My mother still held firm against modern technology.

The heat of Union Market wrapped me in a welcome hug as I wrangled a basket from its pile and headed to Produce. Smokey Robinson sang "The Tracks of My Tears" through the speakers from a retro seventies station as I passed the expensive Honeycrisp apples and stopped at the Macintosh bin, which were fifty percent off today. I leaned over, occasionally swiping my scarf out of the way, checking the calyx at the base of each apple. If the star-shaped end was closed, it was fresh; open, and I tossed it back, a secret I'd learned during an apple-picking outing long ago. I chose four, lifted my head to see what the navel oranges cost this week, and saw a young couple with their noses pressed together, moving them back and forth while they laughed softly. My sister and I used to call it Eskimo kissing when we were young.

I returned to my task, working to ignore them, and settled on one more apple.

The same couple was in the cereal aisle ten minutes later when I reached for my Lucky Charms. This time, he nuzzled her neck, and she pretended to push him away with one hand while clutching his open coat with the other, and I cringed at this public display.

Yes, yes. I see you're in love. You're happy. Good for you.

I tossed my Lucky Charms in my basket and strode onward.

My phone rang in the dairy aisle. Right. My missed text earlier from my sister.

"Stella," Charlie said above the sound of her husband's voice in the background. "Lance will drop the kids by you at one."

"No problem." I nudged the cell phone between my neck and shoulder so I could grab a carton of milk. "I'm at the market. What should I pick up for them?"

"Hold on. Myles, no! Take that out of your nose. Okay, I'm with you. Nothing. I packed them lunch."

In the bakery section, I put cookies and donuts in my basket.

"Please don't buy them snacks. Don't let your embedded teenage junk food habits leak onto them. Promise me."

It was uncanny how well my sister knew me. I put the cookies back but kept the donuts. Aren't aunts supposed to spoil their siblings' children? If we'd had one growing up, I'm sure she would have snuck us donuts.

"Thank you for taking them today," Charlie said.

"My pleasure. What are you going to do with your spare time?"

"I have big plans."

"Laundry?" I said.

"And vacuuming. I'm taking down the Christmas tree."

I laughed. "Come on. Do something for yourself."

"This *is* for me." She said as her husband mumbled something incoherent in the background. "Not now, Lance."

"What's he saying?"

She hesitated. "He wants me to tell you about a new guy who started at his company. He's good-looking and single—"

"Not interested."

"That's what I told him you'd say."

"Thank you."

"But you should still consider dating," my sister said. "He seems great."

"Charlotte—" I groaned, then stopped short in the bread aisle when I spotted the canoodling couple and retraced my steps back to the bakery section.

"His name is Lucas," she went on. "He's a little older than you, thirty-nine, never been married, and has a good job."

"Are you finished?"

"Yes."

"No, thank you."

"Stop being so stubborn. Take a chance."

"I'm not stubborn, Charlie. I'm guarded." I pinched the bridge of my nose. "I'm guarded against life."

My sister paused. "No, you're guarded against men. You have to try to get over it."

"I love you, but no. See you later."

I dropped my cell in my pocket and looked up at the baked beans, positioned on the top shelf in the canned vegetable aisle. I glanced left and right. An elderly gentleman passed the aisle, leaning heavily over his cart. When he was out of sight, I put my basket down, stepped on the bottom shelf, hoisted myself in a semi-jump, and swatted a can. I smiled triumphantly when I'd managed to catch it but yelped when another unexpectedly tumbled after it.

Hitting me smack in my right eye.

Stunned, I pressed a hand to my socket, knelt to absorb the pain, as if lowering myself toward the ground might somehow help me—it didn't—and took a few breaths.

"Only you, Stella," I mumbled, and wiped a rogue tear. Trying not to outwardly grimace, I grabbed a bag of frozen peas from a freezer in the next aisle and pressed it against my face until the pain died down to a dull throb.

The honeymooners were on one of two open checkout lanes, unloading their basket between kisses, so I moved to Rhonda's lane. I normally avoided her register because Rhonda was very judgy, always eyeing me as she rang up my simple food selections every week. At the other register, the couple bagged their capers, steak, artisan bread, and specialty cheeses.

I knew what she was thinking: This poor woman, always alone.

Today, she weighed my apples on the scale, eyes shifting to me quickly, then scanned my five frozen dinners (Lean Cuisine was on sale this week. Score!), same eye shift, and rang up my donuts, milk, cereal, and boxes of macaroni and cheese (Kraft—somehow that powdered cheese tasted so good). Last, she added my cans of baked beans and the thawed peas into my bag.

"You alright?" Rhonda said. "Looks painful."

"Oh, this? I can hardly feel it." My eye socket had a heart-beat of its own at this point, but I was too embarrassed to admit it.

The couple passed us, holding their bags, and he held her hand in his and kissed it as they walked out.

Rhonda smiled. "Adorable, right?"

"Oh my God, so cute!" I nodded.

Paid, I shouldered my full recyclable shopping bag and made the short voyage across the parking lot, wondering what Doug might be doing at this very minute while I walked home with a throbbing black eye and food for one. According to his last Facebook post, my ex-fiancé was at a Rangers game last night with his boyz. That's how he spelled it, with a "z" like he was twenty-three and not on a freight train hurtling toward forty.

The market in question sat in Cobble Hill, Brooklyn, a ten-minute walk from my apartment. I lived in a tiny part of the borough no one knew about, nestled between Cobble Hill and Brooklyn Heights, called Harbor Crest. It's a hidden jewel with no post office, no fire department, no large supermarket, and no library. We borrowed those from the surrounding neighborhoods.

My breath came in short gasps as I reached the last step

to the third floor of my walk-up. Maybe I should eat less mac and cheese. Holding my grocery bag in one hand, I searched my crossbody purse for my key and stepped over the envelope on my foyer floor, likely slipped under the door in my absence.

I left the groceries parked on the counter as I filled a dish-towel with ice cubes and sat down at my half-table propped against the wall, in a kitchen the size of a closet, and pressed the pack against my aching face. I kicked off my low boots, twitching when I noticed a rip in the faux fur along the top edge of one. I scrolled through Facebook to see what was happening.

There was a new post.

It was a selfie of my ex, trying to be contemplative, though I knew he wasn't considering life's big query. He sat on a large boulder somewhere and stared ahead, not quite into the camera, but to the left, as if he were Thoreau questioning his existence instead of what he was probably thinking, which was, *Do these biking shorts make my junk look big?*

Below the picture was a quote: *"It is in your moments of decision that destiny is shaped." Tony Robbins.*

You've got to be kidding me. This is from the guy who backed out of our wedding as I rode in the limo to the church. In my twelve-thousand-dollar wedding dress.

I typed a comment. *"Better three hours too soon than a min-ute too late." William Shakespeare.* I stared at it long enough that my good eye started to blur and finally, deleted it, shut the app, and dropped the phone.

Ten a.m. Three hours until I saw my two favorite tiny peo-ple in the world. After taking extra-strength pain medicine and trying but failing to relax on the couch with my current book, I texted my sister and asked her to have Lance drop the kids off at my shop. I put my boots on and walked out.

My commute to work took twelve minutes by foot in sneakers, twice as long when I wore my low-heeled boots, and forever when I wore two-inch heels, which I did once and never again (shin splints for days). I had a car, but it was easier to walk than fight for a parking spot and as a result, I lost fifteen pounds in the past year that I've kept off with the exercise, despite my juvenile palate.

Between the Covers, my bookshop, was on Gruber Ave., tucked between a high-end boutique and an upscale hair salon. As I passed the boutique, The Closet, with clientele that I'd hoped would start to spill into Between the Covers, I looked up to see the well-dressed forty-something shop owner waving me in.

"Hello, Jeffrey. Happy New Year."

Jeffrey had walked into my shop early on to welcome me to the neighborhood and went out of his way to be kind, always asking how business was doing. I longed for the day he wouldn't have to ask, or that I'd have a different answer. The first half of the year, business was tough—mostly in the red, but the past few months showed improvement. I was *almost* there, barring some unforeseen obstacle.

"Stella! What brings you here? Aren't you closed today?" He grimaced. "What happened to your eye?"

Oh right. Must put some foundation on that before the kids come. "I'm watching my niece and nephew later, and thought I'd get some work done. I'm too impatient to wait at home."

"Look." He held my arm and guided me to a rack holding six items, all in various shades of cream. "Your size." He held the sleeve of a dainty, knit sweater that would show more of me than anyone needed to see. The beauty notwithstanding—the piece cost $280—I shook my head. My days of decadent purchases were behind me.

"I have one like it at home," I lied.

"Okay," he said. "Try something." He gestured to the rest of the sparse but beautiful clothes displayed around us. In leggings, a long wool sweater from a thrift shop in the city, and knock-off boots, I belonged less in this place than a dog in a zoo.

I said goodbye, and went to my bookshop, where everything I knew about the world made sense. In the quiet darkness amid the warm wood shelves and navy walls, stood me and every story I needed to get through life, holding onto my mantra: If you have a book, you'll never be alone.

After a productive but uncomfortable morning of covering my bruise with makeup and paying bills in my office, a modest fifteen-by-fifteen square space tucked in the rear of the shop, I returned up front as my brother-in-law knocked on the door. Two pairs of eyes amid hats and coats peeked in the picture window, and I sprinted to unlock the door and let them in.

Maddie jumped into my arms.

"Hello, my darling girl," I said, reaching down to rub Myles's loose curls as he hugged my leg.

"Aunt Essie! We going to the 'quarium!"

"Yes, we are. I'm so excited!"

When I was a baby, my sister had trouble saying s-words, calling me Thtella so my mother worked with her, emphasizing the letter S: *Es*-tella, *Es*-tella. Charlie started calling me Essie which sounded like Ethie at first, until she mastered the letter. Essie stuck as my nickname and her children adopted it too.

Maddie let out a small shriek, which Myles echoed, and my world felt complete. Today, I was going to introduce them to the aquarium.

Lance, dressed in dark navy slacks and a crew neck sweater over his shirt and tie, leaned over to kiss my cheek. "They've been talking about this all morning. Thank you."

"My pleasure," I said, letting Maddie down and lifting two-year-old Myles to my hip.

Lance leaned over, looking at my eye. "Get in a fight?"

"I did. I won the purse. What's that?"

He handed me a large brown lunch bag. "Strict orders not to feed them anything *you* eat. Your sister's words, not mine."

"I got those instructions already." I made no mention of the donuts I'd hidden in my office. Myles shimmied from my arms and followed his sister to the children's section.

"So, what do you think about Lucas?" Lance said.

"Who?"

"The new dude at my company. Single, good-looking, has money."

"Single, good looking, and wealthy? Not my type."

"Come on, Stella. Get back on that horse."

I opened the brown bag and glimpsed two sandwiches, two clementines, and two granola bars. Poor kids.

"I quit horseback riding last year."

Lance smiled. "But this guy is perfect."

"There is no such thing."

My brother-in-law pointed to himself, making me laugh.

"Ah, now see, if you only had a brother," I said.

"You wouldn't date him either."

"Then we understand each other." I winked, and he shook his head. "I'm happily married to this shop," I said.

Lance crossed his arms over his chest.

"No more, Lance."

Maddie walked up front. "I wanna go now, please."

"Sure thing. Where's your brother?"

Maddie shrugged.

He wasn't in the children's section. "Myles! Come on, babe."

"Myles. Come here," Lance said in a firm voice. "This kid," he muttered.

I walked up and down the aisles and found my nephew crouched against the Romance shelf, flipping through Austen's *Persuasion* as if he were a two-year-old speed reader. I knelt in front of him.

"Another hopeless romantic," I said.

He smiled and kicked his foot out, banging against my kneecap. *Ooof.* I hoisted myself up, leaning on my good leg, and brought him up front.

At the door, my brother-in-law turned around. "Don't let your past dictate your future."

"Go."

CHAPTER 2

An hour later, Maddie, Myles, and I meandered through the aquarium, past enormous tanks full of iridescent fish while I called my mother.

"Where are you?" she said.

"The aquarium with the kids. I'm giving Charlie a day off."

"A day off." Mom chuckled. "She'll clean."

"The apple doesn't fall far from the tree."

"Not always true. You fell into another time zone."

I ignored mom's (spot-on) implication that I was allergic to housework, the antithesis of my sister. "I was going to stop by later to say hi after I drop them off at Charlie's."

No response.

"Mom? Did I lose you?"

"I'm not free later. I won't be home."

I nearly dropped my phone, which was currently supported between my head and shoulder while I held both the kids' hands. I let go of Maddie to readjust it and grabbed her again. "What do you mean? Where will you be?"

"I'm going to the library," Mom said.

"The library closes at six. I'll be there after."

"Stella, I have plans. Come Friday. For dinner."

"Friday is my late night at the shop. I'll call you tomorrow."

Positioned between my niece and nephew, I continued through the rooms, oohing and aahing, appropriately responding to their unbridled excitement while I wondered what my mother was doing. I was happy she was going out but confused. The woman had a schedule like clockwork. Dinner at six. Dogs walked at six-thirty. *Jeopardy!* at seven. *Wheel of Fortune* at seven-thirty, and depending on the night, *Law & Order* or *NCIS* at eight. I couldn't remember the last time she broke routine and went out during the week.

Myles shrieked in wonder as we passed the turtle tank. The three of us watched an enormous sea turtle glide through the water. I wished I could remember being so young, so curious, so...not yet ruined. Myles's resting face was a half-smile. A beautiful, unabashed half-smile. He jumped up and down, pointing to the tank, yelling, "Tuttle!"

Maddie led us toward the touch pool, and I held Myles to me as he emulated his sister, leaning over the open water, gently petting the stingray along its smooth gray gills. My nephew clapped his hands in delight, and I hugged him close, wondering what it would be like to have one of my own. I sighed and kissed his head.

At the shark exhibit twenty minutes later, I noticed Maddie gravitating toward a girl her age. The girl said something to my niece who pointed to a sand shark swimming toward them. As it approached the glass wall, it suddenly veered to the side and swam away. They both covered their mouths and giggled. Before long, they moved together down the length of the immense tank where a hammerhead glided through the dark water.

"Wow. Talk about fast friends."

I turned toward the voice behind me. It belonged to a tall guy with chestnut hair, dark brown eyes, a day's growth along his square jawline, wearing a beat-up brown leather jacket and worn jeans. Good looking. No. Handsome. Very.

"Impressive." I shook my head. "Um, the girls, I mean." I averted my eyes toward the children while my face cooled. They tentatively smiled at each other and stepped closer together.

Myles banged on the glass tank in front of us. I took his hand and bent over, whispering close to his ear that he might scare the sharks. He stopped and stared up at them. I tugged him with me toward Maddie who was still engaged with the other little girl. Both were pointing to a small cluster of baby sharks and jumping up and down.

"Maddie, let's go see the octopus."

My niece moved closer to her new friend. "Aunt Essie, can she come?"

"Hi there." I squatted down in front of Maddie's new companion, placing my arms around Myles' and Maddie's waists. "What is your name?"

"Sam," she whispered.

"Hi, Sam. How old are you?"

The little girl found her father and partially hid behind his leg, a sudden shyness overtaking her. He gently nudged her with his knee. She spent some time figuring out how to hold up four fingers.

"Four? Wow, Maddie is four, too." My niece gave her a bright smile, and Sam returned it with her own shy one. "And this little beast is Myles." I tickled him and he squealed, throwing his head back into my chin.

Stars appeared before my eyes followed by searing pain. I blinked back tears.

"Ouch," the guy said above me.

I stood, rubbing my smarting chin, and wiped my eyes while trying to cover my embarrassment. As the pain began to subside, I noticed Myles reaching for one of Sam's braids. I grabbed him before he could ruin the moment further and lifted him onto my waist. He put each of his hands on my cheeks and squeezed. "Ow. Myles, do you want donuts later?"

He nodded enthusiastically. "Then please don't hurt me anymore, okay?" I returned his attention to the tank as a zebra shark swam toward us. Myles pointed to the intimidating fish, different from the others, sporting tan skin with dark spots, and let out a shriek.

I forced a smile to the man who was still next to me, working to compose myself.

He pointed to my eye. "Looks like it hurts."

"It does." The foundation I'd put on my eye at the store failed to fully cover my growing bruise. Apparently.

"Is this little guy responsible for that, too?"

It took me a second to understand the meaning behind his question. He was asking if someone hit me.

"I belong to an underground MMA ring. Occupational hazard."

He stared at me so long, I turned to check on the girls. Side by side, they gaped at the array of marine life around them. The multi-colored coral and smaller iridescent fish made for a gorgeous backdrop as the sharks glided through the tanks. Sam's long hair was chestnut like her dad's, and her big brown eyes over a smattering of freckles resembled his, too. She was beautiful in a different way than Maddie was, with her unruly dark curls and blue eyes.

"Sam is adorable," I said.

"Your niece and nephew are cute, too."

I leaned toward him conspiratorially. "I'm really their mother. I make them call me 'Aunt', so I appear younger."

He hesitated and then laughed.

"I'm Theo."

"Stella." I nodded, unable to shake his offered hand with Myles in my arms.

"*A Streetcar Named Desire*?"

I grinned. "Dad's favorite movie."

He smelled nice, like leather and musk. I took a subtle step away. Myles squirmed in my arms, angling to get down, so I set him on his feet and took his hand.

"Have you been to the octopus display yet?" Theo said.

"Not yet. We've been here since two. I don't know how much longer they want to stay."

He nodded toward the girls. Maddie and Sam were holding hands, walking to the next tank. "We can learn a lot from four-year-olds."

I sighed. "So true."

We let the girls lead the way through the aquarium, keeping a few paces behind to match Myles's abbreviated footsteps. I gazed at the fish as we walked, wondering where this guy's wife might be. If I had to guess, she was on a beach in Tahiti getting prepped for her *Sports Illustrated* cover shoot.

"You have a question," he said, as if reading my mind.

"Are you giving your wife a deserved day off?"

Theo smiled. "Samantha, Sam, is my sister's kid. They moved from Arizona last month, and Denise has an interview so I'm watching her. I have a lot of catching up to do." He looked around the darkened room. "I haven't been to an aquarium in years."

"I love it here. It's so peaceful."

"The brochure mentioned a bug habitat?" he said.

"I know. I'm avoiding it at all costs." I shivered at the idea of bugs surrounding me, even protected in tanks.

He laughed out loud.

We walked farther, keeping behind the girls, into another enormous dimly lit room where the Giant Pacific Octopus pulsed through the water in a highlighted center tank. His was surrounded by smaller tanks along the perimeter of the room, filled with an array of other spineless creatures like the jellyfish and cuttlefish. Myles tugged at my hand, wanting to follow his sister. I let him go and watched him lumber along behind her and her new friend.

We watched the eight-legged mollusk in awe.

"Look at the tentacles," Theo said. "Can you imagine getting caught up in those?"

I glanced at him, that handsome face with those brown eyes focused on the tank and thought, no way, never again will I get caught up. Then I shook it off and cleared my throat, turning to the octopus. "It's harmless. It prefers flight to fight. Highly intelligent. A solitary creature. Spends most of its life alone. Even after it finds a mate." It was my favorite exhibit.

"Wow."

"I know. So geeky."

We slowly circled the exhibit, watching the octopus change color when Theo spoke. "I hope you don't mind us tagging along for a few minutes. Sam can use a friend. She wants to go home. It's been hard on Denise."

"I don't mind."

Maddie's high-pitched squeal carried through the room as Theo checked on his niece. His hair fell in a thick curl below the collar of his jacket.

"It must be hard to move from home and start over." Charlie and I lived in our small cape on a quiet cul-de-sac for our entire formative lives.

"Where they were was harder. She left a mean SOB behind. I finally convinced her to come home to New York."

That would explain his earlier question about my eye. "Will he try to get them back?"

Theo returned his attention to the octopus. "He'd better not. I'm more of a fight than flight."

I envied his sister, having someone to protect her. For much of my life, it's been Mom, Charlie, and me, looking out for each other.

In companionable silence, we enjoyed the mammoth beast as he floated through the water effortlessly. The octopus watched me, its humongous eye leaning in as if to say, *Hello, Stella. It's been a while.*

Maddie and Sam stepped up to us.

"We want to see the turtles again," my niece said.

Theo turned to me. "You up for some turtles?"

"Sure." I turned around to grab Myles. But he wasn't next to the girls. "Maddie, where is your brother?"

The four-year-old glanced behind her and then looked me, wide-eyed. I grabbed her hand and pulled her with me as we circled the center display, thinking Myles must be crouched behind it, resting. Theo saw what I was doing and walked around the other way with his niece. We met in the middle. Adrenaline started to pump through my body.

"Where the hell is he?" I whispered.

I teetered, unsure what to do while Theo visually canvased the room. Three small groups of people stood around us, all preoccupied with the tanks. Still holding Sam's hand, he walked to each group while I waited in disbelief, turning slowly, trying to see where a little boy would have gone.

"Have you seen a toddler boy, this high? He's wearing a

gray sweatsuit." Theo asked. All shook their heads and looked around.

I started for the exit when Theo stopped me. "Let Maddie stay with me."

"Are you kidding? I don't even know you."

He stepped in front of me as my cheeks burned. His eyes quickly shifted to Maddie, who blinked up at us, the fear evident on her face. "I got her," he said quietly.

Did I trust this guy? This kind, handsome stranger? My gaze covered the room. I needed to look for Myles.

"Please," I said. "Please help me."

"He couldn't have gotten far. Retrace your steps and I'll have security lock the doors so he can't leave."

He'd barely finished talking when I ran up to the mezzanine, running past the Amazon rainforest and Amphibian Alley. Myles wasn't there. I screamed his name, stopping everyone in my path. "Have you seen a toddler boy in a gray sweatsuit with a red truck on it?"

With each shake of the head, my terror grew. I returned to the café and bathrooms, pushing into each unlocked stall, not caring who I bothered or saw. I couldn't lose this boy. I'll die. His mother will surely die.

The doors leading to the outside seasonal displays were locked but I stared through the windows to make sure. I ran past the coral reef, screaming for Myles as people watched me in horror. A few started to search the room with me, asking questions, which I could no longer answer because my brain stopped working and when I tried, all I did was scream his name. I ran downstairs to the octopus and stopped short.

He stared at me, his long tentacles writhing in the water. I froze, stunned, locked in his gaze. *Is it you, Oliver? Do you remember me?*

Suddenly, he darted to the back of the tank, and disappeared behind a boulder, leaving a flurry of bubbles behind him. My body shook, and I sprinted to the shark exhibit, circling the tank when I ran directly into Theo.

He grabbed my shoulders and leaned over to look me in the eye. "Stella. Stop."

"I can't! If something happens to him…"

"Stop!" He held me firm. "We will find him. I promise. Take a breath. Please!"

I shook. Couldn't take a breath. Didn't know how. I'd forgotten. In. Out. In. Out. My head spun, and I gasped.

He pushed my upper back so that I was forced to lean over and whispered, "Breathe. I promise he's here somewhere. I have the entire security team on it. No one's leaving. You need to breathe and then we'll keep looking." His hand stayed on my upper back until I started to take deep breaths and felt myself gain some control.

He pulled me straight and looked me in the eyes until I could finally focus on him. "I can't lose him."

"We won't. Let's go." He grabbed my hand, and we ran upstairs, each of us quickly scanning the groups standing in front of the displays I'd passed minutes ago. Now, everyone seemed to be aware of what was happening, and all started to look for Myles. "Let's head to the other side. We'll hit each room until we find him."

I nodded, my mind racing, thinking of all the things I'd heard that happen to children when they're kidnapped, how their hair and clothes are changed before they're even taken out of the building, and I almost gagged in fear. "Maybe the bathrooms again," I managed.

"Way ahead of you. I instructed security to check each one and then close them so no one can go in."

"The girls!" I had forgotten what he'd said about Maddie and Sam.

Theo squeezed my hand. "They're in the lobby with a guard. Let's go see them and I'll check in with the manager for any updates."

I swallowed the stinging bile that rose in my throat, not reassured that we'd find Myles. I didn't feel Theo's confidence.

I didn't even know the guy, though I wanted so badly to believe my nephew hadn't been taken.

But my mind played horrible thoughts that nearly paralyzed me as we ran to the lobby.

Maddie and Sam were rolling a pink ball back and forth, occupied and distracted by the security guard watching them. My niece clutched the ball and asked about Myles. Her eyelashes were dotted with pearls of leftover tears, which is when I figured the ball was introduced. I told her everything would be all right, though I knew it wouldn't. Theo was across the room, speaking with the guard. He held a map, and the two of them talked quietly. Theo pointed at something on the map, and the guard answered. Then Theo stepped over to me. "I'll be right back."

He ran into the aquarium while I went to the front door and stared out into the parking lot. Were any cars leaving? Were we too late? I gripped the door bar, carefully searching for movement, ready to pounce, when I felt someone grab my arm.

"Come with me," Theo said.

"Where?"

Without answering, he led me past the displays again. "We checked this three times." I was losing my mind. Let the floor break open and take me.

"They covered the area but didn't see anything concerning. I saw the room on the map, but we must have missed it on our search." He brought me to a door near the corner tucked behind the Penguin Pavilion near the shark room. He was right. We'd walked right past this door each time. It was painted and looked like part of the wall, but for the unlit muted sign above it. PARTY ROOM. Theo led me through the door, and we walked into a birthday party in progress. There, in the middle of a long table full of small children, sat my nephew, wearing a party hat and eating a cupcake.

My knees wobbled with relief. I ran to him and knelt by his chair while Theo went to speak with one of the adults watching from against the wall.

"Hey, Myles," I said quietly to the boy, my eyes full and burning from unchecked emotions. "You can't walk away from Aunt Stella, do you understand? Come."

Wearing a smile covered with chocolate icing, he took my hand, no questions asked. From the corner of my eye, I saw Theo shake a man's hand and point to me. Then he said something to a woman, who frowned and responded, before he made his way to us. I quickly swiped at the tears that threatened before he reached me.

"Those are the birthday girl's parents. They thought Myles was the little brother of one of the kids here. He walked in with a group. They don't know all the kids because they invited their daughter's entire first grade class. They feel terrible. They saw a worker walk in and look around but then he left. They would have alerted someone if they'd known." He leaned down to Myles. "You gave us quite a scare, little man."

We headed toward the lobby, me holding tightly to Myles's hand, Theo beside me. I stopped suddenly outside the restroom and shook. Theo searched my face and without a word, took Myles's hand from mine and stepped aside. He raised his hand to a guard asking him to unlock the door.

"Take as long as you need, Stella. We'll wait. Don't worry. You're okay."

I pushed into the bathroom and crumpled in a heap to the floor, sobbing, my arms wrapped around my aching stomach. I dry heaved over a toilet. I'd never been so scared in my life. Visions of showing up at my sister's without her son played on an endless reel in my mind. Squeezing my eyes shut, I rocked back and forth, breathed in and out as Theo showed me earlier, until I could stand and control my emotions. I splashed water on my face, patted it dry with harsh paper towels and when I saw my reflection, my black eye puffy from crying, I terrified myself. It took several minutes until I felt sure I could walk out of the bathroom and appear in control.

As promised, Theo was outside with my nephew, holding him in his arms. He spoke softly to Myles, pointing across the room to a tank when he saw me. He lowered the toddler to the floor. "Okay?"

I nodded and reached for Myles. But before I grabbed his hand, I wrapped my arms around Theo, this stranger who suddenly turned friend, unable to articulate all that was swirling inside. After a few seconds, I felt his hand on my back. The hold was gentle but enough to say, *I got you.*

I don't know who you are, I wanted to say, but you're my favorite person right now. Instead, I gave one last squeeze and pulled away. I lifted Myles up and led us to the lobby and to the girls, still waiting with a security guard. They ran to us as we neared them, fussing over Myles, who reveled in the attention. I took Maddie in my arms and apologized for scaring her. When she smiled, I sighed in relief.

"All is okay, Mad," I said. My throat felt as if there was a sock in it. I lifted Myles onto my hip.

Theo patted him on the head, holding tightly to Sam. "Did you enjoy your cupcake?"

Myles looked at him and burped. Then he rested his head on my shoulder.

Theo glanced at his watch. Of course, he wants to get out of here, away from the woman who can't keep track of the two-year-old in her care. I opened my mouth to give him an out, to say *I got it from here, thanks for your help*, when he surprised me.

"Do you want to walk around a little more? Better to stay a bit than leave with this being the last memory for them." He nodded to the girls, still recovering. He was concerned for the children, his niece included.

I longed to leave. I wanted to bring these babies home and run out of Charlie's house and to my apartment, dive under the covers of my bed, and put this day behind me. I glanced at Maddie and caught the residual hiccup of her scare. Theo was right. Best to leave on a more positive note.

"Okay. Thanks."

Before we left the lobby, I thanked the guard for watching the girls, and we went to the bug exhibit, not so scary to me now.

"I spoke with the head of security," Theo said as the three children stared at the tarantula's tank. "He's going to talk with his staff. That shouldn't have happened. The worker who went into the Party Room should have ID'd Myles and he didn't. A lot of undue stress could have been prevented."

"No." I shook my head. "It's no one's fault but my own. I don't know what I would have done without your help. You saved him. You saved me."

He shrugged. "I'm glad I could help."

"That's never happened to me before."

"It happens more than you know. Trust me. Half of my time is spent searching for little people. Today was easy. The building wasn't on fire."

It took me a minute to understand. "You're a fireman."

He nodded. Of course. He'd remained calm and in control the entire time.

"How can I thank you?"

"No thanks necessary." He smiled but I couldn't return it.

"I have a bookshop on Gruber in Harbor Crest. If you're in the neighborhood, stop in. You've earned a lifetime of books." Sam whispered something to Maddie, who had returned to her happy, worry-free self. "Or if not you, Sam can have anything she wants."

"You own that one? I pass it on my way to work. I keep meaning to go in but I'm usually running late. Something with covers?"

I nodded, certain he was being gratuitous. "Between the Covers."

"That's right. Catchy."

"Thanks."

We stayed another hour, until the girls resumed their happy jaunt through more rooms, pointing, screeching, and laughing. Myles, having no idea of the strife he'd caused, continued with his carefree day. Relief consumed me. I kept telling Theo he could leave, certain he was tortured staying with me longer than expected, but he insisted he wanted to stay. We talked about growing up in New York, me on Long Island, him in Queens, and the music of our youth: Pearl Jam, Christina Aguilera, Red Hot Chili Peppers, which confirmed that we were of a similar age.

Theo and Sam left first, and I took Maddie to the bathroom, keeping Myles in the stall with us. Her legs swung a foot off the floor. Myles rested against me, sucking his thumb, and I pushed away the feelings of attraction to the man who seemed to show up in the nick of time. Like some sort of hero. My heart fluttered. I have no time for a hero. Besides, Stella, they only exist in fairy tales.

"Can we go to the gift shop?" Maddie said as I leaned over to help her wash her hands, tucking Myles firmly between my knees.

"Sure, but then we'll go home."

On the drive to Charlie's, I felt Theo's hand on my back and my eyes filled again.

CHAPTER 3

Charlie had texted me while I drove out to Long Island that she'd run to the store and would be home soon.

She walked in when I had the children in the bathtub.

"Mommee!!" squealed the two-year-old, splashing like a walrus and soaking me.

"Hi, Mommy. Guess what? We went to the 'quarium. And we saw fish. And we saw turtles. And I saw Sam. And we had hamburgers—Myles! Stop! You're splashing!"

Charlie leaned against the door, looking relaxed. "You look like you had a day," she said.

"Do I?"

"Wine?"

"Please," I said.

She stepped into the bathroom, gave each of her charges a kiss and left me to finish what I'd started. When I'd dried and dressed them both in their pajamas, I settled them in front of the television, tuned to *Bluey*, and found my sister in the kitchen with two glasses of wine poured and pasta on the stove.

I dropped down onto a kitchen chair and pulled a glass of wine toward me.

"What happened to your eye?" she said.

"A can dropped on me at the food store."

Charlie leaned in for a better look. "That doesn't make sense. Were you juggling?"

"Yes, that's right. It's a little side gig I do instead of using coupons. Did you get everything done?"

"This house is clean," she said in a squeaky voice, doing a poor imitation of the tiny woman in *Poltergeist,* a movie she'd forced me to watch with her that kept me up at night. She'd finally had to sleep in bed with me until scary scenes no longer filled my dreams.

Charlie smiled as she swirled her glass and took a sip. "I finished early so I ran out to pick up lingerie for our anniversary." Her face turned pink. I had to turn away, my heart aching for this kind of connection. A life I would probably never experience. Charlie and Lance have been together for fifteen years and married for ten. He's one of the good guys while I seemed to discover the not-so-good ones.

I played with a postcard on her table— a reminder Charlie needed to schedule her next OB/GYN appointment.

"What's wrong, Essie?"

"Did you make your appointment?" I asked, holding up the card, though I didn't care.

"I will." She took it from me. "I get more mail from Dr. Harris than holiday cards." She laughed at her joke, in a happy mood. "When's the last time you saw a doctor?"

"I can't remember."

"You should, especially the way you eat. We're not getting any younger." Charlie sipped her wine. "So, how did it go at the aquarium? They look happy and nothing is broken, so… success."

I nodded while struggling with wanting to tell her what happened, wanting to admit I couldn't handle two children on my own, but the words wouldn't come. I longed to keep my title as "helpful, reliable sister" for as long as possible before I let her down. I'd already let myself down. It was enough for one day. "Yep, good day today. Nothing to report."

"Who's Sam?"

"Samantha. The girls met and latched onto each other, forcing me to walk around with her uncle for a bit." I rolled my eyes as if it were work.

Charlie stared into her glass. "Is he cute?"

"Not really." Gorgeous was more apt to describe him.

"Is he, you know, nice?"

I shrugged. "He's all right. Nothing to write home about."

He was damn near perfect. He saved your kid and kept me from going over the edge with worry.

Something was definitely wrong with him.

CHAPTER 4

I no sooner walked into my apartment after leaving Charlie's than my neighbor, Philippe, walked in. He refused to knock and got annoyed when I locked my door. Wearing a deep green turtleneck, a complement to his copper eyes, skinny jeans, and raven hair mussed perfectly, he handed me the still ignored envelope from my foyer floor. I put it on the kitchen table and sat down.

"What the hell happened to you?"

"I caught a mugger, and he got in one shot before I took him down." Sounded so much better than I reached for a can of beans.

He dropped onto the other seat. "'Splain, please."

I gave him the abridged version of the truth.

"You know you're vertically challenged, so why didn't you ask someone for help?"

"I didn't need help. It would have been fine if I'd stuck a cleaner landing."

"You're a pain in the ass."

I pushed the envelope holding my rent notice away from me.

Philippe lived in 3D, across the hall. Born and raised in Poughkeepsie, New York, his given name was Filiberto, after his grandfather who emigrated from Cuba. He was very thin and tan, had a deep voice, and didn't color his hair, though he made a living coloring other's. He owned the uber upscale hair salon next to my shop. He enjoyed tight jeans, snug V-neck tees and Italian shoes with no socks, believed in true love and thought he finally found it. He was great company.

"Why are you here?" I said.

He frowned. "We have to work on your welcoming skills."

"It's Monday." On Monday nights, Philippe and his partner, Rog, dressed in velour sweatsuits, poured champagne, and noshed on Bourdin cheese and water crackers while watching *Dancing with the Stars*.

Philippe pulled my nearly empty glass of wine toward him. "Rog was called into work, and I don't like to watch by myself."

I filled him a glass of red, refilled mine, and led him into my small den. We nestled onto the denim loveseat and waited for the screen to light up.

We were into our second rumba performance when I felt Philippe's eyes on me.

"What?" I said as he pulled my crocheted Afghan over us. "Is it getting worse? Purple? Black?" My hand covered my eye, still holding a dull throb.

"You seem, I don't know." He pulled my hand from my face. "What's wrong?"

"What makes you think something's wrong?"

He tucked his leg under him and turned to fully face me. "Your skin looks stressed."

"My sk—? How does it do that?"

"Never you mind. Speak, woman."

Philippe has quickly become my favorite person outside of my sister and mom. He found me this apartment last year, across from his, while I was preparing to open my shop and commuting back and forth to Long Island. With his salon next door and his apartment across the hall, we became instant friends, which I'd needed as I'd lost my best friend a few months earlier.

"When I was young, my favorite place to go was the aquarium."

Philippe smiled.

"My dad used to take me. His favorite exhibit was the Great Pacific Octopus. We'd stand in front of the tank and watch him, and Dad would tell me all about him." I felt my smile form as I pictured it. "I wasn't afraid, I remember, even with those long legs covered in tentacles and the misshapen head that seemed to change with the water. Maybe it was because he always held my hand."

"The octopus?"

"My father. Anyway, Dad called him Oliver. On our last visit, he told me he had a special ability to communicate with Oliver, which is how he knew his name, and I believed him. Why wouldn't I?"

"Look at him, Es. Isn't he the most gorgeous creature?" Dad's eyes were pinned on the tank.

I nodded.

"Look at his eyes. He's sad. Do you know what he's telling me?"

I shook my head.

"He wants to go home to his family. He needs to be free. He's dying in that tank, captured like a prisoner." Dad knelt in front of me and wiped my tears. "Don't cry, Stella. I have a plan."

"What was his plan?" Philippe said when I'd paused with the memory.

"We stayed until closing and hid in the bathroom until the building was locked and safe for us to move the octopus."

Philippe stared at me. "How, pray-tell, did he expect to move a Great Northern octopus?"

"It's a Great Pacific octopus."

"Irrelevant."

"I can't answer that. I probably didn't ask. I took him for his word. I was six. We were in that bathroom for so long, I started to wonder if my mom was worried about us. Dad assured me she knew about the plan, and I felt relieved." I shifted to cross my legs, and Philippe adjusted himself to accommodate my new position, pulling the blanket back over us.

"A guard found us and spoke into his walkie-talkie. Then he and my dad stepped outside, leaving me in the bathroom."

"Why?"

"I don't know, but I was there for a long time before Dad came in to get me. He was upset the whole ride home."

"How could they not understand, Essie? He's dying in there. I wasn't doing anything wrong." Dad looked at me and back to the road, gripping the steering wheel with both hands. "You know that, right? I wasn't doing anything wrong."

I nodded, my bent legs pressed against me on the passenger seat, unable to see the road over the dash.

Philippe put his hand on my knee.

"It's strange," I said, "there's so much I can't remember of those years. I can't remember his different character voices when he read to me, or the smell of him, but I remember that afternoon vividly."

The music of a rumba played from the television.

"Your father sounds like an interesting fellow."

"He was. Adventurous, full of life—so much fun."

A minute passed and Philippe squeezed my knee. "Honey, why are you telling me this?"

I stared at the screen. A man in a tight silk shirt twirled a stick-thin woman several times before lifting her leg over his shoulder. How was she not nauseous?

"I lost my nephew in the aquarium today. In the middle of the craziness trying to find him, I stopped at the octopus's tank and for the briefest moment, thought to ask him if he saw where Myles went. It's what my dad would have done." I stared ahead. "Stupid, I know. I'm a grown woman, and this octopus didn't know me from Adam. In fact, my dad and I went to a different aquarium, but part of me still wants to believe the unbelievable."

Neither of us spoke for a bit until finally, Philippe blew out a breath. "Well, that's a day, huh? How did you find him?"

"Some guy helped me."

"Must be quite a guy."

He was.

We watched a waltz until a commercial break when Philippe said, "How come I haven't met your dad? I've only met Marion."

"He left."

"Where did he go?"

"I don't know." I rubbed my eyes. "He left while we were at school, and I never saw him again."

"How old were you?"

"Seven. The aquarium incident was close to when he left, I think."

My neighbor whistled. "That's rough."

It's been twenty-nine years.

"Did you look for him?" Philippe said.

"No. He died a year later."

Later, as I climbed into bed, woozy from the bean attack, the aquarium, and the Pinot, I stared at the oversized gown that took up more than half of my small closet. The soft folds of silk draped down the front looked like melting marshmallows in the dim moonlight through the bent slats of the window blinds.

I rolled over, away from the dress and the memories it hid and revisited my day, thinking of Theo, how I suspected I wouldn't see him again.

CHAPTER 5

The next morning, Gina and I were straightening shelves to Simon and Garfunkel's "Bridge Over Troubled Water" when she told me she sold her first painting.

I paused and looked at her. "That's amazing. Congratulations!"

She focused on the books, though she appeared pleased.

"Did you have a show? Is there somewhere I can see your work?"

"Not yet. My boyfriend brought someone to the apartment, and he asked to buy it right off the wall. I don't have enough ready for a show."

"I think it's incredible," I said, still reeling that she sold a painting she made herself.

Gina disappeared behind Science Fiction.

When I'd first opened the shop, I'd had no intention of hiring an employee, preferring to handle everything by myself. Charlie and Philippe hounded me continuously to hire help. "What if you get the flu? What if you break a leg or worse? You can't close the store every time something happens."

My response had been, "Nothing is going to happen. I don't do anything. I don't go anywhere. I want to do this myself." And, I couldn't see adding even a meager employee salary to my intimidating expenses.

But then, I got pinkeye a month into my opening, most likely a gift from Maddie, who I'd babysat the previous week, swallowed my pride along with antibiotic, and put a *Help Wanted* sign in the window.

Two people applied. Gina and a middle-aged, well-dressed woman from Cobble Hill with a pleasant demeanor. Gina was young and so unlike me that I hired the other woman, making my choice before I'd even interviewed either. I'd called Gina and told her the news and thanked her for applying.

Within two weeks of my decision, I'd understood my mistake. My employee thought work hours were "suggestions" and showed up when she felt the desire, usually after a shopping stint, as evident by the full Bloomies bags she always carried. Though very sweet, she wasn't a reader and therefore couldn't help customers with recommendations. When I'd observed a customer asking her where the King novels were, she'd searched the shelves, finally giving up and asking me where I kept books on the royal family.

One month after I hired her, I let her go and took it harder than she did. Back went the *Help Wanted* sign in the window. Gina walked in again, still dressed head to toe in black clothes; thick black eye makeup; indigo-black dyed hair, shaved on one side; enough piercings to command awe right before disgust, and tattoos along one entire arm, the only color on her, like a sleeve. I couldn't stop looking at her. She was gorgeous beneath all the darkness, but I still couldn't see her in a customer service position.

As we spoke, keeping to superficial topics, me in my head knowing I would keep that *Help Wanted* sign up longer, a customer walked in. He'd approached us, not put off by the appearance of my applicant, and inquired about a title that eluded him. He'd explained the plot, a Russian man was exiled in his own country, forced to live in a hotel, and Gina immediately knew the book, found it in record time, and presented *A Gentleman in Moscow* to the man while I'd watched, impressed.

When he'd paid and left, I asked her if she could show me where the King novels were. She immediately found an assortment of Stephen King books in the thriller section, put her hand on her hip, and said she read a book a week. Wide, from every genre. She hated television ("mind-numbing garbage"), lived a short subway ride away, and as an unknown artist, was available to work any hour, any day. The cherry on top: she was fine working for minimum wage. Gina shared an apartment with two other people, to keep her rent low, she'd explained. In short, she was perfect. I'd learned the hard lesson not to judge a book by its cover.

Now, my employee of ten months, Gina peeked out at me from the Science Fiction aisle.

"How did it go yesterday?" she said, switching the subject from herself.

"Fine. Nothing to report." I returned to the counter as a woman with two little boys paused outside to read my chalkboard before walking in. I waved hello and the woman, who I'd guessed to be their grandmother, led the kids to the children's section.

"Gina," I whispered.

She looked at me.

"How many boys did we have at the last reading hour?" The third Saturday of each month, we devoted an hour to reading children's books aloud in our quest to convert new readers. It had started out slow.

She came over to the counter and pulled the sign-in sheet from the lower shelf. Together we reviewed the list from the previous Saturday. Only eight children showed. Six of them girls.

"We have to entice more boys to come," I said.

"Easy. Hire a superhero."

"Sure. I'll look through my superhero contact list and see who's available."

"You'll figure something out," she said.

The customer stepped to the counter but only one of the boys held a book. The older of the two was empty-handed. The woman pointed to the shelf over my head. "How much for *Charlotte's Web*?"

I inhaled and forced a smile. "That's the only book in this shop that's not for sale."

She frowned. "Do you have another one?"

"We sold our last copy on Sunday," Gina said.

"I'll order more. I can call you when it's in, if you'd like."

"Why can't you sell me that one?" the woman said.

"It's my own personal copy. I've had it since I was his age."
I pointed to the older boy of around seven or eight years old.

"Why do you have it up there? What's so special about
Charlotte's Web?" the younger boy asked.

I leaned over, resting my elbows on the counter so I could
speak to him. "It's the story of a friendship between a spider
and a pig. The pig lived on a farm and was supposed to be
killed for food when the spider, named Charlotte, saved his
life."

Both boys listened, their eyes wide. "How did she do that?"
asked the younger one.

"Well, she wrote special notes in her web for the farmer to
see. I won't give away anymore so you can read it for yourself
and find out what happens."

"What's so special about that copy?" the older boy persisted.

"Someone important gave it to me." I stepped around the
counter. "And while I don't have any other copies right now, I
do have another book you might like. Come with me." I led
him to the children's section, pulled out a book, and handed
it to him.

He held it. "*The Trumpet of the Swan*?"

"By the same author who wrote *Charlotte's Web*. It's a cool
story about a trumpeter swan who is born without a voice and
to overcome his handicap, he learns to play the trumpet to
impress a swan named Serena."

The boy stared at the cover unconvinced, and I was ready
to take the book back, when he nodded. "Okay."

"If you don't love it, let me know and I'll give you something else. But I think you'll love it."

While ringing up the woman, I suggested she sign up for
our mailing list, telling her we offered coupons monthly. "And
I have reading hour every third Saturday morning at eleven
a.m. for children."

"I'll tell their mother," she said.

"Do you think she'll bring them?" Gina said when they
left.

"I hope so."

"You went with an oldie. The newer ones might be better suited for the kids today."

I didn't agree. If we'd only hold onto some of the past, maybe the present wouldn't be so...hard.

"I'm running to the deli. What do you want?" Gina said.

"What are you getting?"

"Latte with almond milk."

"I'll have the same."

Alone, I lifted *Charlotte's Web,* touching the aged, cracked spine, and with it, the last memory I had of my father. The nights he'd read to me, his voice changing with each character, how hard I'd laughed when he interpreted Templeton, the rat.

How in love with books I'd become because of him.

At four o'clock, the place was spotless, and our last customer walked out as a postal worker entered wheeling three boxes on a pushcart. Gina led him to the office, to the waist-high shelf lining the inside wall, our workbench, where he'd deposited the boxes. My desk sat perpendicular to the exterior wall and the rear entrance metal fire door.

Gina ripped the top flaps open, and we dove in, pulling out gently used copies of old and recent titles I'd ordered, sight unseen, from a bookstore in Queens that was closing.

I pulled at my turtleneck. "Hot in here or is it me?"

"Well, you are wearing clothes that cover almost every inch of your skin. Crack that door open. Let some air in."

"I've only opened it once. Too creepy." I'd checked out the alley when I did a look-through of the shop before renting it. The ten-foot-wide space was home to little more than discarded bottles, trash, and weeds whose growth was now stalled by the frigid weather temps. I'm sure several varieties of vermin lived there, too.

After ten more minutes of discomfort, I unlocked the rear door and propped it open several inches with a wooden stopper to help circulate the stuffy air.

Gina read the spines, doing a cursory investigation of the books before piling them next to her. She pulled one out and then another with a frown and separated them from the rest.

"Add it to the pile," I said, referring to an amassed tower of discarded books we couldn't sell. It was growing to a substantial height and the source of frustration for my employee.

She read the back cover of one. "I'll take this home. Oh, I almost forgot." She pulled a paperback from her camo backpack and handed it to me. "Read this."

I took the offered book. *Where I've Been and Where I'm Going* by Olivia Connelly.

"Never heard of it," I said.

"She's an indie. Self-pubbed. My girlfriend got it for free from a Goodreads giveaway and told me to read it."

"I'll add it to my TBR pile."

"Put it on the top. Trust me," she said.

The bells over the front door jingled.

"I'll get it." She was already moving before I could react.

I nodded, slipped Gina's recommendation into my bag, and continued to organize the books on the table. I put the ones that didn't meet inspection on my desk to bring home as well, and broke down the cardboard boxes, adding them to a pile for some future use.

A cold breeze blew through the door opening, and I shivered as every paperback cover flapped. Beyond letting all my paid-for heat out, it was far too windy for an open door in January. I'd just kicked the stopper free when I sensed movement in the alley.

"Who's there?" The hair on my neck rose. I peered into the narrow space but didn't see anyone lurking about. A few pieces of garbage. Must be a rat. Another shiver ran through me, and I pulled back in but not before I glimpsed a pair of green eyes in an orange, striped face staring at me from a few feet away.

It croaked a mew.

"Hey, little buddy, are you lost?" I cooed, holding the door open. Do cats get lost? I leaned over to see he had no collar. "You must be cold."

A quick scan of the alley assured me this cat was alone. Bony and unkempt. Poor thing. I propped the door open and stepped inside, wondering if it would accept my invitation to warm up. I leaned against my desk and waited, but it didn't approach the door.

I grabbed my ignored lunch bag and pulled a piece of turkey from the hastily made sandwich I'd thrown together this morning and laid the meat on the ground.

"It's okay. Here." I retreated a step inside the door, out of his line of sight, hugged myself to ward off the chill, and waited. I was rewarded minutes later when I glimpsed the tips of his ears and heard him eating. I waited a bit longer to see if he'd come in, but he never did. I closed the door.

* * *

A few minutes before closing, the dark sky was lit up by streetlights. I was counting the register receipts when a young man wearing jeans and a black turtleneck walked in. His jet-black hair accentuated the two silver earrings in each ear. He stayed at the front display with his hands in his front pockets.

"May I help you?"

Before he could answer, his face lit up as Gina walked toward him. "He's with me."

She greeted him with a full kiss. His arms circled around her, and I watched while they communicated without words as I disappeared from their world.

When she pulled away, Gina said, "This is Aaron. See you tomorrow, Stella."

Hand in hand, they left the shop, stopping once more outside to kiss again, exhibiting that new, rose-colored fresh love that is much sought but can never be replicated.

I waited until they were down the block before I moved the quote board inside from the sidewalk. As I did, someone walked in behind me.

"Closing?" the person said.

I turned and found myself face-to-face with Theo. "Oh! Yes. No." Oy, Stella, get a grip. "No. Hi! Come in."

"Okay." He smiled and took another step further inside.

As we faced each other, I had no idea what to say. I'd hardly expected him to show up.

He read the board over my shoulder. "I like your quote."

"Thanks." The message of the day was a favorite of mine: *There is no friend as loyal as a book - Ernest Hemingway.*

I wiped it clean, and he whispered, "See ya, Ernest," which made me laugh.

"Do you want to help me think of tomorrow's quote?"

He shoved his hands into his front jeans pockets and furrowed his brows as if in deep thought. I waited, trying not to laugh again, feeling embarrassed as I thought of how we left each other at the aquarium, me on the verge of a breakdown.

"How about, Lit Happens?"

Relief covered me. "I love it."

As we moved away from the updated chalk board, I was very aware of Theo behind me.

"I didn't expect to see you again," I said.

He hesitated. "I wanted to see how you were after what happened yesterday."

"I'm okay."

"Good."

As he canvassed the shop, I enjoyed the proud feeling that accompanied every new customer. This business had kept me emotionally afloat when my world crumbled last year. I enjoyed seeing it through the eyes of new visitors: the walnut-stained shelves along the walls, the full display tables in front of the large window, the Dr. Seuss-inspired artwork I'd salvaged from a tag sale and hung over the multi-colored walls of the children's section, framed book covers over Fiction: *To Kill a Mockingbird, The Great Gatsby, A Tree Grows in Brooklyn.* I'd picked every book myself. Every tiny detail in this place had my hand on it.

"This is a great store," Theo said.

"Thanks."

He stepped to the first shelves and looked at the spines, pulled a book out, read the inside flap and put it back.

I dropped the chalk in the box near the register and dusted off my hands. "So, you live nearby?"

He pulled his attention from the shelf to me. "Carroll Gardens. We have a bookstore there, too. Can't have enough. Your shop is on my way to work. That way." He pointed in the direction opposite of where Gina and her boyfriend walked, which is probably why I hadn't seen him approach.

He meandered down an aisle, scanning a shelf, moving slowly toward Literature and Fiction. His intense focus brought forth feelings of vulnerability as if he were going through some deeply personal part of me, like my closet or lingerie drawer—I mean, if I *had* lingerie, which I didn't. With my dating life, that would be pointless.

At the counter, I tried to appear busy while every fiber of my body was aware of him. I picked up my phone, opened Facebook and scrolled through the day's posts, hoping to appear preoccupied. I stopped on a video of a familiar racecar as it crossed a finish line. I'd experienced this scene personally too many times. One of Doug's many extracurricular activities included racing his beloved Charger in Englishtown, New Jersey, while I'd cheered from the sidelines. It was fine until midway through the season as each weekend was sacrificed, and it got harder and harder to feel enthusiastic about cars racing down a track. The noise, the fumes, and one too many sunburns. I'd never complained. Climbed into his car every weekend and endured more races.

Once, I'd asked Doug if we could spend a weekend upstate in the mountains after a race, in a cabin in the woods. Where we could take long walks. Sit in front of a fireplace with some wine and talk. Be together without distractions of work, his friends, his sports and hobbies. *Sure!* was his response but we never quite made the plans, never could find the time.

I replayed the thirty-second video, watching the car cross

the line while a gorgeous woman jumped up and down, cheering and thrilled for my ex.

Marcy, my best friend.

My *former* best friend.

Marcy, who never had an interest in cars or racing. But now, she was loving it.

"You look like you got bad news," Theo said.

I jumped back in surprise and quickly stored my phone on the shelf under the counter.

He squinted and stared at my face.

"What's wrong?" I resisted the urge to check that something wasn't sticking out of my nose.

"I'm looking at the bruise," he said, motioning to my left eye. "It looks a little better."

My hand went up to my eye. This morning I'd applied a good layer of concealer hoping to look more natural. Well, as natural as "medium wheat" can look over my skin.

"I'm looking forward to it turning blue and purple. I have the perfect blouse to match," I said.

Theo chuckled and cleared his throat. He laid a book on the counter. *The River We Remember* by William Kent Kruger.

"Have you read it?" he said.

"Yes. Have you read his Cork O'Connor series?"

"Every one. I thought I'd give one of his standalones a try."

Something fluttered in the lower part of my stomach. "That's a good idea."

He took his wallet out as I slipped the book into a canvas bag. "I told you, free reading for life after what you did for me."

He pushed a twenty-dollar bill across the navy half-moon Formica counter, salvaged from a curb in Queens last winter. "Never give away a sale."

I rang him up and handed him his change. "If you won't accept my offering, how can I thank you for saving me yesterday?"

"You can have dinner with me tonight." When I didn't respond, he cocked his head to one side. "Don't tell me. You're married."

I hesitated, and then said, "No. You?"

"If I was married and asked you out, would I tell you the truth?"

"So, that's definitely a no for dinner."

A shadow passed through his eyes. "I was married. I'm not anymore."

"Phew." I pretended to wipe my brow.

He smiled, and it was really...nice.

"So...dinner?" He toed the rug, waiting. When he lifted his gaze, those eyes and that wavy chestnut hair and beaten-up brown leather jacket made me want to say yes. But my heart was still recovering.

"I'm going to head home. Thank you, though."

He nodded, and a pang of regret rang through me. He's trying to be nice. He helped me find my nephew, for Pete's sake. He bought a book.

"But if you're not in a hurry, maybe you'd like to walk a bit?" I added. "I'm closing and wouldn't mind the company."

Theo waited for me on the street while I moved around the store, shutting down for the night, locking the register, switching off the lights and radio. I peeked into the alley to see if the cat was there, but it was too dark. The poor thing could have been hanging around all this time, unprotected in the cold. I pulled the door shut and locked it. I'll check again tomorrow.

Up front, I locked the shop door, pocketed my key, and turned to Theo, who now wore a beanie. His curls flipped over the back making him appear youthful. And so damn cute.

"I'm in this direction. What about you?" I pointed south and tried not to stare.

He nodded. "Same."

We strolled along the sidewalk. The air was cold but with no wind, bearable.

We passed a bustling pub where music from a live band spilled out onto the street as someone walked out. He gazed at the empty booth in the front window, with lights along the perimeter adding to the coziness inside.

"Are you sure you don't want to grab a bite?" he said.

Dinner here would cost well more than a book. I couldn't possibly let him treat me after what he did. And it would feel like a date.

"I'm sure." My growling stomach betrayed me, and I coughed to mask the sound.

We walked on, our pace slow but steady, neither of us in a hurry.

"How's your nephew?"

"Unperturbed, as opposed to his aunt who is scarred for life." Nightmares of Myles walking away into a dark tunnel as I screamed for him, my leaden legs unable to move, kept me up all night.

Theo choked on a bottled laugh. We crossed the quiet street, the pedestrian light flickering over our heads. "How did your sister take it?"

I sniffed the air and self-consciously shifted the scarf around my neck. "I didn't tell her."

He stopped at the next intersection, and I felt his eyes on me.

We waited for a car to pass. "I couldn't. She can't think her children aren't safe with me. And I'm humiliated. They were my responsibility. If something would have happened to that boy…"

He didn't respond. Maybe I should have said yes to dinner at the pub.

I adjusted my scarf again. "Please don't judge me. I'm having a hard enough time with this as it is."

He put up his gloved hands. "Judge free zone here."

I believed him, and my eyes stung with gratitude.

As we crossed the icy road, I said, "Despite what happened, the aquarium was a big hit with Maddie and Myles. Did Sam have a good time?"

"She did. Totally enjoyed the few minutes she got to spend alone with Maddie while we ran around the aquarium. Completely oblivious."

"Ah, what I wouldn't give to be oblivious again."

He laughed again and it made me smile.

"My sister found a job in Queens, so it looks like she's staying and will be close to me. I can help with Sam on my days off."

"It's nice of you to help her."

He focused on the street. "She's helped me through some stuff. So..."

"I get it. I don't know what I'd do without Charlie. When my dad left, she was my rock. I wouldn't have survived if not for her."

"Where was your mom?"

"Working. Always working. If I've learned nothing else from Mom, it's to always be financially and emotionally independent." And I hoped to be both eventually.

"Denise is learning that the hard way. I'm relieved she drew up the courage to leave her husband. She did it for Sam. Once a child is in the picture, everything changes."

"Do you have kids?" I said.

"No."

We came to a hot dog vendor on the corner. A man behind it smiled and nodded his head. The odor made my stomach grumble again.

"Hot dog? On me." I motioned to the cart, my tastebuds already craving a dog with sauerkraut and ketchup.

"Sure."

"How do you take it?"

"The works, of course," he said, as if I should know this. As if there were any other way to eat a hot dog.

I bought two hot dogs fully loaded and handed him one. "Dinner is served."

"Perfect." He bit into it and sighed as onion juice trickled down his chin.

I'd have to watch myself around him. He was too freaking adorable—even with schmutz on his face. We continued to walk as we ate our dinner. I wanted to ask him why he wasn't married anymore. Did his wife leave him? Or did one of them cheat? Or perhaps he secretly had a dark side, went into unexpected raging fits and she decided to walk away? There were hundreds of possible reasons. Instead, he directed the conversation to the safe topic of my bookshop, asking when it opened (a little over a year ago) and how I decided what titles to stock (it really depended on my budget and demand).

We both steered clear of anything personal, and I felt relaxed and comfortable. I hadn't intended for him to walk me all the way home, but before I realized it, we had reached the apartment building next to mine.

I stopped, so he stopped, and I wondered if he could detect disappointment hidden behind my smile. Or hear my stomach telling me I'd pay for the spicy mustard and onions later.

He pointed to my face. "You have some mustard…"

"Where?" I swiped at my chin.

"No." He reached over and gently brushed the corner of my lips.

I pulled back as if stung, shocked by the feathery feel of his fingertip. I roughly wiped my lips and cheek with the scratchy napkin I still clutched.

"I didn't mean to…"

"Sorry. Gut reaction." I offered him a half-hearted smile, knowing I'd overreacted. Better to end this night before I embarrass myself further. "Thank you. This is me."

He looked at the building. "Oh, right, well…"

"Thank you for the walk," I quickly inserted.

"Thank you for dinner. And the conversation. I enjoyed both."

I did, too. "Have a good night."

"See you around, Stella."

I reached the top step and gave a last wave as I pretended to fumble in my pocketbook for my key, waiting for Theo to walk away. When he'd turned the corner and was out of sight, I let out a shaky sigh. As I ran down the steps and to my actual apartment building next door, I worked to hold the sensation of his feathered touch against my cheek. It had been a long time.

CHAPTER 6

At nine o'clock the following morning, after ingesting a weak cup of coffee, dressed in wool pants and a long sweater under a wrap-around shawl, with my hair in a ponytail, I stepped outside and got slapped by the cold air. My commute this morning was consumed with thoughts of my unexpected company and walk home last night.

Almost at my shop, I heard someone call my name. I retraced my steps and turned to greet Jeffrey, in front of the open door of his boutique.

"Stella, come in! Come see what's new."

"Oh, I know it's all lovely, but it's not for—"

"Come in!" He guided me in, refusing to take no for an answer, though I had been in yesterday. A sales tactic I should adopt.

Today, the boutique smelled strongly of cardamom, a pleasant scent if you're not exposed to it long. He brought me to a bony mannequin wearing a blouse and held the garnet sleeve. "Feel."

I ran my fingers over the silk. This probably felt as if you were wearing nothing with it on, which was tempting. "This is the softest material I've ever felt."

He beamed, exposing a thin gap between his two front teeth. "I know. Made in India. Exquisite. Try it on."

"Oh, no. Thank you, though." I glimpsed the price tag and pulled on my turtleneck to air my neck that heated from the number—$179. "I much prefer my scratchy wool."

Despite my droll refusal, he started pulling the blouse from a nearby hanger.

I put my hand on his arm. "You know what I need?"

He abandoned the blouse to give me his full attention.

"A white camisole." It was the least expensive article of clothing I could come up with. I'd bought a black one last week and didn't see any more, so I felt confident I'd leave today with my savings intact.

"Ah!" He clapped his hands and disappeared behind the door to the fitting room, returning a minute later with a white camisole draped over his forearm.

Really?!

"Oh, perfect," I said, trying to sound sincere.

He wrapped it in tissue paper and slipped it into a small plastic bag. Why was he still using plastic?

"Keep the bag, Jeffrey." I took out my wallet, reaching for my bills.

"Fifty-two dollars. I included a little friendly discount." He winked at me.

I swallowed my self-loathing and handed my credit card over. His "friendly" discount for my last cami was a tad better, but I kept my mouth shut. A discount, no matter how much, was appreciated.

Minutes later, as I walked into my shop holding a large coffee from the deli two doors down, I texted Charlie, *You're not going to believe what I did last night.* Not watching where I was going, my foot caught on the door saddle and I tripped and flew forward, sprawled across the floor, my much-needed coffee ejected from the cup, staining the rug, seeping through the tissue paper wrapped around my now not-so-white cami, and soaking the sleeves of my sweater.

Serves me right for texting and walking simultaneously. I could have waited five more minutes to check in with my sister, but five more minutes seemed too long.

I placed my half-full cup on the counter and sprinted to get a rag from the office. After soaking it under the bathroom sink, I rushed to the front to blot the setting stain as quickly as possible. While on my knees, I glimpsed up and gasped.

Forgetting my task, I sprung up and closed in on the empty shelf above the register where my *Charlotte's Web* book should have been. I spun around searching for it, growing more stressed, looking on the display tables, and then along the shelves to the Children's section where I scoured every single title until it was clear it wasn't there.

I tore through everything under the counter: bags, tissue paper, notepads, sign-in sheets, but it wasn't there. Panic set in as I forced myself to resume the work on the carpet.

There had to be a logical reason for it not to be in the store, though I couldn't think of one. Could Gina have sold it? Did it fall into the garbage can and unknowingly get thrown away?

I scrubbed the spot with the damp rag but could still detect a light brown circle on the tan speckled Berber. I sniffed, not caring as much as I should, my worries on my missing treasure.

Gina walked in an hour later as I inched along the second shelf against the western wall, reading every spine, my growing panic becoming more than I could handle.

"What's the matter? What are you looking for?"

I swallowed. "I can't find my book."

She put her backpack and jacket on the counter and watched me with concern. "Which book is that?"

"*Charlotte's Web.* It's not on the shelf. I'm losing my mind. I don't remember moving it."

"That's because you didn't. I did." She walked purposefully to the office and returned with my dog-eared, broken-spined childhood book in her hand. "I cleaned that area when you were visiting Philippe, and I forgot to put it back. I'm surprised you didn't notice yesterday."

I must have been so preoccupied with Theo coming in that I didn't even see it hadn't been there.

Gina held the book out to me. "Sorry. I shouldn't have moved it. I know how special it is."

I took it, averting my gaze. "It's fine. I overreacted." I pressed the book to my chest, relief filling me like a well. "Such a silly thing, right? To be so attached."

"It's not silly. Though, I think you should protect it better than leaving it on the shelf if it means so much."

"I'll think about it." I returned it to its place, overlooking the store, overlooking me. I wouldn't alter it, and Gina knew it. The only protection it needed was to stay where it was.

"Spill coffee?" she asked, eyeing the rug.

"More like ejected."

"If you want, I'll go get some carpet cleaner after we open," she said.

I was grateful for her calm demeanor.

"Thanks." I nodded and Gina flipped the sign to *Come In! We're Open!*

I opted to go to the pharmacy around the block during our first lull. Carpet stain remover in hand, I stopped into Philippe's salon. My friend was sipping coffee, playing with his hair in front of one of the many long mirrors propped before the cutting stations. I plopped down on the chair next to where he stood.

"How goes it, chickie?" he said, eyes still on his artfully disheveled coif.

"I tripped into my store and spilled coffee all over my rug this morning," I said, instead of what I wanted to say, which was I had a nervous breakdown because my employee did a nice thing and cleaned my shop for me and forgot to replace my most treasured item and I thought I'd die.

Philippe sat in the chair and spun to me, placing his long leg on my footrest. "The stain will come out. Oh! I almost forgot to ask if you want a used couch. My friend Peter is moving to Albuquerque and getting rid of his furniture. He's going from shabby chic to Aztec chic. You know, when in Rome, and all that. Anyway, are you interested?"

"Yes! I could use it for the shop. A couch will be so much better than the folding chairs we've been using." Between the Covers had been hosting book clubs for the past six months. No one wanted to host at their house and displace family members for the evening. It had been working out well. The caveat to meeting at my shop was that the books were purchased through me. And I got to stay while they met and avoid sitting home alone.

Philippe frowned. "I was thinking you could add it to your sparse, white, unimaginative apartment."

"How much is he asking for it?" Did I have enough in petty cash?

"Nothing. He's tossing it."

"That's the right price," I said and leaned forward. "And my apartment is not *that* bad."

"Honey, even Andy Dufresne's cell had a poster of Rita Hayworth."

"Are you comparing me to a character in *Shawshank Redemption*?"

He kicked at my chair and spun me round. "You know what I mean. You put all your energy into your business, your personal space is ignored." Behind me, he ran his fingers through my hair. "Speaking of personal, I'm having a gathering in three weeks. Come over. And please, for the love of all that is good, don't show up in oversized wool pants and a bulky sweater. Put something on that shows you're an actual girl. I promise you'll have fun."

I pulled myself from the chair and faced him. "I might be busy."

"And I might be Arnold Schwarzenegger. You're coming."

I grinned. "I'll take the couch. Thank you for thinking of me."

"Great. I'll have Peter bring it up this weekend."

"No. I'll take it for the shop." I blew him a kiss and walked out as he yelled behind me, "You need balance, girl!"

Balance. Little did my friend know, I'd been searching for balance my entire life, living off-kilter in a world of abundant estrogen and unanswered questions. Questions I wouldn't ask for fear the truth would render my weakened self-worth irreparable. For years Mom and I were passing ships. She with her overloaded work schedule and me navigating my school years with few friends, holed up in my bedroom with my books.

Charlie was my surrogate mother, cooking for us, doing laundry, helping me with homework, trying to lighten Mom's load. Charlie had been the perfect daughter, still was, which was why she was gifted the perfect life— perfect husband and perfect kids. She'd earned it, had prepared for it, while I couldn't get the man I'd dated for six years to meet me at the church on our wedding day.

There were three customers browsing when I returned to the shop. I sprayed the stained area of the rug as directed and left it to set in.

Gina was helping one of the browsers, so I went to the office to store the carpet cleaner and peeked out into the dim alley to check for the cat, but it was empty. I propped the door ajar and left a small bowl of milk and a can of tuna on the threshold and returned to the store.

Someone had walked in asking for the popular New Adult books for her daughter. I showed her to the shelf, rang up two more customers and returned to the office, worried that I'd left the door open too wide, therefore inviting more than a stray cat inside. The temperature in back had dropped significantly as cold air came in, and visions of heated dollars flying out the door disappeared when I saw both bowls were empty. But that's not what surprised me. The cat sat regally at the opening, with his bones protruding through his fur, and the left half of his whiskers missing, as if waiting to thank me.

"Hi," I said softly, not wanting to frighten it.

It mewed, the same croaking sound it gave me the first day we met. I pulled the door open further and stepped out of view, pleased when I glimpsed his nose stretching forward toward the heat. I stayed put until he fully stepped in and gasped when I saw he had half a tail, and amid the matted fur on his lower torso were two bald spots.

"Poor guy," I whispered. He mewed again as if admitting he knew how he looked, saying *Don't judge me*, as I'd said to Theo last night.

The front door jingled again.

"I have to work," I told him. "You're welcome to stay, but I have to close this." He watched me without complaint as I gently closed the alley door, keeping him inside. I'm not sure, but I thought I heard him purring as he circled a few times in the corner and nestled down against the cement wall to nap.

At six, Gina went home, and I flipped the sign to *Closed*, locked the front door from the inside and went to the office to check on my new furry friend who was waiting for me. While he ate a second bowl of tuna, I texted Charlie.

> Me: How was your day?

> Charlie: Living the dream.

The funny thing was my sister *was* living the dream.

> Me: Can I come by tonight?

I skimmed Facebook while waiting for her response and came across a picture of Doug and Marcy in Colorado, at Breckenridge, skiing.

In the years I'd known Marcy, she'd never wanted to try skiing. Couldn't understand why someone would want to be brought to the top of a mountain only to have to find their way down. In the cold. We'd laughed about it when I told her Doug was finally taking me for the first time. He'd been enjoying annual trips with his buddies since high school and spent much of his winters away, and I'd been asking him to take me.

Further down the post, I learned he had taught her to ski through an array of pictures, of him guiding her from behind, rooting for her as she'd passed him. Cute.

The one time he'd taken me, he'd brought me to the top of an intermediate run at Killington Mountain in Vermont, gave me some half-assed directions, and left me. It took me an hour to get down the one run. I kept falling, scrambling to catch rogue skis each time one disconnected from my ill-fitted boots. One skier had taken pity on me and stopped to help me gather my belongings across the mountain after a particularly devastating tumble. *This is what we refer to as a yard sale*, he'd said to me, handing me my pole, both skis and mitten. I had decided at that point not to put the skis back on and slid down the rest of the run on my ass, taking out a little kid in the process. Doug had had a good laugh when I told him, but I had been hurt, emotionally more so than physically. Following that failed debacle, he continued skiing almost every other week throughout January and February with his friends and didn't ask me to join him again. He was doing me a favor, he'd promised.

I couldn't stop staring at the pictures of Doug and Marcy. Who took them? Did they go with his friends? There was no mention in the posts. My heart clenched. He didn't work harder to share this experience with me that he was clearly sharing with her. In fact, in hindsight, I wonder if he purposely turned me off to the sport by what he did so that he could keep going without me.

How could I have misjudged our relationship so badly? What was wrong with me?

My cell phone rang, startling me so that I dropped it. I picked it up and quickly wiped the screen on my pants before putting it to my ear.

"Hi. What time are you planning to be here?" Charlie said when I answered.

"I'm locking up now, and then I'll head over."

"Can you pick up flour? I promised the kids we'd make cookies since we didn't at Christmas. And I need some extra time. We had a little mishap."

"What kind of mishap?"

"Myles decided to stick a marble up his nose and I'm running to the walk-in to get it out. Lance is here with Maddie if you show up before I get back."

I touched my nose, feeling Myles's pain, relieved that something like this happened on Charlie's watch and not mine. I bid the cat goodnight, let him to return to the wild, and closed the door behind him.

The flour was on the lower shelf in the market's baking aisle for which I was grateful. On my way to check out, I grabbed a container of multicolored sprinkles and a box of Lucky Charms.

Someone lightly poked my shoulder while I was waiting to pay. I turned to find Theo behind me, holding a wrapped deli sandwich.

"Hey, what are you doing here?" Heat traveled up my neck and spread to my cheeks.

"I'm off work. Can't wait to get home. Too hungry." He held up his hero. "How was your day?"

"I spent my day in a book shop."

"Sounds like a good day to me. And it appears you're getting out of here unscathed."

Oh, how I wished I hadn't come clean about the source of my black eye at the aquarium. "I gave up baked beans for life," I said. His deep laugh made me flush with pleasure.

Theo looked at my groceries. I lifted the flour. "Heading to my sister's to make cookies with the kids."

"And the Lucky Charms?"

"Oh." I glanced down as if I didn't realize the cereal was there. "Special request from Maddie."

As the customer in front of me bagged her food, the register next to us opened and the cashier motioned for Theo to move to her counter. He finished before me and waited near the door as I put my stuff on Rhonda's conveyor belt.

She took the sprinkles first.

"Can you tell what I'm doing tonight?" I said.

Rhonda took the cereal next and scanned it. "Trying to raise your A1C?"

Clever. "I'm making cookies."

"With?"

"My sister."

Rhonda frowned. I'm not sure why. Maybe she doesn't have a sister.

I met Theo at the door, and we walked out together.

"So how is it I've been here a year, and we've never run into each other, and now I've seen you three times in a week?" I asked as we paused under the store's awning.

"I transferred from another station last month."

Lucky me. A handsome fireman in my neighborhood I get to run into sporadically and embarrass myself when I least expect.

"Transferred from where?" I said.

"Manhattan."

"Do you like it?"

"In Brooklyn?"

I nodded.

"Sure. I don't really know anyone yet outside of the guys, but it's okay."

"You know me. Sort of."

Theo smiled. "That's true."

"Consider me your first new friend."

He turned to me. "Friend?"

"I don't buy just anyone dinner. Only a friend gets a hot dog with the works." And I can use a friend.

He gazed over the parking lot. "I like it. Sure. Friends."

CHAPTER 7

Forty-five minutes later, I pulled onto my mother's street. Her car was in the driveway, the lamp in the den window was lit, and the rest of the house was dark. I pictured her in sweats on the couch surrounded by her rescued posse of animals waiting for *Jeopardy!* to start. I pulled past the house to park in my normal spot on the curve of the street, since her car left no room for one behind it and had shut the engine when headlights appeared in my rearview. At seven p.m., the sky was indigo, so I waited for the car to pass before I climbed out. Except it didn't pass. It pulled up to Mom's driveway, blocking it.

"What the...?" It was too dark to see who it was, so I waited, and was rewarded when the passenger door opened and the car's interior light went on, illuminating the passengers. Mom climbed out of the car and closed the door. Then to my astonishment, the driver stepped out, too. It was our neighbor down the street, Pacer Wright, who was Charlie's age!

I watched him escort her to the side door, which led into the kitchen. She opened the door. He said something, and she laughed. Marion laughed! To my great relief, she said a quick goodbye and disappeared into the house. Pacer returned to his car and did what appeared to be a two-step dance, where he slipped and went down. I strained my neck to see where he was, and eventually, he pulled himself upright, turned his head toward the house to make sure he wasn't seen, and climbed into his car. Poor Pacer. He'd always been socially awkward, answering a simple hello with a soft reciprocation in the other direction, away from the greeter, often to a wall. The guy who chose the rear corner desk in the classroom, pocket organizer poking from his breast pocket, ill-fitted corduroy pants that eternally reached for his ankles, year-round nose-blower. Nice guy. We were friendly, but never friends.

I waited until Pacer had driven down to his own house before getting out and walking into Mom's. I knocked as I walked in. "Mom? It's me!"

She still lived in the small cape my parents bought when my mom was pregnant with Charlie. The house had not been updated since, which I loved. The linoleum kitchen floor wore the footprints of our childhoods, and the original wallpaper absorbed countless dinner conversations and the scent of fried chicken cutlets.

This was where a small herd of animals greeted me. I pet the three dogs as they pushed into each other, vying for my attention. By this time, the two cats had lost interest and mo-seyed away. My mother walked in from her bedroom wearing sweatpants and a sweatshirt, a far cry from the nice slacks I'd just seen her wearing under her coat.

"Stella, I didn't know you were coming out."

"I'm heading to Charlie's, so I thought I'd stop by. But clearly you were busy."

"What do you mean?" She reached for the leashes hanging on hooks by the door, sending the dogs into a happy frenzy at the prospect of a walk.

"I saw Pacer drop you off."

She clipped the leashes on each of the dogs and handed me one. "Why didn't you say hi?"

"I didn't want to disturb you."

"Disturb me? Why would you disturb me?" She led the way outside, avoiding my eyes.

The streetlamps and post-holiday lights along some of the houses lit up our path. It felt celebratory beneath the starry, inky sky. The dogs pulled at the leashes and my mom held firm. I was walking Margie, a mutt with three legs who worked to keep up.

"You've been out a lot lately," I said.

"No, I haven't."

The idea of my mother with our young neighbor was unsettling. She was my last holdout for eternal singledom. I had no right to judge. But Pacer? I couldn't wrap my head around the idea.

We stopped so Mabel, her Pekingese, could pee. Not to be outdone, her Lab, Henry, lifted his leg and sprinkled on the curb. Marion was forced to look at me.

"Are you dating Pacer?"

She gently pulled her charges to continue moving. "What? Stella, no! Stop talking nonsense."

"He dropped you off. He looked happy. He did a little dance on his way to the car."

Her mouth formed a slight upward curve. "I was at the library, and he gave me a ride home," she said.

"How did you get to the library?"

Marion sighed. "Enough with the questions. What's going on at Charlotte's?"

"We're making cookies. Do you want to join us?"

"I'm tired. And I'm babysitting tomorrow while she goes to the doctor."

"Myles stuck a marble up his nose, and she took him to the walk-in to get it removed."

We stopped at Pacer's house, a small, dark green cape decorated tastefully with white lights along the front overhang and a candle in each window. His mother had passed away a few years ago and he stayed, fixing it up after a lifetime of no improvements. We turned around.

"Again?" She shook her head. "That child."

The dogs led us up the steps and into the house. She took Margie's leash from me, hung it on the hook with the others and began to pour food into two large steel bowls as her brood watched in anticipation. "I ran into my friend, Sophia yesterday. Her nephew is single. He's widowed."

"That's a shame." Why was she telling me this?

"She said he is very nice." Her back was to me.

And then I understood. "I'm not interested, Mom."

"Just meet him. He could be a friend."

"I had a friend. She's now sleeping with my ex-fiancé."

Mom turned, and the wounded look on her face cracked my heart. The food was still on the counter. One of the dogs whimpered.

"I'm sorry. I don't want to talk about this. I have my shop. It's enough for me." I brought the full bowls to the floor. The dogs shoved each other aside to reach the kibble and chicken.

"I don't want you to be alone," Mom said.

"I'm not alone. I have you and Charlie. And Philippe."

She sighed and filled another, smaller bowl with cat food. "Did I mention he has a good job?"

"Oh! Well, in that case, tell him I like moonlit walks, junk food, and emotional trauma."

"Don't be sassy."

"Sassy is the only way I know to be." I kissed her cheek, and she patted mine. "Let's talk about this another time, okay? I'm happy with my life now. I promise." I walked to the door when I'd remembered the cat. "Oh, Mom, there's a tabby that's been showing up at the shop. He's very thin, matted with some bald spots. No obvious sores."

She leaned forward, listening. When it comes to animals, Marion is all in. "Wait here." She stepped to the hall closet off the kitchen, and pulled something out, handing it to me. A foldable carry case and a collar. "For fleas," she said. "If you can get him in the carrier, you can bring him to Felicia." Felicia was the veterinarian Mom's been working for, for the past twenty years. "He's got to be dirty."

"We're not close enough for me to give him a bath," I said.

"You can spot clean him. Baby wipes are fine. Damp washcloth."

Then she opened one of the kitchen cabinets and pulled out a small stack of cat food, which I took as well.

Finally, she opened her purse and pulled out her wallet. I watched her rifle through her bills and pull some out. She reached them out to me. "Take this."

"What for?"

"More cat food. And, you know, anything else." The woman had worked two jobs through my formative years trying to scrape together some semblance of a life for the three of us. The sacrifices she'd made so Charlie and I didn't feel deprived were one of the innumerable reasons we appreciated her. The last thing I'd do as an adult was to take money from the woman who allowed herself so little while giving me so much.

And I needed the money.

"Thank you, but I'm fine."

She glanced at the clock, laid the money on the table. "What time is Charlie expecting you?"

"Soon. I'll leave now." I kissed my mother lightly on her soft cheek.

CHAPTER 8

The next hours at Charlie's were spent in a chaotic plume of flour, sugar, sprinkles, and occasional tears as she patiently guided the children in cookie making. In between the stirring and shaping of dough, I filled her in on our mother's young fling, or whatever it was she was doing with Pacer. Charlie, who seemed preoccupied, perked up as we discussed the craziness of Mom dating a man half her age. Or any man, for that matter.

"When have you ever seen Mom with a guy?" Charlie said.

"I don't know if I'm happy for her or worried about her. Maybe she's lonely."

"She's been lonely for a long time, Stella."

The day our father left, Charlie and I were at school and Mom was working her shift at the department store. We'd all returned home, as normal, Mom having met us at our bus. She'd prepared dinner while we sat at the kitchen table doing our homework to the song of sizzling chicken cutlets on the stove. I'll never forget it. We'd put our books away, set the table, and waited for Dad to come home to eat. When the sky darkened and our stomachs rumbled, Mom finally convinced us to eat. Dad had started another new job working in downtown New York City as a truck loader in the meat district. He'd walked home from the station (Mom used our only car to get to work) after his first day earlier in the week, exhausted and reeking of raw meat and blood and wouldn't allow us hugs and reading time until he'd scrubbed off the residue from his day. A broad man with large, calloused hands, he volleyed between eating mounds of food where he couldn't get enough to barely eating and going right to bed, depending on his day. Our mother had tucked us in that night and Dad still hadn't come home.

He never did. We never saw him again. To this day, the

odor of frying cutlets in the pan reminds me of the last day I felt safe.

As it often did when Charlie and I were together, that memory seeped into my mind.

"Pacer's harmless," Charlie said. "His mom really helped us out after Dad left."

"She did?"

My sister nodded. "She brought food over all the time and picked us up at the bus stop when Mom couldn't. We used to stay at her house until Mom came home. I didn't like it because Pacer used to try to kiss me."

"At that age?"

She smiled. "He was a mature eleven-year-old. I convinced Mom to let me watch you so we wouldn't have to go over there anymore. She said no until I told her about the kissing."

For some reason, tears filled my eyes. "I don't recall any of that. I only remember you taking care of me."

When the last tray was slipped into the oven, we slumped in our chairs while Myles banged his hands together, sending tiny sprays of dough around the room. Maddie was busy pressing her pointer finger against the table to catch the last dough beads and sucking on it, until finally, I announced the table was officially clean.

"You know, they sell those tubs of cookie dough already made," I said. "All you have to do is scoop it out and onto the pan."

"It's not about being easy. It's about the experience and the memory."

I looked around the kitchen. A cyclone would have done less damage, making the lasting memory for me of standing over a sudsy sink.

"I have to give them a bath," my sister said through a yawn. "I can't believe I let them stay up this late."

"Can't you do it tomorrow?"

She gave me a level stare. "I guarantee there is sugar in every crevice of that tiny body." She pointed to her son who was now rolling on the floor. "I'd rather a bath now than to have to turn this house upside down tomorrow."

"Okay, you bathe, I'll clean up." I pulled myself to stand as my brother-in-law walked in.

Lance came home from work every day to have dinner with his family and then worked a few hours more in the spare bedroom they'd made into an office. Charlie told me he was vying for a partnership in his firm.

"Enter at your own risk," Charlie said to him.

At the door, he assessed the situation and gave a low whistle.

"Have you come for the goods, Sir Lance-A-Lot?" I said.

He hugged me hello and reached over to grab a cookie cooling on the rack on the counter. He put the whole cookie in his mouth, his eyes rolling in bliss as he chewed and swallowed.

"You've outdone yourself again, my love." He leaned over to give his wife a long kiss. I turned away toward the children who were now clamoring for their father. When he pulled away from Charlie, he lifted Myles and announced he was the bath king and had come to rescue all sugared children, at which they yelled in glee.

I washed the bowls and pans while Charlie dried them and put them away.

"Do you remember making cookies with Mom?" she said.

"Vaguely. I don't recall it being the circus we ran today, though."

"That's because Mom was very controlled, and we were not a two-year-old toddler who can't sit still." Charlie smiled. "You were like Maddie, sneaking pieces of raw dough and pressing your finger onto the table and sucking on it. I felt like it was a reincarnation of sorts tonight."

I scrubbed the baking pan and tried to remember but my recollection of those years was shrouded in snippets of scenes that I couldn't decipher.

"You were young. Maddie's age, I think. We stopped making cookies when he left."

"We stopped doing a lot of things when he left," I said.

My sister slid the clean pan into the narrow space in her cabinet. "Mom worked all the time. She couldn't help it."

I squeezed the excess water from the sponge and put it in its holder. "She suggested I date her friend's nephew."

Charlie frowned. "She's worried about you."

"She shouldn't be. I'm fine. Besides, why would she push a guy on me when she's been living her life all these years without one? Why can't I be like her? Independent and strong?"

"You can. But companionship is nice, Stella." She leaned against the counter and looked around the now clean room. "Experiences are so much richer shared."

My eyes shifted sideways to my sister. "Like making cookies."

"Like making cookies." She leaned into my shoulder. "Do you want coffee?"

"I do."

We moved to the living room couch after coffee was poured. Voices of sleepy children drifted in toward us.

"I punished Maddie yesterday for lying. I've never done that before." She sipped from her mug.

"Charlie, kids lie."

"I'm trying to teach her that it's not right."

"What did she lie about?" I brought the cup to my lips.

"She told me you lost Myles in the aquarium and Sam's uncle helped you look for him. I don't know where she gets this. I thought maybe she wants him to be lost."

I lowered my head. Poor Maddie. What have I done?

"I did lose Myles. She didn't lie."

Charlie's eyes widened. "Are you kidding? Where?"

"At the octopus's tank. I let his hand go, thinking he'd follow his sister and he kind of walked off."

"Why weren't you watching him?"

"I was talking to Sam's uncle."

Charlie's eyebrows lifted in revelation. "So, she had that right, too?"

I nodded. "The girls latched onto each other, and me and Theo were following them around. I held onto Myles, until I didn't. It took us fifteen minutes to find him." My eyes welled. "I've never been so scared in my entire life. How do you do it, Charlie? How do you take them everywhere you go and not lose them? They have to be watched *every second*."

"Last month, Lance and I were in Bloomingdales buying him a new suit and we couldn't find Myles. They had to close the store. He was hiding under one of the clothes racks. I didn't sleep for three days."

I stared at my sister in disbelief. "Could you have warned me that he walks off before I took him for an entire day?"

"Here's your warning. Two-year-olds walk off. The little bastards aren't aware they can't go everywhere they want."

It gave me some solace to know my own sister, the mother of these children, also made mistakes. Now that she knew, I felt a weight lift from me. "I made a complete fool of myself. Theo finally found him. Your son infiltrated a seven-year-old's birthday party. He managed to swipe and devour a full cupcake before we got to him."

Charlie rested her head against the cushion. "Why didn't you tell me?"

"I was embarrassed. Everything was going so well until it happened and then the day fell apart."

My sister laughed though no humor accompanied it. "It's easy for something to go from wonderful to disastrous in an instant. It's life. But you need to let me know what's going on with my children. I'm their mother, Essie."

I put my coffee down and pulled myself from the couch.

"Where are you going?" Charlie said.

"To apologize to your daughter."

In bed, two hours later, still hyped up on sugar (I'd eaten half my weight in sugar cookies with zero regret), I pulled Gina's recommended novel from my pile on the nightstand though it was near midnight. My plan was to read a chapter or two to relax so I could fall asleep. Three hours later, my dry and blurry eyes forced me to put it down and I fell deeply into slumber.

CHAPTER 9

As I ate my second bowl of Lucky Charms the following morning, I finished the book. Staring at the cover, pale blue with two arrows pointing in opposite directions, the title, *Where I've Been and Where I'm Going*, fading as if disappearing, I shed tears as I savored the ending of a most delicious story. I hugged it to me.

A comprehensive search for the author on my laptop found little information. Olivia Connelly had no website or blog site, a huge miss for such a talented writer. But I did find her book available for purchase through one of the distributors for indies, and I ordered three copies for the store. Then I texted Gina.

> Me: Wow. Just wow.
>
> Gina: You read it?

She knew exactly what my message meant. This was a connection I didn't see coming when I hired her.

> Me: It's unbelievable.
>
> Gina: ☺
>
> Me: It's four years old! How are we only discovering it now??
>
> Gina: Unfortunately, there are thousands more we'll never find because these authors suck at marketing. C u ltr

As I suspected, she'd tried to find the author online, too.

That afternoon, Gina and I were in the rear corner of the shop in front of my new, used couch from Philippe's friend.

The muted patchwork quilted cushions fit perfectly and set the tone of a comfortable, relaxed setting. After I'd painfully parted with my rent money, I used my remaining savings to pick up a small table at Goodwill and placed it in front of the couch. Its corners were worn down to raw wood, so I filled them in with permanent marker. It took shabby chic to the next level.

"What do you think?" I said.

She crossed her arms. "I think you're going to have a problem. People with nowhere to go will plant themselves here. Especially during the winter."

"People should have somewhere to go. To escape. I was thinking for the book clubs."

Gina leaned over to better inspect the table. "Is that marker?" She shook her head.

"Anyway," she said, "are you okay to host tonight's club? I have dinner with Aaron's parents."

"Bummer." Another point for singlehood. No enduring awkward meals with the parents. I'd only seen Doug's parents on a few occasions as he wasn't close with them. They preferred brunches and refused to drive into the city to see us. So, we'd driven to Connecticut on the rare Sunday mornings they'd invited us. Over omelets with capers and goat cheese (I hated capers. Too salty), I'd worked overtime to gain their acceptance. I'd choked not only on the capers but my disdain for their political views, nodding my agreement through dessert. The old saying "fake it till you make it" stuck in my mind. "Just agree and get home" became my personal mantra.

Gina looked at me. "I like them. I enjoy their company."

I swallowed. "Anyway, I picked up *petit fours* at lunch." The book clubs didn't so much focus on snacks as they did their wine.

"You're going to lose money if you keep that up. The point of the clubs is to make money."

"Gina, money is at the bottom of my reasons for doing this. Sharing a love of books, people gathering in a community, giving back to readers, that's the fuel that feeds my fire."

Her gaze lasted a beat too long before she said, "That's why you're the boss."

After Gina left, I went to the office to check on the cat, who'd stopped in for his meal and nap. Wearing his new flea collar, he was still sleeping so I quietly returned the shop.

Philippe came in to check on the couch. "You need something on that wall, dear." He pointed to the bare navy wall above the seating area.

"I know. I'm still deciding what to put there." And I had no spare money.

He leaned over to inspect the table. "Is that marker on the corners?"

I winced. "Should I dump it?"

"I'll see what else Peter is giving away. I'm sure we can fill this space up."

"Thank you."

While waiting for the book club, I watched through the picture window at the pedestrians passing, returning waves to some familiar faces.

I'd no sooner turned to set up the back, when the bell over my door jingled, causing my heartrate to increase. I spun around to see Jeffrey from The Closet standing at the door. I forced a bright smile to welcome him.

"Stella! Philippe is having a party."

"I am aware. Are you going?"

"No. You buy something from me. I'll make you look gorgeous."

"Thank you, but I have something to wear," I lied. "I am loving my camis, though." I lifted the bottom of my sweater to show him the cream one I wore beneath it.

"Ah!" He clapped, pleased. "How is business?"

Stop asking me this question! He asked out of kindness, but it was tiring.

Three women walked in, saving me from this conversation. Joan, my best customer, gave air kisses to Jeffrey. She was also *his* best customer. I'd been open about a week when she'd first walked in and told me how happy she was that the scrapbook store I'd replaced was finally closed.

"Now I don't have to go to Cobble Hill to buy a book. This is so convenient." She'd praised the shop and bought three books that day. Hers was the first book club I hosted (she was in two clubs).

"Stella," Joan said to me, "What a fabulous story. Thank you for recommending it. I flew through it." Clutching the book, she headed to the back with the women she walked in with, and Jeffrey left.

The women drifted in one by one, each holding a copy of this month's choice.

One woman, Tara, found me at the front counter. She was smartly dressed in a pressed button-down chambray shirt tucked into flat front chinos and brown loafers. Her short brown hair was tucked behind her ears.

"Hi, Tara, did you enjoy the book?" She hadn't read the last few, from what I could remember, but never missed a meeting.

"No." Two red circles appeared on her cheeks.

"You didn't like it?"

"I'm not a strong reader. I think I have an attention problem. I can't get through them. In fact, I haven't read a single book since I joined three years ago." She glanced over her shoulder to make sure she wouldn't be overheard and lowered her voice. "I like to see the girls. It's a nice escape from my life. My husband's not much of a talker and the boys sit in their rooms playing video games." She pressed her hair behind her ear and looked at her feet. "I'm not sure why I told you that."

I held my arms up and gestured around the shop. "Think of this as Las Vegas. What happens here, stays here. It's a no judgement zone. Besides, I only pretend to listen. I have no idea what you said." I winked and her shoulders relaxed.

"No, Stella, you're a good listener. I think it's why people talk to you. You're like a bartender who doesn't serve drinks."

"The worst kind," I said.

She tilted her head upward and laughed out loud, and in that gesture, I glimpsed a fun girl beneath the buttoned-up exterior.

"Anyway, can I use your bathroom?"

"Of course. Jiggle the handle after you flush until it stops running."

She nodded.

As I opened my book, my cell phone rang, and my mother's face lit up the screen.

"Hi, Mom." I flipped the opened novel down on the counter.

"Stella, what are you doing this evening?"

"I'm working late. Do you need something?"

I heard shuffling on Mom's end. Queen of multitasking, I envisioned her cleaning the kitchen or tidying up her bedroom while talking to me. "Sophia called me again. What should I tell her about her nephew?"

"Tell her I have gonorrhea."

"That's disgusting."

"Mom, please don't try to set me up. I want to focus on my career and live a simple life. That's all I want."

"That's not true. You want more than that."

"Mom—" I looked up in time to see someone walk across my field of vision and stop. Theo waited in the center of the window with his beanie on, his curls below it, and a smile that made something catch in my throat. He waved. I waved back.

"I have to go, okay?" I said into my phone. "I'm sorry. I'll call you tomorrow."

Theo pushed the door and walked in as I disconnected the call. "Am I interrupting?"

"Not at all. My mom is on a mission to set me up. You saved me from another attempt."

He shoved his hands in the pockets of his canvas coat. "I get it."

"You're not interested in meeting someone, either?"

"I prefer an organic meeting. On my own terms."

"Exactly," I said, "which for me, means I'll remain happily single."

His eyes canvassed the shop. "Late hours today?"

Before I could respond, a sudden uproar erupted followed by heavy laughter. Theo turned toward the noise.

I smiled. "Book club meeting. Are you off work or going in?"

"My shift starts in an hour." He met me at the counter.

"So, you're going to save some cats in trees tonight?" He smelled awfully good. Lucky cats.

"That's right. It's pretty much all I do."

"I'm sure. You firefighters don't work hard at all." I offered what I hoped was a playful grin. "You do make a lot of noise coming down the street though. Those trucks scare the stuffing out of me when I'm walking. Do they have to be so loud?"

"Yes. Otherwise, you might not get out of the way." Theo leaned against the counter. "How did the cookies come out?"

I sighed. "Sugary. Delicious. How is Sam adjusting?"

His expression darkened. "She's still giving Denise a tough time. Adjusting to nursery school and having a working mom now has been rough. Denise is struggling, too."

I couldn't speak for the single working mom, a role I humbly admired, but I did understand the situation from a child's perspective. "My mom worked my whole life. It's like having two full-time jobs. Working moms are true heroes." I thought of Charlie, giving up her career to raise her children so Lance could keep his. "Stay-at-home moms are, too. I guess being a parent in any capacity is no easy task."

"No, it's not," he said.

"Aren't we the lucky ones." My words fell flat between us. I'm not sure what Theo's story was, but my plan had been to be a wife and mom by the time I was thirty.

I shook off the pity-party that tried to envelope my heart. That ship has sailed, Stella.

He turned toward the shop and then to me. "I'm going to look around."

I gestured for him to go. "Please do. If you need help, you know who to call."

He pointed to me. "My friend."

"Exactly."

Twenty minutes later, he walked up front holding *Cathedral* by Nelson DeMille. "I thought I read everything he wrote. I never heard of this one."

"It's old. Written in '81. But his powerful narrative is gripping which is no surprise. It was a great find for me."

I rang Theo up, at his insistence, and he stayed with me for another twenty minutes, chatting about books (my favorite subject) before leaving to start his shift.

It was the nicest twenty minutes of my day.

I'd barely read a page, my mind consumed with my unexpected visitor, as the meeting lasted for three hours. When the wine was gone, the ten women moseyed up front, chatting. Tara lagged so I pulled her aside and pressed a book into her hands. "Try this." A woman who seemed lonely at home was the one who needed stories the most. Tara looked at the cover. *Where I've Been and Where I'm Going* by Olivia Connelly. "This is about the power of friendship, the beauty of true love, and one woman's struggle to choose. It's her debut. I couldn't put it down. It's my new favorite book."

Three picked up books to purchase on their way to the front. I rang them up and ordered their next group selection.

"What do you think of our choice?" Joan asked.

"It took me a while to get the courage to read it, but once I did, I was enthralled."

"We dubbed your new couch the 'couch of shame' for those of us who don't finish the book in time. This month, Tara was the only one on it."

"It was very comfortable," Tara said.

CHAPTER 10

Gina walked in a week later as I finished the day's message on the welcome chalkboard.

"You cannot find peace by avoiding life."

If you can tell me who said this, you'll receive twenty percent off your next book.

"Virginia Woolf," she muttered, walking to the office to take off her backpack and jacket.

I erased the board and wrote a new message I stole from the internet.

Cold? Buy a book.
You'll still be cold
But you'll have a book.

I moved the sign outside and had stepped in when she returned up front. "The gnarly beast is in your office."

"I know. He's visiting. I decided to call him Hemingway. He's got that gray beard and looks like he has tales to tell."

"How do you know he doesn't belong to someone else?" Gina said.

"If he does, that person doesn't deserve him. Was the toilet running?"

"No."

The toilet was a headache that needed to be addressed, but last month I gave my employee a deserved, though modest, Christmas bonus which set me back a bit. I've been diligent about checking it several times a day. It's probably an easy fix, but the two plumbers I'd called informed me there was a fee for them to walk into the shop on top of the cost to fix it. So, I'm prolonging my problem until I can afford to address it.

At lunch, I went next door to the salon and watched Philippe finish a blowout. His customer looked gorgeous as she paid, and I told my friend as much.

"You can look that gorgeous, too, with a little work." He assessed my hair. "A lot of work."

Philippe pulled my hair from my ponytail and spread it across my shoulders resurrecting a memory of Doug doing the same. Doug had thought my hair was my best feature.

"Put those scissors down."

Philippe frowned and dropped his scissors. "One day you'll let me have at it."

"One day."

"Peter has a cocktail table and an end table for you, so you can get rid of that sad excuse in your shop."

"How can I thank you?"

He smiled and did that thing where he lifted one eyebrow much higher than the other. Then he lifted my hair.

I shook my head, so my hair fell from his hands.

"You're impossible. So, what brings you in? You want to show me what you bought for my partay?"

"You invited Jeffrey? He keeps pulling me into his boutique to sell me something. My underwear drawer is filling with overpriced camis."

"Just say no, my dear."

I ignored the fact that Jeffrey has been in my store a handful of times and has never bought a book.

"Anyway," Philippe said, "he declined to come. Something about his wife being anti-social."

"An orange tabby keeps coming around. Do you know if he belongs to anyone?" I said, moving from the subject.

"A cat?"

I nodded.

He played with the ends of my hair and scrunched up

his face. "I think the scrapbook lady fed him here and there."
Philippe caught my gaze in the mirror. "You made a new friend,
did you?"

"I did. I want to make sure I'm not luring him away from
anyone. Though he doesn't look cared for." I put my hair back
up.

"You're your mother's daughter. That's for sure."

Don't I know it.

As I updated the Covers website to include new titles in
stock, Gina said, "We're getting snow."

The weathermen had been warning of an impending
snowstorm moving in from the west. The European model
forecasted a few inches while the American model predicted
several. I chose to go with the Europeans, ignoring the other
option and put it behind me so I could focus on next Saturday's
reading hour, choosing *If You Give a Mouse a Cookie*, or my
backup, *Dragons Love Tacos*, depending on who showed up.

"How do you want to prepare for it?" she said.

"Huh? I don't think it will be that bad. We have shovels in
the office. We can put salt down in front."

"We don't have salt."

"I'll pick some up." I finished my task, signed off the computer, and turned to my employee. "Positive thoughts, Gina."

In the office, after confirming I had two snow shovels, I sat
with Hemingway and scrolled through Facebook, pausing at
photos of Doug and Marcy. They posed in front of a hot tub
on a snow-capped ridge, flanked on either side by mountains,
heads touching and jubilant expressions, showing me how ri-
diculously happy they were together while I sat in a turtleneck
and wool pants, in a cement room with a homeless, partially
bald feline.

I'd helped her buy that bikini. Marcy, not the feline. In
hindsight, I shouldn't have. It's much too small. I wanted to
post a comment showing them that I was okay with this whole
situation (*"Looking good guys! Enjoy!"* Thumbs up, smiley, winky

emoji) but my fingers took on a life of their own. *"Hoping you'll get hypothermia"* seemed unfriendly, though justified. I stared at my words, my finger hovering over the Send button, but deleted it before I could press it and look like a bitter woman.

Gina poked her head in. "There's some old guy up front looking for you."

A small man with thick salted hair and a black mustache waited at the counter. He held a thin, brimmed hat, running his fingers over the rim. My landlord. I'd only met him once in person, the day I signed my lease. I've since been paying rent through my bank.

"Hi," I said with a smile, though inside questions swirled through my mind. In the year I've been here, he's never stepped into this shop.

He smiled. "How are you, Stella?"

I positioned myself behind the counter, facing him. He laid his hat on the Formica and pretended to look around in interest.

"What can I do for you?"

Gina positioned herself behind him a few feet away, her arms folded over her chest.

"Place looks great. How's business?"

My eyes flitted quickly to Gina, to the empty shop and to him. "It's going well. Are you looking for a book?"

I caught a subtle shake of Gina's head.

"Never been much of a reader." He inhaled and blew out a breath. "This is always a difficult conversation for me."

I swallowed. "Feel free not to have it. I wouldn't want you to feel uncomfortable."

He laughed. Gina rolled her eyes.

"I have to increase your rent." His shoulders dipped as if the weight of his delivered message had lifted.

A burning traveled up my esophagus. Increase? "I signed a two-year lease. I have nine months left."

"Our agreement is based on the Consumer Price Index, if

you remember. I haven't raised your rent yet. Last year, interest was low." He shrugged. "It's high, so I have to pass it along."

I hadn't negotiated for a fixed rent. My broker at the time thought this approach would save me money assuming the CPI wouldn't surge. I'd assumed my rent was stable through October and hadn't been paying attention.

"How much?" I said.

"Four percent."

I closed my eyes but was too wired to make the calculations in my head. "When does this take effect?"

He lifted his hat and twirled it in his hands. "Next month. I'll send an email tonight." He averted his gaze. "It's not personal, Stella. It's business."

"It's very personal to me."

He frowned. "I'm sorry. If it makes you feel better, you're not the only one."

It didn't.

I loved this bookshop—put every last penny I had into it.

"Excuse me," I whispered, leaving him to help two new customers.

When he left, Gina met me at the Self-Help shelf. "I can have him disappear for three hundred dollars."

I blinked several times and swallowed. "Don't be ridiculous." I didn't have three hundred dollars to spare. "We'll make it work, Gina."

CHAPTER 11

The next morning, I pulled myself from bed, my eyes stinging from broken sleep. The landlord's visit was still fresh on my mind when I glanced out my window to see a snow-filled scene outside. The street was dotted with soft, car-shaped mounds, and I couldn't decipher where it ended, and the sidewalk began. The news reported the shift in wind brought the snow in early and exceeded their expectations: nearly sixteen inches with more in the forecast. Trains were shut down and the Governor declared New York City and its surrounding boroughs a state of emergency, requesting cars to stay off the roads to allow the plows to clear them. On the plus side, most people, myself excluded, wouldn't be trying to get to work on a Sunday, so cars would stay put.

My impending rent increase on the forefront of my mind, I called Gina and told her to take the day off, saving me one day of salary. She gave me the *we-forgot-to-sprinkle-salt-on-the-sidewalk* comment, to which I rebuffed by pointing out a little salt held no power over a foot and a half of snow and ambled my way to the kitchen.

Coffee in hand, I returned to the window, taking in the quiet beauty outside. It felt like a Northeast winter, the kind from my youth where drifts towered over our heads and the entire scene was one huge, soft playground. My earliest memory of snow was when my mother dressed Charlie and me in confining snowsuits and slipped our feet into plastic sandwich baggies before shoving them into the thin snow boots handed down from a neighbor, battling our complaints by telling us it was how she used to keep her feet warm. Technology for snow boots had greatly improved by the time we were kids in the nineties, but we didn't have the money for them, so Mom

engineered her tried and true method. Old ways were sometimes the best ways, she'd said. She still says it when we ask her
to use an iPhone.

I remembered trying to stay outside with Charlie to wait
for Dad to come home, but his train had been delayed, and I
couldn't feel my fingers and toes, so Mom brought me inside.
Charlie had staying power and was the one to greet Dad at
the bottom of the short driveway when he trudged toward her,
lifting his legs past knee height. I'd watched out the window
as he lifted her into the air, like a stiff doll, and twirled her
around, dropping her gently into a snow mound. I'd screamed
for my mother to dress me quickly to go out to him, but he and
Charlie walked inside before she could finish and I stormed
to my room, angry with myself, Charlie, Mom, and especially
Dad, for not waiting for me.

I shook my head of the memory. Another chapter in the
story of why our father walked out the door, never to return.

The last drops of coffee splashed into the sink when
a thought struck me. Hemingway! He must be freezing. In
frantic haste, I dressed (leggings under jeans, long socks, and
turtleneck) and twisted my knotted hair in a ponytail. Slipped
into Sorel boots—my best thrift find to date—and threw two
cans of cat food and the last of my yogurts into my tote.

Minutes later, I was at the door when I found myself face-
to-face with Philippe.

He frowned. "Where are you going?"

"To look for Hemingway."

Philippe raised his eyebrows. "Sweetie, Hemingway is
dead."

Impatience brewed within me. "I'll explain later. I need to
go."

He hesitated, looking relaxed in his black joggers and
sweatshirt that said, *Chop it like it's hot* in neon pink. "I'll go
with you. Wait two secs."

"Are you sure?"

"No, but Rog is sleeping and I'm restless." He ran into his

apartment leaving the door open. I stepped inside and canvassed the room, a flip of mine across the hall. The differences between our apartments were vast. His walls were painted in a creamy butter, thick cream area rug in front of a hunter green leather sectional couch beneath an enormous new painting of a Paris scene centered on the wall. A lone woman in heels and a dress partially hidden by her red umbrella— the only color in the gray, muted picture—walked away, along a sleek sidewalk, passing empty, wet outdoor tables and chairs. The Eiffel Tower loomed ahead. I stared at her, wondering where she might be going. Was she meeting someone?

The television was hidden behind the slick wooden doors of an armoire opposite the couch. The space was cozy and inviting, and I agreed with Philippe comparing my apartment to a Shawshank prison cell: white walls, a thoughtless gray area rug, a coffee table I picked up from a curb on Long Island, and one five-by-seven framed picture on the mismatched side table next to my denim couch. I'd focused my energy on Between the Covers, which, to me, rivaled Philippe's apartment. I spent most of my time there anyway.

Philippe returned to the living room dressed like me, in jeans, scarf, hat, and boots.

"Ready, Freddy," he said.

"New painting?"

"Rog picked it up. His new obsession."

I turned at the door for one more view of the mysterious woman. She's not meeting anyone. She's taking a walk in the rain.

Philippe and I braved the elements and headed to my shop. The silent street lay before us, resplendent in fresh snow so deep, it took effort to get to the corner where Philippe loosened his scarf and unzipped his coat to his collarbone.

"Jaysus, it's deep."

I nodded in agreement. The sun shone, making the carpet sparkle. "I love it."

A walk that normally took less than twenty minutes took us forty.

"Why is Rog still sleeping?"

"He got home a few hours ago. Something about a new system isn't working for a client. He spent half the night trying to figure out what went wrong and the other half trying to get home."

"He works Saturdays?"

"On call twenty-four seven lately. If the client needs him, he's there. I hate it."

Roger was a lead technician for a computer company, a quiet, serious type, the antithesis of my witty hairdresser here. How these two worked was beyond me. But then, I knew so little about men and relationships, based on the tragic experiments of my own.

I was grateful for Philippe's company.

"I rescheduled my appointments last night. Let me put some keratin in this." He gently pulled my ponytail poking out from below my hat. "Good God girl, did you even brush it today?"

"I didn't have time. And I can't afford you."

"You can't, but I'll give you the special friend's discount."

Now was not the time for frivolous spending on such luxuries as a trim or keratin treatment. And I'd just as soon go bald than accept a free service from a friend.

The entrance to Between the Covers and the boutique next door on the right was completely blocked by a plowed wall of snow. The sidewalk in front of the deli and Philippe's salon on the left had been cleared.

"You have to wait," Philippe said. "Yours didn't get here yet." I shared the same landlord with the boutique. Philippe owned his space. He'd hired a removal service while, according to my contract, my landlord was responsible for clearing snow "within a reasonable time."

"I can't wait," I said.

He turned to me and then swiveled his body to face the

problem in front of us. "Stupid question," he said, "do you have a shovel?"

We stared at the looming mountain of snow. "There are no stupid questions. Of course, I have a shovel. I have two." I pointed to the door. "They're in there."

"This animal better be here," Philippe mumbled as we started to use our gloved hands to pull some snow from my entrance, ignoring the occasional snowplow who passed followed by one blaring fire truck.

We'd barely made a dent an hour later when I abandoned the task and climbed over the mound, pulling snow aside enough to make a narrow path to the door. I reached for the doorknob, falling inside the shop like an unpracticed acrobat, and taking snow with me.

Philippe followed and helped me throw what snow we could back outside. "I'll call my people and have them do this," he said.

"Don't. Thanks anyway."

"Stella, it's on me. I should have asked yesterday."

"Seriously, it's okay. It's supposed to be done for me." I'm sure the cost of snow removal was somehow hidden in my rent.

"When?"

"No idea." If I managed to survive enough to reach the end of my contract, I'll re-negotiate the lease to allow me to have control over snow removal. It'll be a bargaining chip. I'll add it to my growing list of things to do.

The store was cool but warmer than where we came from. We strode directly to the office. Philippe helped me to push the alley door open against the snow, enough for me to fit outside and look for Hemingway.

He waited in the doorway while I scanned the alley. "I like this rear entrance. Mine is on the side of the building. So many idiots try to get in that way when there's a clear sign saying *Entrance around corner.* You'd think they'd see the cutting station in their way."

I listened as he ranted, trying to entice the cat to safety with whistling noises.

"This door, however, is hidden," he went on, "And, if you need to, you can make a getaway."

I paused my cat whistle noises to stare at my neighbor. "Getaway? You must be confusing me with someone who has an interesting life."

I resumed whistling, intermittently calling for Hemingway until I was chilled to the bone. My jaw shook too hard to call anymore so I finally relented and sought heat in the office as Philippe stepped out from the bathroom.

"Your toilet won't stop running."

"I'll take care of it." I pulled the door shut and shivered. "I'm worried. Where would he go?" I stepped into the bathroom to stop the running water.

"Animals are resourceful. He's hunkering down until this blows over. You'll see."

I hoped so. This cat had been coming daily to my door looking for food and comfort, and today, I felt as if I'd failed him. It was eleven in the morning. He can't give up on me. He can't think I've abandoned him.

"Let's go to the deli and then try again," I said. "I want to open today."

Philippe frowned. "To think, two hours ago, I stopped over for a relaxing afternoon. Thought we might have a hot toddy. Or perhaps some wine. Chips. Animal rescue in the tundra, or *work*, never entered my mind."

We climbed back over the mountain of snow, leaving my shovels outside the entrance, and went to the deli next door. It was the only business on the block that was open. The owners lived upstairs, Philippe told me.

Philippe passed me a steaming cup of whatever he ordered while I used the deli bathroom. I expected sweet hot cocoa, testing it through the hole in the cover with the tip of my tongue. Coffee. The heat singed my taste buds. Not what I'd wanted, but at least it was hot.

He cheerfully gossiped with the woman behind the register while he waited for his drink. She handed him a small bag.

"I'm closed today, but this one," he said, jabbing a thumb in my direction, "wants to open, too. It doesn't make sense. I mean, for you... yes. But for her? It will take hours to clear away the snow. Besides, who in their right mind would be out today?"

The woman arched her eyebrows.

"Present company excepted," he bowed.

"I have to try," I said. "I'm closed tomorrow." Two days of no business was unthinkable. Maybe I'll open tomorrow, too. Maybe I'll go to seven days a week again. "You can go home. Rog might be awake. Besides, the cat might be trying to get here."

Philippe looked at me like I had three heads but shrugged.

Outside, I coveted my drink. The warmth seeped through my mittens. I was consumed with worry about how I was going to make my entrance safe for customers when Philippe said, "Well, I'll be damned."

"What?"

He held my arm to keep me from moving forward as we watched two guys shoveling my front walk.

"Is it your guy?" I said.

"Uh-uh." He was entranced.

I leaned forward, shielding my eyes from the glare of the snow to see that I didn't recognize either person. "I don't know them. What am I supposed to do?"

"You act grateful and say thank you."

I approached the men. "Excuse me?"

One stopped and wiped his nose with his sleeve. He couldn't be older than twenty-two.

"Hi. I'm not sure you're at the right place. Do you work for my landlord? Patrick Halloran?"

He shook his head. "Are you Stella?"

I nodded.

He jutted his thumb toward Between the Covers' door,

where I glimpsed the handles of my own shovels still waiting. "This your store?"

I nodded again.

"We're in the right place."

He resumed shoveling when I said, "You can stop now. I appreciate it. But I'll take care of the rest."

The two paused and looked at me. The younger one spoke again. "No, we can't. If you can step aside, we'll finish and be on our way."

"May I ask who you are?"

"We work with Theo. He asked us to do this."

"I'm sorry."

The kid shrugged. "Don't be. We're off shift. Not a big deal. And besides, I gotta listen to him or he'll try to kick my ass."

The other guy snorted. "Try nothin'. He can take you down with one hand and you know it."

The young one rolled his eyes and smiled.

We watched them for a few minutes when Philippe handed me the bag and announced he'd go home. "I'm going to see if Rog wants to make a snowman. We like to make them with big...feet." He took two steps and turned, giving me an exaggerated wink. I ignored him, hoping the guys didn't see and ran into the shop, through to the office. I pulled out my petty cash box and counted the bills. I stared at the meager amount for a minute, struggling with what to do. I could hardly afford to give them what they deserved and didn't want to insult them with what I could spare. I closed the box. As I walked to the front door frustrated and empty-handed, I glimpsed my deli cup and bagged muffin that Philippe bought me on the counter and had an idea.

Returning to the deli, I bought two oversized muffins and hot chocolates and put them inside the shop before grabbing a shovel and working alongside the guys. A few minutes in, sweat already tickled down my spine with the effort. How would I have done this on my own?

"It's not much but, thank you," I said, handing them the food and cocoa when the portion of the sidewalk in front of my store was completely cleared.

They took my offering, and the younger one said, "Our pleasure. Thanks for this."

In the alley, my teeth chattered, and I hugged myself with one arm. I spilled the last drops of my coffee in the snow next to me and waited for the cat to return.

Inside, while warming up, my phone chimed, and a picture appeared of two small, rosy-colored faces mostly covered by wool hats and scarves sprinkled with snow. A lump formed in my throat. If that wasn't the most beautiful sight I ever saw, I didn't know what was.

Losing hope, I went outside again as Hemingway reached the pinnacle of a snow mound. He paused atop the drift when he spotted me. His mouth opened but he was too far away for me to hear his mew, and my entire body sagged with relief.

I whistled for him to come to me, though it was wasted effort. He had every intention of doing so. He greeted me by rubbing his cold body against my leg over and over while I pet him with my gloves. Then we went inside, and I closed the metal door.

Up front, I updated my welcome board and put it outside so passersby would see I was open.

Hey! You made it!
Come inside and warm up.
I have snow many books!

I glanced up and down the sidewalk. The shops on either side of mine were closed and dark. I felt as if I were an island today, floating in a sea of white.

CHAPTER 12

The next morning, I sat in my office poring over my receipts, Hemingway at my feet, grateful that I'd opened yesterday.

My familiar joy at being surrounded by books in my own business was overshadowed by the threat of higher rent looming over me. How would I do it? *Could* I do it?

Though it was Monday, I flipped the lights on and had turned the sign on the front door to *Come In! We're Open!* when my cell phone rang. My sister's face appeared on the screen, and I was happy for the distraction.

"Hello, sister."

"Auntie Stella!"

My face bloomed into a happy smile. "Maddie!"

I listened for the next few minutes to a four-year-old rant that her brother was sick and now she couldn't go outside. When she finally relinquished the phone to her mother, I was laughing hard.

"She's not happy," I said.

"Understatement." Charlie sounded tired.

"What's wrong?"

"The baby was up all night. He has a fever and a croupy cough." She yawned. "It was Maddie's idea to call you. I know you're closed today, so I allowed it."

"Doesn't she have preschool?"

"They're closed."

I gazed around the shop, out the window as people walked by, mentally arguing about whether I should open or help my sister and spend time with my niece. I longed to unburden my financial worries with someone, but I knew I would never. This was my path. My struggle.

Maddie's tearful voice filled my ear. "Auntie Stella, want to play in the snow with me?"

I flipped the sign on the door to *Sorry! We're Closed!* and turned from the window.

"I would love to, Mad. Put your mom on, please."

"I'll come over and take her out," I said to Charlie. "I can get there by noon."

"Lance can drop her off by you and he'll head to the office. He has a meeting he can't miss otherwise he would have taken her somewhere."

I did some quick thinking, taking into consideration where Lance's office was. "I'll meet them at the south entrance of Central Park, so he doesn't have to cross the bridge."

"Bridge. He's using public transportation today, Es."

I hung up the phone and locked the register when I spotted Theo walking outside the front window. Without thought, I burst through the door and caught him as he passed the dry cleaners.

"Hey!"

Theo turned and smiled. Something deep inside of me fluttered. Now that I had his attention, I felt tongue-tied. He waited but didn't seem to mind or to be rushing off.

"Thank you for having your friends shovel me out yesterday."

"My truck passed, and I saw your entrance covered. I asked them to shovel you out if it still wasn't done when they got off work."

"They were very nice, but they were probably silently cursing me. I'm sure they had their own places to clear out."

Theo shook his head. "I would have done it if I weren't on a twenty-four. They said it took no time." He hesitated. "Isn't your landlord supposed to take care of that?"

"In a 'reasonable amount of time'." I used finger quotes. "It's in my contract. Anyway, thanks to you I opened and had a pretty good day."

I looked around at the mounds of snow made by the plows, the edges black with soot and dirt, marveling at how quickly something so beautiful could be tainted. "What does your niece think of all this? Being from Arizona, she must be thrilled."

"She hasn't been out yet. Denise works until six and I just got off duty."

Before I could stop myself, I said, "Do you want to meet me and Maddie at Central Park? I told my sister I'd take her while her husband is at work."

He looked down at his phone and I immediately began backpedaling. He must have plans. "It's short notice, so don't worry about it. Next time," I added.

He dialed a number and started talking, so I turned to give him privacy and walked into the shop, embarrassed. In the few times we'd seen each other, I'd lost a kid and didn't plan for a snow day for my own business. I felt like a walking catastrophe when around this guy, so I didn't expect him to accept my offer.

Theo walked into the shop. "I spoke to Denise. We'd love to meet you, but she doesn't have appropriate snow clothes for Sam yet."

I relaxed. "Leave that to me."

After a brief call with Charlie, Theo and I agreed to meet at one o'clock at Bethesda fountain. He suggested we exchange phone numbers in case we couldn't find each other. I practically ran to my apartment to change and caught the subway to Manhattan, still disbelieving that I'd coordinated an outing with a man. No. *A friend.* I'm sure he agreed to the afternoon to please his niece, but still, it was a big step for me.

As I waited on the platform, doubt plagued me. Did I overstep in asking Charlie for winter clothes for Sam? Was it Theo's excuse not to spend the day with me?

I climbed the steps up to 57th. Next time, I'll simply say thank you and keep my mouth shut. Oh, if I had a nickel for every "next time," I'd be able to cover the raised rent and then some.

Maddie looked like she'd stepped from J.Crew Cuts magazine in her matching pink snow pants and coat. Her navy hat and mittens picked up the navy accents of the lining of her pants. Her dark curls fell from her hat past her shoulders. She was precious to see.

Lance handed me a canvas tote filled with a lavender snow-suit with pink hat and mittens and a pair of dark purple boots for Sam to use.

"Charlie hopes it's the right size," he said.

"Sam's smaller than Maddie, so even if it's a little big, it'll be fine."

Lance hugged me and pressed money against my palm.

"What's this for?"

"For today. You're saving us. We hope Maddie doesn't catch whatever Myles has."

I pushed the money into his hand. "She's my niece."

He insisted. "Exactly. Please take it." I opened my mouth to protest when he said, "Did your sister tell you she wants to plant a large garden in our yard in the spring?"

I shook my head.

"Guess who's helping her do it? Take the cash."

Central Park looked like a winter wonderland. I felt well protected from the cold in the chocolate brown down coat that covered the thighs of my faded jeans, and my light brown Sorel boots tied below my knees.

Maddie and I sauntered through the park and still arrived a few minutes early, giving us the advantage to watch as Theo and Sam made their way toward us along the lower Terrace toward the fountain. Sam wore a bright orange jacket with the hood over her head and tied tight, cream wool leggings, and short boots that would surely fill with snow in minutes. She stared open-mouthed at her surroundings, as Theo guided her toward us. The sun shone, making the snow-covered tree limbs glisten like diamonds and the grass into a sparkling white bed. I was excited for her. For both the girls.

They faced each other, happy to be together again. Theo and I agreed it was the perfect day to be outside, as I secretly enjoyed the way the sunlight highlighted his hair and the stubble along his jaw. He seemed moved when I showed him the snow outfit and boots I'd brought for Sam, and we helped her into them before taking the girls hands and heading toward the path leading to an open space.

Along the way, Theo and Sam stepped ahead to let others pass, so I softly tugged Maddie's hand.

"Hey, Maddie," I whispered. "Let's have some fun." Her eyes sparkled with excitement as we ducked behind a large rock. I gathered snow, patting it into a neat round ball and handed it to her before making one for myself. "When they turn around, toss it at Theo, okay?"

Theo and Sam walked only a few steps before Theo realized we weren't behind them. He turned, frowned, and pulled his niece closer to him.

"Now!" I said. We jumped out and Maddie's ball made it a few feet, landing impotently well before our target. But mine hit him in the shoulder, startling him. Maddie and I began to giggle.

Theo immediately relaxed when he saw us. He let Sam go and she ran to Maddie.

They jumped into the snow, well past their knees, and licked icy clumps from their mittened hands. Theo stepped over to me in his tan canvas jacket.

I clutched a new snowball, and he held his gloved hands up in surrender. "Sorry about the attack. I couldn't help it." I smiled and shrugged. "When there's snow, you kind of have to."

"Oh yeah?" He took a step toward the girls and bent down to grab a fistful of snow. He turned around, threatening to throw it, and a squeal escaped me as I ran for cover behind a rock. Through fits of giggles, we managed to include the girls in our snowball fight until finally, I called a truce.

"No more," I said, bending over, working to control my laughter and catch my breath. I hadn't felt this playful in years. Theo dropped his last piece of ammunition and leaned against the rock, trying to contain his laughter, too.

He turned to the girls. "Sam, have you ever made a snowman?"

Sam and Maddie looked at each other, their eyes bright, their cheeks red, and their smiles full. "Please, Uncle Theo, I want to make one!"

"Me, too!" Maddie and I added in unison.

It took us a long time, but together, we managed to build a lopsided Frosty.

"He looks ornery," I said, as we assessed the mound of snowy orbs with eyes of black rocks. The girls were now lying on the ground, making snow angels.

"Wouldn't you be if you had to stand out here in public naked?" Theo said.

"He needs a pipe. That's why he's ornery. He quit smoking and he's cranky."

"Smoking'll kill you," he said. "He's going cold turkey."

We lifted our nieces up and made our way to Wollman's rink at the southern end of Central Park. I rented ice skates as Theo bought us hot chocolate. We found a table and sipped cocoa while watching the skaters glide effortlessly with the New York skyline as a backdrop.

"I've never been here," I said, squeezing my feet into skates. I'd originally rented three pairs for them, and Theo went to the rental kiosk and returned with a pair for me, too. He wouldn't accept my refusal to join them.

"I used to come here all the time with my father."

"Well, be warned. I'm not as graceful as I appear." I gripped the entrance wall while Theo held Maddie's and Sam's hands guiding them around the rink's perimeter. He finally deposited them near the wall where he could keep an eye on them and told them to stay put. Then he skated to me. It took a bit of coaxing on his part before I relented and let go.

He gripped my forearms and, skating backwards, pulled me to the center of the ice.

"Don't look down. Look at me." I lifted my head, and he laughed. "You look terrified."

"Don't let my face fool you, I passed terrified three weeks

ago." My face flushed and I looked down at my skates. *Why did I say that?* I wobbled and clutched his arms, certain my full body would meet the ice. He tightened his hold, and I stopped weaving, once again securely in place. I pulled my gaze up to his.

"What do you mean?" he said, staring into my eyes. "What do you mean you passed terrified three weeks ago?"

"Did I say that? I meant three minutes ago. I passed terrified three minutes ago." I stared at him to hide my lie. The truth was I had been terrified of what I felt when I saw this guy for the first time three weeks ago—and every time since.

"Where'd you learn to skate like this?" I separated my legs to better support me.

"Hockey. Stop looking down, Stella."

"You're good." He glanced over my shoulder to check on the girls. We locked eyes. *What am I doing?* "I'm ready to let go."

"You're not," he said.

"Let me try." Before he could protest, I pulled my arms from his capable hands, made two elegant glides (akin to Michelle Kwan in my mind), until my feet betrayed me and went skyward, bringing my rear onto the ice. *Ow.* Splayed on my back, I recoiled as Theo's face appeared above me. He bent over, his hands on his thighs.

"I'm sorry. I shouldn't have let go." He pulled me to my feet, held the sides of my face in his gloved hands, and checked my eyes.

"You didn't," I said. "I let go." I looked to the side to avoid his scrutiny, my ego more bruised than my body.

"Did you hit your head?"

"No."

He pursed his lips, as if he wasn't sure I was right.

"I didn't, Theo. I landed on my built-in cushion."

He guided me to the girls, who'd stayed in place as directed, asked me three times if I was okay, and then took them for another spin around the rink. I watched from my bench as he pulled his arms forward, bringing them together and then to his sides. They squealed in delight and for a moment, the throbbing of my hips, ass, and back dulled as I reveled in their childlike joy, their oblivion to everyone around them, wishing we could hold onto it forever.

We returned our skates and formed a small circle.

"Do you want to grab something to eat?" Theo said.

"I'm hungry!" Sam.

"Me, too!" Maddie.

"It's unanimous. We're hungry," I said.

We argued over who would pay for the food until finally, Theo told me I was the most stubborn person he'd ever met, and he'd met some doozies. He also countered that I was the reason his niece was having the best time, her first time in snow, and I relented.

Over pizza and soda, while Maddie and Sam talked about what they loved the most about the day, I told Theo that snow days like this reminded me of when I was young, and my mom would make chili for dinner when we came in.

"My mom makes the best chili," I said.

"Impossible."

"Are you dissing my mother?"

He shook his head. "With respect, I will treat you to the best chili you've ever had. If you still think your mom's is better, then I'll personally buy her a new stove. That's how confident I am." His enthusiasm was contagious.

Maddie yawned, and Sam rubbed her eyes.

Theo and I smiled at each other.

"Success," I said low.

He nodded. "Today was a great day. I need to get her home. I need sleep, too."

After declining Theo's offer to call me an Uber, Maddie and I walked two blocks when she started complaining her legs hurt. I texted Lance, who responded with an apology that he'd be another hour or so. I hoisted Maddie onto my back and carried her to the subway and then to the Long Island Railroad to Charlie's.

CHAPTER 13

Maddie and I walked into Charlie's house as she prepared dinner. Our mother was setting the table in the dining room.

"How was your day?" Mom said, lining the forks on the left on top of the linen napkins. To see her fuss with place settings seemed unnatural to me. Being raised on Mom's modest salary, we'd enjoyed no frivolous dinners with linen napkins or fine China. But we always had a warm meal in our cozy kitchen with the same unadorned flatware Mom still used. Granted, there were a lot of Hungry Man dinners and food Mom took home from the diner after Dad left, but it was delicious because we were together. I'd hated the charity people gave to us when my father left; the casserole dishes and pies left on our doorstep, the passed-down clothes from neighbors. It made me feel we were weak, and I vowed at a young age to be self-sufficient. If Theo thought I was stubborn, he was right. Behavior born of a lifetime of practice.

"It was great. Maddie loved it. We spent the entire afternoon at Central Park with her new friend, Sam. If she's not sleeping within the hour, then I've failed my duty as an awesome aunt."

In the kitchen, I helped Charlie finish chopping carrots for the salad. She yawned.

"How's the little man?"

"He finally fell asleep around three. I managed two loads of laundry before Mom came."

I tossed the last shreds of carrot into the bowl and turned to my sister, who yawned again. "Do you want to rest? I'll put the fish in the oven and get you when it's ready. You look terrible."

"And you look wonderful. The outdoor air agrees with you."

I blushed and turned away.

Lance came home as Mom set the plate of salmon on the table, flanked on either side with broccoli and roasted potatoes. Charlie, who had agreed to lay down, still looked tired when she walked in a minute behind her husband.

We settled around the table in our usual seats. "How is your friend?" Charlie said. She remained standing, assessing the table.

"He's fine."

I felt Lance's and Mom's eyes on me. "What friend?" Mom said.

My sister winked and went into the kitchen.

"No one. Me and Maddie met him and his niece at the park today."

"Are you dating?" Mom tried to act nonchalant, straightening her already straight napkin. Lance covered his smile with his hand and received my warning glare as a result.

"We're friends."

She nodded and said nothing. Charlie returned, holding the bowl of salad. Maddie sidled up next to me.

Myles called for his mother from his bedroom, and Lance jumped up to check on him so Charlie could eat. He returned with a red-faced little boy on his shoulder, and I felt guilty for all the fun we had today without him.

Despite Charlie's obvious exhaustion, she lovingly took the time to help her daughter by cutting the fish into small pieces, ensuring every hidden small bone was removed while Maddie recanted her day with her new friend, remembering much of the activities, including the snowball fight, the ice skating, how Auntie Stella kept falling, the hot cocoa…basically everything we did. When she finally ran out of steam, her meal barely touched, she yawned wide and asked to go watch television.

"Take three bites," Charlie said.

"Two," countered my niece.

Charlie leaned closer to Maddie's small, pink face. "Four."

Maddie enjoyed this game. "Two and one."

Charlie pretended to think about it. "Fine. You win again."

When Maddie was out of earshot, I held my hand out for the potatoes and said, "You're not helping her to attain math skills, you know."

Charlie passed the dish to me. "Right now, my priority is to get her nourished. The math will come later."

"I can't believe she could recall the day in that much detail at her age. She takes after me," I said.

Charlie nodded. "She does take after you. She doesn't know when to stop talking."

Mom smiled into her lemon water.

"I disagree. Maddie makes Stella look like a mute sometimes," Lance said.

"Thank you, Sir Lance-A-Lot."

"Sometimes," he said. I threw a piece of broccoli at him and was awarded with a tired grin from my ailing nephew.

Mom held her hands out to Myles, who whined and reached for his mother.

"So, Mom, I stopped by at six on Wednesday with Myles and you weren't home. Have your hours at work changed?" Charlie said, settling her son against her.

"No."

"Where were you?"

"What do you mean? Nowhere." Mom picked at her chipped, unpolished nails.

I waited for Charlie to poke fun at her for going out with our young neighbor, but she didn't. In fact, she didn't seem to be in a playful mood. The rough night with her son was wreaking havoc on her.

Marion gathered the plates. "Dinner was delicious. I'll bathe Maddie. Stella will help you clean up."

I saluted my mother. "Yes, ma'am."

Lance took Myles, leaving Charlie and me alone. When the table was cleared, I washed the dishes. She dried and put them away.

"I thought you'd push Mom. She's seeing Pacer," I said.

"So what? She deserves to do what she wants, with whomever she wants."

I soaped the last plate and stared out the darkened window. A half-moon had risen, giving the swing set an ethereal glow. "Why do you think she never got involved with anyone after Dad?"

Charlie moved beside me. "Raising two kids alone didn't give her much time to think about romance. I have Lance and we're both always tired." She paused. "She never talked about him. She must have been so hurt."

"Maybe that's why we didn't talk about him either."

Charlie sighed. "You talked about him, Stella. All the time."

"I did?" How could I not have remembered?

"You talked about the things you'd tell him when he came home. Grades, pictures you made, books you read, stuff like that."

Our silent reflections watched us in the window.

"I was so relieved when you finally stopped. It was hard to watch Mom when you did."

I swallowed the lump in my throat. Did I block it out? How far back did our memory go? "I remember the last night he was home," I said. "Mom let us watch *The Wizard of Oz* even though it was a school night. She let us play it loud so we could sing along."

"No. She turned it loud so we wouldn't hear them screaming at each other."

I turned to my sister.

Charlie kept her focus on the window. "Someone came to the door, and Dad was angry, and then Mom started screaming."

"Maybe it was that old Mr. Hutchens. He used to yell at us for crossing his lawn to get to the bus stop. Maybe we did something again."

"Maybe."

"I don't remember what happened after that," I said.

Charlie put her hand on my shoulder. "Our brains try to protect us, I guess."

"But you remember."

"Yes," she whispered. "I was eleven. You were only seven."

I dropped the saturated sponge into the sink and slumped onto a kitchen chair. "I spent the day with a man, and I had fun."

Charlie sat next to me. "That's wonderful."

"No. The whole day I kept pushing away feelings that I don't want to feel." I picked at my thumbnail. "I tried to have a lasting relationship and look what happened. I was literally left at the altar."

"Did you love Doug?" Charlie said.

"Sure. I could have made it work."

"I'm not sure you could have."

"What does it matter? He made a promise, and he broke it." Charlie watched me. "Maybe I didn't love him. What does it feel like?" I've read every love story I could get my hands on, but the descriptions were so far-fetched, who could possibly believe them?

Maddie's laughter trickled in from the bedroom. Our mother's voice was muffled, but her tone told us she was enjoying her.

Charlie took my hands and squeezed them. "I imagine it's different for everyone. Remember when Dad used to spin us around in the yard until our feet flew behind us?"

"I think so."

"Love to me feels like that. Like I'm floating in air, exhilarated but safe in someone's arms, knowing I won't fall."

My heart twinged in pain, missing my father. How could I miss a man who hadn't been in my life in almost three decades?

"You'll know it when it happens," Charlie said. "Believe me."

"I'm not sure I will. I'm thirty-six and haunted by an extremely embarrassing, expensive mistake brought on by poor judgment." Not to mention a shattered heart. My wedding dress came to mind. "Leave me once, shame on you. Leave me twice..." I half-smiled and shrugged.

"Well, you have me and Mom. You have the best kind of love. It's unconditional."

Tears filled my eyes. "Thank you."

"No, thank you, Es."

I wanted to believe my sister, but over the years, hope for my happy future with someone had been chipped away by bad decisions. She stood and began to wipe down the countertop.

"What's wrong?" I said. She was frowning and didn't answer. "Charlie?"

She turned, and my gut filled with dread. Something was wrong. I knew whatever she was going to tell me would alter our lives. Her expressions mimicked mine, her fear radiated to me. "I found a lump in my breast and went to the doctor."

I felt as if my chair had tilted sideways. A lump?

"I had a mammo and a sono. I have to go for an MRI." She threw the sponge in the sink. One of her cheeks sunk in, which meant she was biting it from the inside, a tell she had when she was trying not to cry.

"When?"

She picked at invisible lint from her sweatpants. "Wednesday."

Two days away. "Do you want me to take you?"

"Lance will take me."

"Does Mom know?"

My sister shook her head. "She's on a need-to-know basis, Stella. I don't want her worried if it's nothing."

I left my sister's an hour later, tired and scared, the money Lance had given me on the kitchen counter.

CHAPTER 14

On Wednesday morning, I texted Charlie before I left for work.

Text me as soon as you get results.

After I opened the shop, dragged the welcome sign outside (*This is your sign that you need to come in and buy a book)*, and was settled at the counter, I texted her again.

Or call. Whichever. xoxo

Keeping up jovial appearances proved difficult, but I didn't want my concerns over my sister to cloud the ambiance of the bookshop, which I strived to be a haven for visitors.

During our first lull, I checked on Hemingway who was taking his morning snooze. Up front, I paced up and down the shelves.

"What's up with you today?" Gina said. "I'm usually the one who paces. Is it that idiot from the other day?"

Idiot? Oh, right. My landlord. With the current worrying about Charlie, and Monday's antics with Theo, I hardly dwelled on the potential demise of my business.

"No."

"Then what's on your mind?"

I paused. I didn't want to tell her that Charlie was going for tests, that she was only forty and shouldn't be going for tests, but I knew it wasn't fair, that so many others have their hardships. And nothing happened yet. People have lumps all the time and it's nothing. That would be the case for my sister. Of course. It was so silly of me to worry.

So, I paced again. Stopped.

"Have you sold any more paintings?" I said.

"No."

"When's the last time you picked up a brush?"

"Last night."

The bell over the door interrupted our conversation. After greeting our customer, I returned to the counter and picked up my phone. No text from Charlie.

"What are you doing?" Gina peeked over my shoulder to see my screen.

"Nothing."

"Who is that?" She pointed to the picture I'd enlarged. Two happy, tanned faces posing under wool hats and matching snowsuits with a cobalt sky above and a ski run behind them, looking…happy. My ex-fiancé and ex-best friend have been in Colorado for almost two weeks. The picture was gorgeous. They were gorgeous.

"No one." I stared at the picture, my stomach turning over.

"Get off his Facebook page, Stella. In fact, get off Facebook." I stared at it.

Gina sipped her coffee. "Does it make you happy to look at it?"

"Of course not. It's torture."

"Then why do you do it every day?"

"I self-sabotage so I don't make the same mistake again."

She frowned. "Do you miss him?"

"No." I pulled a picture closer with my thumb and pointer finger. Marcy's smile filled the screen. "I miss her."

When Doug called off the wedding, we went to Mom's house. Charlie eventually had to go home to take care of her children, and without question, Marcy had sat with me through the night while my self-esteem lay splattered on my bedroom rug. She'd quietly passed me tissues and listened as I wondered why I'd ignored my innate warnings and agreed to get married. She held her tongue when I bashed Doug for his insensitivity and poor timing. By dawn, when I was spent and at my lowest, she made me laugh and I knew I wouldn't die. She was my friend, and as close to someone I loved outside of my nucleus.

A text came in from Charlie.

Just got back.

I stared at the words. In my life, Charlie was my constant. My sister and eternal friend. She would be with me forever, unlike outside friends and lovers, who came and went with the seasons. If she got sick, I wouldn't get over it. I would have nothing.

I responded,

Okay. I feel good about this, Char.

Three dots kept appearing and disappearing, playing with my emotions. Gina must have noticed me waiting.

"It's a brilliant feature, really, the elusive three dots. They're meant to keep us from putting the phone down because we think we're getting another message," she said.

Charlie responded.

Me, too. Let's cross our fingers and toes to be sure.

Me: Everything's crossed!

I put my phone down. I had Gina's full attention.

"What?" I said.

"Everything okay?"

"Oh, fine. Charlie went for a test and it's…the waiting is hard."

"You should take her mind off it. You know, distract her."

It was an excellent suggestion.

Hey, do you want to help me find something to wear to Philippe's party next week?

Three dots again. I looked at Gina who rolled her eyes.

Yes! How about Saturday?

Me: I'll be there after work. xoxo

Theo walked into the shop, carrying my sister's canvas tote bag, and an idea hit me like a can in the head. Suddenly and unexpected. Gina mumbled she'd check on Hemingway (though she referred to him as "the mangy creature").

He held out the bag. "Denise washed everything. She really appreciates what you did. I do, too. It's all Sam talks about."

"I'm glad. I'll let you in on a secret." I leaned toward him. "It was the best time I've had in a long time."

"Same. I've been in work mode for the past couple of years. I haven't played outside like that since..." He paused. "In a while."

"Why don't you hold onto the clothes? We may get more snow." I held up crossed fingers. "Our snowman needs a pal. You can bring it at the end of the season."

He hesitated. "Are you sure? Your sister wouldn't mind?"

"I'm sure. She's generous that way." Reminder to self: ask Charlie if she minded not getting winter clothes yet.

Andy Gibb sang *Shadow Dancing* through the speaker as we lingered awkwardly. Joan passed by the window, saw us, and opened the door. She leaned her head in. "The book is depressing."

She was referring to her book club's choice.

"But it's engaging," I said.

"I can't put it down!" She closed the door and walked away.

Theo watched the exchange. "Customer," I said.

He nodded. "She's the third person to wave at you through the window."

"I'm trying to get a patent on a moveable sidewalk that brings them *into* the shop when they approach my window. They won't know what brought them in."

"Sort of like a *Field of Dreams* enticer."

"Or a moving floor like in the airports."

He laughed. "Do you have plans tomorrow night?" he said. "Thought maybe we could grab dinner. There's a hot dog cart on Monroe we could try."

I hesitated.

"It's my way of thanking you for the snow clothes," he added quickly.

"I do have plans. I'm sorry." I had a date with my couch and a book. I wanted to spend time with Theo, but my uncertainty held me back. The sting of my desertion still flared.

He ran his fingers through his hair, leaving chestnut trails along his scalp. "Okay. So, how can I thank you?"

"Let's call us even."

He circled slowly gazing around. "Looks like I'll have to come in every day and buy a book."

His warm smile drew me closer, but I stopped, keeping a few feet between us. Time to verbalize my idea. "I have a reading hour the third Saturday of every month for children. The ones who come seem to love it. But we don't attract enough."

"What do you propose?"

"Would you be open to coming in next month?"

"Absolutely."

"Wearing your uniform?"

He blinked.

"Children are enamored by firefighters, for good reason. I think they'll come in if you're here. I'll read something fireman related." I shrugged. It sounded like such a better idea in my head, as usual. "Or maybe not your whole uniform, just the jacket and the hat."

He seemed to relax. "Good, because what I wear would probably scare most kids."

I doubted it.

He held his hand out. "Deal. I'll be here."

I took his hand, and he squeezed mine lightly. Why was I blushing? "Bring Sam."

CHAPTER 15

The kids were out with Lance when I arrived at Charlie's on Saturday evening. The quiet was disconcerting. Rarely do I enter this house without the raucous jubilee of two happy children. Was this a premonition of what was to come?

Dressed in bootcut jeans and a light blue silk shirt, Charlie slipped on her coat, and we left the house. I started the car, unable to read her guarded expression, and suspected she wanted to celebrate and was making me wait. She liked to do that when we were growing up. She'd walked in from school on more than one occasion looking glum, waiting as I'd interrogated her as to what had happened when at long last, she'd burst into laughter announcing she'd aced her math exam or won the first prize in the science contest.

This was one of her typical moments and I was ready to play the part.

"You okay?"

She nodded.

"If you're hungry, we can go right to dinner. I don't need to shop for an outfit. I'll wear something I have."

"No, you won't. All you have are loose pants and turtlenecks. You need to change it up. Let's go."

After a brief argument of where to shop—I refused to go to one of her boutique stores and suggested the thrift shop in town—we finally settled on TJ Maxx. Ten minutes later, I pulled into the parking lot.

My sister stared through the windshield. "You should have let me take you to the other place."

"One, I'm on a strict budget. Two, I'm comfortable here. I've never been a boutiquey kind of girl." My looming rent increase hid in the corners of my mind, like the new wallpaper of my life. Not always on the forefront of my thoughts, but *there.*

Charlie snorted a laugh. "That's not what the price of your wedding dress said."

"A different girl bought that dress." That girl made an appearance and disappeared.

In the quiet car, I tried to think of something funny to say, to lighten the damp mood around us, but my mind came up empty.

"I'm having PTSD, remembering when we shopped for your prom dress," Charlie said.

"It wasn't that bad."

Charlie had taken me to the Roosevelt Field Mall, and we'd scoured ten stores, with me trying on fifty dresses until we finally gave up and sat in the food court eating tacos and churros.

"Can I wear your dress?" I'd said between sips of soda. I'd managed to find something wrong with every one Charlie made me try. *Too Little Bo Peep, too slutty, too loose, too tight, too blue, not blue enough, too shimmery*, and on and on until finally, Charlie asked me if I wanted to skip the prom altogether.

"I can't. I already told Ricky I'd go."

"I thought you broke up."

"We did. But he didn't have enough time to ask anyone else. So…"

"Let me get this straight, you're going to your senior prom so your ex-boyfriend, who broke up with *you*, has a date?"

"That's right."

In the end, I wore Charlie's prom dress. An hour into the night, I'd gone to the bathroom and spent too much time in the tiny stall contending with the long gown. I'd found Ricky on the dance floor making out with Vanessa Peterson to Aerosmith's "I Don't Want to Miss a Thing," and though heartbroken, I felt grateful I hadn't spent the money.

If only there were a way to erase our memories, I would have let the good go with the bad if it hurt less.

I opened the car door. "Let's go try to make me beautiful for less so I won't be judged by my neighbor."

We linked arms as we crossed the parking lot.

Charlie, with more of an eye for fashion, pulled outfits and dresses from the depths of overstuffed clothes racks that I'd passed over. With an arm full of clothes, I followed her to the try-on room, feeling better than when I'd headed to pick her up. I'd convinced myself that we had another few days of happy ignorance until I was in front of a three-way mirror wearing a piece of material that barely reached my mid-thighs, and caught Charlie staring ahead, not seeing me.

I knelt to where she sat on a stool and put my hands on her knees. "You heard?"

She nodded.

But it was Saturday. What doctor worked on Saturdays?

"Tell me."

Her full eyes moved to mine, and I knew. At that moment, I wanted to turn back the clock, to before she got a phone call that would change her life.

"I have breast cancer."

The blood in my body plummeted to my feet. I tightened my hold on her to keep from falling. How could this be happening?

"Is this one of your fake news jokes because I'll tell you, it's your worst yet."

Tears spilled down her cheeks.

Oh, God, no.

"He called today?"

"I had the biopsy yesterday. He told me."

"We've been together for two hours. How have you been keeping this to yourself?"

"I wanted to have one last conversation before everything became about cancer."

The rims of her eyes were red and her cheeks blotchy. She

sniffed. I looked around for a tissue, found nothing, and handed her a blouse. "Cotton."

We stayed in the fitting room while the news filled the air, suffocating us. Charlie swallowed over and over, as if trying to keep her fear down while I worked hard not to vomit.

"Let's get out of here," I said.

I bought the cotton blouse, feeling guilty that we'd used it as a tissue, and dumped it in the garbage on the way out.

"That was a waste," Charlie said.

"I never want to see that blouse again."

We couldn't pull ourselves from the car to walk into the restaurant, so I took us through the drive-through lane of a fast-food place, ordered burgers, French fries and two chocolate shakes. Charlie didn't complain. We sat in a dark parking lot of an office building and quietly ate. Normally, I'd relish the taste of the greasy, fatty, salty goodness, but tonight, everything tasted like cardboard.

My phone rang and I quickly silenced it. It was our mother.

I gave a side glance to my sister, who stared ahead.

"Should we have gotten salads?" I said.

Charlie slurped her shake in response, which was so ridiculous and out of character that I started to laugh, which made her laugh. It didn't take long for a convulsing hysteria to overtake us. For several long minutes, we couldn't gain control and succumbed to the manic delirium that comes with something very funny but at the worst possible time.

I'm not sure when the laughter morphed into sobbing, but it did, and we held onto each other until finally, the hiccupped residue of sadness was the only sound in the car.

"So, what now?" I said.

"We're going to discuss the plan for my mastectomy and whatever follows."

"One or both?"

She poked at her remaining fries. "The tumor is in only one. But I don't want the other one."

A siren sounded somewhere nearby, growing louder as it passed and then softened.

"Which boob?"

She looked at me. "Does it matter?"

I shrugged, not knowing what else to say.

"Left."

We put the wrappers in the takeout bag and tossed it in the back seat. Charlie explained to me what happened. She'd noticed her nipple sucked in months ago and had ignored it, not knowing it was a symptom of cancer. Finally, she'd forced herself to get checked out. The doctor told her the growth started in a duct and spread. "It's called carcinoma in situ."

She turned to me in her seat, her beautiful eyes pained. "I should have gone to see him right away. I waited." A new tear fell down her blotchy cheek, and I gently wiped it.

"It's okay. It's going to be okay. I'm here. I'll be with you, Charlie. And you have Lance and Mom."

She wiped another fallen tear. "I have to tell her."

I nodded. It would be a hard conversation. How did you tell your mother that her child was sick, that the mother of her grandchildren had cancer?

"Do you want me with you?" I said.

"Yes." It was a whisper.

"She's the one who called."

Charlie looked at me. "What did she want?"

I played Mom's voicemail on speaker.

Stella, I saw Sophia again today. She mentioned her very nice nephew. I have his phone number if you want it. I knew enough not to give her yours. Think about it.

"She's relentless. She, of all people, trying to set me up."

Charlie shook her head. "Maybe she knows how nice it is to have a family of your own."

The drive to Mom's was silent. I'd called from the parking lot and asked her if we could come by, so when we pulled up to her house, she was standing at the door. I think she knew before we even got out of the car.

The three of us sat in her tiny living room, surrounded by her animals. I pulled Margie onto my lap for protection and lost my fingers beneath her floppy ears, scratching the part that made her lean her head into it. If reincarnation were possible, I wanted to return as this dog. Henry took his post beside Mom, and Charlie sat alone with her hands clasped in her lap. I noticed for the first time since picking her up that her nails had been bitten down, and her thumb cuticle was bloody.

"Tell me," Mom said. Her strong voice pierced the silence.

I tipped my head to Charlie. You got this, sister. She lifted her chin and told Mom what she told me in the fitting room. *I have stage two breast cancer, Mommy.*

There was the briefest crack in Mom's veneer before she walled up and announced that Charlie would be okay. She was so sure of it, that I believed her.

We sat in the room where memories whispered our past, holidays spent on the couch, watching the Thanksgiving Day parade on television, around our small Christmas tree, preening over our modest but beloved gifts, holiday carols, and the scent of baked bread filling the house, sick days spent watching game shows, and sipping homemade soup under a cozy, crocheted blanket. Maybe the good memories were worth keeping the bad. Ours were endless, and I knew how fortunate we were to have each other in the face of our early loss, how we'd banded together to stay strong and survive, and how we would do it again.

I took Charlie's hand and squeezed it. She squeezed back and smiled at me.

She felt it, too—the positivity emanating from this woman we were privileged to call *Mom*.

I walked into my apartment at midnight after dropping Charlie at home. I stripped out of my wool pants and sweater and immediately climbed into bed, wrapping myself in my comforter. My body shivered uncontrollably. My sister must survive. Maddie and Myles need their mother. They had no idea how lucky they were to have been given this woman to love them and raise them. No one knew that more than me. Every memory I've ever had included her. Charlie helped to raise me and pulled me from my abyss of despair after what happened last year. She was my biggest advocate when I announced I wanted to open my own business.

Giving up on sleep, I turned on the news and listened as the anchor described how tough and horrible the world can be; robberies, attacks, murders, fires, but the news paled by comparison to what I learned tonight.

I waited for the weather report and turned off the television. Snuggling down under my comforter, I couldn't get warm. My mind raced as I recalled pieces of our conversation. Charlie said little about Lance. How did he react, I wondered?

She was dismissive when I'd asked. "You know Lance, he's a rock. He said I'll be fine and locked himself in his office."

I grabbed my phone and scrolled mindlessly through Facebook, stopping at the latest post from Doug. It was a selfie of him and Marcy sitting at a bar, toasting to happy hour. Smiling faces, sparkly eyes. How could you smile when my heart was breaking all over again?

A text appeared at the top of my screen. Theo.

> Would you believe Sam is still talking about the snow day? We're getting a lot of mileage on this one.

My eyes filled. This was what I needed. A distraction. I typed:

> Who dis?

I watched the three dots appear and disappear until he finally sent:

> Wiseass.

I smiled, and a tear meandered down my temple.

> Me: I'm glad she's happy. We'll have to do it again. They get along so well.

> Theo: They do. Friends in an instant.

> Me: Imagine that.

> ☺

I closed my eyes and rested against my pillow. I wanted to tell him I was upset, that my sister was sick. It's what I would share with a friend.

He texted again:

> Hey, funny story. I saved a kitten today. Somehow, he managed to get to the top branch of an oak, and I could only reach him using the bucket (the thing attached to the end of the truck ladder).

I let out a breath.

> Me: I knew that was all you firemen did.

> Theo: You're right. Easy peasy.

> Me: My sister is sick.

I hit send and tossed my phone on the side table. I could no longer tell Marcy. And Gina didn't like texting or talking on the phone, for that matter.

His response came immediately.

> I'm sorry. Do you want to talk?

> Me: Not yet. But I needed to tell someone. Thank you.

> Theo: I'm glad you did. What are friends for?

I stared at the screen when another text came through.

Theo: Cancer?

Me: Yes.

Theo: We're living in a time of advanced science and technology.

In other words, he was saying, Charlie has a good chance of survival. I needed to hold onto that.

Me: Yes.

Theo: If you need to talk, call anytime. I'm here.

Peeking through the folds of my comforter, I stared at my wedding dress, too full to fit the confines of my small closet. My eyes trailed the intricate lace along the bodice and the hand-stitched pearls. I sighed. I'd spent two months pushing doubts aside as I'd shopped for the perfect gown to start the perfect life. The more I'd searched, tried on, scheduled appointments, the weaker my apprehension, until I was convinced the answer to the rest of my life was in a bridal boutique. Twelve thousand dollars later, I was ready to show the world I was worthy of marriage. My life would be my own, as a wife and mother. Thousands on a piece of material.

I stared at the massive silk anchor taunting me.

Enough. Time to let go.

I grabbed my phone and signed onto eBay. Several drafts later, I had a listing:

FOR SALE

Vivianne Westwood Gown. Features a back cuff and illusion beading with a cathedral train. Size 8. Brand new (worn less than two hours). Original price: $12,000. Best offer.

I pressed the submit button and exhaled.

CHAPTER 16

On Tuesday morning, I struggled to ignore the surprised and curious glances as I walked to work. With my lunch in my satchel over my shoulder and a full wedding dress in my arms, partially blocking my view, I stopped several times to push it down or risked walking into traffic.

The wind had died down, making the chill bearable, and I was almost at Gruber Ave. when the harsh wail of sirens interrupted me. I stopped, clutching my dress to my body, and kept close to a building as two fire trucks drove past, followed by a truck with a single swirling light on its dash. One of the firemen hanging off the second truck found me funny and said something to his friend, who gazed at me in wonder.

In the dry cleaners, the dress was positioned on the counter like a ghost bride who'd fainted. Ms. Roselli, the owner, leaned her head close to the fabric, to the intricacy of the beaded work, and marveled. I agreed, it was a gorgeous piece, and asked how much to clean it.

She continued to scour the material, poring over the train, and asked if there were stains. I pointed out the faint blotches along one sleeve and the chest area. She brought her nose toward the bodice. "What is it?"

"Um, it might be salt, or it might be something else," My eyes flitted to the rows of plastic-wrapped clothes behind her, avoiding her scrutiny until she returned to the blotches.

"I see," she said.

"Please take them out, carefully. I'd like to sell this."

She nodded and pulled the whole thing with her so that she disappeared under a sea of silk.

As I passed the boutique, I glimpsed the owner speaking with a customer while another sifted through a rack of clothes.

I wondered how Jeffrey was doing. We shared the same land-lord. Was his rent being raised as well? Was he as stressed as me?

He caught me watching and waved me in. I waved back and continued, pretending not to understand his gesture, and escaped into my shop. My wallet would remain closed for an-other day.

I dropped my bag on the counter and breathed in the si-lence. Hello, books. My friends and companions.

I wasn't going to lose this shop. It was my life. Speaking of, I texted Charlie to see how she was doing, even though I'd talked to her four times yesterday.

I poked my head out the office door into the alley in time to see a man pushing a shopping cart past the opening on the other street as Hemingway approached. The man, wearing oversized dark green pants and an open parka, turned to look at me, his unruly beard twitching in surprise. He slowed, and then continued. I quickly lured the cat inside with a bowl of fresh cat food and closed the door. He greeted me with a rub against my leg. As he ate, my stomach growled, pining for my morning muffin, which I'd forfeited the past several days in preparation for my monthly increase. I pulled out my petty cash box and counted what I had left. Two hundred forty dollars of emergency money, which may not cover the cost to clean the dress. I slammed the top down, alarming Hemingway whose ears pricked up in fear.

"Sorry. It's not you."

The cat finished his bowl, cleaned himself, circled the cor-ner and promptly fell asleep.

Charlie called me as Gina walked in, reminding me to re-turn to TJ Maxx and buy the green silk dress she'd picked out for me, the dress I'd discarded and left in a heap after her news.

She sounded better today— everything looked better in the daytime. But I was worried about her. There was no way I was going to a party.

"I'm going to blow it off," I said. "Philippe will understand."

"He would tell you it's not going to do me any good to have you sit there at home with some book when you could be enjoying his friends and socializing. And I would agree. Get your butt to the store or I'm going for you."

"Forget the dress. When do you go to the doctor?"

"Noon," Charlie said.

I stared out the front window, but all I could see were the faces of my niece and nephew on the bodies passing by.

"Stella?"

"Sorry."

Charlie sighed. "It's okay. I'll call you later."

I checked the shop's voicemail, noting the numbers to call back. One woman left a message asking if we carried a copy of *The Beautiful and the Damned* by Fitzgerald.

After returning the calls (No, I did not currently have a copy but would call her when I did), I updated the chalkboard near the door.

Gina arrived and noted the message on the welcome board.

Fiction...
Because real life is terrible.

She looked at me, at the sign, at me again. I turned away and started organizing the shelf behind the counter. My stomach growled. I pulled out a book that took me three weeks to find for a customer who'd never returned to pick it up and placed it on the counter.

Gina lifted it and read the spine. "No deli? Again? Did you finally find a roach in your cup?"

God forbid. "I'm eating gourmet breakfast at home now." My stomach growled again, reminding me to pick up more cereal.

She stared at me. "You okay?"

"Peachy. You?"

She eyed me closely. "Coffee and muffin are your favorite thing. You're frowning and you never frown."

I straightened and took a deep breath. "Sure, I do."

She leaned on one leg. Put her hand on her waist. "You always smile. Even when you're not happy. Trust me, it's annoying, but not nearly as annoying as giving up something you like because you think you'll be run out of business by that jackass landlord." She glanced at the welcome board again. "Explains today's message at least."

"You don't like it?"

"I love it. And I agree with it, but it's a bit cynical for you."

Gina flipped the sign on the front door to *Come In! We're Open!* and went to put the book away while I moved the message board outside. Chilled wearing only my sweater, I stared at the words on the board until they swam in front of me. Jeffrey called my name as he peeked out the door of his boutique.

"Stella! Happy Tuesday!"

I returned his smile and waved. Before heading into the shop, I made a slight change to the day's quote.

Fiction...
Because real life is terrible.
☺

Charlie called me midday, after her appointment. I took her call in the office while Gina covered the shop.

"Well?"

"I met with a plastic surgeon and spoke with the general surgeon. Now we need to coordinate their schedules for my mastectomy."

"They both have to be there?"

"The plastic surgeon puts the expanders in when the other guy takes off my breasts. It's like a tag-team."

I grimaced, distressed by the thought. "When?"

She hesitated. "They'll call me to let me know when. Then pre-op."

"Did they say when they'll call?" I unwrapped my liverwurst with mayo on a roll and stared at it. Hemingway stretched from his nap and sauntered to me, his one-sided whiskers working overtime to smell the meat. Having lost my appetite, I shared my lunch with him.

"No. I asked three times. Lance and I fought on the way home. He told me I annoyed the doctor. And I started screaming at him that I would have kept asking until I got an answer if he didn't stop me." She sniffed. "He pulled over on the parkway, so I didn't jump out while he was doing seventy."

This was the first time she'd admitted to fighting with her husband. They'd had disagreements, sure, but minor and quickly resolved.

Charlie put Myles on the phone, so she could put on sweats. I opened the door to let Hemingway out as I asked Myles questions, to which he provided "yah," "no," "boo!" and inaudible answers until Charlie retrieved the phone.

"I'm going to take him to a playgroup. I need to get out of here."

Charlie's motto with little boys was like Mom's with dogs: the more tired they were, the better behaved.

I tossed my wrapper in the garbage and opened the shop door to return to work. "Lance is trying to process this, too. Try not to be so hard on him," I said.

"I'm going to be hard on everyone. I'm beyond angry, Es. I'm enraged."

"Consider me warned," I said, forcing a smile I didn't feel, and waving to Joan as she entered the shop. I hung up with Charlie in time to greet her.

"Stella." Joan reached me and grabbed my arms. Her brown eyes were red and watery. Her dark hair, typically styled loose past her shoulders, was pulled into a severe ponytail. With minimal makeup on, in light gray leggings and long gray sweater, she appeared younger today. And sad.

"What happened?"

Joan sniffed and blinked, releasing a single tear down her smooth cheek. "Do you have a minute? I need to talk to someone."

"Of course." I glanced at Gina, who nodded and went to help another customer. I led Joan to the couch of shame in the rear corner.

"My husband is cheating on me."

"Oh." I wasn't sure what to say. "Are you sure?"

"I followed him today to her apartment. Then I came here."

I pulled a box of tissues from the cocktail table and handed her one. "Does he know that you know?"

She shook her head. "You're the only one I told. I can't tell the girls because it's too embarrassing." Tears trailed her cheeks in earnest now.

"You shouldn't feel embarrassed. You didn't do anything wrong."

"I did something if he's bringing another woman into our marriage."

"I'm not sure that's how it works." Or does it?

"I'm so angry." Her fisted hands pressed against her eyes.

"What made you follow him? What made you think he was seeing someone?"

She blew her nose. "He had yogurt and blueberries for breakfast again today."

What?

Joan grabbed more tissues and wept quietly. I rubbed her sleeve until she'd calmed.

"Can you explain how his breakfast was the tell-tale sign?"

She swallowed. "Every morning for the past eighteen years, Patton has eaten three eggs over easy and two pieces of rye toast with butter. He dips his toast into runny yolks and reads the news." She began to cry again, and I waited, still not understanding.

"A few weeks ago, I walked into the kitchen to find him eating yogurt and blueberries." She turned to me. "*Yogurt and fruit!*"

I nodded. Go on.

"He's been eating it every morning since. And he was smiling as he read the news. Smiling! Oh, God." She dropped her head and let out a wail that attracted the shop's attention. I glanced over to Gina, who gave us the evil eye. I returned it with my wide-eyed "sorry" expression.

"But I love him. I don't know what to do."

She explained how there were signs, new behavior she'd excused, blaming his stresses at work for suddenly needing to go the gym, or the kids' busy schedules making him cranky because he didn't have enough time to "relax." She used finger quotes here.

"I mean, we have kids who are involved. Since when do we relax?"

She went on about not wanting to listen to the worried thoughts that something else was going on. He became short with her, spent an inordinate amount of time in the bathroom with his phone. He'd purposely stayed up later, so she'd be asleep before he climbed into their bed. They stopped making love.

"Did you talk to him about your concerns?" I said.

She blew her nose. "I couldn't. I'd hoped it was a passing phase." She shifted her body to fully face me on the couch, her nose red, her breath uneven. "We had the best life. Why would he fuck it up?"

I shrugged. What stayed with me was that she picked up on insignificant behavior that only two people who shared the intimacy of marriage could detect. Doug and I had sex right up until he ditched me on our wedding day. When he didn't show, I was blindsided. Yet, there had to have been signs. No one ups and leaves without explanation and doesn't give something away in the days leading up to it. I saw nothing. I knew... nothing.

A small group of young women walked in. Gina was busy at the counter, so I excused myself to help them, leaving Joan on the couch with her sorrows.

I led them to the young adult contemporary fiction, as they'd requested. "I have a recommendation for you." We walked to the Staff Picks shelf. "This author writes more in the

New Adult genre, which means her characters are a little older than in YA, but she's so gifted. You won't want to put it down once you start." I pulled a copy of Olivia Connelly's *Where I've Been and Where I'm Going.* "If you don't love it, I'll reimburse you."

One took the book from me while the other three looked over her shoulders. She shrugged. "Okay."

Gina intercepted me before I could return to Joan. "We need more cash for the register."

"In the petty cash box in my desk drawer."

Joan met me at the counter. She held a book in her hand. "Have you read this?" Her eyes were puffy, and my heart ached for her.

"You'll love it, Joan. It's a nice escape." She held her credit card out to me, but I shook my head. "It's on me. No charge today."

She gave me a sad smile. "Patton is loaded. Please, let me pay. He's going to be sorry he did this to me. I feel the need for diamond earrings coming on."

"Whatever you do, sleep on it first. Things look better after a good night's sleep."

I met her at the end of the counter. She hugged me. "Thank you, Stella. You're a good friend."

Gina poked her head from the office. "Stella, can you come here for a minute?"

I went to see what Gina needed. She pulled me into the office and shut the door. "We have a problem."

"We have many problems. Can you narrow it down?"

She pulled my bottom desk drawer open. "Look."

It was empty. "Where's the cash box?"

She crossed her arms. "It's probably with the person who walked in while we were up front."

"What are you talking about? We would have noticed." I was sitting on the couch right in view of the office door. No one walked past me.

Gina sighed, exasperated. "They didn't walk through the

shop to get here. They came in through *that* door." She pointed to the metal door that led to the alley.

"It was unlocked?"

"No. It was *open.*"

I started to shake my head and deny that possibility when I remembered shutting the door but not locking it after letting Hemingway in. How could I not have locked the door? I'd been preoccupied, but it was no excuse. I closed my eyes and exhaled. Did I even put the cash box back in the drawer when I took it out this morning?

"How much did you have in it?" Gina said.

"Only a few hundred dollars. It's okay." But it wasn't okay. I needed every dollar I made. And my employee knew it, too.

The bell over the door rang. "I got it," she said, and turned at the door. "We have to report this."

I shut the drawer. "I will." It wouldn't make a difference. We didn't have cameras. But I didn't want to upset her more.

I stepped into the alley and paced the five steps between the buildings. What else could go wrong? I needed the money to pay for a dry-cleaned dress that I desperately needed to sell. I needed to pay Gina this week. I needed Charlie not to be sick. I needed my rent not to increase. I needed...I needed...I let out a scream in the center of the alley, my head back, arms out, as frustration, anger, and hopelessness washed over every nerve. I was drowning with no life preserver in sight.

Finally, my voice cracked, and my throat began to burn. I fell against the brick wall.

When I pulled away, straightened up and reached for the door, a stranger at the end of the alley watched me in horror. I held up my hand as if to say, "It's all good."

She shook her head and scurried onward.

CHAPTER 17

Two policemen left my shop as Theo walked in.

"What's going on?"

"Someone came in through the rear door and took my petty cash box." I shrugged as if it wasn't a big deal when what I wanted to do was punch everything I saw.

"That sucks. I'm sorry."

The door jingled, and we moved a few steps aside to let a young couple in. "Are you on your way to work?" I asked.

"Just got off."

A woman approached the counter to make a purchase. I rang her up and waited while she added her name to the mailing list.

"Would you like to have dinner tonight?" Theo said, filling the spot the customer had left.

I thought of the small stack of books in my bag to fill the hours in my apartment while I dined on Lean Cuisine. Alfredo Pasta with Chicken and Broccoli was on deck tonight.

Theo shifted to his other leg.

My eyes met his. I opened my mouth to tell him I was busy when I stopped myself. I didn't want to be alone.

"Yes," I said. "I'm having a crappy week."

He smiled. "It's Tuesday."

I squeezed my eyes. "Is that all?"

He met me outside the shop at closing. He'd changed into jeans and a navy sweater under his worn leather jacket.

"Where to?"

"Are you ready to taste the best chili you've ever had?"

I put my hands in my coat pockets. "I'm not going to your place." Going to his place was the very last thing I needed in my life.

"I'm not taking you there, Stella."

He led me across the street and one block over to the subway. Two stops later, we climbed up to the street and walked east.

"We're here," he said, stopping us in front of a fire station.

"What do you mean? We're here for what?"

Theo guided me inside and upstairs to a second floor.

I'd never been inside a fire station and was surprised by what I saw. If you'd blindfolded me and put me at this spot, I'd be hard-pressed to tell you where I was. We stood in what appeared to be a large living room, with a huge, flat screen television, couches, side tables, and a pool table off to the side. It was an aboveground man cave. The only giveaway would have been the large, glass cabinet that boasted all the trophies and plaques, helmets and photos of firemen and chiefs that I found out of eye's reach at the entrance.

The empty living room was warm, and conversations drifted from inside. Theo took my coat and scarf and hung it in the closet near the door. With his hand on my lower back, he guided me into the kitchen, where eight men were gathered around a large, rectangular table, talking. Another stirred a pot of what smelled like delectable chili on the stove. At our arrival, the group silenced, and all eyes were on me.

What was I doing here?

I smiled awkwardly and gave a small wave. "Hi, guys."

"Well, who do we have here?" This came from the oldest of the bunch, a friendly looking, squat man with a shock of white hair and blue eyes. He stepped toward me, holding out his hand. "I don't know what you did to deserve being brought here, but I apologize. Name's Fitzsimmons."

I took his offered hand and introduced myself. Theo whispered in my ear, "Chief Fitzsimmons. We call him Fitz."

"You should call him, Chief Fitz, no?" I asked, to which the group at the table responded in a chorus of loud approval, and a toothy smile from the older gentleman, breaking the awkward initiation immediately.

"Boys, this is Stella. Stella, the boys," Theo said.

The rest of them stood one by one to give me a mock salute or shake my hand, as Theo listed their names. "Paddy, Troy, Mikey, John, Frank, and this," he stepped over to the man at the stove and put his arm protectively around him, "is Hoagie."

When Hoagie turned around, long wooden spoon in his hand, I recognized his youthful face from in front of my snowed-in shop. His familiar brown, almond-shaped eyes were bright and became slits when he smiled, which he did now. His cheeks reddened, and he shrugged off Theo to reach over to me with his free hand to shake mine.

"I know you," I said, taking his hand. "Thank you again for the other day."

"My pleasure. The name's Salvatore, by the way. They call me Hoagie because it has less syllables."

The group laughed, and Theo practically hugged him. "No, we call him Hoagie because this guy makes the best sandwiches of anyone we've ever met. He's our probie and our cook. It's why we keep him around."

Hoagie pushed Theo away and went to his pot, turning to say over his shoulder, "You keep me around because I can haul a hose farther than any of you seniors."

Theo put him in a mock headlock while the men around the table retaliated vociferously. "Put him in his place! No respect!" But Theo play-wrestled the boy, and I watched as he did so with affection, while Hoagie complained that his chili was burning. As we settled around the table, one of the men rose to leave.

"Where is he going?" I asked Theo amid the clamor and noise.

"His shift ended. The earlier shifts stick around to see the relief. The others left."

He walked to Theo and shook his hand. "Good stuff today."

Theo nodded and hit him on his shoulder.

"What did you do?" I asked.

One of the men sitting on the other side of me leaned over, his hand around a mug of coffee. "Oh, the usual crazy shit he always does."

"Frankie…" Theo said, giving Frankie a look of warning.

"What? Are you kidding?" Frankie said, ignoring Theo. "I can't wait to tell my wife. Stella, this boy right here is the first one in. Every time. No one faster." He spoke with pride as he regaled the story of a multiple-alarm fire in a four-story apartment. While the hoses were pointed into the flaming windows, a woman screamed on the sidewalk pointing to the top floor saying her baby was still inside. Theo ran into the building, to the top floor, and searched every room. Outside, they heard loud splintering and fresh flames started to spew out of the upstairs windows.

"Fire goes up, see. Tries to get to unlimited oxygen. Anyway, the place is going up and still, no Theo. Finally, we see him hanging out of a window and damned if he wasn't lucky to jump to that ladder."

He looked at Theo. "Pretty lucky it was swinging that way, right?" To me, he said, "The irony was that as he was gasping for breath, the woman was holding her baby. She didn't know a neighbor had grabbed him on his way out and was safe on the street." He drained the mug and put it down. "Close call, that one."

"Frank, enough." Theo shook his head. "Overreactor."

"Yeah, right." Frank turned to another guy. "Paddy, what'd Theo say on the ride to the house?"

The guy looked at Theo. "He said, 'Got pretty warm.'"

Frankie winked at Theo. "Wuss."

I sat at the table with eight men, eating the best chili I'd ever tasted from mini crockpots, over rice with crusty bread, (Theo was right—Mom's chili couldn't compare) listening to them insult each other until tears fell and my sides ached. Their primary focus tonight was, of course, on Theo, who brought a guest and therefore earned the jibes they doled out.

The noise from the non-stop ribbing and talking helped to

keep my worries at bay for the moment and I was grateful to be here. I glanced at Theo.

"I thought you could use the distraction," he said.

Clean-up was on Hoagie, who was still on probation. When the bowls were empty, he brought everything to the sink and began to wash the dishes. Everyone else went inside.

"Does he need help?" I nodded my head to the sink.

"No. And you're my guest, so you don't do anything. I'll show you around."

"Before you do, can you direct me to the bathroom?"

At the first of three sinks lined along a brick wall, I looked at my reflection in the mirror. My cheeks were red. Too red. I splashed cold water on my face. Better, but still flushed. I pressed a damp paper towel against my forehead and neck. It had been a long time since I'd laughed all evening. The woman in the mirror stared at me. *First one in. Every time.*

When I walked out, I approached an open door to an office and heard a voice. It sounded like the chief, and he was angry. "I'm not going to warn you again. Do something that stupid and I'll pull you off the truck."

"I had to check." Theo. I froze before I reached the opening.

"I *ordered* you not to go in."

"And a baby might have died if I didn't."

For a moment, there was no sound and I wanted to peek my head in the door to see what was going on.

"Theo, I love you like a son, you know I do. But your behavior again today put everyone at risk."

"I never ask anyone to go in with me. In fact, I make sure no one does. It's my job."

"It's not your job to get killed. It's your responsibility to use your logic, assess the situation, and let us decide what to do together. This is a team. You are not an island. These boys would walk through the fire for you. You know that."

An island. This is how Philippe had described me only days ago.

"Chief, if there's a chance someone is inside and I can get them out, I'm going."

"Consider this your final warning."

A long moment passed.

"Nice to see you keeping company. Finally. Took you long enough," Chief said.

Theo cleared his throat. "She's a friend."

"Still. I'm glad."

"Me, too," Theo finally said.

I heard footsteps and quickly retreated into the bathroom where I slowly counted to twenty before taking a deep breath and venturing out.

He was in the living room speaking with Hoagie, who smiled at me as I entered.

Theo turned to me.

"I'm ready for the tour," I said.

He showed no sign of being reprimanded by his boss as he led me downstairs and through doors to the garage. There were two large firetrucks parked, one ambulette, and two smaller trucks, all in pristine condition. The floor was spotless, as well. I whistled.

"Everything is so clean," I whispered, as if speaking out loud would somehow interrupt the calm serenity of the space.

"Yeah, we work hard to keep it this way."

There was a row of open metal wall-mounted lockers, each with a personalized plate above it. Reading each name, I stopped at Theo's and touched his hanging jacket gently. It held a slight odor of smoke. At the base of the lockers were pants with boots already in them. I pointed to them.

"Time is crucial," he said.

"Oh."

I reached up to touch his dented helmet on the upper shelf. "You don't fix the dents?"

He shook his head and pulled it out, looking at it. "No. Every dent tells a story."

I nodded and watched him place it back. "What else do you have in here?"

"My gear, some rope, vise-grips, stuff like that." He stepped away. "Come here. I'll show you more."

He led me to a wide closet that could fit two of me vertically, filled with shelves of hoses and storage cylinders. Tools hung along a storage rack, and each hose was folded neatly against the wall of the closet. Theo pulled a rack out, exposing axes and tools I couldn't begin to comprehend. He pulled an axe from its holder, his biceps working as he did. He handed it to me, and my arms pulled toward the floor with its weight. He chuckled and grabbed it before I could do any damage and carefully hung it up.

"This allows us full visibility and fast access. Every second counts when the sirens go off. We need organization, or there would be chaos and lives could be lost needlessly."

Standing beside him, I watched his smooth hands hold the nozzle, his long fingers point to the parts of the hose as he explained them. I barely heard a word, but instead, briefly lost myself in the soft sound of his voice, the musky smell of his skin, the brush of his strong arm against my head, for I was standing so close to him.

"Stella?" he said softly.

"Hm? Oh, sorry." I cleared my throat.

Theo smiled. "I tend to go on. I'll take you home now."

I made no effort to move. "Did you always want to be a fireman?"

He nodded. "I lost my brother in a house fire when I was nine and Denise was six. We were with a sitter. My sister and I were watching television, and she smelled the smoke first. I grabbed Denise and pulled her outside while the sitter looked for Jake. We hadn't realized the other half of the house was already in flames. She came out without him, and I tried to run in, but she held onto me. I screamed and fought but she was stronger, so I watched while it burned until the firetrucks arrived. The men ran inside, and I wanted to tell them where to look for him." Theo paused, focused on the nozzle. "There was an alcove behind Jake's closet he liked to hide in when he was afraid." He shook his head. "Anyway, an eternity passed before one ran out holding him, but I knew it was too late."

"Oh, God."

"In high school, I told my father I wanted to take the test and skip college. We fought. He wanted me to go to school, but my mind was set. The day after I graduated high school, I applied, took my tests, went to the academy, and here I am."

My hand went to my heart. If I'd lost Charlie as a child, I don't think I'd have recovered.

"Where was your mom?"

His eyes lifted to the ceiling in thought. "She kind of checked out when we lost Jake. Denise and I helped my dad take care of things. It was a lot for Denise, too. The day after graduation, she followed her first boyfriend across the country to get away. He was never good to her, but the pain of being home probably hurt worse."

I supposed pain shaped all of us.

Theo placed the nozzle in the closet and closed the door. "I don't share things about myself, Stella. Certainly not with someone I haven't known for very long. This is a first for me."

I thought of the men upstairs. He'd told me he transferred here a month ago, yet they had the camaraderie of guys who seemed to know each other all their lives. Do men share with each other? Maybe he needed a new set of ears. Someone for whom he could paint his own truth.

"You haven't been here that long."

He ran his fingers along the top of his locker. "A month and a half. Why?"

I couldn't tell him I eavesdropped on his conversation with the chief. "*I love you like a son.*"

"You seem close with the guys. And the chief. That's fast bonding."

"We go through a lot on each shift. The bonding is quick and tight. It's the only way I like it. When I was a probie eighteen years ago in Manhattan, Fitz was there, but he wasn't a chief at the time. He was a chauffeur." My confusion must have been clear. "Fire equipment operator. He drove the truck, among other responsibilities."

"He came here first?"

Theo nodded. "We kept in touch as he rose through the ranks. He called me a few years ago and tried to get me to transfer here. I refused."

"Why?"

"I wasn't ready to let go of my other life."

"And you're ready now?"

He looked at me, his gaze canvassing my face and shoulders and finally resting on my eyes. "I think so."

We stared at each other. I'm not sure who leaned in first but the next thing I knew, our heads were closer together. I felt his warm breath on my skin, felt the urging need to press my lips against his, and would have if the doors hadn't banged open. We heard voices on the other side of the trucks and pulled apart as the guys walked through the garage and out the door, taking their conversation with them.

Theo cleared his throat. "I'll take you home now."

We decided to walk to my shop instead of taking the subway. To cover my regret at not kissing him, I asked what the probability was that we'd find the person who took my money.

"You won't," he said. "Be careful. You're a single woman with a business. You're a target."

Even without my business, I was a target.

We covered a few blocks in companionable silence. The streets were mostly empty, yet I felt safe beside Theo. At my shop, he told me he'd walk me all the way home and refused to take no for an answer, for which I was relieved. I didn't want our evening to end.

"I'm sorry about my message the other night," I said, as we continued. "About my sister." Theo hadn't brought up the text, or Charlie. He'd waited for me to mention it.

"Don't be sorry. How is she?"

"Who knows? It's new. But we're all broken up about it."

He slowed down. Touched my arm. "Anytime you need to talk about it…"

I nodded. "You said before that you don't share things about yourself with someone you don't really know. I don't share myself easily either. But there's something about you that makes it easy for me to be open. Maybe it was the trauma of losing Myles?"

He looked at me.

"Bonding. Quick and tight, right?" I said.

"You were listening."

"More than you know."

As we reached the building before mine, Theo stopped. Right, I'd told him I lived here the last time he walked me home.

"I'm over there." I pointed to the apartment building next door. "I was being cautious."

The corner of his mouth lifted in a half smile. "Smart."

At the bottom of my steps, I faced him. "How old was he? Your brother?"

Theo took a deep inhale through his nose. "Four."

No more. "I was having a shit day until you showed up."

"I saw."

"Please promise me one thing."

He frowned. "I'll try."

"Never mention to my mother that I swooned over some-one else's chili."

Relief splayed on his face though he was serious. "You got it."

CHAPTER 18

One of the best things about having a sister was the chance to relive the memorable experiences we didn't already share, like, say, an unexpected evening with a nice man after a ten-month drought. Though Charlie would call it a "strike" or a "self-imposed drought" since I'd pulled away from the few opportunities presented to me after the non-wedding. She'd be floored, I thought, as I called her on my walk to work the following morning. I was hoping to distract her, if only for a moment.

I got her voicemail.

I held a stack of books in my arms, canvassing the aisles, returning them to their shelves as Gina sprayed the counter, erasing the fingerprints from the morning hours. It was a ritual we'd fallen into, a quick cleaning of the store midday, so the hour before closing would go smoothly.

She turned and lifted *Charlotte's Web* from its special post, wiped the counter, and placed it. I smiled at the care she took with the book, as old and used as it was. When I looked at the cover—the little girl holding the piglet as they watched a spider drift down on her delicate web—I saw my father sitting on the edge of my bed, the book open on his lap, turned to the page we'd left off the evening before. I tried but could no longer hear him reading to me—his voice lost to time. He'd bought the book for my sister, because she shared the spider's name, but it was me who treasured it, wishing my sister and I could trade names.

"Gina?"

"Hm?"

"Do you still have your dad?"

"He's in Boston."

A few hours away by car. "Do you see him often?"

"No," she said and put the spray bottle below the counter as a customer entered and pushed her dripping hood off her head.

I continued my task and held the last title to bring home. The pile on my nightstand was dwindling. Nights had been long lately, sleepless with worry, and reading was the only medicine that worked.

The customer paused to read my message board: *Interested in group therapy? Join a book club.* Today, it was inside due to rain. I stepped toward her.

"I don't belong to a book club," she said. "I moved here a month ago because my husband was relocated with his job from Nevada." She fondled a novel in her hand "I miss my club at home. I miss everything." Her lower lip quivered, and she breathed through her nose. I averted my eyes, pretending to straighten a shelf of books, to give her a moment.

"One of my customers is in two clubs," I said, when she seemed to recover. "I'll talk to her to see if she has room in one if you'd like. I'm happy to talk books as well. You can stop in anytime. I have a comfy couch in the back."

She brightened. "That would be lovely. Thank you. I'm Marie."

"Stella. Anything you need, stop in."

Marie turned the book she held so I could see the title. "Have you read this?" she asked.

"I have. It's excellent. Are you a fan of this author?"

"I read another one of hers a few months ago." Marie's eyes flitted around the store. "I've been doing a lot of reading."

"I know what you mean. I find different authors get me through different phases of life. Judy Blume helped me through puberty." I walked to the romance section and held up a Danielle Steele book. "She got me through my teens."

Marie laughed. "You seem too young to have grown up with those authors."

"Are you kidding? I can't wait to introduce my niece to Ms. Blume. She's timeless."

I led her to the modest indie shelf next to literary fiction and pulled out the last copy of Olivia Connelly's paperback. I needed to order more. "When you finish that, try this one. It's stunning."

She took the book and read the back cover. "I've never heard of this author."

"She's an indie. Harder to find, but worth it. I promise."

Marie smiled. "I'll take it now. Thanks, Stella. I'm so happy I stumbled in here."

"Me, too."

When Marie paid and left, Gina nodded. "Nice sale."

"Thanks to you and that gem you discovered."

"Speaking of, if you keep recommending it, we should order more copies," she said.

"You read my mind. And we should move our Top Picks table more toward the center. We can write little blurbs of what we loved on pieces of paper and tuck it into the books." I'd seen that in another bookshop when I was out with my mom on Long Island and liked the idea.

Gina considered my suggestion and walked to the table in front of the picture window that displayed our new inventory. "This one?"

"Sure."

We scoured the shelves for our next picks and rearranged the display, adding our notes on each title, occasionally inter-rupted by customers. Satisfied, we stepped back and enjoyed our work.

"So, why don't you see your dad?" I said.

"We don't talk anymore." She adjusted one of the books.

"Why not?"

She pulled the carpet sweeper from the office, sweeping the rug whenever our conversations veered into uncomfortable territory.

"He doesn't support me."

"Financially?"

"He thinks I'm ruining my life, trying to be an artist."

I wasn't a parent, but I imagined he was worried about her making a decent living. You couldn't fault him for that.

"So, you stopped speaking to him? What about your mom?"

"She died a year before I left."

Gina was alone. Brave and alone. My mom was a lifeline for me. Especially without my father.

"It's not my business, so you can ignore this," I said, "but I'd give anything for a chance to speak with my dad."

Gina held the sweeper still. "What would you say?"

I blew out a breath. "First, that I miss him." And I needed answers, like, how could you tell me you love me and walk away as easily as you did? Gina waited. "I'm not sure," I said, instead.

"We're different, you and me. I'd have been pissed off if my old man walked out. If they leave, who gives a shit? Good riddance, I say."

I was going to tell her it wasn't easy to be angry when the pain of abandonment hurt so much. But I didn't. Maybe she knew better. She was the one in a relationship while I failed my whole life to have one that stuck.

Gina started on the rug again. At least the shop would be clean.

"Aunt Essie!"

The scream echoed through the quiet shop, causing a customer to drop the book she was holding in the self-help aisle. I ran over to pick it up, handed it to her, and advised her to make herself comfortable on the couch, which she did.

I'd stepped into view in time to catch my niece as she hurtled into my arms.

"Aunt Essie! Guess what?" Maddie took a dramatic breath, and my heart squeezed with love for this child.

"What!"

"We're getting hot chocolate and," another deep, dramatic inhale, "going to the children's museum!" Her eyes were large circles, exemplifying her excitement. I hugged her tight.

"You're a lucky girl, Mad."

"Can I have a book?"

I lowered her to the floor. "Pick what you want."

"We have some new ones you might like," Gina said.

My niece accepted Gina's hand, not put off by her dark clothes, makeup, tattoos, or piercings.

Charlie waited up front at the counter in her raincoat and rainboots. She held a paper bag.

"Here." She thrust the bag at me.

"Where's the little monster?"

"He's with Mom. Today, Maddie and I needed a dose of Essie."

I pulled my sister to me. She squeezed me once and let go. "Wear this on Saturday."

I peeked into the bag to see the green silk dress I'd tried on when she broke the news. It was folded neatly in tissue paper. "Thank you, but I don't want this."

"You look amazing in it and you're wearing it to the party. If you don't, I'll go next door and buy something else."

"Don't you dare." I sighed. "I don't want to go."

"You're going. Be social. You're alone too much."

"I'm hardly alone. I'm at your place every week." I spread my hands out. "Does this look like I'm alone?" For the moment, the store was empty but for the woman sitting in the corner on the couch. "You know what I mean," I said. "And I spent last evening with a man."

Charlie's eyes widened. "Sam's uncle," she said.

"How do you know?"

"I'm your sister." It was all the answer I needed. "Tell me."

"I wanted to kiss him, but I didn't." My eyes filled, surprising the both of us.

"Why?"

I shook my head. Because I was afraid.

"Oh, Stella. I'm so happy for you."

We spent time in the children's section, poring over the new books I'd found and stocked until Maddie decided on two. I managed to convince my sister to squeeze a quick visit next door to see Philippe before they left.

"Does he know about me?" she said.

"No."

"Good."

Philippe finished with his client and propped Maddie onto his chair on a large cushion. While we chatted about general news and listened to Philippe complain about the bridesmaids he'd worked on over the weekend (*"The drama! Oy! I felt like I was in Jersey Shore but without the hot, disturbed guys."*) I noticed Charlie relax and enjoy the conversation. Philippe, having no idea of her sickness, took her mind off her troubles for a spell and my love for him grew exponentially. He invited Charlie to his party, and she declined.

When we left the salon, Maddie had a beautiful haircut, shoulder length with soft curls that framed her delicate face, making her look like a doll. Philippe refused payment, and Charlie promised to return to visit. When we hugged goodbye in front of my shop, Charlie told me she'd left a healthy tip for Philippe at the counter.

CHAPTER 19

I crossed the hall to Philippe and Rog's at nine o'clock the following Saturday night and walked into the soft stylings of subdued jazz music. There were about two dozen people, mostly men, milling about the dimly lit living room, drinking Cosmos. Rog explained this was how Philippe's parties started out: softly and elegantly, until his guests imbibed enough vodka and wine to loosen them up, gaudy disco would scream from the hidden Bose speakers, and clothes would start flying. That, I figured, would be my cue to leave.

The host walked around with a pitcher, filling glasses dangerously close to their rims, while Rog followed behind carrying a tray of bacon-wrapped dates stuffed with cheese.

He was pleased to see me, and his warm welcome filled me with enough courage to enjoy the evening.

"Honey, you look positively divine! I approve. And I didn't even have to come over and dress you!"

I did a little twirl to show my snug, emerald green wrap dress that fell mid-thigh. It was my first, and most likely my last, time wearing this outfit, only brave enough to carry it over here among the anonymous fashion elite. I'll regress to my Gap clothes once the clock strikes midnight, Cinderella, but in sensible pants.

Philippe leaned in. "Sweetheart, why are you hiding yourself in horrible pants when you have those legs? I am so proud of you!"

I blushed. "Charlie made me buy this."

"I'll be sure to call her tomorrow and congratulate her. Our very own Eliza Doolittle. As I live and breathe." With that, he handed me a glass, filled it up, kissed me on the cheek, and left me to fend for myself.

Guests had arrived throughout the evening and by eleven, the party was in full swing, music blaring, dancers all over the room and each other. I was into my third Cosmo, hanging out with my new friends, Carmine and Arthur, a couple who flanked me on both sides.

"Tell us your story," Arthur said. Carmine leaned in.

"I'd rather hear yours."

Carmine raised his eyebrows and Arthur smiled. "It's the tale as old as time."

"I'm an ER doctor."

"I'm a barista."

"I was working a mobile blood donation drive."

"I delivered a large coffee order to the staff."

"I didn't want him to leave, so I convinced him to give blood."

"I abhor needles, but he was cute and offered an extra tip." Wink, wink.

"Got him to the table. Took a pint. Got to talking."

"Stood up to get my cookie and OJ and dropped like a weight."

"Needed six stitches in his chin, which I did right there."

Carmine lifted his head and pointed to the faint scar running perpendicular to his chin.

"Nice work," I said.

"Thank you," they said in unison.

"We've been together since."

"End of story."

"Or is it the beginning?" They gazed at each other.

"How many years?" I said to break the awkward sexual tension I was suddenly a part of.

"Two," they said again in unison, eyes still locked.

As I was about to extricate myself from this private lovefest, Philippe grabbed my hand and pulled me to a stocky guy standing by himself in the corner.

"Stella, this is James. He works with Rog." *Straight* he

mouthed behind him, rolling his eyes as if he wasn't even sure how this person managed to infiltrate his fiesta.

"Hi," I said to James.

"I'm not sure what just happened," James said, watching Philippe walk away.

"I think we're the only two straight people here, so we belong together," I said. "I live across the hall. What's your excuse?"

"Rog and I went to happy hour last week and he invited me. He told me I had to come for at least a drink and meet his neighbor." James held up his beer. "So, here I am. Feeling like an awkward outcast."

"You're feeling awkward? I think I'm the neighbor." We both turned toward the main room and saw Philippe and Rog next to each other, smiling and waving. James and I waved and returned to each other. "I hope you didn't give up a better offer for tonight. This neighbor isn't looking to get set up. I'm sorry."

James lowered his eyes. "No worries. I'm recently separated. I think Rog felt sorry for me. It's too soon."

I held up my Cosmo. "Here's to our matchmakers. Thank goodness they have day jobs." We clinked glasses. "What do you do?" I asked.

"I'm in IT with Rog. We're working on the same project. I'm trying to get it done before the Paris deal."

"What's the Paris deal?"

This seemed to perk James up. He widened his short stance as if he needed the support to explain. "There's a huge opportunity the company is vying for. If it goes through, which I think will happen, then they're going to need a team to set up the new office in France. There's a rumor that there are limited spots and I want to get my ass over there. You know, make a fresh start. Meet a French woman."

"Is Rog hoping to go, too?"

"He's the most driven of all of us."

I glanced toward Rog; his head leaned in to say something to Philippe. Philippe touched his arm as he did and then threw his head back and laughed.

Poor Philippe. Nothing lasts.

"Well, good luck." I threw in a yawn. "I'm beat. Nice to meet you, James."

He leaned close to speak in my ear. "Would you like me to walk you home?"

"No thanks." I pointed to the door. "I'm practically home already."

My hand was on the doorknob when Philippe caught me trying to make my getaway.

"Honey, where do you think you're going?"

"Home. I drank too much and I'm tired."

He gave me a hug and a kiss and relented. Right before I closed the door, I glimpsed Arthur and Carmine in a passionate embrace, exactly where I left them, in front of the painting of the Paris scene.

* * *

I have a simple wall clock in my kitchen. A square piece of wood with two coffee mugs that hang below a painted A.M. Halfway down the "clock" are two hanging wine glasses below a painted P.M. A rather efficient way to tell time. I was reclined on my couch, staring out the window, sipping my morning coffee, when Philippe, gifter of my neat clock, walked into my apartment. Without a word, he went into the kitchen, took the other mug off the hanger, filled it, added milk, and returned to the den, forcing me to sit up to make room for him on the other cushion.

We sipped quietly until finally, I was ready to converse. "Thank you for last night. Great party."

"You didn't like James?"

"No, I didn't. No more setting Stella up."

"How long has it been since you've been with a man?"

"Describe 'been with,'" I said, using my fingers as quotes.

He put his mug down and pushed his pointer finger through a circle made by his other finger and thumb.

"Ah. What decade are we in?"

Philippe frowned.

"I'm joking. Let's see. My wedding anniversary is next month..." I lifted my eyes in thought, mumbled, "carry the one...," and finally looked at my neighbor. "About twelve months."

"You should've taken James home. I'm not saying you had to speak to him. Shit, you don't even have to like him. But you need someone to rock your world before you forget how to do it."

I dropped my head onto the cushion, my mind going directly to Theo, to his thick, wavy, finger-raked chestnut hair. Crooked nose. Only one dimple. Godiva eyes. My world had never been rocked. And James was not the one to do it.

"I wasn't feeling it," I said.

"You have to let him stand closer to you."

I went to the kitchen to dump the remnants of my coffee in the sink. Philippe followed.

When I turned around, he hugged me.

"What's this for?" I said over his shoulder.

He drew back and met my eyes. "You're going to have to let someone in eventually. As amazing as I am, I'm not enough for you."

"I have news," I blurted, unable to keep it to myself any longer.

Philippe's face dropped. "Spill it."

I told him about Charlie. "Oh baby, no," he said, putting his hand to his own heart. "I'm sorry." His eyes fell to the floor. "She looked so good the other day."

"Sometimes I look at her and think the doctor made a mistake. That he read someone else's test and Charlie is fine and she'll call me and tell me, and I can stop worrying every minute of every day."

He took my hand in his and held it. "Whatever you need from me, dear. I'm here."

"You are enough," I said.

CHAPTER 20

I ducked into the dry cleaners on my way to the shop. The owner, Ms. Roselli, seemed happy to see me. I pulled out my credit card to pay for my wedding dress, knowing it was too early to charge more this month, but I needed to pay for her service.

She agreed to hold the dress for me a little longer. The pain of having it at my apartment was more than I could handle, and I still hadn't gotten a viable offer on eBay for it.

I let the cat into the shop office. While he ate his tuna, my eyes lingered on the growing pile of discarded books on the workbench. As a former copywriter, I knew how much work went into writing and publishing a book, so when Gina suggested we toss them, I couldn't.

The mess stretched across our workspace—easily a couple hundred stacked haphazardly. Each one a story saved from being forgotten.

A job for another day.

Gina left at closing and Hemingway bid me farewell shortly after, leaving me at the counter in front of the store. While I waited for the scheduled book club to arrive, I checked Facebook and subjected myself to my ex living his best life.

Today's post was taken in the red velvet seats of the Majestic Theater, holding up a Playbill for *Hamilton*. I stared out the window. Unbelievable. He hated musicals. I couldn't get him to a single show in the six years we were together, going instead with Marcy, who now sat beside my ex-fiancé holding her own Playbill and looking as radiant as ever.

As the women arrived, they greeted each other and meandered through the shop. I surprised them with pastries from an

Italian bakeshop on the next street. Several brought a bottle of wine and plastic cups.

Joan walked in. I hadn't seen her since she discovered her husband's infidelity.

I met her at the door. "I'm so happy to see you. How are you doing?"

She hugged me. "I'm okay. Still not sure what to do."

How could she not be sure? Leave him. He cheated. But I said, "You'll know when the time is right."

She nodded, looking gorgeous in her cashmere coat, her silky hair in waves past her shoulders. Maybe it's hard to leave that kind of money. As I took her coat, Marie walked in.

"Oh! Marie! You came."

She widened her eyes as if to say, I'm not sure what I'm doing here.

Joan pasted on a smile. "I'm Joan. We spoke on the phone. Welcome."

"Thank you." Marie's eyes flicked to me. I winked in encouragement.

"Did you read the book?" Joan said to Marie.

"Yes. I loved it."

They continued to talk as they walked toward the women already assembled, and I resumed my spot behind the counter.

Philippe walked in, backlit by a dark sky and streetlights outside. He sidled up to the counter and leaned over.

"How goes it?" he said.

"It goes. Are you finished?"

"Yepper. My late client rescheduled. How long are you going to be?"

A roar lit up, breaking the silence, surprising us both. The women fell into a fit of laughter, which made us both smile.

"Laughter is contagious, isn't it?" I said.

"One of the good things that is."

"They have until ten."

He grimaced. "Oy." Two more hours.

He sauntered through the aisles, peeked to the corner where the women were vociferously engaged, and returned to me. "The furniture looks good. I like the table much better than yours. That bare wall, though, is screaming for attention." Still the blue painted wall above the seating area.

"I know."

He walked to my chalkboard, read today's message: *You'd look better with a book in your hand.* Philippe glanced at me over his shoulder, erased the message with a tissue he pulled from his pocket, and wrote something.

Marie approached us. "This is so much fun, Stella. I can't thank you enough for introducing me to Joan and the girls."

"I'm glad."

"Where is your bathroom?"

I pointed toward the office, explaining it was through the door, to the right. "Please jiggle the handle when you're done, or the toilet will keep running."

"Will do."

Philippe raised his eyebrows. "Still?"

I didn't answer.

"What are you waiting for? Get that fixed."

"It's on my list." Mental note: add toilet to growing list.

Philippe decided he didn't have the patience to stay and went to meet Rog. I returned to my book, wondering if or when Rog would tell him about Paris and what kind of friend I was by not saying anything.

An hour and a half later, my phone dinged, and I quickly picked it up when I saw it was a text from Charlie.

> Charlie: If I have Maddie's party on a Sunday, can you make it?

> Me: When and what time?

> Charlie: Two weeks. Two pm. Sorry. I can't expect people to come on a Monday. Some moms work.

I hesitated. I knew this would happen. People had parties on weekends, weddings, showers, birthday parties, brunches. In retail, weekends were my lifeline. I planned it this way. But how will I tell Maddie I can't go to her birthday party?

Another text pinged on my screen.

> Maddie wants to invite Sam. Do you think you can ask your friend?

I picked up my phone to text Theo:

> Hey, Sam is invited to Maddie's birthday party on Sun, Feb 15th. Do you think she'd like to go?

I pressed send when the women walked up front, ordered twelve copies of their next book choice and took their leave, none of them noticing, thankfully, the note my cheeky friend left on the chalkboard.

"Go Home!"

Alone in the shop, I headed to the office when Theo answered.

> She'd love to go. I'll take the address and bring her.

I stared at the words as I flipped the light switches and radio off.

Another message followed.

> If it's easier, we can meet at your shop and go together.

My heart sank. I'd expected his sister would want to bring Sam since I assumed she had weekends off. With a sigh, I sent Theo Charlie's address as I walked through the shop to the front door to leave. I paused at the door and added:

I can't go with you. I'm going late. Work.

Three dots appeared and disappeared on my phone as I locked up and started my walk home. Finally, he responded.

Okay. See you Saturday.

Most of the way home, I wondered how I could get to Maddie's party on time without sacrificing my shop. In the end, I couldn't.

A siren alarmed and a fire truck followed by an ambulance and two police cars zoomed past me, breaking my indecisive trance.

CHAPTER 21

I was ringing up two new customers to the tune of *Mr. Bojangles* when a man walked in carrying a dirty canvas bag and asked for the owner.

"I'm Stella. Can I help you?"

"I'm a plumber. I was next door, and the guy sent me here to look at your toilet."

Gina chimed in, "Go through to the ba—"

I held up my hand, cutting her off, and handed change to a woman who'd purchased two historical fiction books.

"There's nothing wrong with my toilet," I said, when she was out of earshot. "I'm sorry he sent you."

The man shrugged. "Are you sure? It's paid for. I can check."

"I'm sure. Thank you."

When the last customer walked out, Gina said, "What the hell, Stella? Why did you send him away?"

"I don't need Philippe to pay for a plumber for me. I can figure it out myself."

"Then do it," she said, through a clenched jaw.

"Has it been a problem for you, Gina? Is the simple movement of the handle too much to remember?"

"No."

"So, let's prioritize what needs to be done. I'll get to the toilet. I will."

I fumed, as upset with myself and my tight budget as with Phillipe for publicly shaming me.

After Gina left, I searched the self-help shelf remembering I'd purchased a book on plumbing. *Plumbing for Dummies* sat between *I Can Fix It* and *Fake it Till You Break It*.

The chapter on toilets was comprehensive, but I begrudgingly used a YouTube video to guide me. I carefully took off the tank cover and sat backward on the toilet, leaning over the open tank. I replayed the video six times, convinced the flow valve was the cause of the running water, before I felt comfortable adjusting the valve and stopper. I replaced the tank cover, flushed the toilet and waited. The water eventually stopped running. It took a bit of time, but it stopped on its own.

Victorious! Why had I waited so long to do this?

* * *

With a sense of invincibility, I went to Charlie's after work and reveled in the enthusiastic greeting and adoration of my niece and nephew, already bathed, fed, and in pajamas, and found Charlie in the kitchen. Tonight, on the menu were tacos. The meat was simmering on the stove, and there were six bowls of fixin's lined along the counter, chopped, diced, and waiting.

Charlie was sitting at the table, scribbling onto a legal pad.

"Tacos? My favorite," I said.

She noted something, not looking up. "Today's your lucky day."

I leaned against the doorway and waited until she finished her task. Her hair hung over the paper, long tendrils waving above the lines. The picture blurred into a memory of the two of us, eight and twelve, waiting for Mom to come home from work late. After cereal for dinner and lukewarm baths, we'd sat on the floor of our small bedroom in our pajamas. Charlie had brushed and braided my hair, and with abundant patience, taught me how to braid hers. Over and over, I'd loosened the crooked braids, threading my fingers through her long hair, growing more frustrated with each failed attempt but determined to match my sister's ability, until finally, she'd declared me competent.

"Sort of late for dinner, isn't it?" I said.

"The kids ate. The tacos are for us."

"Us— you and me?"

"Originally, me and Lance, but sure. You, too." She stopped writing and looked up at me with tired eyes.

"I was thinking of that night you taught me how to braid your hair."

A flicker of a smile appeared. "You were intolerable. You refused to quit trying until you got it right. I was exhausted. And my head hurt from you pulling at it."

I laughed. "What's ironic is we never really braided our hair after that."

She laughed with me, but it quickly faded. "I got a date for my surgery."

"Great! And?"

She sighed. "February 28th."

I sat down across from her. "Okay, that's only three weeks away."

"Do you know what it's like to have something inside of you that can kill you? I want this tumor out of me now. I feel like with every passing day, my odds decrease."

"I'm sure three weeks won't make a difference."

"That's what the doctor told me when I called the office yesterday. Hysterical." Charlie had begged them to schedule her sooner and his nurse repeatedly told her no. He's booked. Finally, he got on the phone, explained he had other patients, and promised it wouldn't make a difference.

"They do this for a living. Other women are going through the same thing as you are."

"I don't care about other women. I care about the woman who is responsible for the two souls sitting inside in diapers and pajamas."

What right did I have to tell her not to worry? When she'd calmed down, she waved the legal pad in front of me. "At least I'll be able to throw Maddie her birthday party while I'm still whole."

"You'll be whole after the surgery."

"Will I? I'm leaving a piece of me there."

"Well, two pieces actually," I said, cupping my boobs.

She rested her head on her hand.

"Charlie, boobs don't make you who you are. That's what your ass is for."

Crickets.

She hiccupped. "Every time I make them dinner, or give them a bath, or read to them, or watch them sleep, I feel like it might be the last time I do it."

I reached over and took her hand.

"I'm planning an amazing birthday party for Maddie."

"What can I do?"

She squeezed my hand. "Show up and make her happy. I'll take care of the rest."

"I can't close the shop. I can catch the last few minutes."

She blinked, thinking it through. "What if I started it an hour later?"

"Don't do it for me. Maddie will be too distracted to realize I'm not there."

Charlie frowned. "Have you met this child? You're her favorite person."

This should have made me feel better, but instead it fed my guilt. What could I do?

"I bought her a dollhouse," my sister said. We locked eyes, both holding the same memory.

Our mom had found a used dollhouse at someone's curb the night before garbage pickup one cold December night. It was three feet tall and was opened on one side, revealing three floors. On the other side was the exterior, on which was painted faded shingles, shutters, and a black door. She'd brought it home for me and Charlie, sanded it down, painted in the wee hours of the night after her shifts, and surprised us Christmas morning. She'd painted the shingles a pale blue, the shutters navy, and the front door red. I'd loved that dollhouse for years—pretended it would be my house and I'd be married. I knew which room would be mine and my husband's and where the children would sleep. And we'd be happy because he'd come home every night and take care of us. My favorite rooms were the bathrooms. I used to rearrange the tiny toilets and bathtubs.

"I woke up in the middle of the night to watch her work on that house for us," Charlie said. "Well, it was mostly for you. Even when he left, she made sure Christmas was special." She shook her head. "How difficult it must have been for her."

I tried to imagine what our mother must have gone through, as a parent with two young children, trying to continue the enthusiastic rituals of Christmases and birthdays, and I couldn't. This thought fueled the energy I spent keeping heartbreak away.

"Maddie's friend, Sam, is coming, too," I said.

"Her mom is bringing her?"

I shook my head.

Charlie's eyebrows raised. "All the more reason for you to be here. Ask Gina to close for you."

"No."

"Why not?"

"I can't let someone else do it." Not to see Theo. Not even for my niece.

When I left after dinner, after bedtime stories, after a quiet glass of wine with my sister, Lance was still not home.

CHAPTER 22

The following morning, I unlocked the shop's front door, dropped the store-bought blueberry muffin I brought from home on the counter, and went to place my purse and lunch bag in the office and feed Hemingway. I surveyed the dark shelves on my short journey, the framed pictures along the upper walls, the accents I'd accumulated over time, feeling the tranquil pleasure and pride that never failed to envelop me before the day began.

Near the back, my feet sank a bit in the rug. That's strange. It's Berber. Feet aren't supposed to sink into Berb—oh crap. The speckled, light gray color was dark gray along the back wall.

I swung the office door open to step in water that coated the whole cement floor. The gurgling sound coming from the bathroom signaled what had happened. I ran to the toilet and jiggled the flusher, but it was too late. The damage was done. Water overflowed over the rim and into the store. I shut the water at the main and then stared in disbelief.

I opened the rear door, relieved the cat wasn't there yet. The alley was clear, so I got to work trying to remove the excess water from the office with a push broom.

Gina walked in an hour later as I was still sweeping the mess. In her black clothes and camo backpack slung over her shoulder, she surveyed the scene.

I swept the floor, unable to speak, waiting for her to flash a neon sign that said, "I told you so!"

Instead, she swung her backpack around to rest against her chest, took her phone from an inside pocket and returned her pack to her shoulders. She sloshed around on the floor and took pictures of the bathroom and the office.

"You might be able to salvage the rug," she said, nodding her head into the shop. The upside, if there was one, was that the office floor was cement and would eventually dry. "We could cut the soaked area and find a remnant."

I kept to my task without answering, berating myself. I did this. Ten minutes later, I looked up and she was gone, along with the pictures she took for the insurance company. What I couldn't think about was that my monthly number was high, so to keep my umbrella insurance reasonable, my deductible was steep. I tilted my head toward the ceiling to catch the tears that threatened when I heard movement from inside the shop. I opened the inside door to see Gina dragging a wet vac across the carpet.

She paused until I stepped aside and took over where I left off.

Up front, I called a plumber and the insurance company. We opened on time and cordoned off the rear of the store where I'd placed two fans that Gina's boyfriend brought to dry the carpet. I spent the day on autopilot, considering my next step. The insurance company would send a check for new drywall and a rug. The thought of replacing the entire rug, moving everything off the floor, overwhelmed me. I couldn't close long enough for that to happen.

I knew what I had to do. I'd known since I moved what I needed to do, but it was difficult for me to come to terms with it. I had no right keeping my car. The parking situation alone was cause for stress, and the insurance and gas money were costs I needed to unload. I had been able to afford a parking spot in Doug's garage when we'd dated because it was my only expense. The money I'd socked away working at the publishing house had since been used for this shop, my apartment, and my car. The fact that I walked to work was enough reason alone to amputate this weight off me.

Six people had my wedding dress on "watch" on eBay. One person offered two thousand dollars. I declined, hoping the dry cleaners wouldn't mind holding onto the dress a little longer.

Philippe stopped in at lunch and started to say something when he saw the cordoned area.

"What happened? What's with the noise?"

I was ringing up a customer, ignoring him when Gina piped in, "Fans. I'll give you one guess." She was furious. I didn't care. No one was angrier at me than me.

His face dropped. "My plumber did that?"

"No. We sent your plumber away," Gina said.

"Gina," I warned.

"You what?! What the hell did you do that for?"

Okay, so someone was angrier at me than me. I headed to the office to distance myself from the few customers in the shop. Philippe followed.

"I don't want your charity," I said, once we were behind the closed door. "Don't do that again."

His arms opened wide. "What? Don't try to help a friend? Oh, God forbid you accept a favor. I'm horrible. I can't believe I did that."

"You know what I mean."

"No, *dear*. I have no idea what you mean. What did you do?"

"I fixed it myself."

He looked around the office, noticed the darkened cement floor and sniffed in the musty odor. "Right, so you finally put all of your plumbing knowledge to work." I didn't answer. He crossed his arms and stamped his foot. "How'd that work for you?"

I pretended to pile the discarded books on the workbench while an uncomfortable silence formed between us.

"Stella, you have issues. I paid the plumber for the hour. It took him six minutes to unclog my drains. I thought I'd help. Your stupid pride is going to kill you." He shook his head at my silence. "You know what? I'm done. I'm out."

Alone, I wiped my nose and bent down to pet Hemingway, who took pity on me and rubbed against my leg. His paws were damp from the floor.

I dropped onto the desk chair and blew out a breath. At the lowest point in my life, this shop sustained me and gave me purpose. The first endeavor I'd tackled on my own after being forced to rely on others my entire life.

Of course, I wasn't going to accept favors. For the first time in thirty-six years, I would take complete responsibility for my life. My dream. Whatever happened would be on me. No one was going to leave me at the altar again. No one was going to tell me they loved me and have me believe he wouldn't leave. The only reliable person in my life would be me.

I'd had enough.

Philippe's words repeated in my mind. *Your pride is going to kill you.*

No. I wouldn't allow it. It may, however, kill my dream.

Charlie texted, interrupting my thoughts.

> I called the moms and pushed back the party so you can at least come for an hour or two. I know how much you love cake.

My eyes welled. My sister was sick. She was throwing her daughter a birthday party. I took a deep breath and typed back.

> Okay.

She answered immediately with a smiley emoji, and tears dripped down my cheeks, clouding the screen.

I wiped my face with tissues to hide my distress and returned to my desk to regroup. Facebook was crowded with posts today. I scrolled down to see acquaintances posing on their various vacations, thanking the world for their birthday wishes, wishing their sons and daughters happy birthday even though they're only three and not yet on Facebook (or maybe they were), until finally, I stopped at a photo posted yesterday, a selfie taken by Doug with his three friends. They were at a Rangers game, each holding up a beer. There was no sign of Marcy and for some reason, this gave me a small sense of satisfaction. He's still going out with his friends.

I should have shut the phone down then. I shouldn't have read the numerous comments, which started with, *Yo! What section are you in?* and *Looking good, dude!*

And there it was. *Where's your better half?* With Doug's response, which gutted me. *She's on her way.*

She's on her way? Since when was a girlfriend invited to a boys' night out?

I stared at the screen and jumped when I realized Gina stood at the door with a frown. "What are you doing?"

"Self-sabotage."

She didn't say anything at first. I expected her to walk out but she didn't. I closed the app.

"I'm sorry about before," she said. "I was frustrated for you. But I think I get why you sent the guy away, and I admire you for it. Even though you fucked up."

"Thanks, Gina. Bear with me. We'll get it right."

She nodded, averting her eyes now that I was facing her. "I know."

We walked up front together. Three customers milled about, searching the shelves.

I walked along the newly released indie shelf, touching but not really seeing the books. I needed a distraction.

"Gina, how did you get into your painting?"

She rearranged some books in Sci-Fi. "It's a boring story."

"Tell me."

"I was an overachiever in school, planning to study law like my father and his father, until I found out he was cheating on my mother. I was pissed, started cutting classes, picked up bad habits, got in with a rowdy crowd. You know, headed down a rough road." She shrugged. "Anyway, I would've kept going, but someone went out of her way to save me."

"Who was it?"

She pulled a book from the shelf, assessed the spine, and moved along the aisle. "An art teacher. She came down to the detention room, where I spent most of my time that year, and convinced me to try her Sculpting class."

"You sculpt, too?"

"No. It wasn't for me. But I liked *her* and the way the silence felt when I worked alone. I was helping her clean a walk-in closet and came across buckets of paints and an old, discarded canvas. She told me to take them home and give it a try. So, I did. And that was it. I'd found my salvation." The way Gina described her art felt akin to how I felt about running my bookshop.

"Soon, my bedroom was filled with brushes and canvases. It became my respite from the cold rooms that surrounded me."

I listened, rapt, as she continued.

"When the old man found out I'd skipped the SAT and didn't apply to the colleges on his list, I came home from school to find my room completely empty. He'd removed everything I'd done, everything I'd loved, and cut me off so I couldn't buy any more to start over."

"Is that why you don't speak to him?"

She placed the book in its right spot. "Yep."

"Gina?"

She started to walk to the counter. "What?"

"Would you like to paint something here?"

She stopped. "What do you mean?"

"Well," I walked to the empty wall over the couch section where the book clubs met, the wall Philippe continuously reminded me needed something. "Right here could use a little pizzazz, don't you think?" I hadn't been able to decide what to do here. Maybe now I knew why.

She met me where I stood. "What do you want?"

I thought a moment. "Anything you see fit. I trust you."

We stared at the blank wall. What did she see there, I wondered? Did she miss her father? Did she ever struggle with the phone, wanting to call him and hear his voice? I thought about my dad every single day, wanting to hear him say my name and ask me how my day was, tell me he loved me. Read with me.

"For the record, you don't need a silly test to tell you how bright you are," I said.

Gina kept her eyes on that wall. "I signed up for the next SAT without telling them. I got a job to pay for it. Got a fifteen fifty."

A near perfect score.

"I got this," I said, heading toward the counter where one of our customers waited to make a purchase. "You stay and ponder possibilities."

The bell over the door dinged as someone else walked in. After a welcome greeting from me, he started down an aisle. I shuffled to Gina so I wouldn't have to raise my voice. "Whatever it is you choose to do, if you do it because you love it, then you're a success." A message I needed to remind myself of, as well.

She grinned. "That's what I've been saying for years."

CHAPTER 23

The day of Maddie's party, I was in the shop assessing my newly spackled wall. I'd been considering an accent wall—a bold, bright color to make a statement, until I could buy another set of shelves to fill.

Gina stepped out from the office. "There are too many books back there. Barely room for new deliveries." That ever-growing discarded mountain on our workbench.

"I know." I had piles accumulated at my apartment as well, the books I'd taken home to read. "I was considering a large bin for customers to take any for free."

She stared into space, possibly considering my suggestion.

"Should we splurge for new shelves here? Then we wouldn't need a new carpet," I said. The handyman who'd replaced the drywall had cut the strip of compromised carpet leaving two feet of bare floor along the wall.

"We could. Oh, your mother called. She wanted to make sure you'll be at Maddie's party."

"My mother? Why'd she call here? Why not my cell?"

"No idea."

"I'll stop there later."

Gina frowned. "It'll be over. I'll take care of the shop."

"It's fine."

"It's not fine. You're missing it."

I glanced at my watch, wanting to be at Maddie's party, yet I didn't want to leave Gina alone. Guests would be arriving soon. I'd sent Theo the address and the new start time a few days ago. His answer had been a short, *K.*

I hadn't spoken to Philippe since his outburst last week. His words had been on repeat in my mind since. *You're not an island. Your pride is going to kill you.*

I cleared my throat. "Are you sure you feel comfortable working the last hour alone? And closing?" She opened her mouth to answer, and I regretted my question. "On second thought, it's been sort of slow today. I'll close early. Don't worry about it. I'll pay you for the extra hour of course, though."

"Stella. Stop. I can do it. You have to go to the party and you're not waiting until five. Go sooner. Go now, even. It's not a big deal. Trust me."

Trust me, she said, not understanding how hard that was for me. "I'll wait a little longer. Thank you."

She smiled. "Thank *you*."

An hour into the party, Gina broke me down, convincing me to go, even promising to watch the cat she couldn't stand. The weather was cold and rainy so there was light pedestrian traffic, and I forced myself to leave with the instructions to call me immediately if something should happen or if she needed me.

Gina practically pushed me out the door, and once I stepped outside, I bolted to the street, directly to my car.

Because Maddie's birthday fell in February, it negated any chance to entertain children outside. For the past four years, Charlie has managed to pull off a successful indoor fiesta with aplomb. Today, I walked into a bustling chaotic scene and was agog. Since Maddie is currently enamored with princesses, Charlie transformed the house into a Disney extravaganza. Dressed in full Cinderella garb, my sister met me inside the door with a wand and a wide grin. "You're earlier than I expected!"

Lance, donned in a royal blue dress coat and crown, walked up behind her, looking for more string for the Princess Belle piñata.

"I couldn't wait any longer."

She hugged me tight. "I'm so happy. Maddie is going to be thrilled." I was suddenly thankful I'd left when I did.

"Can you tell I need to keep busy, so I don't think?" she said, as I took in the scene before us.

"Oh, Charlie. It's beautiful. You've outdone yourself." Last year, Maddie's party followed the *Dora the Explorer* theme where little guests, and parents, had to locate a map and follow clues in Spanish throughout the afternoon in search of goodies, cake, and games.

Our mother was across the room, carrying a paper grocery bag and picking up discarded napkins, plates, and cups. I scanned the den, pretending to scrutinize the decorations when Charlie said, "He's in the other room."

"I'm not looking for him."

"Sure, you are. Go."

I wandered in awe through the rooms, pointing and clapping as if I were one of the twelve little girls donning a costume. The kitchen was decorated with pink and lavender streamers and balloons hanging from the ceiling. Decorated cupcakes and juice boxes lined the counters. Not one to pass up a cupcake with pink icing and sprinkles, I swiped one from the counter and ate it in two bites.

The living room was draped in pink and blue. A hoard of balloons in various shades of pink hugged the ceiling while blue throw blankets lay on the couches and a pink shag rug rested on the wood floors in place of the area rug. On the shag rug, a table displayed gorgeous, delicate faux-porcelain tea settings for twelve princesses. Cookies and more cupcakes drowning in pink and blue icing filled the center of the table and awaited the small guests to sit down for dessert.

I found Theo tucked in a corner surrounded by four moms. As I approached, he looked over their heads to me and my stomach dipped when he smiled. I elbowed my way between the women, introducing myself to the few I didn't yet know, and announced that I wanted to show Theo something inside.

"Thank you," he said when we'd entered the kitchen. "They ask so many questions."

"Come on, you have experience with women."

"Not in this element, and not without alcohol."

I laughed. "I'm out of my element, too."

The women were where we left them, heads together, watching Theo, whispering. I'm sure I could guess what they were saying. He was worth talking about.

"I didn't think you were coming," he said.

"I can't say no to my niece. I'm surprised you're still here. Especially being one of only three men in the entire house."

"I gave Sam my word that we'd stay to the end."

I turned toward the noise in the next room, the happy screeches that accompanied each swat at the candy-filled Princess Belle pinata.

"We should try the cupcakes," I said.

He kept a straight face, but his eyes sparkled with amusement as he pointed to my cheek. "You have some pink icing there."

"Oh." I wiped the icing from my face as it burned with embarrassment.

"Where are the girls?"

I took him to the living room where the party girls were slowly entering, each clutching a small bag of pinata treats. They sat around the square table in the center of the room. Maddie protectively sat Sam next to her.

"I have no idea where Charlie learned to do this. Our birthday parties included the twins across the street and washing a brownie down with a plastic cup of lemonade at a peeling, redwood table in our tiny, postage-stamp sized lawn in the backyard."

"I've never seen anything like it. She's got a gift."

"She does, along with the cooking gene." I nodded to my sister, who was speaking with a small group of moms near the table.

Theo stared at Charlie. "What gene did you get?"

I spotted my mother across the room, still at work, picking up after the guests, trying to help my sister. "I'm not sure."

He kept a protective eye on his niece.

"Are you having fun?" I said.

"Let's just say I'm more comfortable at work than standing here."

"Of course. That's because most of your time is spent climbing trees."

We laughed as Charlie approached us.

"Sam's adorable," my sister said. "And Maddie loves her." The table slowly filled as Maddie reached out to a cupcake on the center plate and licked the icing from her finger while Sam watched. Lance, holding Myles, leaned over to whisper something to Maddie.

"I appreciate the invite," Theo said. "She's shy and has no friends, other than Maddie. It means a lot to Denise. And to me."

Charlie smiled. "I'm so glad." Her eyes canvassed the room. There was something on her mind. I could feel it. And sure enough, she said, "I'm going to steal Stella for a quick sec."

Theo held out his hands as if saying I wasn't his to take. Or perhaps I was deflecting.

Charlie led me into her bedroom.

"Can you drive me to my surgery next Monday?"

"What about Lance?"

She shook her head. "Please. You're closed, right?"

"Of course," I said. "You know I will."

She fidgeted with the shoulder pads of her costume. "They're going to put a port when they do the mastectomy."

"What do you mean?"

Charlie pulled her gown aside and pointed to her collarbone. "Here. Under the skin. It's like a box so they can give the chemo."

I stared at the spot, unable to fathom this reality.

She adjusted the gown. "It's getting real."

We exchanged a grave, silent stare until the kids started yelling for cake. Without another word, Charlie moved to the door to return to her daughter's party when I stepped behind her and hugged her. She gently patted my hands.

"I put some food aside for you. It's in the fridge, wrapped."

"Okay."

"He likes you, you know," she said.

"What are you talking about?"

Charlie turned around and brushed a loose strand of my hair from my forehead. "He's not here for his niece. He'd have sent his sister. What man wants to endure a princess party?"

I looked into my sister's eyes, eyes that have been seeing me since before I knew who I was. She's thinking about me, and she has cancer.

"A man who loves his niece more than anything. And we're friends."

"He got here early, so we put him to work. He helped Lance put the table together and hang the decorations. Thank God for him or we wouldn't have been ready." Charlie kissed my cheek. "When you accept it, please, sister, enjoy it."

"Charlie? Why did you have Mom call the shop today?"

She looked confused. "What are you talking about?"

"She called to see if I was coming."

"I told her you were but that you would come at the end." Charlie smiled and shook her head. "You know what she did, right?"

"Mom?"

My sister nodded. "She made sure Gina knew you were missing the party."

Gina, who forced me out of the shop early.

"She's a genius," I said.

"Always was."

Charlie left me in the bedroom. I texted Gina for the third time since I'd arrived to see how she was doing.

> Gina: OMG So much has happened since you
> texted fifteen minutes ago.
>
> Me: Really?
>
> Gina: No. Not really. Please stop.

I returned to the living room and took up my post next to

Theo again, while Maddie, surrounded by her guests, opened my gift of an easel and paints. Her face lit up, and I'd wished my employee was here to see my niece's reaction.

Maddie immediately lifted her head from the gift and searched the room until she found her mother. "Momma!"

Without warning, my eyes filled, and dread came over me. Charlie needs to be okay.

Theo did a double take, seeing me. "Are you okay?"

I nodded, unable to speak. Instead, I covered my angst with a clenched grin and watched Maddie tear open the last of her gifts.

Theo and I were the last guests to leave the party. Sam and Maddie were in Maddie's bedroom, assessing her presents, and Myles was put into bed following a mild meltdown, which Charlie attributed to his sugar spike and drop. We helped Lance and Charlie break down the small tables, wrap the leftover food and cakes, and bring the garbage bags to the outside bins.

The rain had stopped as I walked Theo and his niece, whom he carried, to his car.

"You have a nice family," he said.

"It's small, but it's mine."

"Family is family. No matter the size."

How true.

"How does it feel to have left your shop?"

"Fine, why?"

He smiled. "You checked your phone at least five times in the first hour you were here."

Warmth crept up my neck and bloomed across my cheeks. "Gina played with me the whole time. First, she told me the place was on fire. Then she said someone came in and bought every book. Finally, she told me to leave her alone or she'd block me. Not easy for a control freak like me."

He laughed and the sound fell like warm rain over me.

Theo shifted Sam to his other shoulder, glanced up and down the street and to me. "Is everything okay?"

"Today, Charlie told me she's getting a port. It's a little box tucked beneath her skin."

"My mother had one."

"She had cancer?"

"Yes." He hadn't told me when I shared my sister's news the first time.

"Did she beat it?"

He paused before answering. And I knew why.

"Never mind. I don't want to know." I shifted my weight to my other leg, trying not to think about my sister. Lance was helpful at the party. Overly talkative and happy, it seemed.

Theo placed a sleepy Sam in a booster seat in his car and buckled her in. He shut the door, and we faced each other.

"She's young. She's strong. She has a good chance," he said, breaking the silence.

"I keep telling myself that. I keep telling *her* that. But…it's just us, and I don't know what I'd do without her."

"I get it." He glanced at his niece already sleeping. "Thank you for today. Maddie is a huge reason Sam isn't begging my sister to move back home."

"I can relate to Sam. I was alone a lot as a child. By choice, mostly, but still, alone." I don't remember moving closer to him but suddenly, we were inches apart. I tilted my face up to his, wanting to push onto my toes to kiss him. He lowered his head, as if waiting for me to do it.

A door slammed from the house. Lance walked down the side steps with another garbage bag. He didn't look our way, but I moved anyway.

"So, are we still on for next Saturday?" Theo said.

The reading hour. "If you're okay with doing it."

"I told you I was."

"Great! See you then."

It took me thirty minutes to find parking near my building. I replaced the For Sale sign I'd take from the side window and finally got to my apartment at eleven, as Rog stepped out in black jeans and a black wool coat, carrying a crossbody messenger bag.

"Hey, Stella."

"Hey. Where are you off to so late?"

"An OS system is down, and the client needs it running for tomorrow."

"Sounds tragic."

"It is." He said, not joking.

"Is he still angry with me?" I nodded my head toward his apartment door.

"He's insulted. Give him some time."

How much time? I needed to talk to Philippe. I missed him. "Are you going to Paris?"

Rog turned quickly to the door. He shrugged.

"Did you tell Philippe it's a possibility?"

"Of course not. Why would I do that? He'll try to talk me out of it."

"You don't know that." On second thought, he was right. Philippe was crazy in love with Rog, and it would crush him if Rog left. "Okay. I guess it's a wait and see."

Rog touched his finger to his nose and stepped toward the stairs. "See ya."

My tiny apartment felt empty tonight, as it had been for the past week, without Philippe's constant visits. I'd welcome him barging in, even at this late hour. With Charlie on my mind, I changed into pajamas, climbed into bed, and fell into a restless sleep.

CHAPTER 24

My mind was on yesterday's party and seeing Theo as I unlocked the bookshop door. Though closed, I planned to spend the day here, avoiding my apartment.

I welcomed Hemingway, who was waiting by the alley door. His loud purr filled the room, and I opened his can of food and placed his bowls on the floor. Keeping him company, I sat at the desk and checked the locked petty cash box when I noticed the office seemed more spacious, the stacks of books on the workbench suspiciously light.

Where did they go?

They were in the shop, lined against the spackled wall in neat piles around five feet apart, the beautiful spines all facing out. I stared at the towers until my eyes blurred and an idea formed. My employee was brilliant.

I quickly paid open invoices, scoured my resources for the next book order, and then got to work with my idea.

I brought the rest of the books from the office to the wall and had run home twice and brought the piles from my apartment as well. So, when Gina walked into the shop the next day, they were all arranged against the spackle.

"Tell me your thoughts about this," I said, while we were in front of the wall.

She put her hands on her waist. "After closing on Sunday, I played around, trying to figure out if maybe we could make a frame of books around it. You know, after we paint it. Thought it might be cool."

I stared at the wall, envisioning Gina's description and then offered her my idea. "I saw what you were thinking. Then I took it a step further. Why not cover the entire wall with books?"

"You mean book covers?"

"More like a 3-D experience. Some we can lie flat, some with the spines out, some open, like they're being held by a ghost." I pulled a rough sketch from my pocket that I'd made before she came in. "Like this."

She studied my amateur drawing and furrowed her black, pierced brows. We faced the wall until our creative spell was broken by the jingle of the front door.

She turned to me. "Let's start after work tonight."

I put the chalkboard sign on the sidewalk announcing that a real, live firefighter would make an appearance at the next children's reading hour on Saturday. I added the announcement to the website as well, hoping to draw more children than the trickle of kids we'd had so far.

I went through the rest of the day excited, though I couldn't pinpoint if it was about the new wall project or my upcoming guest.

At closing, Gina drew a more detailed, comprehensive picture of my idea, making changes over and over until we both finally agreed on a combined vision. We put together a list of what we needed, and I went home at midnight, super excited to begin.

CHAPTER 25

Saturday morning, Theo arrived an hour early as I helped a customer find Kristen Hannah books. After perusing her choices, she realized she'd read every one, so I suggested she take a gander at the staff picks for the week, suggesting an author to follow Hannah.

Theo waved to me from inside the door. I waved back, as my whole body heated from my center. Wearing jeans and a deep brown sweater that brought out the warmth of his complexion, he held up a bag, and Gina directed him to the office while I remained with the customer.

The woman was chatty, and I enjoyed our conversation, but I eventually pulled away to allow her some privacy to peruse. I was pleased when she met me at the counter with my recommendation, *Where I've Been and Where I'm Going*. The last two customers who'd bought it had stopped in to tell me they'd loved the book.

I found Theo in front of the new wall.

"Hey, thanks for coming in early. Where's Sam?"

"Denise is taking her clothes shopping. I'll bring her next time. This is awesome. When did you do it?"

"We finished this week. It's getting a lot of attention. The shop has been tagged twice on Instagram already." It looked better than we'd imagined—full of color and depth with a personality all its own.

"I love the way these seem to be floating." He pointed to the books we'd propped forward, opened and suspended by heavy glue and small support clasps underneath, invisible to the eye. Gina and I were most proud of this feature.

He turned to me. "What time should I change?"

Reading hour started fifteen minutes late because there

were so many little seats to find. Many parents were forced to prop their children on their laps and hips as there was no more room for small tushies on the carpet.

Gina typed a note on her phone and showed me the screen. *Buy more tiny chairs!*

We smiled at each other; our shared enthusiasm obvious. Theo stepped out from the office dressed impressively in his fire jacket, boots, and helmet. The children, ages ranging from two to twelve, stared, open-mouthed, as I did, at the sight of him, his tall frame, his hair exposed beneath the helmet, the way the jacket hung on him like it had been made for him – sturdy, solid and perfectly right.

Working to cover my awe, I waved him over to where I stood in front of the group.

"This is my friend, Theo. He's a firefighter here in Brooklyn. Does everyone want to say hi?"

A round of hellos echoed through the room, and Theo offered a humble wave in return. I had him sit next to me and the children watched him, captivated, as I read the first book, *Firefighters to the Rescue!* Theo read the second one, *Jimmy, the Firefighter, A Dream Adventure*, for the older children while I tried my best to focus on the book. A part of me relished the scent of him so close, mixed with the smoky odor of his jacket.

After the books were read, Theo patiently took questions for another hour while I hung behind the group, enjoying the spectacle. He ended with some basic tips on fire prevention and what to do if there was a fire. Then he let the children touch his jacket and try on his boots (which covered most of their little legs) and hat, allowing their parents to take photos.

"You've done it," Gina whispered beside me. "This place is packed." Unbeknownst to me, people were pulled into the shop, intrigued by the crowd inside. "While you read, I sold more books in the hour than we usually sell in three days."

I thought of my landlord, and my increased rent. I could do this. I *am* doing this.

"The question is, can I keep this up every third Saturday? I can't pull a celebrity in for every reading."

"You don't have to. We had to bring them in once to keep them. I know it. This place is an escape, Stella. For adults and children. It's beautiful in here."

"I hope you're right."

When I felt that Theo had done enough, I announced that our firefighter had to go out and save animals stuck in a tree, as I'd read in the earlier story. They collectively screamed goodbye to their hero, and I pulled Theo to my office to escape.

Alone with him, I gushed. "You're awesome! I can't thank you enough for doing this. I know the last thing you want to do is wear your work clothes on your day off."

"I had fun. I didn't expect all these people."

"Me neither. This is the largest crowd we've seen here. Thanks to you."

He lifted his duffel. "I'll change now." He started for the bathroom when I stopped him.

"Don't squeeze into the bathroom. Change here. I'll give you some time. Hemingway, turn around."

His deep chuckle followed me as I left him to go into the shop, where Gina was ringing up the line that had formed. Many of the parents were buying books for their children. I practically floated on air to the register to help her.

Twenty minutes passed, and Theo hadn't come up from the office. I knocked on the door, wondering if he'd left through the rear exit into the alley to escape unnoticed.

I opened it tentatively and the sight before me almost melted my heart. In his dark brown sweater and faded jeans, he was on the floor holding Hemingway, who had fallen asleep in his lap.

"I'm sorry," I whispered, "I was looking for a brawny hero-type. I didn't mean to disturb you." I went to leave when he said, "Wiseass."

I laughed and entered, squatting down to sit next to him. "You made a friend."

"I have a way with animals."

"Right. Occupational benefit."

He elbowed me gently.

I pet the cat, who purred loudly. For a quick moment, I was jealous of the feline, nestled on those muscular thighs.

"Thank you for what you did today."

He turned to me. "It was my pleasure, Stella." He held my gaze until I pulled away.

"I'm coming up on an anniversary that I'd like to forget," I said.

He didn't ask what it was. I suspected he knew. The one-year anniversary of my wedding—*non-wedding*—was in two weeks.

"I would normally rely on my best friend to get me through it, but I don't have one anymore. And Charlie...well, she's pre-occupied, as she should be."

"So, let's forget it," he said. "I'll take you out somewhere. We can go dancing, or to dinner, or a show or movie, or anything you want. Or you can get drunk, and I'll make sure you get home."

That's what Marcy would have done. I was sure of it. If she weren't sleeping with my ex-fiancé.

Did I want to do any of those things? I didn't know. Still, I said, "Okay," anyway, because I didn't want to be alone.

"Okay." He gently moved the cat from his lap and offered his hand. I took it and he pulled me up close to him. I swallowed as I stared into his brown eyes. He leaned over and touched his lips to mine. They were softer than I'd imagined. He placed his palm against my cheek, barely touching me. Tiny sparks flitted along my skin. It felt so nice to kiss a man after not doing so for so long. I almost lost myself in the moment.

Almost.

I pulled away.

"I'm sorry. I'm not looking for that." I blew out a breath, mortified.

"You don't kiss all your friends that way? Where were you brought up?"

I let out a laugh, relieved that he didn't let my aloofness offend him. He was different from the other men I've known, and I was enjoying discovering how much.

He touched his fingers to my chin, raising my face to his. "I apologize. It won't happen again."

"Make sure it doesn't." I teased, though something in my chest ached.

CHAPTER 26

I pulled into Charlie's driveway at five a.m. Monday morning. The sky was pale pink, window shades were drawn on neighboring homes, cars were immobile, no dogs barked. She walked out before I could get my car door open and climbed into the passenger seat. We were the only ones awake, it seemed. Charlie and me. A team.

As I drove down the street, I peeked in my rearview mirror to see if Lance looked out the window to watch his wife, but the blinds stayed down.

"Does Lance mind I'm taking you?"

Charlie laid her head against the seat and closed her eyes. "Stop asking."

"Sorry."

She opened her eyes so that she watched the ceiling of the car. "It was his idea. He wants to take Maddie to school and Myles to Mrs. Baxter's. He'll meet us there." She was quiet the rest of the way, kept rubbing her legs and staring out of her passenger window. The gorgeous pink sky remained impotent against the bleak mood in the car.

"You'll be fine, you know," I said. "I read the statistics, and your odds are higher now than they've ever been. It's a good time to be a woman."

She turned her head away from me.

Mom was in the hospital waiting room when we arrived. "I told her she didn't have to come," Charlie said. "We could have picked her up."

"She's probably been here an hour already." Poor Mom. She clutched her purse on her shoulder. Wisps of dark hair fell out of her bun, and the track lighting paled her complexion, making her appear disheveled and slightly older looking. She was worried, but the words would never leave her lips.

We weren't a family of over-talkers. Certainly not prone to emotional sentimentality. While I'd stayed wrapped in my cocoon of sheets and blankets in my dark bedroom for days after my aborted wedding, my mother brought food, my sister brought wine, and neither said much more than "He's an idiot. You're better off." Hardly the boost someone might need, but I did appreciate their input and knew they were telling me they loved me.

Lance arrived at nine o'clock to find the three of us in a room. Charlie wore a thin robe, the television tuned to Kelly Ripa, who unknowingly tried to take our minds off the inevitable by regaling us with another story about her children.

Lance paced the room, stopping at a box of surgical gloves attached to the wall. He took one out, blew it up, and put it by his pants zipper. "John Handcock," he said.

Charlie rolled her eyes and our mother sighed.

Lance glanced in my direction. I winked. It was a good try, however inappropriate.

At eleven, the nurses arrived to wheel my sister to her operation. She left us with instructions for the kids for the afternoon as she was wheeled away.

"She'll be fine. She's got this," Lance announced when his wife was gone.

Mom walked to the door, then turned around at the threshold and glanced at him. He smiled and gave her a thumbs up. Her eyes flitted to me, unreadable. Then she left.

"Welp, I have to check on Myles at Mrs. Baxter's. He was crying when I left him. I'll be back soon. Will you call me if there's any news before that?" Lance said.

I nodded and watched him leave. In the waiting room, I took a first sip from my third cup of coffee when I saw the news flash on television of an apartment fire somewhere in New York City. Over the anchor's shoulder, firemen convened, pointing, hoses aimed at the building. I stepped closer to the TV to hear it, paying careful attention to the update.

Flames poked out of the windows, reaching up toward

the roof like orange fingers. I thought of Theo on Saturday, wearing his helmet and jacket. How was that any match for what I was watching on television? I walked to the other side of the room and settled in front of the other television which was showing Dr. Phil speaking with an angry teenager. I sipped my coffee, ignoring the screen.

Two hours later, my sister still in surgery, Lance returned as Mom and I were in the surgical waiting room. I received a text from someone asking about my car. I answered his questions and then checked for offers for my wedding dress on eBay. There was another offer. I didn't accept.

My phone pinged with a text from Theo.

> Hey, thinking about you and hoping all goes well today with Charlie.

I'd told him about her surgery after reading hour. He remembered.

I typed back.

> Who dis?

Even under the circumstances, I smiled while texting Theo.

> Wiseass. Keep me posted.

Ten hours later, I trudged, bleary-eyed, up the last steps to my apartment floor almost missing Philippe leaning against the frame of his open door.

I stopped and faced him. His arms were crossed over his chest. I hadn't seen or talked to him in two weeks and felt the deep loss of his company.

"You sound tired," he said.

"I haven't spoken yet."

"Your footsteps. Extra slow. Still walk like an elephant, but a tired elephant."

I leaned against the wall across from him. "I don't take help well. It's always been an issue for me."

He listened.

"When my father left, neighbors dropped off food or clothes constantly, and I hated it. It embarrassed me to open the door to find a box or Pyrex dishes with instructions on how to heat. Like my mother couldn't handle it on her own. I refused to wear the clothes, thinking the girl down the block would see her T-shirt on me and pity me."

"It's nice that you had support in your community. Not everyone does."

"I was young. I didn't see it that way."

"And now?"

"I should have accepted your help." I kicked at the floor. "At least I should have thanked you for trying."

He rested his arms by his sides. "You can try now."

"Thank you for sending your plumber."

"You're too late. I don't accept."

My laugh brought heavy tears. "Charlie had her double mastectomy today."

His face dropped. "How is she?"

I wasn't even sure. She'd been in surgery longer than expected. She had excessive bleeding, the doctor had explained when he finally came out of the OR. She'd needed two blood transfusions, news that caused even Lance, who'd been trying to entertain us with Myles' latest antics, to sway between my mother and me, and we held him upright. We found out later, after she'd woken briefly, that she'd taken an aspirin a few days earlier and had forgotten to tell the surgeon.

The doctor was optimistic that he removed the cancer, but who could know? People say things they don't mean all the time. I found it hard to trust anyone— even a doctor.

Before I could utter another word, Philippe had me in one of his signature bear hugs. I collapsed against him, feeling better and whispered a sincere apology over his shoulder.

"It's forgotten," he said, and I closed my eyes, relieved.

CHAPTER 27

Three days after the surgery, I left work early, allowing Gina to close again, for which she announced she was proud of me. Though it was difficult to do, being away from Charlie was even harder.

I let myself into my sister's house and paused in the foyer, acutely aware of the silence that greeted me. I took a deep breath and walked through the house, finding her sitting on the couch in the den, the muted television tuned to the news.

Her eyes were closed, but she wasn't in a slack sleeping position. She was resting.

"Hi. It's me," I whispered.

Charlie opened her eyes. "Hey, you."

I put down the small stack of books I'd brought for her on the cocktail table. "Be right back." I scurried to the kitchen and put the soup and sandwiches I'd bought from the deli on the counter and milk in the fridge. I poured her a glass of green tea I picked up, at her request, and put the rest in the fridge, too. Then I placed two oversized cupcakes in the center of the table, an impulse buy from the bakery.

I brought the tea to the den to find Charlie in the same position. Her flannel shirt was buttoned to her collarbone, but I could still glimpse the top of the wrapping around her chest. Her cheeks were still a bit sunken, though her color had returned, thankfully. Chemo was scheduled for next month, after she healed, if all went well. Two tubes led from under the bandages on each side, reaching below her shirt, so I could see them filling up with a murky, yellow fluid.

I sat beside her and handed her the tea, trying not to stare at the bulge below her shoulder.

"How are you feeling?" I asked.

"Same." Her hands went gingerly to her chest. "It hurts."

"How does it feel compared to childbirth?" I can't imagine anything hurting more than giving birth.

"Nothing compares to childbirth, Stella. But at the end of that pain, there's a gift like no other. In this case, I'm in pain and there's no gift."

"Yes, there is. The gift is life."

"Let's hope so."

I leaned over to see the discharge from her tubes. "This is disgusting."

"You're disgusting."

"You are."

She smiled, but I could still see the underlying discomfort beneath it.

We both turned to the news. There was footage of an auto accident on the FDR from the view of a hovering helicopter.

"Where is everyone?"

"Mom took the kids to McDonald's. They were getting antsy. I keep reminding Myles not to climb on me. But it's all he wants to do."

"And Lance?"

"He hasn't been climbing on me."

"Oh good, your sense of humor is still terrible."

She shifted and grimaced. "He's at work."

She sipped her tea. Two fire engines were on the scene, a slew of fighters working on removing a portion of the car partially trapped below a truck. Charlie glanced at me. I stared at the screen, trying to understand how they were going to extricate the driver.

"Can we watch something else?" she said.

She handed me the remote, and I found a harmless cooking show. "This is because I love you," I said.

"You should try paying attention now and then. You need to start eating better. Cooking can be cathartic."

"I'd rather read."

She let out a soft snort and then grimaced.

"Theo is taking me out to do something fun for my anniversary, so I don't sit home and dwell on it."

Her head swiveled to face me. "Oh, really. What are you going to do?"

"We didn't decide yet. Something outlandish and different."

She nodded. "That's perfect."

"Mom called me last night, and for once didn't mention Sophia's nephew."

Charlie's eyes widened. "Wow. She's not one to give up."

"Why, though? All these years she's enjoyed being on her own. Why does she feel the need to set me up? I told her I'm fine."

"Did you tell her about Theo?" she said.

"There's nothing to tell. We're friends. He was married and it didn't work, and I'm turned off to marriage."

"But you agreed to go out with him."

"To avoid the dwelling."

"I'm happy for you."

I stared at the screen.

"You like him," Charlie said.

"It doesn't matter."

"Of course, it does."

"Do you remember who I went to the prom with?"

Charlie lifted her head, surprised by the random question. I had a point and needed her to answer.

"Ricky."

"That's right," I said. "Ricky, who I dated for two years."

"So? Why are you bringing that up now?"

"Stay with me. Do you remember who I left the prom with?"

She thought a moment. And then, "Didn't I pick you up?"

"Yes. Yes, you did. I never told you why."

"You said you were sick."

"I wasn't sick, Charlie. The DJ hadn't gotten through the second song after we'd arrived when Ricky started kissing Vanessa on the dance floor." I watched my sister process this.

"Do you know what he said before he broke up with me a month earlier?"

Charlie shook her head slowly.

"I was too clingy. I was suffocating him. Needy, was the word he used."

"What the hell is that supposed to mean? How did you suffocate him? You were hardly needy. In fact, you were the most independent person I knew."

"Don't confuse independent with alone. Anyway, I asked him. He said I was always around. Everywhere he looked, there I was. I was too available and had no opinion. He said being with me put too much pressure on him."

"So why did he ask you to go to the prom after breaking up with you?"

"He didn't have a date. What's worse is I went with him, hoping we'd get back together. I was so desperate to be in a relationship."

I could see my sister recalling the night, how in the car on the way home, she'd asked me what happened, how I told her I felt sick and didn't want to force Ricky to leave his prom. At the house, I ran into our bedroom and crawled into bed where I stayed for the entire weekend. She never questioned my explanation.

"Why didn't you tell me, Es? I'd have helped you."

"I was mortified. Who gets left at their prom? How clingy could I have been to make him leave me? I'm not clueless. And I wasn't independent. I had no real friends after the twins moved."

Charlie stared at her lap.

"Now, a year after I'm dumped at the altar," I said, "this guy suddenly comes along. He's good looking and kind. Do I like him? More than I want to. But whenever we seem to be on the verge of something more than friends, I sabotage the moment. He's easy to talk to. I don't feel like I have to be anyone but myself. Like with Philippe. Or you. And I don't want to lose that."

Charlie took a deep inhale and blew out a breath through narrow lips. "Every guy isn't Ricky or Doug. Theo is different. He's upright and good."

"They all *seem* upright and good at first, don't you see? They're all hiding behind a mask that I fall for. Then the mask comes off and the monster appears. Only, *I'm* the monster they run from."

My sister took my hand.

"A part of me will always be that girl in high school," I said.

"I wish you would have told me then."

It was easier to act like nothing bothered me. "I brought soup," I said, tired of the subject. "Do you want me to do your hair before or after we eat?"

"Let's do it now," she said, pushing herself up. I helped her to stand, and she flinched.

"Do you have painkillers?"

"I'll wait until Lance gets home to take something."

I held my tongue to keep from expressing my disapproval of my brother-in-law, who returned to work one day after Charlie came home. She'd had her mastectomy four days ago.

She shifted her weight and held her tubes and bags. I felt her discomfort as if it were my own.

I matched Charlie's glacial pace toward the bathroom. We were in the hall, surrounded on both sides by walled pictures of the kids, Lance, mom, and me. There was one sepia picture framed on the end. While Charlie paused to take a breath, I stared at it. The photo was of our father's back. He held Charlie's hand as they faced a large, illuminated Ferris Wheel not far in front of them. She couldn't have been older than four. I loved this picture—her small, thin legs below her dress, her hair falling to her waist as she held onto his hand. In his other arm, he held a baby, six months old. Me. It was the only picture Charlie had of him in the house—a different shot than the one framed in my apartment. At my place was a full-frontal photo of Dad holding me on his shoulder as my hair blew across my face, partially covering my laughter. Proof I'd been a happy, carefree child once.

In the bathroom, I covered her shoulders with a towel and gently guided her back in an office chair until her head was over the sink. I shampooed and rinsed her thick hair, and gently pulled her up. She couldn't lift her arms at all yet.

"I've been thinking about him a lot lately," I said.

"Who?"

"Dad."

She stared ahead.

"Do you still wonder why he took off?"

"Not anymore," she said.

"I keep thinking about the last night he was home. What you said about someone at the door and the screaming. It must have to do with that."

"Maybe. I asked Mom about it the next morning. She didn't want to talk about it. Said Dad was tired and sleeping and everything was okay."

I gently squeezed the excess water from her hair and pulled a comb from the shelf behind the mirror. "But you asked."

"Yeah." Charlie paused. "I was relieved to be told it was okay. I was afraid." She leaned her head into the combing motion.

I finished and wrapped her head in a towel. "How did you stop thinking about him?"

"I still think about him, Es. I just don't wonder why he left anymore. I decided not to put myself through it. Too painful. I look forward now."

Oh, how I wanted the strength to make that decision too.

I had filled two bowls with soup and placed them on the kitchen table when my phone pinged with a new text message from Theo.

Hey, Lucky Charms Girl, how is your sister?

Me: I'm never going to live that down, am I?

Theo: Most definitely not.

Me: I'm with Charlie now. She's looking dandy, thanks to me.

Theo: You have that "dandy" effect on people.

Me: I get that a lot.

"Who are you texting?" My sister walked in from using the bathroom.

I put my phone in my pocket. "Gina."

Charlie gently lowered herself onto a kitchen chair. I don't know why I lied to her. I guess I don't want her to think too much into harmless texting between me and this guy.

The front door opened, and the squeaking voice of Myles wafted in, followed by Maddie's in the middle of a story to her grandmother. Charlie's face lit up, proof that the strength of love could pull anyone to a better place.

Mom walked into the kitchen and seemed startled to see me.

"I didn't know you were here. Where's your car?"

Charlie turned to me, confused.

"I took the train and Uber'd from the station. I'm selling my car and wanted to see how hard it is to get here using mass transit."

"But you still have your car," Mom said.

"That's right."

Charlie shook her head.

"What?"

"Use the car until you sell it. Why make it harder on yourself before you have to?"

"Exactly," Mom said. "You're living a future problem before you even have it."

CHAPTER 28

Theo walked into the shop near closing time.

"You like to push the hours, don't you?" I met him by our display tables up front. I hadn't expected him to stop in. He'd been here twice this week already, minutes before closing. Bought a book each time.

"I like living on the edge."

"And you like to read."

He shoved his hands in his front jeans' pockets. "I'm off work and wanted to check in. How is Charlie?"

"She's doing as well as can be expected considering it's only been a week since her surgery."

He leaned in. "But?"

"What makes you think there's a but?"

"You still seem worried."

"I am. I worry she won't beat it. And Lance has been working longer hours at his office and when he does come home, he won't let her feel scared or unsure or even talk about it. He insists she's going to get over this and things will return to normal. He's over-optimistic."

"Has he been unsupportive in the past?"

We slowly made our way down the center aisle, toward the couch of shame. "Raindrops Keep Falling on My Head" played through the speakers.

"No. He's been the ideal husband."

I gestured for Theo to sit on the couch. I took the upright chair opposite.

My cell phone rang from inside my pocket. I checked it quickly.

"Take it," Theo said.

"I want to be available for Charlie if she needs me."

The bell over the door jingled as a couple walked in.

"Was that Charlie?" he said.

I stood up to assess if my customers needed assistance. They didn't. Holding hands, they stopped in front of the Literary Fiction section. Heads close together, they whispered while he touched a spine.

"No. It was my mom."

"You should answer your mom's call."

"She's trying to set me up with some guy. A widower, no less. The last thing I want is to get involved with a widower."

Theo crossed his arms over his chest and wore a grin. "Why?"

"First, no setting up at all. We've both established that it's awkward and never works out." He nodded in agreement. "Second, I can't compete with a dead wife— to be compared to a perfect person he didn't want to lose. My track record with men is low as it is. I see a widower walking my way, I run."

I checked again on my customers. They found the 3D wall and he took her picture. I winked at Theo. He gave me a thumbs up. This wall was amazing for business. As the couple walked toward the counter, I said, "I'll be right back."

They bought three books, signed onto my mailing list, and after some pleasantries, walked out. It was past six, so I flipped the sign to *"We're Closed"* and returned to Theo, who was now in front of the historical fiction shelf. He reached for a book.

"Don't buy anymore."

"That's the worst sales tactic I've ever heard."

I covered my face with my palm. "I'm not a salesperson."

He canvassed the shelf in front of him but spoke to me. "On the contrary, you're friendly and approachable and people gravitate to you."

My cheeks blazed.

"Are you still okay with going out Sunday?" he said.

"Absolutely. Operation Forget My Anniversary is confirmed."

He turned from the shelf, leaving the book. "So, have you given any thought to what you want to do?"

I had. A lot. On Monday, I wanted to cancel. On Tuesday, I wanted to see him. All week I wrestled with my indecision. Seeing him now, I realized I wanted to spend time with him. Being alone would make me sad. And Theo made me laugh.

When I didn't answer, he said, "If you're closing, I'll walk you home. It's on my way. I'm not being chivalrous or anything."

"I'd love it. I'll lock up."

I met Theo outside, and we started the walk home.

"It's okay to be worried about Charlie," he said when we'd covered half a block without speaking. "Your brother-in-law is handling it the way he knows how. We're not given an instruction book on what to do in situations like this. Be patient with him. His world is rocked right now."

"I know. I've learned not to expect too much of people."

Theo looked at me.

"My sister is my hero. My past, my childhood, my memory. I can't picture my life without her."

He didn't comment and a moment later, I realized why. He'd lost his brother, cutting their childhood short. I grabbed his arm. "I'm sorry. I didn't mean to say that. That was rude. I'm...sorry."

He stopped. "Stella, it's okay."

We slowed our paces more, as if we didn't want to reach our destination too soon.

"Life is so hard. It feels like it's one test after another. How are we expected to endure all this without losing hope?" I said. "I'm thirty-six, and one of the two people I love most in my life could be taken away from me."

Theo ran his fingers through his hair. "You find the right people who help you endure it."

Like you, I wanted to say. But fear of the unknown prevented me.

The lights along the street shone against the dark sky.

"Thank you for letting me vent."

"What are friends for?" he said. We paused at the corner

of my street for passing traffic before continuing. "You didn't answer my question."

Right. About Sunday.

"I'd like to do something different than anything I've ever done."

His eyebrows rose in anticipation. "I'm ready. Hit me with it."

"I would like to cook dinner for you."

His head lifted in shock. He wasn't the only one surprised. "You don't owe me anything. In fact, you bought me dinner, remember?"

"A hot dog?"

"It was delicious."

I elbowed him and he nudged me, a comfortable, communicated agreement.

As surprised as I was by my own offer, I knew that's how I wanted to spend the anniversary of the second worst day of my life. Not out getting hammered, or seeing a play, or jumping out of an airplane (yes, I'd thought of that at one point). I wanted to make a new, nice memory.

"I thought you didn't get the cooking gene."

"I didn't. This will be your true test of bravery. From what I understand, you're a risk-taker."

He glanced up and down the street and then to me. "It might be safer running through fire."

I tried to act hurt, but my grin gave me away. Lord, he was fun.

He poked me in the shoulder. "Sure. I'm up for the challenge." Then he returned my smile, and I waited for butterflies to take flight inside my belly. Instead, an unfamiliar sense of calmness overcame me.

"So, Sunday," he said,

It was dumb luck that I closed early on Sundays and didn't open on Mondays.

I nodded. "Six?" It would give me enough time to get home from work and prepare this inconceivable meal.

"I get off work at six. How about seven?"

"Fine," I whispered.

I started to walk into my apartment building when Theo called my name from the sidewalk. I turned around.

"Life isn't all about tests, Stella. There are parts of it that are beautiful, too. The tests make the beautiful worth it."

CHAPTER 29

Charlie called me on Sunday morning at work.

"Do you have everything?"

"Yes." After I invited Theo for dinner, I'd called my sister and asked her what I should cook.

"Linguine with scallops and Caesar salad. Simple. Easy," she'd said, "and so tasty."

"Can I make that?"

"Yes. I promise. I'll walk you through it. When is this happening?"

"Sunday."

So, here we were, on Sunday, the anniversary of my non-wedding, and my thoughts were on this dinner I had to prepare. It was the perfect distraction. In fact, it was all I could think about for the past three days. I'd purchased the scallops yesterday, as well as the ingredients for the salad and necessary spices. I'd had to go to three stores to find everything.

Charlie was almost three weeks post-surgery and preparing to start chemo, so my unusual endeavor helped to distract her, too.

I closed the store at five, as usual, and had most of the dinner for Theo prepped by seven, thanks to a half dozen phone calls with Charlie. I hummed along to the music coming from the stereo as I pulled the lettuce out of the fridge. The pan sizzled on the stove, browning the scallops to a caramel hue. I threw a handful of salt into the pot of boiling water. Occasionally, the music from the living room was drowned out by the glorious symphony of sizzling and popping of garlic in oil. I smiled to myself as I imagined Theo's reaction to the meal, happy I'd set low expectations on my cooking ability.

I pulled a bottle of Chardonnay from the fridge, uncorked it, and poured two generous glasses. Sipping one, I surveyed my work. Not too bad. The scallops were just about done, and the linguine would follow shortly. Charlie had warned me that timing was everything, and the most difficult part of a successful meal. No kidding. I stepped from the kitchen to check my apartment, pulling overlooked clothes crumpled in the corner of the couch and throwing them into my bedroom closet. I ran a finger over my dresser and pulled it back covered in dust. No time to fix that now. I closed the door to my bedroom. He wouldn't be seeing it.

It would be dinner. That's all. Friends sharing a meal. At my apartment. Making a new harmless memory to replace the other one.

At the kitchen counter, I carefully followed Charlie's directions for the Caesar salad dressing, trying not to gag while I chopped the little hairy anchovies. I checked the clock on the table and mentally calculated when the linguine should hit the water. Charlie said to time it right before Theo was due over, so the pasta wouldn't stick together. It was seven ten and his shift ended an hour ago. I quickly changed into my hunter green wrap dress, the one I wore to Philippe's party, figuring I'd get one more wear out of it before it was relegated to the untouched portion of my closet. I was straining the linguine and simultaneously enjoying a facial steam when I glanced at the clock again. Seven twenty-seven.

Theo was late.

I set the table, barely fitting two plates, utensils, and napkins on the small surface. I moved the settings twice. First, I tried them next to each other, but one of us would be facing the tiny, blue and yellow flowered wallpaper left here by the previous tenants. Then, I moved them so that we'd face each other. Was it too romantic? Perhaps. My heart did a little thump. What was I going for here? Did I even know?

I left the table as is. I sat in one of the chairs in my green dress, minimal makeup, hair left down to fall past my shoulders, and sipped my wine. I lit two tapered candles I'd bought yesterday.

I blew them out and moved them off the table.

I grabbed them again and re-lit them, putting them back on the table.

He was forty-five minutes late.

I scanned Facebook, scrolling down the posts when I saw a new one. A picture taken on a tropical island, Doug and Marcy, arm in arm in bathing suits, in front of a large waterfall.

On what would be our one-year anniversary. Why would he post this today? Why not wait until tomorrow? How callous.

My phone rang in my hand, and I jumped, my heart pounding. I looked at the screen. My mother.

"Hi, Mom." If I let it go to voicemail, she would have called Charlie to find out where I was, and my sister would have told her I was home and she'd call me again anyway.

"Stella. Am I interrupting anything?"

I looked around the kitchen, down at my dress and empty wine glass. I didn't want her to know what happened tonight. That my first attempt at a date in a year (is that what it really was?) failed.

"No."

"I spoke with Sophia yesterday."

"Mom—"

"No, I wanted to let you know that her nephew met someone and isn't interested anymore so I won't be bothering you about him."

"Oh good. What a relief." Tears threatened to erupt. Theo was an hour late. No call. No apology. Ghosted.

He's not coming. The fear that this might happen had occurred to me, yet I'd pushed it away, believing he might be different than the rest. I made my first full dinner and got dressed in a swanky get-up.

"Can I call you tomorrow? I'm not feeling well."

Mom hesitated. "I'll bring you soup."

"Definitely do not bring me soup. I love you for offering, but I'm going to get into bed and read a book and close this day. I'll call you tomorrow."

I tossed my phone on the counter and went into my bedroom, catching my reflection in the mirror. What was I thinking, putting on this stupid dress? I pulled roughly at the bow to untie it, ripping the seam as I pulled it off and threw it in the bathroom garbage. Who am I to think I can be with a man and have any sort of relationship? Why do I even try? Even a "friend" wouldn't keep his promise.

I wiped my running nose with a tissue and put on stained sweatpants and a T-shirt. In the kitchen, I mixed the now congealing scallops with the clumping linguine in the pot, adding olive oil to loosen everything, grabbed the pot and the bowl of Caesar salad, placing it precariously on top, and walked across the hall to Philippe's apartment.

Philippe opened the door, eyed me up and down, and frowned.

"For you and Rog." My voice shook but I managed to keep my eyes from leaking again.

"Come in, love." He took the pot from me and put his arm around my shoulders. "Why are you dressed like a homeless person? You weren't going to wear that, were you?"

Philippe and I had discussed this dinner a few days ago. He'd suggested I wear the green wrap dress.

"What does it matter? He's a no-show."

Rog walked into the kitchen where Philippe and I placed my dinner. "Smells amazing."

"Have at it," I said to Rog. "Stop looking at me," I said to Philippe. "Or I'm leaving."

I couldn't read Philippe's expression. Was it shock? It shouldn't have been. Or confusion? It wasn't pity, and for that, I didn't turn around and walk out. If he so much as dropped his shoulders and said, "Oh baby," I would have lost it and hated myself for doing so.

Rog gave me a half-hug, obviously informed of my dinner

date, and grabbed a bowl while Philippe frowned. "Do you want to stay with us? Have you eaten?"

"Not yet. Sure." I grabbed a bowl, served myself, and was about to take a seat in the kitchen when Philippe said, "I think you should come inside and see something."

I followed Rog into the den where he and Philippe had been watching television. Philippe stayed at the den entrance and waited for me to look at the screen.

"Check this out," Rog said, raising the volume. "It's like watching a car wreck. We can't stop."

I stared ahead, clutching my bowl while a blaring fire that seemed to take up an entire block filled the screen. Then I gasped.

The newscaster droned on soberly as behind her, a row of apartment buildings in downtown Brooklyn burned. The woman adeptly let the viewers know that firemen from all nearby stations were called in. The blaze, origination not yet known, started at 3:30 p.m. and escalated to a five-alarm blaze within an hour. Two firefighters had already been taken by ambulance to the nearest hospital.

"Let's hope we learn of no other casualties," she said, before the camera panned around the scene. Theo was there. That's why he didn't show up to dinner.

I didn't realize Philippe had sat beside me on the couch until he leaned in and said, "Methinks he got caught up at work. I was really hoping he got to you first."

Theo had said running into fires was who he was. I put my bowl on the cocktail table and tried to identify any of the stained, somber faces walking across the screen.

"That's got to make you feel better, right?"

I couldn't answer. I'd rather he be doing anything else but this.

After thirty minutes of watching an out-of-control fire, I pulled myself to stand. "I'm going to my place."

I turned on my own television, climbed onto my couch, and covered myself with a blanket. Minutes later, Philippe walked in, sat next to me, pulled a portion of the blanket onto his lap, and said nothing.

We watched the footage, covered by news programs that shifted off, resumed by the next wave of broadcasters. This was big. It preempted any other news of the night. Philippe switched through the channels, trying in vain to get some clear picture of who was hurt. Still, they mentioned only two firefighters who were taken to the hospital.

My phone vibrated on the coffee table at ten o'clock, and both of us jumped and looked over. I felt deflated to see Charlie's text.

> Well? How did it go?

> He got held up at work.

Three dots appeared and disappeared for several seconds until her response came.

> Don't look into it, Stella. I'm sure he has a viable reason.

> I do, too.

> Do you want to talk?

> No

> Ok. Invite your neighbor over and enjoy the meal anyway. xo

The anchor updated viewers with news that one of the firemen brought earlier to the hospital was confirmed dead, according to a hospital source. His identity would remain anonymous until family was notified. My stomach lurched and nausea washed over me. I pulled in deep breaths until the feeling passed. If something happened to Theo, his sister would be called— his next of kin. Did he have other family? I would find out with the public. Who was I to him? A friend? An acquaintance?

At midnight, the newswoman looked how I felt: exhausted, worried, and worse for wear. Unable to eat, the dinner I'd planned was left untouched, congealed and cold. At some point during the night, Philippe put a glass of wine in my hand. I held it, untouched. Rog stopped over, carrying the salad bowl and pasta pot. He washed them and put them away before joining us in my den.

The three of us sat on the couch, mute. Philippe occasionally moved to and from the kitchen to refill his wine glass or get a cup of water, while I remained seated, staring at the screen, praying I wouldn't see Theo's name scrolling along the bottom. Rog left at one a.m., saying something about an early meeting in the morning. Two more firefighters were hurt and taken to the hospital. Four down. Three alive as far as we knew. The rest? In or around the building, working to squelch the flames that seemed to be continuously fed by some unseen demon.

At three a.m., seven hours after I walked into Philippe's apartment with my shattered vision of a promising night, I managed to convince him to go home to sleep.

"Are you sure you're okay?" he said.

"I'm sure. I don't know why I'm so worried."

"I do." He kissed me on both cheeks, assuring me he'd be back in a few hours. Alone, I crumpled onto the couch and watched the moon in the starless sky, wondering if Theo was one of the ones in the hospital or the one who would never make it home.

The news cameras panned the area showing the fire was finally under control, smoldering in the early dawn, as a fresh-faced news anchor summarized the events of the evening, occasionally showing snippets of familiar footage. The name of the fallen firefighter was still withheld, but the three in the hospital were identified. None were Theo. I recognized a name, though, from his fire house. Salvatore. The probie who shoveled my shop entrance without complaint, who made the best chili I'd ever tasted. Who Theo seemed to favor and watch over. Hoagie. How do people put up with this stress? Was this why

Theo was no longer married? Did his wife get tired of waiting for him to walk in the door after every shift, wondering if he would?

Through the window, darkness gave way to the dawn, leaving me numb and exhausted. Natural light cast an ethereal glow to my neighborhood, but I refused to see the beauty splayed before me. I won't acknowledge that another day would begin with one less hero. Stay dark, I told the sun. I'm not ready. Someone gave their life tonight.

I thought about the past few months of getting to know him, the way we met at the aquarium, his visits to the bookshop, our walks and conversations, the day we spent in Central Park. Despite not wanting a relationship, we'd built one, and now, I wasn't sure how I could wake up every morning to a world without him in it.

Philippe knocked at my door. I ignored him. Stared at the sky. The sun was coming up, and with it an unbelievable palette of colors. He knocked again, this time with more force. Irritated, I turned to tell him to go away until a realization fell over me.

Philippe never knocked.

I ran to the door and flung it open.

CHAPTER 30

Theo stood in front of me in jeans and a long-sleeve T-shirt with his firehouse emblem over his heart. His hair hung in his eyes, his large browns bloodshot. His hands and face still held the residue of grime from the night. He reeked of a cologne of black smoke, sweat, and fear. I froze in place, taking him in, in all his beautiful, filthy, very alive splendor. He was here, in one piece. Emotion filled me. My throat constricted.

"You're late," I said softly.

"I'm sorry I missed dinner." His voice was raspy, as if he'd been screaming for hours.

"Yeah, well, you'd better have a good excuse."

He exhaled. "Stella…"

When he whispered my name, my emotions overtook all logic, and I leaned up to kiss him. As I did, he grabbed my face with both hands and returned my kiss deeply, roughly, long, and my own suppressed longing betrayed me.

He took one step in, kicked my door closed and brought me down to the foyer floor. He pulled his mouth from mine leaving me gasping as he moved down my neck and along my collarbone in a heated rush. In seconds, my ratty T-shirt and sweatpants were in a crumpled heap next to us. He pressed his lips to my breasts, his hands tight on my arms, holding me in place while his mouth sought my body, until I groaned with pleasure. His mouth moved along my stomach, hungrily, seeming to taste every bit of me. I grabbed his shoulders, moved my fingers into his hair and knew all that I felt for him had changed in this instant. Or maybe it was there all along, hidden behind the fear I wore like a cloak.

Everything we'd been feeling but denying rushed forth

in a sensual wave of touching and grasping, biting, sucking, pulling. He was between my legs, hands holding me up so I could meet him, and he could explore, his tongue hot and merciless. I grabbed fistfuls of his hair roughly—responding to him, knowing I was probably hurting him and not caring. His response became more urgent the harder I tugged. I writhed under his touch, and he held me in place with his hands, his fingers pushing into my skin so hard I could already feel the bruising, until I could control myself no longer and let go in a cry of ecstasy.

Theo placed my shaking body down, and languidly kissed my inner thighs, hips, and stomach, moving at an excruciatingly slow pace to my flushed face. He bit along my chin and jaw as I reached down until I could feel him, throbbing and ready. Holding himself above me, his full eyes gazed into mine with a look of longing, hunger, and need that terrified me.

"Stella," was all he said when he entered me.

While we were connected, I succumbed to my fears and needs, desiring him, wanting this to never end, yet wanting to push him away, to stop all that was happening between us. He whispered my name over and over, and as he rose to his own climatic peak, I managed to clear my mind of all thoughts but one. Never have I experienced lovemaking like this. I cried out in pleasure, letting go of all but him.

Sated, we lay on the floor, catching our breath. He held himself up on his elbows and stared at me intently. I couldn't read his thoughts, and I wasn't sure what my own were.

I swallowed and caught my breath. "You've had quite a night." My voice was little more than a whisper from lack of sleep.

He frowned. "Are you okay? I didn't mean to do that."

"What did you mean to do?"

"I came over to apologize for not showing up when I was supposed to."

I stared up at him, not sure if I should touch his face like I wanted to, or his arms, or any part of him.

"Well, that was one of the better apologies I've ever received."

His eyebrows pulled together. "You look tired," he said.

"I'm…relieved." I shifted my body to try to get comfortable.

He lifted me beneath my knees and my shoulders and carried me effortlessly to my bedroom. He set me down on the bed and went to stand, but I pulled him to me. "Theo," I whispered. "I thought you were…" dead, but my voice caught before I could say it.

He fell onto me, and we were lost in each other once again.

It was as if a dam burst, and we couldn't get enough of each other. He brought out feelings in me I thought were unattainable, and I bit his shoulder as he rocked with me, taking me places I'd never been.

Finally, he pulled himself from me and got out of bed. I took in his body, his muscular stomach and arms, the pulsing of his veins beneath his skin. His face was raw with emotion, and it frightened me.

He lifted his arms and hands, still grimy from the fire. I'd hardly noticed. "I'm sorry," he said again.

"For what?"

"Can I shower? I came right here after work. I didn't expect…"

I nodded.

"I'll be right back."

Several minutes passed before I heard the water running. I closed my eyes and took a deep, shaky breath. I felt overwhelmed, wanting, and afraid of my pull to this man. When I'd calmed, I sat up, listening to the shower run and noticed my chest and legs were smeared with soot. That's why he apologized.

On shaking legs, I walked to the bathroom, pushed the door open, and saw him under the cascading water through the clear glass shower door. He leaned against the wall, his arms supporting him, and his head hung down. My movements were lost in the sounds of the spray until I reached the glass.

He sensed my presence and turned to me. Pure exhaustion mixed with the dirty water dripping down his face. What did he see tonight? I stepped into the shower, put my arms around his waist, and rested my head against his chest. "If you need to talk…"

He held me tight as the warm spray poured over us. Stepping out of the shower, he dried my body first and then his. I took his hand and led him to my bed. He settled behind me, holding me, until we both dropped off.

I rolled over sometime later to find the bed empty and lifted my head toward the window. Natural light poked through the blinds.

"I'm here," he said behind me from the chair in my room, fully dressed. A heap of my clothes sat on the floor beside him, but I was too exhausted to feel embarrassed by the mess.

"Go back to sleep. You didn't get enough rest."

"Neither did you," I said. "You must be hungry."

"You have nothing but Lucky Charms for breakfast."

I covered my hot face with my hand. "It's not mine."

Theo laughed softly and pulled my arm, exposing my flaming cheeks. "I don't like you less because you eat Lucky Charms." He shrugged. "It's not Peanut Butter Captain Crunch, but not everyone has my refined palate."

I sat up and pulled the sheets to cover me, suddenly self-conscious. "I think the milk might still be good."

We ate overflowing bowls in the small kitchen, me in a T-shirt and boxers, and Theo dressed in the clothes he'd showed up in last night.

My desire fought with my urge to push him out the door, close it, and never open it again, for the same reason. I watched him spoon his cereal, wondering how often he had work shifts like last night. How often was he in imminent danger?

Still famished, I lifted the bowl and drank the remaining milk. When I finished, he stared at me.

"What?"

He shook his head, a glint of humor in his eyes. "I've never met anyone like you."

And I've never reacted this way to anyone. Ever.

"I need to go to the hospital," Theo said, all humor gone. "Hoagie."

He nodded. "I need to make sure he's okay."

I put my empty bowl in his.

"Can I see you later?" he said.

I hesitated, then stood to put the dishes in the sink. "Did you call your sister?"

Something flickered in his eyes. "I called her on my way here. Can I come back, Stella?"

No. Yes. I wanted to weep. I wanted to tell this man that what we'd experienced together changed everything I thought we'd had. This was no friend. I understood that now. Is this what love felt like?

As if reading my mind, he said, "I think we left the friendship station."

"I think we're miles past it." I blew out a breath. "I was comfortable at that station. This is a trip I didn't pack for."

I couldn't embrace this new realization. Especially after the last twelve hours of my life. I couldn't survive another night like the last. Even with the promise of a connection that made me feel, for a few glorious hours, like I was part of another world. Finally.

He frowned. "Are you sorry you answered the door?"

Theo moved close enough for me to place my palm against his cheek. "When I said I wanted to pass this anniversary and make a new memory, I didn't expect this. You're an overachiever."

His eyes held mine. "Talk to me."

"I'm happy you're okay."

"No. Tell me what's on your mind."

"I can't," I said.

"Of course you can."

"I need some time to sort out my thoughts. I can't do it while you're here."

A thick silence fell over us. I stared at the wall over his shoulder, feeling his eyes on me.

"Stella, I have to go to the hospital. Tell me when I walk out that door that you'll let me in."

My throat closed and I forced down a swallow. "I make no promises."

He smiled at first, until he realized that I was serious. "I'm sorry I was late for dinner."

"Me too." I walked inside and waited in the bathroom until the apartment door closed behind him.

I spent my entire day off in fitful sleep, dreaming of flames surrounding Theo as I tried to get to him, my reaching hands and arms burning as I did. I awoke in tears and heat, my newly discovered desire battling with my fear of the unknown. I wanted Theo in my bed, wanted his body on mine, but I couldn't. I wasn't ready to feel the feelings that I was battling over this man who risked his life every day to save others.

Theo texted me after he'd returned from the hospital, asking to come over to talk. I'd asked him about Hoagie (stable, thankfully) and then told him I was too tired.

Later, I opened my apartment door to a delivery of a large basket of mini–Lucky Charms and Capt'n Crunch boxes and containers of whole milk. The note attached read, *Try them together, Lucky Girl. It's delicious.*

He texted me three more times that day. I answered his last one, telling him I'd been sleeping, which wasn't far from the truth. I thanked him for the basket.

My sister asked me to take her to chemo next week. I told her I would.

CHAPTER 31

On Thursday, as I returned change to a customer and took pictures of another in front of the book wall, I could still feel the warmth of Theo's body against mine. While straightening a shelf, I relived the exhilaration of his lips along my neck, making me feel woozy. So much so that I had to hold onto the bookshelf to catch my breath. I'd never made love with anyone with such a hungry intensity, never with my entire being so in tune with another.

It was an awakening that I yearned to undo. I felt at once euphoric and ruined, and I had no idea what to do about it. I picked up my cell phone five times to text him, to tell him I wanted to see him, but each time I did, a voice in my head told me this would not end well. And who was I to get involved with a man who risked his life every day, who probably had a backlog of women who filled his singlehood? He was only married for eighteen months. Did he leave her?

I've experienced loss in my life. Pain and disappointment that took a long time to get over. This time, though. This time, with Theo, would hurt. I've had a taste of wonderful. And more than the intimacy we'd shared, I felt a kinship with Theo, a comfort and ease with him. More than I've ever felt with anyone else. I was falling in love, and I needed to catch myself before I fell too far.

Gina stepped into the office while I was dining on liverwurst with Hemingway. She carried a box with a bow.

"This came for you."

It was the second delivery to the shop since I saw Theo on Sunday. On Tuesday, he'd sent a box of hot dogs with the works, the message attached: *I'm sorry (again) I missed dinner. Raincheck?*

Gina watched as I opened today's box. Inside was a dozen freshly baked chocolate-peanut butter cookies. "He knows you well, that's for sure," she said.

"How do you know who it's from?" I hadn't even opened the small card yet, though I knew.

"Who do you think delivered it?"

I dropped the envelope and turned to her. "Is he still here?"

"No. I told him I'd get you, but he's on his way to work and couldn't stay."

I stared at the cookies. My favorite flavor. How did he know?

Gina went into the shop while I read the card.

Let's talk.

As I picked up my phone, wanting to tell him all that I was feeling, wanting to ask him how his friend was doing, a text came through.

> I'm off my shift tomorrow evening. I'll meet you at closing?

I put my phone down and dusted the entire store under the dark scrutiny of my employee. And what if I closed the shop and waited for him again? What if he got caught up in another huge fire, which I would expect to happen at some point? The not knowing...No.

"I can't understand why he keeps trying," I said, more to myself than Gina, but she heard me.

"Maybe you're worth the effort."

I paused. History didn't support that thought. My dad, Rick, Doug. I returned the duster under the counter and strolled through the shop, trailing my finger down book spines, breathing in the scent of inked paper, and decided.

> I'm sorry, I can't. I hope Hoagie is okay. He's in my prayers. Thank you for the cookies.

After work, I drove directly out to Mom's to take my mind

off my situation and because I hadn't seen her in a week. She'd missed our last weekly call, and I was starting to worry about her.

I needn't have. When I stepped through her kitchen door at 8:00 p.m., I heard music playing from her portable radio inside. Music! I couldn't remember the last time I'd heard anything but the television.

Her furry posse gave me away before I could see where Mom was, what she was doing, or who with. I leaned over to greet each of the welcoming committee, Margie, Mabel, and Henry first, followed by the two cats, Ben and Jerry, as Mom walked into the kitchen. She'd shut the radio and appeared flushed, as if she were working out in her housedress.

"Stella! You must let me know when you're stopping over."

"I do? Since when?"

"Since I almost had a coronary, thinking a stranger walked in!"

"I'm sorry." I straightened and kissed her cheek. "Did I interrupt something?"

She shook her head, her flushed cheeks starting to return to their natural color.

"Were you exercising?"

"No, I was straightening the den. That's all."

"To music?"

"Is that a problem?"

I smiled, trying to defuse the tension that had formed on her part. "Not at all. I'm happy you're able to listen to music with all that's going on. You make me hopeful." Of course, Marion would refuse to succumb to worry and grief. When had she ever in the past?

She looked as if she was going to say something but stopped. Then she said, "What do we have if we don't have hope?" Marion gave some love to her dogs, avoiding my gaze. "Are you staying?"

"Sure. For a little while."

She finally looked at me and tilted her head in question. "What's the matter?"

"Why do you ask?"

"Well, you're here, for one. And you have a look."

"A look?"

"What's going on?"

I dropped my coat onto the back of a kitchen chair and fell onto the seat. "I'm confused."

She went to the stove and lifted the tea kettle. "Would you like coffee or tea?"

"No." I took a deep inhale, ready to ask the question I'd been avoiding for too long. "Mom, there's something I need to know."

She put the kettle down and grabbed the sponge from the sink. She wiped down the countertop, facing away.

"Mom?"

"Hm?"

"Charlie remembers something happened the night before Dad left. Someone came to the door. She heard you and Dad fighting. I don't recall any of it, but she does."

My mother continued to wipe the counter. "Why are you both talking about this now?"

"I don't know. Since last year, I've been thinking of Dad more. Wondering how he could have loved us so much and then disappeared. It doesn't make sense." Mom played with the sponge. "Mom. What is it? Can you look at me?"

She turned around, but her eyes still avoided mine. "You never asked. It's in the past. It's done."

"Maybe. But my past is affecting my life."

She reached for my hand, but I pulled it away, upset.

"We wanted to talk about it, but we were afraid it would upset you," I said. "You were left, too. It was devastating. He walked out. Did he have an affair?"

My mother dropped the sponge in the sink and pulled a chair from the table. It seemed to take her a long time to sit. She faced me.

"No, he didn't cheat. There was no one else. And he didn't walk out." She swallowed. "I asked him to leave."

The blood in my head dropped to my feet. "What?"

Mom blew out a breath, ran a hand down the side of her neck. Her left eye twitched. "He struggled with a sickness that I didn't understand."

She picked at her cuticles.

"Tell me, Mom. Please."

"When I met your father, he excited me. He was larger than life. Our first date lasted twenty-four hours. He took me to Niagara Falls for dinner. We drove nine hours straight for dinner. He said he wanted the date to last, so he wasn't going to drive to the Olive Garden ten minutes away. My mother was livid."

He was adventurous. I remembered.

"We had to eat at a diner because nothing else was open when we got there at four a.m. We didn't see the falls—they were closed, too. While he drove, he talked nonstop, jumping from topic to topic, and I could hardly keep up. I was exhausted and exhilarated. I'd never met anyone like him. After we ate, he drove us home. I'd begged him not to, asked if we could find an inexpensive place to rest and go home in the morning, but he insisted. He drove the whole way home and dropped me off the next night." Mom shook her head. "My mother told me something was wrong with him. Who could stay awake for twenty-four hours like that? She could see it, but I disagreed. Your grandmother was an overreactor. We disagreed on everything. Why should this be different?" She ran her finger along the edge of the table. "I didn't hear from him for two weeks. When he called again, I asked him where he'd been, and he said he'd been tired."

"What happened?"

"Against my mother's wishes, we eloped less than a year later. I was twenty-one. At first, it was wonderful.

"He played music loud and we'd dance in the living room, skipping dinner, drinking wine. He was handsome, carefree, and fun. It was such a departure from my controlled upbringing." She brought her fisted hands to her chest. "I craved him.

I was young. Inexperienced. What did I know about men? We threw parties we could hardly afford that lasted into the morning in our tiny house before we even got furniture. He was reckless and wild, and romantic."

"What was the problem? It sounds like an ideal situation."

"As the years passed, I saw an increase in that erratic behavior. He kept quitting jobs, searching for the perfect career, said it would take time. In the meantime, he'd wake up early, make two dozen eggs for breakfast that we couldn't eat. We were living on my meager waitress salary. A few months into our marriage, I went to see him at work, at a warehouse, to bring him a sandwich and found out he'd been fired three weeks prior for threatening another employee. When I confronted him about it, he went crazy and accused me of checking on him. Then he cried because he was sorry and promised to find something else." She sighed. "He always did. He was charming when he was on."

"What do you mean, 'on'?"

Mom put water in the kettle. From the counter, her shoulders sloped downward. "He was unbalanced. He had severe mood swings. His highs were high, but those lows, when I saw the first one, scared me."

That's not Dad.

"He stayed in bed for four days after one of our parties," Mom continued. "He wouldn't eat, or talk, or go to work. I didn't know what to do. I kept asking him if he was sick. At first, he didn't answer. Buried himself in blankets. When I asked the last time what I could do, he threw his alarm clock at me."

I stared at her. She pointed to her temple, to the slim scar that ran along her hairline.

"Why did you stay with him?"

"I was pregnant. How could I leave? Go back to my mother? No." The kettle whistled. I waited while Mom steeped her tea bag. "There were periods of quiet and I thought maybe having children would keep him steady. And it did for a bit."

She brought her mug to the table and sat, tired. "It got worse over the years instead of better. They were manageable until they weren't."

A memory of Dad waking me up at dawn to watch the sunrise materialized. Outside, it had been still very dark, and I'd been cold in my pajamas. I'd asked how long until the sun came up.

"Soon," he'd promised. "I know the perfect spot to see it."

He put me in the car and drove us to Bear Mountain. Just him and me. He'd carried me up a steep path, and we rested on a flat rock overlooking an expanse of trees, he in a robe and me still in my Tweety Bird cotton pj's. When the sun rose, he'd held me. I hadn't recalled that night in years.

"I don't remember the lows."

Mom nodded. "We kept them from you as best we could. When you were maybe four, he didn't get out of bed for two weeks. By then, I knew better than to try to help him. I left him alone and slept on the couch."

"That's when you went to work."

"When you started school. Yes."

I tried to process this as questions formed in my mind.

"I got a call one day from the owner of an apple orchard upstate threatening to call the police if I didn't get your father to leave. He was disruptive and loud and scaring the other patrons. The man didn't want to involve the police because it would scare you and Charlie. I had no idea you were there. You were supposed to be in school."

I vaguely recalled that day. The sole memory I held onto was when Dad showed me how to tell if an apple was ripe. The calyx of a ripe apple, the blossom end, he'd explained, should be closed. He'd leaned over, blocking the sun so that its light shone around him, pointing to the fruit, his head close to mine, his patient explanation cemented in my memory. I don't remember if Charlie was there or anything that happened before or after. In fact, until this moment, I thought I'd imagined it.

"How did the owner get our number?" I said.

"Charlie gave it to him."

Did Charlie remember him this way? She'd never let on.

"Tell me about the night before he left."

Mom closed her eyes.

"Mom, please. I should know this."

I waited for whatever thoughts she struggled with in her mind. Finally, she blew out a breath and her entire body sagged. "Charlie was right. The person who came to the door that night was Pacer's mother. She'd made soup because when I'd picked you girls up from her house after my shift, she saw I was sick. Your father was insulted. He believed she thought he couldn't take care of me. I saw the episode start before I could prevent it. Charlie walked in to see who it was, and I told her to go into the bedroom, to you, to put the volume up on the television. She ran away. I'd often wondered if she knew what was happening, but she never asked.

"I told Pacer's mom to leave and to take the soup. But your father followed her down the block, screaming and threatening her if she ever stepped foot on our property again."

"Why did he do that?"

"He'd started to have unpredictable hallucinatory pockets that frightened me. I convinced him to come home and begged her not to call the police." Mom stared ahead. "The neighbors watched us through their windows. No one came out. They watched."

"Oh, Mom." Tears filled my eyes.

"That night, he threatened to leave with you and Charlie. He thought I was conspiring to take you away. I locked him and me in our room and tried to calm him, telling him anything I could to keep him from thinking we were against him. It took hours until finally we fell asleep." She paused. "Something woke me in the night. He wasn't in bed." Her hands shook as though the memory was fresh. "He was in your bedroom, standing over you with a bat in his hand." She swallowed. "I put myself between him and you and hugged him as tightly as I could until his whole body sagged, and he dropped the bat."

I tried to picture this happening but couldn't. This wasn't my father. This wasn't the man who sat at the edge of my bed, reading me books in different character voices.

"I'd never been so scared in my life. Something switched off in me. I had to do something. I told him he had to leave. I told him he wasn't allowed to come home until he got help."

"What did he do?"

She lifted the mug to sip, but her hand shook so badly that some tea spilled over, so she put it down. "He started to cry and couldn't stop. I got you and your sister ready for school while he stayed in our bedroom, packing, unbeknownst to me. He didn't fight me. He knew he needed to go."

"Why didn't you tell us? All these years have passed."

Mom brought her eyes to me, and the pain I saw in them pierced my soul. "How do you tell your children that you sent their father away because he might hurt them?"

"He must have been so sad." It was too much for me to digest. I leaned over my arms, taking deep breaths. "Was he bipolar?" Memories of my father picking us up from our beds and taking us on adventures without my mom flooded my mind. Sudden trips to Six Flags, arriving before the park even opened. The aquarium. Apple picking.

"Maybe? I begged him to get help. I watched you and your sister closely to see if you exhibited similar behavior, but you never did."

I felt as if an enormous hole opened, and I was teetering on the edge. I stood.

"There's more," Mom said.

"Do I want to hear it?"

She looked up at me. "I don't know."

"I can't hear anymore right now. I need to go."

"Stella, what I did, I did out of love. Not a day goes by that I don't regret what happened, but if given the same situation, I would do it again. My priority was to you girls. If he would have hurt you, I'd never have forgiven myself."

Dazed, I walked out.

CHAPTER 32

Twenty minutes later, I called Charlie from my car.

"What's wrong? Are you crying?" she said.

"I'm outside."

"Come in. The kids are sleeping. Come, Stella."

Charlie opened the door wearing her robe. Her tired face morphed quickly to concern when she saw me. We went into the living room.

"Where's Lance?"

"Work."

I looked behind us to the office.

"No, he's at the Manhattan office."

"This late?"

She sighed. "Stella, what's wrong?"

I repeated my conversation with our mother, reciting every word. Charlie listened, clutching the lapels of her robe the whole time. When I finished, we sat in silence.

"Wow. Poor Mom," she whispered.

"Poor Dad."

Charlie looked at me. "I can't imagine how hard it was for her to protect us like she did. Were you aware of any of it?"

"No. You?" I said.

"Some things make sense now. Some things I remember make sense."

We sat on the couch for three hours, dissecting what we'd found out, trying to piece together the memories we'd shared with Dad. So much was clearer now to Charlie. His behavior was reminiscent of psychosis or something similar. But I was still in the dark. My memories were happy.

"I remember when he took you to the aquarium. He pulled you out of school without telling Mom. I remember because she came to pick us up at the bus stop and you weren't there, and she started freaking out. She dropped me at Pacer's house and then when she picked me up later that night, you were with her, but she was different. She took my hand to walk us home and didn't say anything. Pacer's mom had told Mom to get help, and when I asked Mom what she meant, she said, 'Never mind.'"

"I remember that day."

"You do?"

I nodded and repeated the story I'd told to Philippe a few months ago, how Dad had me hiding in the bathroom with him well after closing until the security guard found us.

Charlie shook her head. "Oliver?"

"Dad called the octopus Oliver. He'd said it was his name."

"The guard was probably going to call the police," Charlie said. "Mom had no idea where you were. She was scared."

I went to the bathroom, took the whole box of tissues, and brought it to the couch.

"How did we not know this our whole lives? How could she keep this from us?"

Charlie took a tissue and dabbed the corners of her eyes and down her cheeks. She shrugged. "How do you start that conversation?"

"You start by saying, 'I have something to tell you.'"

"When would she have done that? While she worked two jobs and you were trying to get through high school? Or college? Or spending all your time at Doug's, planning your wedding? When would be the right time to tell you she made your father leave when all you wanted was for him to come back?"

I swallowed a lump of grief. "I miss him, Charlie. I miss him every day."

She pulled me to her, and my head rested on her shoulder. She ran her fingers down my hair while I cried.

"You're so strong," I said. "Don't you miss him?"

"I did, for a while. But Stella, I wasn't close to him like you were. I was sort of afraid of him. I didn't understand his personality. It was off-putting. Until now, I thought it was me."

I hiccupped and sniffed, calming down.

"I see this through a mother's eyes," Charlie said. "I would do anything to protect my babies. Even if it meant leaving Lance, if he was a threat. And Lance is the love of my life. When you're a mom, you become a warrior."

Lance met me on the path to the house as I was leaving. His tie was askew, and his hair was mussed as if he'd run his hands through it one too many times. The bags under his eyes matched his wife's.

"What's wrong?" he said, frowning. "Are you crying?"

I shook my head. "It's too much to go into now. Ask your wife."

His eyes shifted to the house, and he paled.

"She's okay, Lance. Mostly. It's about our dad."

His demeanor relaxed but his frown seemed to have become a fixture of his face.

"You're working late again."

"We have lots of bills, Stella."

I crossed my arms, thinking of my sister inside, a warrior herself. "Stop hiding behind that excuse and face it."

* * *

Philippe walked into my apartment and found me on the couch.

"Good Lord, woman, you look like you were run over by a train."

I smiled through my tears. I'd been crying ever since leaving Charlie's. "Oh good. I thought I looked bad."

He sat next to me. "Tell Papi. What's wrong."

"Be careful what you wish for."

"Consider me warned."

"I found out tonight that my father didn't leave me. He was thrown out of his house by his wife."

"Marion?"

I nodded.

He stared at me. "Without hearing any more, I know Marion had a reason."

"Even so, I feel betrayed. Like I should have known earlier."

"So, you know now. You probably weren't open to hearing it earlier. Maybe hearing it at any other time would have been the wrong time."

I hugged my knees to my chest. "The man I knew was thrilling and funny and exciting and happy. I can't see him any other way. I can't see him deserving of losing his family."

Philippe crossed his legs on the opposite end of the small couch. "Tell me the story. I want to hear it if you can bear to repeat it."

When I finished telling him what I'd learned, he whistled. "That's a mouthful."

"No kidding."

"Want to know what I think?"

I nodded. Of course. He was my friend.

"I think you protected yourself from the bad memories to keep loving him. It's a gift you gave yourself. It's a gift your mother coveted for you. If she'd told you what happened earlier, you'd be a different person."

I laughed without humor. "Maybe being a different person would have been better. I'm a mess, Philippe. I don't trust anyone. I almost married someone I didn't love because I didn't believe I'd find someone else who'd want to be with me. And he left me anyway."

"Tell me about Doug. You never talk about what he's like."

"How does this help at all?"

"Humor me."

I stretched my legs and wiped my nose. "He's uber active. Loves to play sports and race cars and ski and go to concerts. He's a successful hedge fund manager. Loves to party. Loves to be the center of attention. He's fun. He's really fun."

Philippe nodded.

"What?"

"It sounds like you found a version of your father you liked.

Someone whose most days were very high with very few lows."

I thought about it. I didn't put Doug and my father in the same category. Not even close. Doug was a successful professional. I looked at Philippe. That wasn't the only difference I could come up with.

"Doug's not crazy."

"Your father wasn't crazy. He most likely had a chemical imbalance that was out of his control." He put his hands on my shoulders. "You were loved. He loved you. That's more than I can say for many people."

What Philippe didn't have to remind me, was that his father threw him out of the house when he came out to the family. How can you disassociate with your child because of who they love? Would my father have done that?

No. He wouldn't have.

"And, with a mom like Marion, you're a lucky girl."

CHAPTER 33

Charlie had her first chemo appointment four weeks after her surgery. Since it was a Monday, I picked her up and we left our mother in charge of Myles while Maddie was at preschool. I stayed in the waiting room of the women's center for a few extra minutes while Charlie was set up.

A nurse escorted me into a large, bright room. We passed privacy cubicles where I glimpsed three other women attached to IVs, lounging in recliners. In my periphery, I saw one flipping through a magazine, another watching TV, and the third quietly chatting with a woman her age.

I sat next to Charlie, as if being seated at a restaurant for lunch and not settling in to watch her accept some cocktail of poison into her blood. The one thing I noticed about the other women in the room, but of course did not mention to my sister, was that they all wore scarves on their heads. Charlie's full head of hair screamed newness to this whole endeavor.

"How long does this take?" I whispered.

"They said three hours. One and a half for chemo, another hour for Herceptin."

I looked around the small space. "It's nice. You have a TV, privacy..."

"It's not so bad," she agreed. "They're giving me pre-nausea medicine. I hope it helps." My sister leaned back and settled for the afternoon. "I'm sorry I'm tired today. With Lance in Orlando, it's only me, and I crawl into bed when the kids fall asleep."

"Don't ever apologize."

She tilted her head. "You look worse than I do. Are you still reeling?"

"I haven't talked to Mom since. I'm having a hard time forgiving her for keeping this from us," I said.

"But you forgive her for telling Dad to leave?"

"I don't know."

Charlie yawned.

"You forgive her," I said.

"Yes. She's our mother."

"For most of my life, I've been killing myself trying to figure how he could walk away when he loved us."

Charlie looked at me. "Does knowing he didn't change anything?"

I'd been thinking about this since our mom told me what had really happened. "I don't know. He could have tried to come home. He didn't fight for us."

Charlie closed her eyes.

"I have not had a healthy relationship my whole life. I choose the wrong guys, guys who don't give enough of themselves, or ask so little of me because it feels safer. And they walked away like he did."

"He didn't walk away."

"He didn't come back." My chin quivered, and a surge of self-directed anger formed in the pit of my stomach. "Since I was seven years old, I have felt unlovable. Do you have any idea what kind of crutch that is to carry? I'm exhausted, Charlie. I'm so tired of pretending I'm okay."

Charlie's eyes opened and I shook my head. "Look at me, whining to you while you're getting chemo. What kind of person does that?"

She pulled my hand to her, and I leaned over to oblige. "You are loveable, my dear sister. You are more loveable than anyone I know. What Mom did, she did out of pure, unconditional love for you and me. *I* love you more than life. Maddie and Myles love you. What more do you need as proof?"

A tear escaped, and I felt it run the length of my cheek to below my chin.

"I've been avoiding Theo since he came over."

Charlie frowned. "No, Stella. You must give him a chance. He's not like the others."

I know.

She let go of my hand and covered another yawn.

"Rest," I said.

She closed her eyes and several minutes passed when she said, "Talk to him. Explain your behavior or he'll think he did something wrong."

It's not you, it's me. The worst words ever to be strung together, no matter how they're expressed. He's probably moved on. It had been two weeks since he stopped texting and calling. There'd been no more deliveries. The truth was, until he showed up that morning after the fire, I spent eight hours with my heart in my throat, thinking he was going to die and the emotion that had gripped me gave me the strength to push him away.

"I hope Mom remembers to get Maddie," Charlie said, eyes still closed.

"She will. The woman forgets nothing." I watched the liquid seep into her and shuddered.

The time went quickly, as it does when we're together. On our way home, Charlie said, "Don't be afraid to open your heart to him."

Tears stung my eyes.

"Love is powerful."

"Powerful enough to ruin me," I whispered.

"You can't base every decision on what happened in our past."

But I did.

I dropped Charlie at home and declined dinner with her and Mom, wanting to be alone with my thoughts. Perhaps Charlie was right. Maybe I should call Theo. At least to explain my behavior.

The question was, would he take my call?

CHAPTER 34

A full week later, I walked home from the shop, protected from the rain under my small canary-yellow umbrella. We'd had another good day, thanks to some promotions on the website and social media. There seemed to be a steady stream of people taking pictures and selfies in front of the book wall.

I still hadn't called Theo.

For the past days, I'd considered what I'd say if I called him.

Oh, hey, checking in to see how you are.

Lame.

About that Sunday, I think we overstepped. Can we go back to being friends?

Yeah, right. Anyone knew once the clothes were shed, the friendship was off the table.

At the corner of my street, I waited for a passing car, trying not to think about Theo and instead focused on my next visit with Charlie. I offered to take her to chemo again so my mother wouldn't have to watch and could be with her grandchildren. As for tonight, I had a small pile of books and Lean Cuisine Sesame Chicken for dinner on deck.

When I crossed to the other side, I looked up and gasped. Theo waited in front of my apartment building in jeans, work boots, and his canvas coat, unprotected as rainwater dripped down his face and jacket. He remained in place while I approached him and pulled his hands from his pockets only when we were face-to-face.

"Hey," he said.

"Hey." He looked good, dammit. Adorable, wet, sexy and...not happy. I kept a safe distance between us, my arms crossed, and chin tucked. No smile. No hug. It didn't feel right to initiate that kind of familiarity after a vacuous few weeks following our night of lovemaking.

He didn't move.

"How are you?" I said.

"Confused. You?"

Oh, you have no idea. Confused was an understatement.

He sighed and ran a hand through his wet hair. "We buried a guy from another station last Wednesday, so there was that."

"I'm so sorry." How many funerals does he attend a year? How much longer before it's his? "How is Hoagie?"

"Back to work next week."

"Oh good." I pushed my tote bag further up my shoulder, ignoring the fluttering in my chest. I should invite him in, at least to dry off. But I knew I wouldn't.

I squeezed the umbrella handle and waited. Heavy drops danced on the canopy. The awkwardness between us crushed me. We lost the easy banter I'd come to enjoy so much.

"You've been avoiding me," he said, "so I figured I'd show up and force you to hear me."

"I've been busy with the store and my sister."

"How is Charlie doing?"

"Fighting the good fight."

He shuffled his feet. "I came to apologize. I overstepped that night and you're angry."

I forced my eyes to meet his. My first mistake. I could lose myself in them.

"I'm not angry. You didn't overstep. *I* did and I shouldn't have. I'm the opposite of angry. I'm remorseful."

His face broke open, and I stepped away before I allowed myself to get pulled in and lost in those arms.

"I like you. More than I thought I could like anyone," I admitted. "What happened between us was…wrong."

"Wrong? Why?"

"I'm not looking for a romantic relationship."

"Yes, you've mentioned that. Yet you can't deny something has happened between us. And I'm not talking about the night we made love. I'm talking about our connection. From the minute I met you, I felt it. Tell me you felt it, too."

Of course, I felt it, and with it, the fear that wormed its way through me the first moment we touched. "I can't." My eyes burned. Don't cry, Stella. Please. The rain tapped my umbrella as the sky wept for me.

He looked around. "I see."

I shifted my umbrella to my other hand so he couldn't detect my heaving chest.

"You've ruined my life. And now you're telling me you don't want to see me anymore because I got caught up at work one night."

"It's not that simple." Or was it? What would have happened if he'd come over for dinner on time? If we'd enjoyed the evening and there had been no stress, or worry, or near-death experience to push us into each other's arms?

"Stella, I never thought I'd want to be with someone again." He put his hands behind his head, heedless of the rain. "You push and pull, and I'll admit, I'm confused. But I don't want to walk away from whatever this promises to be."

"I'm not playing games with you. It's not my intent. I want to be alone."

"No one wants to be alone."

"I thought so once. But I end up that way. And I've accepted that this is how it will be."

He stepped closer.

"Stop there," I whispered. "Please."

"You have the power to not be alone. Surely you must know that."

I shook my head. "I've been burned before."

He cracked a smile. "I have a solution for that."

"You're a hero." He lowered his head, but I continued. "You are. You firefighters all are. You run into burning buildings while everyone runs out. Heroes, every one of you. And we need you. But I don't. I have no room in my life for a hero."

His head lifted. "Don't say that. We just found each other."

"I can't, Theo. I'm sorry. I can't do this." I moved around him, toward the steps.

He sidestepped, forcing me to stop. "You knew what I did all this time. What changed?"

I swallowed. "My feelings for you. I have too much to lose."

"I know you're scared. I'm scared, too, but I'm not going anywhere."

"Don't make promises you can't keep." I blinked back tears. "Believe me, I'm doing you a favor. I'm a mess, weighed down with baggage you don't deserve."

"You don't have to carry it yourself."

I stepped back, remembering his chief telling him he was reckless. "I do. You can't understand the pain I went through. The way I can't understand your pain."

"I'm not in pain anymore."

"You are."

His face hardened. "How would you even know?"

"You run into fires trying to save a child that can never be saved. You can't bring your brother back and you're going to kill yourself trying." His head snapped back as if I'd physically hit him, and I immediately regretted what I'd said, but the words were out there and there was no turning back. "Is that why your marriage ended?"

"You know nothing about it."

"You're right. I don't. But I know enough to understand you're carrying the loss every time you put on the uniform. That you'll be forever trying to save someone despite your own safety and that scares me." I sniffed. "I'm not brave enough to love a person like that."

With his jaw clenched, wearing a look I'll never forget, Theo turned and left. I watched him walk away as the softened rain trickled down my umbrella.

My cell phone rang as I entered my apartment. I wiped my eyes before checking to see who it was.

"Stella?" Charlie's voice shook on the line when I answered. "Can you meet me? I need you."

"Where are you?"

"I'm trying to buy a wig, and the owner said he can't fit me for one with the hair I have left. I need to shave it off. Here. Now." She sniffed. "Can you come?"

Still in my jacket with my pocketbook on my shoulder, I left the apartment and ran to my car, exhaling a breath of gratitude that I'd scheduled to give it away next week. Perhaps I don't have to sell it. I made a mental note to call the buyer in the morning. Before pulling out, I entered the address into my GPS.

My worries about Theo were overshadowed by my sister's illness. I would survive. Would she? Forty minutes later, I walked into the wig shop and sat next to Charlie, holding her hand as the shop's owner shaved what was left of her rich, shiny, glorious hair. She gripped my hand tightly as the last locks fell to the floor in a soundless cascade.

"Okay," the owner said, putting his hands on her shoulders. "You're ready. Be right back."

Charlie and I sat before the mirror. I touched her soft scalp. She was beautiful.

CHAPTER 35

Charlie continued to schedule her chemo sessions every other Monday so I could join her. On our third visit, there were no longer differences between my sister and the other women there, save for the designs on their bandanas. Her eyes were dull, and she seemed waxen. *This isn't Charlie*, I kept thinking. *What is happening to my sister?*

"Hey," Charlie said, and I looked up to see her looking at me. "What?"

I shook my head, deciding not to worry her further by telling her what she might already know: that she seemed to be melting before my eyes. "Nothing. Do you want the TV on? Or a book?"

She shrugged. "I might nap. I didn't sleep well last night."

"When does Lance get back?" He was away on business, again.

"Friday. But it doesn't really matter anyway. He's consumed with work. He's trying to get a promotion, so…"

Work wasn't what was consuming my brother-in-law, but I didn't have the heart to say it. She knew. Charlie was protecting him. It was her nature to protect those she loved. I didn't get the protective gene. I wanted to beat the crap out of him.

Before she got sick, I'd never seen a couple more fit for each other or more in love. I'd wondered if Lance would ever let Charlie down, or if he was the exception to his gender, but now that he was, it hurt me to see my sister in pain.

"When he's home," she told me, "he's jubilant. Refuses to express concerns or worries about my health. He won't talk about it. He won't let me talk about it. When I ask him how he's feeling, he gives me the same answer. 'I feel fine. You're going to get through this no problem. We're good, babe.'

"I'm exhausted trying to be so optimistic. His focus on the kids was taken to a whole other level." She closed her eyes. "When he's home, anyway."

Would Lance leave her? Can true love be extinguished like that? Is no one immune to the inevitable demise of the heart? My sister's marriage was the one beacon of light in my cloudy vision of romance. What was going on here? If she can't keep it together, what chance in hell do the rest of us have?

Three hours dripped by while she slept, and I stared at my phone, scrolling through Facebook, at the happy posts of family gatherings, children's photos, vacation scenes, changing statuses of some from "single" to "in a relationship." Why should we care what your relationship status is? Except I did. I looked up to find Charlie staring at me.

"What?"

She nodded toward my phone. "How are your 'friends' doing?" She used finger quotes for friends, which stung. She was right. How many of these people are my friends? Who of these people would I call in times of trouble? Not one. "You want to rock their world, Stella? Take a picture of me."

She rested her head and watched the ceiling. Charlie was not on social media and couldn't understand my attachment. Nor could I, really.

"Okay." I crouched next to my sister on her chair and took a selfie. Added a comment, *Current situation: fighting the fight with this beauty*, and hit post. I looked at Charlie and smiled.

"You didn't."

"I so did."

"You're terrible, little sister."

I brought Charlie home in time to see our mother pulling in the driveway from picking up Maddie at preschool. The child bounded out of the minivan, holding up a fresh piece of artwork which I was delighted to learn was for me. I scooped her up into a bear hug and made all sorts of noise over my gift.

Finally freed from his car seat harness, Myles lumbered down from the car toward us, aiming right for his mother with a wide, drippy grin. Charlie bent over and wrapped him in her arms, whispering something for only him to hear. He put up his arms to be lifted, and I reached over to hoist him onto my waist so I could talk to him as we walked into the house.

While she rested and read books to Maddie and Myles on the den couch, Mom and I prepared dinner. It was the first time we were in the same room since she'd unloaded the truth of my past in her kitchen.

I could cut the tension with the knife in my hand.

"Stella, you can't be mad at me forever."

I paused what I was doing. "I won't be mad forever, but I am upset and angry that I only found out the truth about my father at thirty-six. That's going to be hard for me to get over. So, you have to give me some time."

She stared at the wall. Then nodded and continued to dredge chicken cutlets in flour.

We cooked in silence. I hadn't called her in over a week—a record for me. I missed her as much as I think she missed me. But I couldn't return to pleasantries and chitchat about life. I simmered as my rage bubbled below my surface. I was proud of myself for even being here.

Marion laid the cutlets in the sizzling pan where they were greeted by a loud popping complaint. It smelled delicious already, and my dad materialized in my mind, as he often did unexpectedly. Tonight, it was the chicken cutlets. Myles walked into the kitchen, and Mom put the spatula down and lifted her grandson, nuzzling his neck with her nose, making him giggle and squirm.

My heart cracked a little, seeing my mother happy with the kids. She'd had so little to celebrate when we were growing up, working so hard. I needed to get over this news. As difficult as it would be, she deserved to be forgiven.

We had chicken Marsala, which was tasty. Charlie managed to sit at the table with us and got down a few forkfuls of food. She looked a little better than she did when I picked her up in the morning, but she still didn't look like herself. My mother said something to me as I walked her to her car after the kids were asleep.

"She looks bad. She shouldn't look this bad. He didn't call her all night. Not during the day either." Mom shook her head at her own mention of Lance, then went to give me a kiss, a normal routine we'd adopted throughout our lives. No leaving each other without a show of love and affection. I hesitated and turned my head, not ready. She frowned and nodded again, understanding.

"I need some time, Momma."

I went into the house to sit with Charlie a bit longer.

CHAPTER 36

My landlord stopped into the shop as soon as we opened. Gina had returned up front after putting the carpet sweeper away, and I was sipping my coffee at the counter, scouring my sources online for more inventory.

He walked around the store and paused at the book wall before continuing. Gina wore a mask of indifference while I fought the urge to escort him out—by his neck. Maybe she took CBD gummies. I'll ask her.

He lingered on the other side of the counter, while I pretended to be finishing something online, making him wait. What I was really doing was checking my wedding dress on eBay. The only offer still standing was the one for one thousand dollars. I swallowed my disappointment. The dry cleaners had been holding onto the dress long enough.

I dragged my focus from the laptop to him. "To what do I owe this pleasure?"

"My daughter saw your shop on Instagram. It's trending."

"Is it now?"

He pointed toward the back. "The wall. Genius."

Gina and I met eyes and then returned our attention to him.

"I got your rent check last week."

"And?" And then I understood the reason for his visit. I'd forgotten to pay the new amount. How could I have forgotten when it was the undercurrent of my existence since his last visit? Then I knew. Charlie. Theo. Life in the interim.

"I forgot the added amount," I said.

He did a half bow, like an old-timer. "I emailed you."

"I must have overlooked it. I'll send it today." Ouch.

"Thank you." He walked out, past my chalkboard sign that said:

*If I can't find the book
you want, it's free.*

and directly into Jeffrey's boutique.

Hours later, I'd been straightening the abbreviated cooking section when the bell rang over the door, and someone entered the shop. My mind was on Charlie and her worsened condition and Theo. I kept going over our conversation, the terrible things I'd said to him, and his angry, hurt expression was seared into my brain. I ached to call him, to apologize, to take it all back, but the words were out there in the ether...forever. I wondered how he was doing, missed his visits to the shop, our conversations and walks.

I pulled a cookbook out and had started flipping through recipes when I heard, "So, my client canceled a few minutes ago and I have an hour to kill."

I looked up to see Philippe standing at the counter where a paper bag rested. "Did you eat lunch?"

"Yes, but I can eat again."

He rolled his eyes dramatically. "Where you put it all is a mystery to me. Do you want to go to the salon?"

"How about we hang on the couch?"

We sat in the corner on the couch while Gina manned the front of the shop.

"What news, lovey?" Philippe said as he unwrapped his sandwich, a thick Cubano.

He'd brought me the same and I was already into it. It tasted amazing— the thick salted ham, Swiss, and pickles caused my taste buds to dance a happy, carnivorous jig. He watched me take another bite and wordlessly handed me a napkin then mumbled, "Born in a barn, I swear," while I wiped a glob of mustard from the corner of my mouth.

"Where did you get these? I've never tasted a sandwich so delicious."

He showed me those perfectly white teeth and pretended to give my jaw a gentle punch. "My mother made them."

I shook my head. "Wait. When did you go visit your parents? I thought you weren't talking to them."

"My old man is in the hospital taking his last breaths and she wanted to see me."

"Oh no! I'm so sorry! I didn't know he was sick."

Philippe shrugged. "Me neither. But it was good to see her. She's getting old but she still has spunk."

"Did you see your dad?"

"Hells no. I hate him. I met her at the house while my brothers were at the hospital."

I pretended not to see his eyes gloss at the mention of his father.

As I sipped my ginger ale, I realized how similar my two friends were. Gina and Philippe both were alienated from their dads.

We finished the sandwiches—I wished I had another one, it was so damned good—and settled on the couch. The bell over the door rang, alerting us of another customer.

"Thank God," Philippe said. "I was getting worried for you."

I stifled a laugh. "We're doing pretty good. I invited three indie authors to do signings and we're booking into October with book clubs."

"Good girl. Now, tell me what's going on. How is that hunky tree you've been keeping company with?"

I blew out a breath. "It didn't work out."

He stared at me.

"What?" I said.

"What about it didn't work out?"

"I don't want to get into it."

He tapped a thin, perfectly manicured finger against my temple. "Methinks Stella might be the problem with men."

"What the hell are you talking about?" He thinks it's *my* fault I'm alone? "You don't know me enough to say that."

"Your idea of a good time is a night at home in hobo pajamas reading a book. You like to hide your fetching body behind thick wool. You're taking care of your sister, running a business from scratch, and have a bottomless appetite for shitty food."

"Okay, you know me better than I thought."

He shook his head and frowned. "I haven't scratched the surface. I don't understand what the hell you're so afraid of."

"I'm not afraid." I returned his stare and held my breath.

"Okay. Why do you self-sabotage?"

"I didn't sabotage my almost marriage. Doug decided to leave me."

"Have you asked yourself why? It takes two to tango my lovely, lost little friend. Once you figure that out, you may be able to move forward." He held out a hand. "Come. I want a selfie in front of this masterpiece."

In front of the book wall, he put an arm around my shoulders. It hurt to smile.

"Beautiful." He typed quickly and slid his phone in his pocket. "There. It's now on my Insta feed." He kissed my temple and returned to the salon.

My conversation with Philippe stuck in my mind for the rest of the day. He was right. I never understood why Doug left. We'd never had that closure.

Philippe returned at closing and waited for me to lock the shop. A few steps into our journey home, he pulled my arm, stopping me in front of the dry cleaners.

"Well, if that's not the most gorgeous gown I've ever seen, I don't know what is," he said.

And there it was, in the window of the dry cleaners. My wedding dress, cleaned, wrapped and tear-stain free staring down at us.

"It's just a dress," I said.

"No, baby, that's a *statement*."

"What does it say to you?"

He put his hand on his chin and squinted his eyes. "It says, Kate Middleton who?"

I pulled him along and let him talk about the dress in the window, while I struggled to keep my thoughts to myself. I saw that dress now, through different eyes. It wasn't who I was, and I knew it. Had I been trying to prove to the world and my guests that being married was the most important thing to me? Did it scream insecurity and misdirected priorities?

Rog met Philippe at the door of their apartment, so I bid them good night as they embraced.

As I sat on my couch in comfy pajamas and brought my first spoon of Lucky Charms to my mouth, my phone rang. I let the call go to voicemail. It was the buyer for my car, following up on our last conversation. I'd since planned on retracting my offer to sell and forgot to call him.

As I spooned the last of the bright soft marshmallows, my landlord's earlier visit sat in the back of my mind. I returned the call and set a date for him to pick up my wheels.

CHAPTER 37

Doug operated like clockwork. In the office by seven a.m. Out by five. His after-work activities awaited and he needed time to change, eat a protein bar, or drink a protein shake and get to his next game, practice, workout, sporting event.

At four fifty-eight, I positioned myself to the side of the thirty-five-floor slate gray building, in mid-town Manhattan, watching as the people poured through the revolving doors to head home. I recognized some faces from Doug's company— guys we'd toasted with at our regular Friday happy hours.

Doug couldn't miss a happy hour. He liked to celebrate the end of the week and let loose. Sometimes too loose. Life was a party to be celebrated.

He stepped onto the sidewalk wearing earbuds. At first, I thought he was listening to music, but he doesn't listen to music. He's a television guy; financial updates by the hour, sports games—any, it doesn't matter the sport. Once, I'd been forced to watch trampoline dodgeball in between hockey and baseball.

Riveting.

No, he was on the phone with someone. He spoke and turned, catching sight of me. He took a few more steps when he stopped and did a double take. We hadn't seen each other since the eve of our wedding.

He ended his call and moved himself out of pedestrian traffic to where I stood.

I thought when this moment arrived that I'd react in some way. That my emotions would operate on overload, my heart would pound in my chest, or perspiration would drip down my spine, those things that happen when you finally face the one that got away.

I felt nothing. My body remained unaffected— all functions accounted for. Weird.

"Hi," he said. "Wow."

"Wow?"

"I didn't expect to see you again. Ever. Least of all, on purpose."

"Do you have time to talk?"

He glanced at his watch. "One minute." I waited, internally rolling my eyes while he texted who I was sure must be Marcy. He pocketed his phone. "Drink?"

"Coffee?"

"Okay."

I didn't call ahead to warn him about a meeting. I wanted him unprepared, unrehearsed, and honest. It was the only way I could do this.

We ducked into a small diner on a corner and grabbed a booth next to a window.

"How have you been?" he said. "You kept your hair long. Looks good."

Now that I had him here, I wasn't sure where to begin. I, too, was unrehearsed. I didn't want to start with pleasantries. Pleasantries were for friends or acquaintances we were still fond of. Doug was neither. I went right for the meat.

"Why did you do what you did to me?"

His eyes widened. "Why are you asking me this now?"

"What?"

"Why now? I tried to reach you for weeks after you showed up at the apartment and you ghosted me."

Three weeks after he'd left me at the altar, after ignoring dozens of texts, deleting too many voicemails, I'd pulled myself out of bed and decided to show up at his place, ready to listen to his apology in person. I'd put a lot of time into the relationship and thought there might be the thread of possibility we could salvage what we had and move forward. Like today, I hadn't warned him I was coming. At his door, I'd envisioned us falling together in tears and apologies, making up with a coital union and me moving back into his bed. So, when my best friend and bridesmaid, Marcy, answered the door wearing his boxers, a thin tank top with no bra and disheveled hair, I ran. He'd tried to follow me, but my adrenaline kicked into overdrive, and I'd lost him quickly.

I'd avoided his attempts to reach me until he finally gave up.

"What changed?" Doug said. "It's been over a year."

"I can't move forward. I'm stuck. I need to know why you ruined my life. What did I do to deserve that ultimate humiliation?"

He looked around the diner. "You didn't do anything, Es."

"Don't call me that."

A waitress walked over and took our coffee orders.

"You didn't do anything. We weren't working," Doug said, when she was out of earshot.

"And you figured that out on our wedding day."

He put his hands on the table. "I admit my timing was terrible. I woke up that morning and couldn't go through with it. I realized I didn't know you any better on our wedding day than I did when we had our first date."

First date? We'd finally introduced ourselves at happy hour one Friday night, after eyeing each other for weeks. Got drunk and went to his apartment and slept together. Hardly counts as a date, but I wasn't going to nitpick.

"What are you talking about? We spent every day together, when you weren't off somewhere with your friends."

He paused as the coffee, creamers, and milk bowl was set down on the table, and waited until the waitress left us again. "We had nothing in common."

"We had everything in common."

He shook his head. "No, Es...Sorry. Stella. You did everything I wanted and never spoke up for yourself. We both lived my life."

"What's wrong with that? Most people would love if their significant others were more involved in their hobbies."

He rubbed his eyes, appearing frustrated, and leaned forward. "When we first got together, I'd asked you where you wanted to go for dinner or what you wanted to do on the weekend, and you said, whatever you want. I thought it was sweet. But the dialogue never changed. Eventually I stopped asking. It was boring. I can do what I want by myself. No need to drag a mute with me. I knew you weren't happy. The only one who didn't know was you. It got tedious."

I felt as if I'd been punched.

"I need more from a partner," he went on. "You tried so hard to make sure I was happy that I wasn't happy. Neither of us were."

"You should have said something. I didn't know." I took a deep breath, trying to see what he saw. Charlie was my go-to if I needed to unload. Or Marcy. And even then, I didn't burden them with my deepest fears and insecurities.

"I woke up on our wedding day and couldn't put that suit on," he said.

There it was. This failure was my fault. It had nothing to do with Marcy, my best friend at the time and Doug's lover now. You don't look outside the relationship if the foundation is solid. I knew that, yet it was easier to blame them both and cut her out of my life than to face the truth.

We stared at each other.

"Did you ever love me?" I said.

His expression softened. "Yes, but I'm not sure you ever loved me."

"Yet, you proposed."

"We were together six years. The sex was great. You made a good living, like me. It seemed like the next logical step. We weren't getting any younger. I didn't want to start over, and I figured we'd get a house, raise some kids. The whole picture. It was easier. But after our engagement, my picture became muddled, and I couldn't see you in it as much as I tried. I knew it was a mistake. But the wedding plans snowballed, and I lost my nerve to say anything. I think you were so excited about the party you weren't focused on what was happening."

I pushed my full coffee mug to the side. Stared out the window at a woman tugging her young child along the sidewalk. What had I been looking for? The marriage. Family. Following in Charlie's footsteps, trying to catch up to life. Trying desperately to form the nucleus I needed but never had.

"The thing is, Stella, we were never friends. We went from strangers to sex. There was no intimacy. Somehow, I sensed it, but now I'm in a healthy relationship and I see that clearly."

Sitting across from him, I realized this was the longest conversation we'd ever had about something other than sports.

"I didn't want to be alone," I said.

Doug nodded. "We were alone anyway."

We parted on the sidewalk. No hug. No well-wishes. I wanted to tell him he was wrong, that the sex wasn't great. It was sex. The beautiful thing about making love with the right partner was that indescribable inner connection that filled your soul, making it almost impossible to imagine touching anyone else. I knew that now. Instead, I walked away.

He didn't ask about my sister, my mom, or my shop. I didn't ask about Marcy or his parents or brother. What was the point? We'd extricated each other from our lives. I no longer cared.

I waited until I was three blocks away and hid in a doorway where I cried.

CHAPTER 38

My favorite time of day was when I was alone in the bookshop, with the natural morning light chasing the shadows away. Just me and all the love stories, mysteries, and fantasies I wanted. It was all here. I needed nothing else. The touch of a bound spine, the smell of inked paper, and I was home.

I observed the street scene through my picture window. Occasionally a customer paused to wave to me on his or her way to work or wherever they were going. Each wave lifted me enough to smile. I loved my customers. I loved this part of my life, this amazing business I've been struggling to make work. It was the most rewarding endeavor I'd embarked on, and I was proud of myself.

I'd turned toward the office when something made me stop. I spun around and there he was. Theo, outside the window, watching me. He blinked, breathed in deeply, and in that moment, a piece of my heart tore away. When I made no move to acknowledge him, aside from my gaze locked with his, he moved on. He was on his way to work. He was running toward danger.

Go. Go and be safe, please.

In the office, I flipped the light on to find Hemingway coming awake. He's been opting to stay in regularly, leaving me in the mornings to return for food and shelter before I close. The animal mewed silently, blinked as he acclimated to the fluorescence, and stretched first his front paws and then his back, languidly, as if I had all day to sit and watch (which I would have done if it was what he wanted). I was growing to love the old, gnarled beast.

"You look nice and rested." I rubbed behind his bare ears. A drop of salty water fell onto his warped whiskers. He looked up at me in question. "Sorry," I whispered, sweeping my eyes with my sleeve. "I seem to be leaking."

Since seeing Doug, I found myself weeping without warning. By understanding what had gone wrong, I was able to properly mourn that part of my life, something I hadn't done. Instead, I'd buried myself in this new business, tacking on new worries about my sister. I'd gained new perspective on myself, and it scared me. Do I know how to be with someone wholly?

Hemingway leaned into me and rubbed my leg with his side, as if to say, "Hey, I get it. I've been there."

I straightened and he walked to the door, slipping outside to face the day. "See you later. Make good choices."

I texted Charlie, my daily message before opening the shop.

> Good morning, sister. How goes it?
>
> Pulled a marshmallow out of Myles's nose.
>
> Marshmallows in the house? When did this happen?
>
> When I ate nothing but nutritious food and still got cancer.

I stared at the screen. *Don't give up, Charlie. Hold onto yourself.*

> When I get there on Monday, I'll introduce you to the Twinkie.

She responded with a laughing face, and I blew out a breath.

In the shop, I stopped in the fiction contemporary romance section to rearrange a misplaced book when I saw it. On the wall, above the seating area where browsers turned to buyers and book club meetings congregated, was a glorious scene of color and imagination.

I hadn't asked Gina what she was going to do. I only knew I trusted that she would make something memorable. I was not disappointed. As I ingested the scene before me, my heartrate quickened, and joy bloomed within me. The painting was extraordinary. Covering the entire expanse of the wall were covers from every story I'd ever loved. The orange dancing horse from *The Catcher in the Rye*, the blond girl wearing an orange and black dress from the 1976 cover of *Are You There God? It's Me, Margaret*, the cover of *To Kill a Mockingbird*, *Anna Karenina*, and the greenery and flowers of *One Hundred Years of Solitude*. A large tree leaning over, dropping an apple to a small boy with his hands held out to catch it, *The Giving Tree*, cornered the wall.

In the center of the organized magnificent chaos was a brilliant, long-legged spider sitting on a delicate web dotted with pearls, the words "Some Store" woven into it. In the story of *Charlotte's Web*, the spider weaves a message to the farmer in her web to save her friend, Wilbur, the pig destined for sale and dinner. Her message: "Some Pig."

Tears fell like rain down my cheeks as I drank in every detail, always resting on the web. I felt the support of this woman, my employee, my friend. *We can do this*; she was telling me in her silent way. *I will help you.*

Gina walked into the store two hours later, at ten o'clock. I was at the counter, lights on, business open, reviewing my inventory and cash flow. She was about to head to the office when she stopped short. "Jesus, you look like shit."

I frowned.

She stared at me. "Seriously. What's up with your eyes? They're swollen and red."

"Allergies."

She pressed her lips together, sensing my lie, but continued to put away her belongings: backpack, flask, and whatever else she carried. When she returned, she started sweeping the floor. No more talk of my current condition. It was just as well. I didn't have the energy to think about it.

"Gina?"

"What?" She kept sweeping.

"The wall. It's…" I couldn't find the right words to explain all that I felt. She waited for me, staring at the carpet. "It's… thank you."

She gave me a half nod and continued, but I could detect a smile on her face.

Tara, the woman who went to book club meetings but never read the books, came in after the lunch rush and directly to me while I was straightening the mystery shelves.

"Stella, I've been wanting to come in to see you for a while."

"What happened? Are you okay?" She was flushed.

"I'm better than okay. I read the book you gave me, practically in one sitting. I didn't make dinner that night because I lost track of time, and my husband and kids didn't eat, and they were angry with me." She covered her mouth while she laughed. "I totally didn't care. It was great."

"Oh, congratulations? I think?" I laughed with her.

"I want something else. What else do you have for me. I'm hooked. I'm so excited."

"Why don't you read the book club choice?"

Tara frowned. "Oh, there's not enough time. We meet in a few days."

"Okay." I led her down one aisle, pausing to pull out a book I thought she might like, wishing Olivia Connelly had written more.

"You know what? I'll try to catch up. What is my group reading?"

"Ah." I took her to Mystery/Crime and pulled out the book they'd chosen. "Give it a try. You already know what the couch of shame feels like. You have nothing to lose."

CHAPTER 39

I had a strong need to see my mother. My anger, weighing heavy within me, was overshadowed by missing her. I wanted to forgive her, *needed* to forgive her. The decision to ask her husband to leave to protect us could not have been easy. Her struggle to give us the life we had was immeasurable, as was my gratitude. Charlie had arrived at this decision right away. She had always been quicker than me. Now that I had, I couldn't get to Mom's fast enough.

Two blocks from my apartment on my walk home from work, I called her from my cell. She hesitated when I told her I wanted to come out to Long Island to talk to her. *Hesitated!* My mother, who spent her entire life devoted to me and Charlie, who waited for our visits and calls, seemed to have something or someone else in her life, and I was interrupting her. I felt gutted all over again. Marion quickly rebounded and insisted I still come when I told her never mind.

"I'll wait for you," she said.

"It's okay. I'll come another time."

"Stella Michelle…" The way she said my name, like she was losing patience with me, brought me back to my youth, and I felt nostalgic for simpler times. "Come. I must talk to you."

When I walked into the house ninety minutes later (extra time for public trans), she was in the kitchen, dressed in nice pants and a pressed blouse. Her furry posse sat at her feet. I hesitated at the kitchen entrance. She came to me and pulled me into her embrace. I hugged her tight, at once confused and relieved.

"You're dressed nice. Where are you going?"

My mother gestured for me to sit. "Nowhere. I'm talking with you."

I slid onto the available kitchen chair next to her. She wore makeup tonight. "You look pretty."

"Thank you. Have you forgiven me?"

"I can't be mad at you. I need you."

"You have every right to be angry with me. I should have told you years ago. When you were planning your wedding, I wanted to sit you down and explain what had happened, so that you'd call it off, but I couldn't summon the strength. I was ashamed of keeping it from you for so long. I'll never forgive myself for that."

"You didn't approve of Doug."

She rested her crossed arms on the table. "For you, no."

Somehow, I knew this. "Why?"

"You didn't love him. I'm thankful he did what he did."

"You could have told me this before I put on that dress."

Her shoulders lifted. "You insisted you wanted to be married. What should I have done? You're a grown woman."

I dropped my head in my hands and stared at the linoleum table. I told Mom what happened with Theo, how he came to me after the fire, but that I ended our relationship before it got more complicated.

Marion shook her head. "Why?"

"I need to focus on my job and Charlie."

"Bullshit."

I lifted my eyes to hers. There was no pity in them. "What do you mean?"

"If you want to end it, that's fine. It's your life. But you're not being truthful. Not with me and not with yourself."

Hot tears burned my eyes.

"Be truthful. For once, Stella, tell it like it is."

"Fine! I'm afraid he'll walk out my door and I'll never see him again. And that fear paralyzes me." I gulped a wet breath and swallowed my grief, but it choked me, and a cough mixed with a sob came out, my admission out there, making me a fool, a weak, pitiful fool.

Mom brushed my hair from my face. "Was that so hard?" she said.

I nodded. Harder than I thought.

"I never finished telling you what happened. You left before I could."

I braced myself for another mind-blowing admission.

"Your father called me several times after he left, asking about you and Charlie. He missed you so much. But he hadn't gotten help, and he knew he couldn't return to us until he did."

I listened, leaning on my elbows.

"A year after he left, his doctor called to tell me he'd been seeing your father for a few months, and he had started medication to help control his outbursts. Your father had asked him to call to prove to me he had some control over his illness. I called him and told him to come home."

I straightened in my seat. "Why didn't he?"

"He was on his way when he had a car accident. He'd collided with another car." Her voice broke. She sniffed and sat back, composing herself.

"Oh, Mom, I'm so sorry. That had to have been so hard."

"I'm telling you this now because you need to know, they don't leave you because of you, my sweet. You are a gift. Your father was coming home to you."

Mom waited for me to gather myself, handing me tissue after tissue.

"I don't think this one will leave," she said, finally, referring to Theo. "If he does, you'll have had something beautiful to carry with you."

"I don't think he'll leave either. Not on purpose. But his job is dangerous. I can't be with someone who risks his life every day."

"If he was an accountant, you would have found some other reason to push him away."

I shook my head.

"Yes, something about too many paper cuts. Or some other excuse."

I laughed, but the tears that fell were heavy. "Am I going to be alone?"

She touched my chin. "Everything is a risk. People leave or die, and sometimes there's nothing we can do about it. If you let your fear keep you from opening your heart to love, you'll have lost anyway."

"I'm tired of hurting. I don't want to risk it."

"Then you won't live. To love is to open yourself to hurt. It's the greatest gift you can give yourself. Nothing is guaranteed."

The clock ticked on the wall.

"Did you love Dad?"

"With my whole heart."

A large knot formed in my throat. And yet, she sent him away.

Like I sent Theo away.

"Do you miss him, Mom?"

She rolled her tongue in her mouth, as if tasting the words before releasing them. "Not anymore."

"I do," I admitted. "Still."

"I know." Mom took my hands. "Everyone needs love, Stella. Stop worrying so much about what might happen and take a chance. Give yourself wholly to whatever makes you happy, no matter the risk. You did it with your career. You're going to have disappointment. It's life. But you're going to find nuggets of magic along the way. The nuggets make it all worthwhile. Don't let fear take that away from you. You get one chance. No one gets out alive." She squeezed my hands. "Start to live."

I blew my nose and wiped my eyes.

"Why didn't you find someone after Dad died?"

She smiled and brought my hands to her lips. "I was busy doing something incredible."

I wrapped my arms around her. "Mom, thank you for making our lives so wonderful. I know it wasn't easy."

She pulled away after I lightened my hold on her. Her eyes

shifted above my head to the clock on the wall. "This is as good a time as any. There's someplace I want to take you."

"I'm not sure I can take any more revelations."

She pulled her car keys from the keyring hanging next to the door. "Come."

Mom had been alone for the past twenty-nine years. Was she unhappy? I didn't know. She worked all the time. I never gave it much thought. How selfish I'd been. My mother knew me better than I knew myself. Yet, I couldn't tell if she was truly happy. Was that how it worked? Your parents made you, knew you inside and out, and the child took and took, then left. My mother was my Giving Tree.

From behind the wheel, Marion glanced at me. "What?"

"I'm wondering what Dad would think of me now. If he was still here. Do you think he'd be disappointed or proud?"

She pulled into the parking lot of the town library and parked near the rear door. It was dark, and the library was closed. The car engine cooled while we sat in the silence.

"Your father was so proud of you. This I know to be true. When you walked into a room, he lit up. But I'm going to tell you something and I need you to listen to me. Don't worry about what other people think. Be proud of yourself. That's all you have to do."

I stared ahead through the windshield. "So, when you kept telling us you were going to the library, it wasn't code for something?"

"No." She climbed out of the car, and I followed. There was a side door I'd never seen. A light was on behind it. Marion led me through and down a set of stairs to the basement. A beating sound drifted toward us. As we descended the steps, the music grew louder. At the end of the hall, we pushed through another set of doors and found ourselves standing at one end of a large room. There were some folding tables and chairs along one wall, an elevated stage at the opposite end to where we were, and a man leaning over the stage, adjusting the volume on what appeared to be a modest boom box.

There had to be thirty people milling about, chatting. When we walked into the room, they looked at us and waved. Marion waved in return.

"Mom? What is this?"

Pacer saw us and strode over, taking long steps to reach us. "Marion!" He kissed my mother on her cheek. "You finally brought Stella. I'm so glad!"

My mother nodded. "It was time."

I watched Mom and Pacer carefully, trying to detect something beneath their innocent exchange when the older gentleman who was playing with the boom box near the stage turned to the small crowd. "All right everyone, let's start." He scanned the room and stopped when his eyes found my mom. He broke into a warm smile, and I felt my mother's posture straighten beside me. She blushed.

Wait a minute. Pacer moved to stand next to me. The gentleman walked directly to Mom. He took her hands and kissed her on both cheeks. "Marion," he said softly.

"Lorenzo." His speckled, silver and black hair was a beautiful contrast to his brown skin. They stood eye to eye.

Without giving me so much as a glance, he said to her, "Shall we begin?"

Wordlessly, she handed me her purse and allowed the man to bring her to the center of the floor. Other couples formed around them. The music subsided, and they all waited. My mother and Lorenzo locked eyes. He smiled and leaned his face closer to hers. I couldn't see her reaction, but my heartbeat went into overdrive. Marion with this man?

The music started again, a smooth, graceful styling, and Lorenzo led my mother into a dance around the floor, the surrounding couples shadowing their steps. They were beautiful together, and I was awestruck as I watched her follow his movements with an elegance foreign to me.

Pacer leaned over to speak in my ear. "She's a natural."

"When did this start?" I asked, my eyes riveted to the dance floor. "I never knew."

"I shoveled her driveway last year and we got to talking. I told her I signed up for dance lessons to try to meet someone, and she offered to come with me for the first time so I wouldn't have to go alone. That was the night she met Lorenzo. It was a done deal from that moment."

I pulled my eyes from them to look at Pacer.

"I know," he said. "I was shocked, too. He couldn't keep his eyes off her. He uses your mom to demonstrate new steps to the group. She can dance."

"Yes," I agreed, mesmerized. "She can."

"She's been my practice partner since."

"And? Have you met anyone?" The crowd was mixed ages, but it appeared most had a partner. There were a couple of single ladies older than my mom.

"No. Still looking. There's someone out there for me," Pacer said. "Until then, I'm having a great time."

When the song ended, Lorenzo led my mother to me.

"Lorenzo, this is my daughter, Stella. Stella, my friend, Lorenzo."

Lorenzo kissed my hand. "It's a pleasure to finally meet you." He left us and returned to the class.

"Mom, you look amazing out there."

She watched Lorenzo. "Everyone has their weakness, Stella. Mine is rumba."

"Rumba? That looked like a waltz to me."

"It was. The rumba is when he comes alive." She patted my arm and walked to the man who'd grabbed her attention. Pacer went with the class too, on the arm of one of the elderly women. For the next hour and a half, I sat at a corner table and watched my mother living her best life in a library basement.

CHAPTER 40

Friday night, as the ladies arrived one-by-one after hours for their book club meeting, I updated my website with new photos from the book wall and listed the new titles we had in stock.

The group loudly exclaimed their greetings. I overhead one compliment about my buffalo chicken dip— a new easy recipe I tried.

Before I shut my laptop, I checked Facebook, telling myself I was curious about the responses to my previous post about new store hours, as I scrolled down my page until I found one that stopped me.

Marcy had posted an hour earlier. She looked positively ethereal. Doug faced her so I could see only his profile, but it was the way he looked at her, a way he'd never looked at me, that opened my eyes. Her hand covered half her face as she laughed. It was a beautiful shot, one even I couldn't deny if it weren't for the massive, emerald-cut diamond gleaming on her ring finger. They were sitting side-by side in the same Italian restaurant he and I used to go to for special occasions. But none of that mattered because what the picture told the world, what it made clear to me, was they were in love. In the six years Doug and I were together, never once did he look at me the way he looked at Marcy in every photo they shared with the world. Nor did I look at him that way.

That was almost my life. Doug did me a favor when he broke my heart.

I called Charlie to tell her about my recent visit with our mother and what I'd learned.

In between yawns, she admitted that our mother had told her about our father wanting to come home. Charlie had pushed Mom to tell me too, believing I needed to hear it. She was right.

But Charlie didn't know about the library dancing and Mom's new romance. So, I relayed in detail about the experience. She laughed, saying she was so happy for her, but her laughter was hollow. I asked where Lance was. Not home.

The book club meeting ended early—the women all deciding impulsively to see the movie version of their chosen book since it was opening night and three of them forgot to bring wine. I called Charlie and told her I was coming over.

She was in the den with the children watching *Nanny McPhee* when I arrived. Forty minutes later, as the credits scrolled up the screen, I carried a sleepy two-year-old to bed while Charlie read a book to Maddie.

My sister met me in the clean kitchen where I sat reading.

"No plans tonight?"

"No." I put my book down.

She fell onto the chair across from me. "When Lance and I started dating, I couldn't wait for Fridays. It was our routine. Work all week. Play all weekend." The clock chimed nine p.m.

"Where is Lance?"

My sister shrugged, and her face fell. "He should be home soon. Can you do me a favor? The pharmacy called. My refill is ready."

"This late?"

"It's the twenty-four-hour pharmacy on Main. Don't go to the other one."

Main Street in town was a quaint thoroughfare, characterized by boutiques, restaurants, and bars. Tonight, it was alive with weekenders enjoying the budding spring weather, looking for some relief from the work week. I walked down the street, holding a full bag of medication when I glanced through the window of McGreevey's Pub and stopped short. I peered in to be sure my eyes didn't deceive me, turned around, and entered.

Lance barely moved when I took the seat next to him at

the bar. He fondled a short glass of untouched amber liquor, staring into it. The bartender approached me.

"She'll have a Chardonnay," Lance told him without looking up.

"Seltzer, please," I said and waited until I had my drink in front of me before I spoke.

"I was skeptical of you, at first, waiting for you to hurt my sister. Then I started seeing you through her eyes and I thought, maybe you're the one who'll come through. They write love stories about someone, right? You're the one who works hard and loves his family more than he loves anything else in the world. Sir Lance-A-Lot." Lance sat, immobile. "Now, I find you in a bar, less than a mile from your house at nine-thirty on a Friday night. I don't know what you think you're doing. But someone I really love needs you and you're failing her. You're failing your amazing, beautiful kids. And I hate you for it. You no longer deserve the title."

He stared into his glass. An older venue, the bar was comfortably crowded, every seat occupied. My raised voice was absorbed into the moderate background noise.

"Say something!"

He turned to me, and I flinched. His full eyes held that same look of sadness and despair as his wife's. Gone was the exaggerated smile he'd pasted on at home. "I'm trying to keep everyone's spirits up. Trying to stay upbeat, keeping the kids distracted so she can rest." He shook his head. "I'm exhausted."

"Tough shit."

"Let me talk, Stella. The other night as she slept, I stared at her bald head on her pillow, and I couldn't see my wife. I couldn't see the woman who could hold a baby in one hand, make dinner with the other, and stop a toddler from careening into a garbage bin. The person in my bed is an imposter who's taken my life and threatens my world."

Every muscle in my body tensed. "You're not blaming her."

He swiped at his eyes. "Who can I blame? She's my rock.

She's the one who's supposed to keep us together. Who am I without her?"

"She's still *her*. Fighting for her life. For *your* life and your children."

I abandoned my drink and spun my chair to the man I've known for a decade and a half. "Ignoring it or diminishing it won't make it go away. Fight with her. She needs you. You're better together. You know this already!" I took a deep breath trying to control my temper. My mother's words repeated in my head. "This is life. Shit happens. How do you think Charlie feels? She's the one going through it. Listen to her. Really listen. She needs to tell you what she's going through. She wants to know you're scared too so she's not so alone. You need to suck it up, go home, and support her the way she deserves. Because right now, you're showing her that you don't love her as much as she thought you did. And that hurts more than cancer."

I pushed my glass away. "Men have disappointed me my whole life. I wanted you to be different. And until recently, you were the closest I could call a hero." I shook my head and tossed a crumpled napkin onto the bar. "Anyone can be a hero when things are going well." I slid off the stool. "I'm going to your house now. My sister needs her medicine. We never had this conversation."

Charlie's house was dark and quiet when I returned with her prescriptions. She was in the den with the television on low, on the corner of the couch under a knit Afghan.

"I was worried you might have gone home," she said.

I dropped onto the couch next to her. "I had a drink at McGreevey's."

Charlie gently nudged me with her toes. "You should have, little sister. You've been working hard and helping me out."

I shrugged and watched the screen.

"McGreevey's is our Friday go-to bar. I can't wait to be able to go to happy hour again. To order a drink without a care in the world." She looked at me. "Will I ever be able to do that?"

"Of course," I whispered.

Charlie put a hand on my hair, running her fingers through it. "Go home, Es. I'm okay."

I was about to say no, that I wanted to stay longer, when I heard a car door outside. I hugged my sister and went into the mudroom to get my sneakers. Lance walked through the garage door into the kitchen, not seeing me. I went to sneak out, but curiosity pulled me into the shadows where I could peek into the den undetected. It was so quiet, I thought maybe Lance went directly to his bedroom and not to see Charlie, but the scene I found froze me. My sister stood in the middle of the room in her flannel pajamas facing him. Without a word, he pulled her to him and wrapped his arms around her. She exhaled and returned his hug.

I slipped through the door, feeling my first pangs of hope for the both of them.

CHAPTER 41

Someone jiggled my doorknob, trying to get into my apartment at nine o'clock Sunday night. My first thought as I jumped off my couch was that I forgot to pay my rent. Beads of sweat formed along my brow as I envisioned my landlord waiting to tell me I'd used up all my chances and would be promptly evicted. My body pressed up against the door.

Wait a minute. I paid the rent this month. On time. I've *been* paying.

"Stella, it's me."

Philippe stood at the threshold wearing one of his signature sweaters over tight pants and a serious expression.

"What's going on?"

He leaned forward and hugged me.

We took our seats on my couch after he declined both wine and coffee.

"You're making me nervous," I said.

My neighbor sighed and dropped his head against a cushion. "Rog is moving to Paris."

Whoa. So, it happened.

"Okay." I watched Philippe carefully. He was more contemplative than distressed. "When is he leaving?"

"Next month." He turned to face me. There's the pain. "I told him I'm proud of him and happy."

"Are you?"

He shook his head. "Of course not. But if I were honest, he would think I'm a shitty boyfriend."

I rubbed his arm. "Honesty is overrated."

He sighed and fell into me. "Oh, what am I going to do? My favorite thing in the world is to wake up smelling his foul morning breath."

I held him and patted his back. "That's quite romantic."

He spoke into my neck. "It hurts so bad."

I thought of what my mother told me. Of course, it hurts. It's love. The reason I avoided it. "Philippe, he's not leaving you. He's going to work. In Paris. You can go visit him. Talk about romantic."

His large brown eyes watered, and he sniffed. "He asked me to go."

My heart sank. Not Philippe. Not when I felt like our friendship was deepening. "You said no?"

"How can I go? I have my business here. I can't leave." He began to cry in earnest. "Rog knows this. I hate him."

Relief swept through me. Relief and guilt. His tears began to soak my shirt. Several minutes passed and I knew he didn't fall asleep on my shoulder because his breathing was still ragged.

Philippe pulled away so I could see his tear-streaked face. He wiped his eyes with his hands while I went to get him tissues. I handed him a box and sat down.

"What are you doing tomorrow?" I said.

"I'm going to wallow. All day. And feel sorry for myself."

"How about, wallow until ten and then come with me? What you need is a good chemo session."

He blotted his eyes. "Wow. Way to put it into perspective, sister."

CHAPTER 42

I was in the shop early Monday morning to get stuff done before leaving for Charlie's. It took me three hours to catch up with my record-keeping and pay invoices while Hemingway slept at my feet.

Checked eBay to find another offer for the dress and shut the app.

Before I left, I let the cat out and watched him saunter down the alley, his tail lifted in a happy gesture as he embarked on his next adventure. "Make good choices."

On my way home, I passed my wedding dress in the dry cleaner's window, a reminder of the jilted bride who'd bought it. I didn't deserve to sell this dress. I deserved this hard lesson of having it watch me struggle day to day.

Philippe was waiting at the bottom of the steps in front of our apartment, and we barely caught the ten fifty-five train to Long Island.

"Why are we taking the train when you have a car?"

"I sold it."

He looked at me.

"What?" I said.

"What's next? A kidney?"

"Don't be ridiculous. How much do you think I could get for one?"

By the time we arrived at Charlie's, there was no time to delay. After a quick embrace between my sister and Philippe—she was thrilled to have his company—we piled into her minivan and left immediately for her treatment. Fortunately, she was now able to accept them at the Sloan Kettering center on Long Island, saving us travel time. Charlie looked much better, considering the treatments were kicking the shit out of her. Her skin was sallow from the drugs, but her demeanor seemed more upbeat, and I felt a stab of optimism. In the car, we kept to superfluous topics such as weather, the kids, jobs, anything but Charlotte's plight.

When she was settled into her chair at the clinic, in her thin robe over sweatpants, attached to the drip, we spent the full ninety minutes discussing Philippe's situation, what he would do about getting a new roommate, plans to visit Rog in Paris, learning how to move day to day without his company. To Philippe, Roger simply chose his career over his relationship, and he found it difficult to accept. In fact, he told us he'd asked Rog to reconsider and stay.

This distraction helped Charlie. To see her so involved in my neighbor's problems made me feel happy, though I tried hard not to show it, for fear Philippe think I was enjoying myself at his expense.

"Philippe, he must go," she said. "You don't want to be the reason he doesn't accept this opportunity. He'll resent you for it if you ask him to stay."

Philippe shook his head, as if not wanting to hear the words.

"Do you love him?"

His lower lip quivered. "I do."

"Then you must let him be the best version of himself he can be. Let him go. He'll come back for you," Charlie said.

"If he doesn't?"

She thought a moment. "Then find someone who can't live without you for one breath. He's out there, if it's not Rog. I promise."

Philippe glanced at me. "Don't ask me." I didn't believe Rog would return to him, that love was fragile and fleeting.

He appeared visibly relaxed, as if Charlie's word was the final resolution. He took her hands, as thin as his own, and gently squeezed them. "Thank you, Sunshine." Then he leaned over and kissed her cheek. "Now I have to survive the time it takes him to come to the same conclusion. And," he exhaled a frustrated breath, "find a roommate."

With Philippe's fears assuaged and fifteen minutes left of her treatment, both turned their focus on me.

"You look tired." This from my sister, who wore a bandana on her head above dark eyes.

"Do I?"

Philippe nodded. "You getting enough rest?"

Rest? Who has time to rest with a business to run and a sister on chemo with two small children? "Sure. Plenty. It's the lighting."

"Have you heard from Theo?" Charlie said.

"No. I don't expect to. It's fine. I'm fine. All my energy is going into the shop." I ignored the unspoken opinions painted on their faces. Let them postulate. I spoke the truth. Did I think about Theo?

Not the point.

Did I miss him so much it hurt, and wonder how he was doing every single day?

It no longer mattered. But I did have something to tell them.

"Guess who I saw last week?"

"Your ex," Charlie said.

Philippe started to shake his head as if that were ridiculous when my jaw dropped. "How do you know these things?" I said.

"Wait, she's right?!" said Philippe.

Charlie nodded. "It was a matter of time, Essie. You had no closure. He needed it as much as you did."

"No, he didn't. I went to him."

Charlie's face broke wide open. "Really. I'm proud of you."

I smiled. I was proud of me, too. The old Stella would have hidden from the truth forever.

"Tell me what he said."

As I reiterated my conversation with Doug, my sister giving

me a knowing smile, I realized she was totally right. We'd both needed closure.

"How did seeing him make you feel?" Philippe said.

I hadn't thought about it. My last conversation with Theo, which broke my heart, was on the forefront of my mind, followed closely by discovering our father, who'd left us, wanted to come home, and Mom was doing the rumba with a man, and finally seemed truly happy, to the ever-present threat of losing my shop, to Philippe dealing with this new life change. My need for closure with my ex was shadowed by my life.

Understanding that Doug didn't walk away because I wasn't worth loving gave me a sense of relief, I suppose. But it also worried me that I would keep pushing people away.

How can I change practiced behavior born of childhood fear?

Philippe declined Charlie's dinner invitation, opting to head to Brooklyn. "I'm blazing mad that he's leaving, but it doesn't mean I don't want to spend as much time as I can with him."

After dropping my neighbor at the train station, Charlie and I went to her place for dinner with Lance, Mom, and the children. On our way, she told me she and Lance had a long talk and that I was relinquished of chemo duty for the foreseeable future. Lance would be taking her. His suggestion.

He returned from work early tonight and surprised his wife by bringing home take-out for all of us. I was pleased to notice an ease in tension between my sister and brother-in-law. She didn't tell him that it was going to be hard for her to see the pain in his eyes during her treatments.

She told me instead.

"He's been more open to expressing his concerns, only occasionally reverting to his cheery 'this is a passing inconvenience' mantra. He listens to me now. And doesn't tell me not to worry about it. He's scared too. I feel validated."

Lance never told her about our meeting at the bar and I was grateful. Charlie loved him fiercely and knew it was returned.

"We made love," Charlie told me while we were in the kitchen after dinner. I was making coffee, and she was sitting at the table. "For the first time since this all started."

I smiled.

"It was a little weird. I left my shirt on. I couldn't help it, and I'm dry down there. They don't warn you about that. They don't warn you about lots of things. But it felt so good to be re-connected. It's so necessary." Through her sallow complexion and dark eyes, she let out a satisfied sigh. "I feel better than I have in a long time."

My sister was living proof that the human connection was integral to our well-being. In this case, love might save her life.

CHAPTER 43

On Wednesday we had a constant trickle of customers. A group of tourists spent half an hour taking selfies in front of the wall, and not one of the eight of them bought a book. Gina and I shared a laugh when they left. One woman commented on the painted scene, and I gave full-deserved credit to Gina, who pretended to ignore me.

Joan stopped in, still undecided about what to do with her marriage. She told me she and Marie, the new addition to her book club, had grown close and thanked me for the introduction. She bought three more books. All romance. If not in life, you can live a happy ending between two covers.

I took advantage of a lull in the afternoon to run next door to the dry cleaners to finally pick up my dress.

"Miss Stella! Someone wants your dress. She left her phone number to talk to you." Ms. Roselli handed me a small slip of paper with the name, Karen, and a local number.

"I came to pick it up."

"I'll hold it until you call her. The dress is making me busier than usual. I have three more to clean."

"Great. Thank you!"

I returned to my shop, where I called Karen. She picked up on the second ring, her voice bubbling with excitement as she exclaimed it was the most gorgeous dress she'd ever seen. She was getting married next year, and when she saw it in the window, she *knew* it was for her. I was pleased. It was exactly what I'd hoped for this dress. To be worn in love.

"I have seven thousand dollars. I know it's probably a low number but it's all I have in my budget."

"It's yours," I said, working to keep my voice steady.

We agreed to meet next week to exchange payment for the

dress, and I hung up feeling relieved. And, ready to let the dress go. Things were finally starting to go well for me financially. Business had improved and with the sale of my car and now, the dress, I had a small cushion to rely on.

I was in a good place for the first time in over a year.

After closing, I settled in my office to finish paperwork and prepare the following month's book club and author signing schedules. My last task before locking up was to prop the alley door open to wait for Hemingway to finish his dinner and leave. I nearly fell asleep reading my book (not the book's fault—it was riveting—but the reader is lacking sleep) when his mew and purring startled me awake.

"Why are you still here?"

Philippe texted as the cat circled his new bed—a soft, gray square cushion I'd picked up for the corner—then curled up and settled in.

> Philippe: Where are you? You're not answering your door.
>
> Shop, I answered.
>
> Philippe: Still? Stop working.
>
> I just did.
>
> Philippe: Can you meet me for a drink? I can't be here right now. His clothes are everywhere waiting to be packed. :-0

I glanced at the cat, sleeping.

> I'll meet you for coffee.
>
> Philippe: Fine. Diner in twenty?
>
> C U there.

Though we'd spent the afternoon together only two days ago, seeing Philippe again was eye-opening. He looked bad. We hovered in the rear booth over coffees and pecan pie.

"He's still packing. I can't watch. He's too happy." Tears spilled down his face. I reached across the table.

He dropped his head on our joined hands. I felt the wetness against my fingers.

"Are you this upset in front of him?" I said.

"I'm worse."

"You can't be like this. You don't want him to remember you as a weepy puddle. Be strong. Cry with me."

Philippe lifted his tear-sodden face to me. I took a napkin and gently wiped his cheeks.

"He needs to know how I feel. Otherwise, he'll think I'm okay with it."

"Exactly. Be strong."

Philippe frowned. "I was strong at first. If I don't share my emotions, how else will he know what I'm feeling?"

"He doesn't need to know."

He nodded, as if something dawned on him. "Even those we love most don't always know what we're not telling them. Transparency, lovey."

He chipped away at the pie while I mulled over what he said. It seemed improbable that showing neediness would change Rog's mind. If anything, it would drive him further away so he wouldn't return.

"Why aren't you eating this?"

"I don't like pecans," I said.

Philippe dropped his fork and let out an exasperated sigh. He raised his hand to get the waitress's attention. When she came over, he looked at me. "Tell her what you want."

"It's fine," I said. Which is what I'd said when he ordered the pecan pie and asked if I'd share it with him.

"It's not. You're abominable. What the fuck do you want?"

I stared at his angry face. Then I looked to the waitress who shrugged as if to apologize for my friend's behavior. "Chocolate cream pie, please."

She walked away and Philippe leaned over. "Was that so hard? I don't love you less because you don't eat my pie."

Over the next hour and a half, we had two more cups of coffee and finished my chocolate pie. "Do you want one of your own? My treat." We had pushed his pecan pie to the side when my luscious piece was placed on the table.

"Not nearly as fun or therapeutic. Besides, calories fall off the fork when shared."

We talked about everything and nothing. Hopped up on caffeine and sugar, yet emotionally exhausted, we paid the bill and headed home arm in arm.

We were a block from our apartment building when three fire trucks sped by, their horns raging in the quiet night. I practically hung onto Philippe when another fire truck careened down the street. As it passed, I watched the men holding onto the rear bumper and thought of Theo, imagining him wearing the coat, the helmet, racing toward the very thing that could kill him.

The truck turned left and sped out of sight, but I could decipher the commotion of the fire trucks not far off.

"It's close," Philippe said. "But not here, so I'm too tired to care."

I looked at my watch. Almost midnight. Stepping onto the first step of our building, the noise grew louder.

"I'm going to look."

Philippe pulled away. "I'm going to bed. You should, too. You look exhausted."

"I'll be a few minutes behind you. See you tomorrow. If you need me sooner, you know where I am."

He hugged me tight and kissed my temple. "Thank you."

"No thanks necessary."

Philippe walked into the building. I remained on the steps, listening to the commotion a few blocks away, feeling nervous though I couldn't explain why. Was Theo there? I shouldn't care or worry. But I did.

Curiosity propelled me toward the action. Part of me wanted to watch firemen at work, to experience the excitement as a bystander, maybe to better understand the job. A couple up ahead picked up their pace, moving in the same direction, and I followed close behind.

The noise grew louder as we continued. When they made another left, my heart leaped to my throat. We were traveling the direction to my shop. The noise decibels grew. Taking the steps I do every day, my heart hammering in my chest, I turned onto Gruber Ave. and froze.

The chaotic scene in front of me— in front of *my shop*— was a scene out of a movie. My feet were leaden as I approached the barricade of trucks and firefighters. I circumvented the crowd that had gathered until I found a spot that afforded me a clear vision of what was happening.

Oh God, no.

Flames were pouring out of the windows above the nail salon next to the dry cleaners. They danced and frolicked and threatened to move to the shops below. I glanced around, but then forgot Philippe wasn't with me. I pulled out my phone.

We're on fire!

Closer to the street, the heat intensified. I tried to see into *Between the Covers* but couldn't make sense of anything in the dark. It didn't appear the fire had spread yet.

My eyes swam, and I wiped them roughly, trying to keep my vision clear. My life was in that shop. I couldn't lose this. I had too much at stake. I didn't realize I was moving forward until a large, black coat with yellow stripes appeared in front of me.

"Don't even think about it." Theo's stern face frowned down at me. "Don't, Stella. It's dangerous and you need to steer clear so we can do our job."

"My shop." It came out as a weak wail.

His face softened a fraction. "I know. I promise we'll do everything we can. Get back." He pushed me toward the sidewalk across the street, which made me angry.

"Stop pushing me."

"Get over there."

"I have my stuff in there, Theo! I need to get my things."

"Forget about it!"

I crossed my arms in defiance, and hot tears filled my eyes.

"I have to work," he said. "Promise me you won't move."

My eyes were fixed on my business. Smoke poured through the windows above the dry cleaners now.

"Stella, don't make me pull a man from the fire to control you."

I couldn't peel my gaze from the horrific scene. They needed all the manpower they could use, and I didn't need a babysitter. "Fine."

As Theo ran across the street, my frustration mounted. Someone shoved me aside, and I pushed back with all my weight, not caring how rude I was. A loud explosion sent us stumbling several paces. Someone screamed. She wouldn't stop —a high-pitched piercing that caused everyone to look. Make her stop!

They were all looking at me. *I* was screaming. Theo! I moved along the periphery, craned my neck, trying to identify familiar faces from his station and went weak with relief when I saw that he wasn't in the building but climbing a rising ladder on top of a truck. It was extending toward the building, and he was racing to it while pulling something black over his face.

The shop seemed intact. Maybe they could contain the fire. Resigned, I accepted my post on the sidewalk when I noticed Philippe walking toward me. At the same time, a thought hit me like a sledgehammer. Hemingway! Did I let him out to-night? I glanced up and down the street. My mind raced with ideas. The noise of the men yelling directions, the horns and sirens of more trucks arriving mixed with my frantic thoughts. The alley!

I ran down the street, away from Philippe. Away from the fire. My breath caught in my throat, but I pushed forward to the street behind my shop. There, the noise was more manage-able, and I was relieved to see little activity on this side. Either the fire was contained to the front of the building, or it hadn't broken through yet.

I raced down the narrow alley. Heard shouting on the roof. Pushed myself close to the wall.

My hands shook so badly, it took several tries before I fit the key into the lock and stepped into my office, into a gray haze. I squinted my eyes to barely make out the shapes of the desk and workbench. There was no imminent heat around me.

"Hemingway! Here boy! Here kitty!" I held my shirt over my mouth, coughing into the fabric as thin smoke surrounded me. The light switch didn't work. My eyes teared, as they strained to see in the dark. *Please let this cat be okay.* I walked the perimeter of the room, forced to close my stinging eyes. Stretched my hands out in front of me and leaned low, trying to feel for the matted fur or half tail.

I hit the door again. Panicked, I re-traced my steps, this time reaching toward the shelves. Something rubbed against me. I dropped to my hands and knees and found the cat shaking near my foot. I lifted him and brought him to the door. In the alley, I sucked in a deep breath and coughed until my ribs ached. The cat squealed and squirmed out of my hands. I turned to go back in. There was something else I needed to save.

Only seconds had passed. The office had darkened with thickening smoke. No flames. The heavy gray air and darkness was disorienting. Using my hands along the desk, I found the extinguisher on the wall. Struggled to pull the pin. Aimed the hose in front of me prepared for fire.

Reached the shop door and pulled it open.

I fell against it— hit with a wall of heavier smoke. Sight was gone. One hand out, the other covering my mouth and nose with my shirt, I felt along the wall leading to the register. Voices from outside. Glass shattered somewhere.

Blackness stung my nose and eyes.

Save the shop.

Save my shop.

Flailed my arms, searching for the counter, but no connection.

Where? Is? It?

I keeled over, coughing.

Swiped my arms around until I hit the Formica, and then the hardcover from the shelf behind it. My book!

Clutched it to my chest. Turned to leave.

Front door too hot. Changed direction.

Office door wasn't there. I hugged the wall. No door. A crash behind me, or was it in front?

Eyes closed, half face covered with cotton, I spun. Hit a shelf. Turned again. A shelf. I dropped the extinguisher. Where was the door?! I backed up. Tried again. No door. Dropped to my knees. Oh, God. Help!

Amid the chaos came a clear voice. "Stella, this way."

"Who is it?"

"Over here, my girl."

"Dad?" My arms extended out to him but found air. "Where are you?"

"Come closer, love."

I moved toward him. Hit a wall. No door.

"This way."

"Dad."

I followed his voice. No door. My chest burned. I…need… to…get…out…Another explosion. Someone screamed. I let myself fall into the blackness.

"Stella." His soothing voice wafted through the thick haze. "Stella."

"Dad." I touched his body and felt at once safe and protected. What was he doing here? How was this possible? He put something over my face. A cup.

"Breathe," he said.

I inhaled. Coughed. Inhaled.

"I've got you," he said. "I won't let anything happen to you."

I wanted to tell him how much I missed him, ask him how he was here right now with me when he's been gone for twenty-nine years. We were wrong. He didn't die. He's here!

But I couldn't speak. Couldn't open my eyes. I relished the feel of his arms around me, protecting me like he did when I was small. Filled with a sense of peace, I fell into black, knowing he'd take me with him.

CHAPTER 44

My eyes opened. I was in a bed.

I'm not dead.

My sister and mother were in the room, talking quietly. Charlie stepped to the right, and I saw Philippe.

"Hey," I tried to say, but the plastic mask over my mouth blocked any sound because they ignored me. I pulled the mask to one side. "Hello?" An unrecognizable sound came out of me. Mom's head shot up and she turned. She smiled. Oh no, I'm going to die. Mom doesn't give out smiles easily. I must be bad off.

"You're awake," Charlie said from my left side. I put my mask back over my mouth and breathed.

Philippe was behind Charlie. "Hey, lovey!" he whispered loud.

The doctor walked in. My family parted to allow her to approach me.

"Ms. Duprey, I'm Doctor Golding. How are you feeling?"

I blinked in answer. I didn't yet know how I felt. "How long have I been here?" was what I wanted to say, but what came out of me was "How lo—" before I became consumed with a painful coughing fit. The doctor waited until I stopped.

"Try not to talk yet," she said. "You've been here for twenty-four hours." She spoke now to my mom and sister across the bed, over me, so I could hear. "She's on a high dose of levalbuterol and racepinephrine to help with wheezing and shortness of breath." She adjusted the drip on an IV above me. "You're very fortunate you got out when you did." To Mom and Charlie, "She seems to be responding to the medicine according to her bloodwork, leaps and bounds better than her original blood gas test yesterday. I'll keep her another night for observation and if all goes well, start her discharge papers in the morning."

When the doctor left, Mom frowned. "I'm angry with you. You ran into a burning building when you were specifically told not to."

To which Philippe added, "She needed to be *told* not to run into a burning building? Don't people know not to do that?"

Mom gave him the stink-eye and turned to me. "Why'd you go do something so stupid? What could possibly be worth getting yourself nearly killed?" Her voice was raised.

Maybe I was going to be all right. I moved my mask.

"My shop." I moved my eyes between them, waiting for someone to tell me if it was still standing.

Charlie and Mom met their gaze over me. Finally, Charlie said, "The place is a mess."

I closed my eyes. My dream, my life. Gone again.

Mom pushed my hair from my face, resting her palm against my temple. "What's important is your health. We'll deal with that other stuff later. You were very lucky you got out of there. Very lucky. The next time you do something so monumentally stupid, someone might not be there to save you."

My eyes shifted to Charlie.

"Daddy saved me."

"What did she say?" Philippe said.

My sister and mother exchanged glances. I've heard of it happening in movies— estranged parent shows up in the nick of time to save the child they'd abandoned. Why couldn't that be me? Dad didn't die. He was here.

I lifted my head to see the room. A searing pain pulsed in my skull, and I dropped against the pillow. Where was he?

"Tell her," Mom said to Charlie.

"It was Theo. He said when he didn't see you across the street where he told you to stay, Philippe"—who raised his hand behind my sister—"told him you might have gone in the shop through the rear door. Theo found you and carried you to the ambulance."

I squeezed my eyes closed. Was it his voice I heard and not my father's? Oh, Freud would have a field day with this. I was so confused. I looked past Philippe but there was no one else in the room. Philippe turned to see where I was looking.

"Honey, he was here. He waited until you were admitted."

"He called me," Charlie added. "He stayed with us until the doctor assured him you'd be okay." She averted her eyes when she added, "He wanted to be gone before you woke up."

"I won't lie," my mother said, "I was grateful when he finally left. Took that stink with him. The man needed a shower something fierce."

"Mmm. I didn't mind the smell at all," Philippe said, prompting another stink-eye from Mom.

"Your salon?" My voice was thick and coarse.

Philippe leaned toward me. "I'm not sure yet. We'll be okay. We will." He held my hand and kissed my fingers. "I'll see you when you get home. Don't worry, I fixed up your place. I convinced the Super to let me in. It's spotless." To my sister, "She'll never recognize it."

My heart ached, thinking of Theo sitting here with Charlie and Mom, waiting to make sure I was okay after the way we'd left each other. I didn't think I could feel worse than I did before. I started to drift off and felt the gentle kisses of my family leaving me to rest.

I slept fitfully all night. One of the nurses told me a woman named Gina called the nurse's station three times to see how I was. I fell back to sleep, worrying that Gina wouldn't have a job. I woke in the darkness as a new nurse adjusted my IV, tweaked buttons and knobs, and replaced a fluid-filled bag I couldn't identify.

Dawn approached through the window, and I abandoned my oxygen mask. I wanted to see my shop, to see if I could salvage any of my business. I sighed and turned toward the room.

I gasped and a sharp pain pierced my chest. Theo waited at

the corner of my bed, looking adorable in a hooded sweatshirt and jeans.

A grim expression splayed on his face. No, not grim. Angry.

"Theo." It came out a raspy whisper, but he heard me.

He looked at the floor. His jaw clenched.

My gratitude eclipsed my remorse. Before the fire, the last thing I'd told him was he was chasing a ghost he'd never catch. Who was I to explain his behavior when mine was questionable? No condolences for what he'd been going through. Instead, I'd ended whatever relationship we'd started. Now, here I lay at his mercy. He saved my life. "Thank you for—"

"Do you have any idea what you did?" He cut me off with his short, clipped words.

"I'm—"

He held up his hand, and I clamped my mouth shut. "Stella. Don't say anything. I need to speak and then I'll leave."

I waited.

"I asked you not to go near the building due to the imminent danger and you deliberately ignored my order. If I didn't come out to check on you when I did..." He shook his head and rubbed his stubbled jaw. "You're lucky your friend was there to tell me where you'd gone, or I wouldn't have reached you in time. I have never been angrier with anyone in my life. What you did put many of us at risk. I had to leave my post to find you."

My eyes filled. "I'm sorry."

"Not good enough."

His anger saddened me. I was foolish. "I needed to get into the shop." I began to cough, a painful, hacking bark that felt like it was coming from my hips. I leaned against my pillow. Everything hurt. He took a step toward me but stopped, shaking his head.

When I'd calmed, he said, in a slightly softer voice, "What the hell did you possibly need?"

I shook my head, trying to remember when I dropped the book. "The cat and a book."

He chuckled though there was no humor behind it. "A book. A fucking book. What the hell, Stella?"

"It was the last thing my father gave me. It's what I have left of him." Had. I must have dropped it at some point. "It doesn't matter."

I wanted to tell Theo I missed him, that I thought about him every day. I wanted to ask if he could forgive me for sending him away, but I didn't want to know the answer.

He kept to the foot of my bed, hands in his pockets. We eyed each other, neither speaking, until finally, he exhaled. "You're a lucky woman. If you weren't by the door, I might not have found you in time and that thought makes me crazy."

So, I *was* by the door.

How'd I get there?

My father.

"I wanted to see for myself that you were okay. And to yell at you."

"Mission accomplished."

He turned to leave and paused, holding the doorknob, staring at the floor until finally, he looked to me. "You know, you did the very thing that you sent me away for."

I tilted my head, confused.

"You put yourself in mortal danger. I never do that. Regardless of what you think, I follow rules and take precautions. I know what I'm running into. I've been trained for it, as opposed to you."

He was right. But his words were hard to swallow.

"What you said to me the last time, about my brother..."

"I'm sorry," I whispered.

"No." He gave a hard shake of his head, his jaw taut. "What you said to me was backward. I know with every breath I take that I did nothing to save him. And I don't run into fires with his face in my head anymore. But if I could save someone else's child or brother or sister, so they never feel the pain I live with every single day, then it's worth it. Even if it means losing you."

His silhouette didn't move. I wondered what was keeping

him here. He closed the door and returned to the foot of the bed.

"My wife got sick and died. That's why my marriage ended. I was devastated and didn't think I'd fall in love again. But four years later, you walked into an aquarium on a Monday afternoon and my world changed."

My eyes burned with grief for him, for his loss. "Why didn't you tell me?"

"You stay away from widowers, you said." He stared down at me, and I cringed. I did say that. How careless I was with my words. "We're both carrying shit, Stella, but you can't get through life without that happening. You take the good with the bad and work it out. You're so closed off you can't accept even that." He exhaled loudly. "Take care of yourself. Please. I miss you." The last words were barely a whisper. And then he was gone.

Through the window, the rising sun slipped between the open blinds. It wasn't my father's voice I heard. Those weren't my father's arms who protected me from harm.

It was Theo, who I sent away.

And he missed me.

CHAPTER 45

The apartments above the row of four shops on Gruber Ave. were uninhabitable. The fire had started by a faulty wiring in the apartment two floors above the nail salon, so that business and the dry cleaners were the only shops to have fire damage. The fire had been contained before reaching my bookshop or Philippe's salon. That's not to say our businesses were spared.

When allowed, Philippe returned to his salon to file an insurance report. Every day for the first week after I was released from the hospital, he checked the alley to look for Hemingway and every day, he came home with a face I couldn't bear to see. It took me another full week before I had the strength (mentally and physically) to return to Between the Covers. I still coughed but the antibiotics were working, and my follow-up appointment showed lung improvement. I was still exhausted but no longer sleeping sixteen hours a day.

I paused first in front of the dry cleaners, knowing my wedding dress was hanging limp, possibly burned, or charred behind the boarded window. Or perhaps it was a pile of ashes. Either way, I'd held onto it too long and ended up with nothing for it. A painful lesson.

My shop's front was boarded up as well and the place had an eerie, ghostly feel. Caution tape crossed the façade, but I was now allowed to go inside to assess the damage.

I crossed the tape and entered the dark shop which still held the haunting odor of smoke. Most of the books were soaked and frayed. I went immediately to the office and opened the alley door, hoping Hemingway would understand that I was looking for him. The alley was empty.

I picked through the aisles, praying I wouldn't come across the cat among the debris. I couldn't trust my memory of that night. Did I really let him out? As I searched, I realized the firemen would have already found him if he'd been stuck here.

There was nothing worth saving. My father's book was nowhere. I knew I wouldn't find it but was unable to stop trying.

The painted wall over the ruined couches and tables boasted the remnants of Gina's work, much of it intact, though darkened, appropriately matching the mood. I stared at the beautiful, intricate web in the center, the words, "Some Store" hovering over me, as if daring me to believe I could succeed in owning my own business. The 3D book wall that had gotten attention appeared to be melting, the floating books resembling sodden novel corpses.

I turned away. Back to square one. I dropped to the floor, my jeans soaking in water, soot, and grime almost immediately, and wondered if I'd ever be able to pull myself up.

The door opened, letting sunlight into the dark space. Gina walked in, dressed in cargo pants, a denim jacket, and that damned backpack. She surveyed the area, walked the shelves, occasionally pausing to touch a sodden spine.

"I don't do hospitals," she said, "or I would've stopped in."

"It's fine. Have you seen the cat?"

She walked the perimeter of the walls again. "No. I'm sure he's annoying another unsuspecting soul by now."

Oh, I hoped so.

She faced the book wall, as I did minutes ago. "I think you should add more LGBTQ shelves."

"Oh yeah?" I barely registered what she was saying, so caught up in my own distress.

"The shop should promote more indie authors, too."

"Mm-hm." Maybe insurance money could keep me afloat while I looked for work. I had been a good copywriter once.

"Also, we can start our own shop book club, instead of hosting other people's. Are you listening?"

I turned to my former employee. "I'll pay you for last week. I'll write you a reference to wherever you want to go. Anyone would be lucky to have you."

Her pouty face frowned. "I don't want to work anywhere else."

"That's going to be a problem."

"You have insurance. And that old guy will get some, too."

My landlord had already reached out. I was only responsible for my personal inventory and equipment. His insurance would cover the structural damage and cleanup. But I couldn't even fathom the loss of income I'd incur over the time it would take to fix the damage here. The smell alone was unbearable. And I could no longer lean on my wedding dress sale. I pulled a soaked book toward me and ran my fingers over the cover. I had to figure out my next step.

"You know," Gina said, "no one drinks tea in my neighborhood. They like their coffee black, usually, not that wussy way you drink it, covering up the taste with all that sugar and milk."

I finally looked her. "So, you're saying I can never drink coffee in your neighborhood?"

Gina rolled her eyes and exhaled. "I'm saying you'd have to make sure to keep a lid over your cup, so your customers don't see what a wuss you are when you take over that tea shop that closed down on my street."

I couldn't muster the energy to laugh. This girl thinks I can do this again? Is she high? "I'm out of the business, Gina. I could hardly afford to keep this place open."

"That's not true. We had a solid three months and growing. You were doing it."

I reached for another book. Where was the cat?

"What if you have an investor?"

I eyed her, wary. "What are you saying?"

"I'm saying, I'm offering to go in as a partner." She gazed around the dank space. "You're good at this. You would have taken this place somewhere. I'll go in halfsies."

I sat stunned for a moment, then shook my head. "Gina..."

"It doesn't make you weak to accept help. It doesn't mean you've failed. Like your friend sending the plumber, or that fireman pulling the kids in for reading hour. My God, Stella! You're the most stubborn person I've ever met. If you weren't so difficult, all of this would be easier! Think of what we can do."

I gripped the book in my hand. She stared down at me with that beautiful, pierced, poker expression. "That's the most optimistic thing you've ever said to me. Do you feel okay?"

She straightened her shoulders. "I met my quota for the decade."

"I don't know what I'm going to do," I said.

"Sure, you do. You're going to start again. No one loves books like you do. Except for me. The people here love you." Gina brought her cell phone out and showed me her screen. "Someone started a GoFundMe page for you. This is how much they raised so far."

My eyes filled. "What? I can't take people's money."

"They're *giving* it to you. No one is forcing them. We can get our inventory this way."

I shook my head in disbelief. "I'm uncomfortable with that."

Gina exhaled a wind of frustration and bent down to where I sat. "The community is speaking to you. They want an independent bookstore. They need a bookstore here. Without one, where is civilization?" She straightened. "Think about it, Stella. That's all I ask."

"Gina? Where did you get the money you're offering?"

She lifted her chin. "I sold some more paintings."

I searched for Hemingway for an hour after Gina left, before giving up.

At home, I climbed into bed and considered my options. Philippe brought me food and then climbed in next to me. I didn't ask him how he was doing now that the departure date for Rog's Paris move was imminent. And he didn't volunteer.

"She wants to partner with me and do this over again."

"Who?" Philippe moved a strand of hair from my forehead and shifted his position on my pillow.

"Gina."

"Well, look who's full of surprises. There's more to her than charcoal makeup. And?"

"A partner was never in my plans."

"What plans are these? You told me you opened your book-shop without forethought, that you quit your job and paid the first month's rent in one day." Philippe nudged me. "Did you enjoy having the shop?"

"Yes, but I don't know if I can do this again."

"You were happy every morning heading there. Even with your fledgling romantic life, you found happiness in that store. Surrounded by your books, doing what you were meant to do."

"I'm exhausted. This will be the third time in as many years that I have to start my life over."

He level-stared me. "You can't be exhausted. You're only thirty-seven."

"Thirty-six."

"Really?" His eyes roved over my face and neck. "Sweetie, more retinol before bed, k?" He clasped his hands behind his head. "I have a question."

"You have many."

"Shut up. Who thought up the 3D book wall?"

"I did."

Philippe waited.

"Well, Gina initiated an idea, and I built it from there. No, *we* built it together."

"And how did it feel?"

I thought of the evenings Gina and I had spent, hours into the night, putting our ideas onto the wall, how seamlessly we worked together, feeding off each other, and how satisfied we were when it was done.

"The wall was quite a showpiece."

I nodded. "It brought in a lot of business."

Philippe pulled his hand from behind his head and reached for mine. He squeezed it. "Two heads...always better, my dear. You are not an island."

"I…always thought I'd be able to do it on my own."

"It's not worse if you have a partner. You'll still be proud and maybe less stressed and more successful. And having a partner will allow you to enjoy a life outside of the shop."

Theo appeared in my mind. His face at my door, grimy and beautiful. One day, he'll show up at someone else's door.

"My shop is my life."

Philippe sighed and pulled himself off the bed. "It shouldn't be." At my door, he turned. "When did Gina come up with the wall idea?"

"When I was at my sister's." I smiled. When I'd finally agreed to let her close the shop without me. "Aren't you a clever one?"

He tipped his imaginary hat and walked out.

CHAPTER 46

On day twenty, I showered, dressed, and ate an overflowing bowl of Lucky Charms. Alone in my kitchen, I chewed while I scrolled through Facebook. Doug and Marcy were still accepting congratulatory posts and messages after their announcement. Again, that picture filled the screen, the one of Marcy holding her diamond-laden hand out to the photographer while Doug stared at her, enamored. For the first time in over a year, I didn't care what these people were doing. I've lived a lifetime since the morning of my wedding.

I typed, "Congratulations." Hit send. And then I unfollowed both so that we could all move forward.

As I was about to sign out, a post caught my eye. The heading: Bring Back Our Bookshop. Beneath the title was a picture of me in front of Between the Covers on opening day. I remembered the feeling that encompassed me the day I took the picture and put it on my website. Pride framed with fear, a picture that I'd carried inside of me all year. The post went on to say how the neighborhood took up a GoFundMe collection to help me reopen with a link to the page. There were four-hundred and seventy comments. Four-hundred-seventy. I hit the link to find that Joan, the woman who became a regular customer and friend, had made the biggest contribution. But who started it?

After drinking the sweet milk from the bottom of the bowl, I threw on sneakers and walked to my shop. I had several unheard voice messages on my phone. Karen. Bride-to-be and soon to be severely disappointed if she didn't already know what happened. Join the club, Karen.

I dialed her number. She answered on the first ring.

When I told her what happened, she was quiet on the other end. Then I heard her sniffling.

"Karen? I know it seems like this is a travesty, but it's only a dress. I'm sure you can walk down the aisle in a paper bag and your husband will beam with love. And if he doesn't, he's not the one."

She sighed in my ear. "He doesn't care what I wear. He just wants to marry me."

My heart twinged in envy. "He's a keeper. You're a lucky woman."

I'm not sure how long I lingered in front of the bookshop, staring at the boarded window and door, but at some point, Gina was next to me. Had she been here every day, waiting for me to come to my senses?

The answer was clear.

"I wouldn't use the tea shop," I said, still staring ahead.

She waited.

"We'll stay where we are. After all, the people…"

She nodded. Her hands clutched the handles of her backpack. I pointed to a hole in the corner of the canvas above her hip. "That's seen better days."

"Like everything."

Our heads angled together upward as if the answers to the reincarnation of the shop were on the roof.

"It's going to take a tremendous amount of work," I said. The idea unnerved me, but I had no choice.

"I'm not afraid of work."

I looked at her. "I know that better than anyone."

Gina shrugged. "When do we start?"

"I have no idea. I'll talk to the landlord, then we'll plan."

"Okay."

"Gina."

She waited.

"Thank you."

I felt a genuine smile bloom across my face for the first time in days. Gina turned to walk away but stopped. "Oh, I almost forgot." She shimmied her overused backpack off her slight shoulders, unzipped it, and pulled out a wrapped box. "Here."

"What is this?" I accepted her offering and stared at it.

"You have to pull the paper off to see it," she said, dryly. "Ever get a present before?"

I tore the simple, brown paper to find the corner of a shadow box. Intrigued, I ripped off the rest and let the wrapping drop on the ground as I stared in shock.

In the center of the boxed frame, *Charlotte's Web*, my twenty-nine-year-old worn, tattered treasure seemed to float. The faded colors of the cover were a strong contrast with the navy backing. My throat constricted with emotion. I turned to Gina, who had picked up the wrapping paper and was squeezing it into a tight ball.

"When did you…?"

"Four days before the fire. I thought for sure you'd say something when I took it, but you were so preoccupied that you didn't even notice it wasn't on the shelf. I was going to return it before you said anything. And, well," she shrugged. "I'm sorry. I was worried it would fall apart."

My eyes overflowed, and I clutched my gift, ignoring people passing. Gina watched me, biting the inside of her cheek. I went to hug her, but she moved out of reach. "Don't make me sorry I did that. Call me when you're ready to start." She walked away and turned. "If I don't hear from you tomorrow, I'll call you."

I remained rooted to my spot well after she disappeared.

Philippe walked through his salon, conferring with a man who took notes on a clipboard. The place looked surprisingly better than I'd expected. The vinyl floor was an easy replacement, and he'd explained the insurance would cover the new chairs and sinks. My business comprised of paper, a significantly harder resource to salvage. And my shop was closer to the fire than Philippe's.

Philippe noticed me and excused himself.

"Who's that?" I said.

He glanced at the man who was now looking up at the ceiling. "Rog hooked me up. He's a G.C. Going to help me make some changes I've been wanting to make. Figured now's a good opportunity to do it."

"How are you handling this so well? I want to cry every minute, and before this year, I never cried."

He pulled me to his thin chest. "Cry all you want, but eventually you must face it. Believe me, losing this is not nearly as devastating as losing my man. This can be replaced. But love?" He sniffed and pulled away, his long lashes dotted with salty pearls. Rog was leaving next week. "He's working tonight. I can't stand it. I already miss him."

"Come over. We'll have dinner."

"Whatcha got there?" He pointed to the shadowbox in my hands.

"A gift. From my partner."

He smiled. "It's nice."

"Yes, it is."

CHAPTER 47

I left Philippe to resume the search for Hemingway in the alley, praying he wasn't scared and knowing that I'd never abandon him. How long would I have nightmares about the fire? Would they ever go away?

I kept thinking about Theo, his expression at the foot of my hospital bed. How I'd wanted him to come closer to me, climb onto the bed and hold me like I so desperately longed to be held. Somehow, I knew that the problems of the world would dim in those arms.

Yet, my fear of the unknown pushed him away.

I felt as if only minutes had past when in fact, it was an hour, before I heard a strained mew and froze. Hemingway was tucked in a shadowed corner. I knelt and waited for him to approach me. He hesitated until I reached into my pocket and pulled out a baggie filled with tuna. While he ate from my hand, I pet his growing coat. He shivered. "How are you, buddy? I'm happy to see you."

He finished the contents of the baggie and brought his gorgeous green eyes to mine. "Mew," he croaked.

"Would you like to come home with me? I'm not very neat, but we don't have an office right now."

The cat nuzzled my hand with his head and circled my bent legs, pushing against them with his body, his loud purring a clear answer.

"Okay, then. It's decided. I'm going to lift you. Try not to freak out." I reached for him in what I hoped was a non-threatening way, in much the same way I'd reach for Gina. It was then that it hit me: how similar she and Hemingway were. I'd needed to earn the loyalty of both, and I did.

He allowed me to pick him up— he was lighter than I'd

imagined— but started to squirm and scratch at me when I moved away from his familiar area. I hurried into the first open store where I was given a cardboard box. With the top loosely closed so he could breathe, I carried him with my treasure from Gina hanging in a bag off my shoulder.

When I stepped into my apartment, we were greeted with a bright, citrusy aroma and the subtle, fragrant scent of white wine.

"Good God, you brought it home?" Philippe was in the kitchen holding a wooden spoon, his mouth in a frown when I put the box on the floor and lifted the lid.

"Not 'it.' Him." I leaned closer to the box and whispered loudly, "You remember my friendly neighbor, right, Hem?" I scratched behind his ears. The cat craned his neck from the box to look around. He'd stopped purring.

"What are you making?" I leaned over the odiferous pot and inhaled. Philippe struggled to stay in his apartment now that it was half empty. Rog had been spending extra time at the office, tying things up in preparation for his move, so my sad friend had been spending more time at my place, for which I was grateful. I enjoyed the company.

"Does our Super know about him?"

"Of course not. I didn't know he'd be here until about two hours ago."

Philippe stared at Hemingway in disgust. We watched the cat, his neck extended, lopsided whiskers twitching, until finally curiosity took over and he ventured from the safety of the cardboard box into the kitchen to sniff the corners of the room. He walked away to investigate the rest of the small apartment.

"How's the search going for a roommate?"

Philippe stirred the pan. "Not good. Met with a guy yesterday. Epic fail. No chemistry."

"You're not looking for chemistry, friend. You're looking for someone who's not too crazy and has an income."

"If I must share my space, sweetheart, I need chemistry. At present, the only person who makes my Boron hot is Rog."

"I've been thinking," I said.

"A scary thought."

I nudged his shoulder.

"I've been thinking something, too," he said.

"You go first."

Philippe put the wooden spoon on the rest and turned the flame low. "How about I move in here? Or you move in with me? We both have a second bedroom."

"You called it a closet. It can't be more than ten by ten. Which one of us would use it?"

He turned to the pot and resumed stirring. "You're right. It was a silly idea."

His profile masked his feelings. If he moved in with me, I wouldn't be alone. We'd talk and he'd cook like this, and we'd have coffee in the mornings and life would be one long sleepover. Maybe this would be enough for me. Friendship. It could be a nice life. It worked with *Will & Grace*. I'd even consider the small room.

Philippe brought the spoon to his mouth to taste the food. He sniffed, and it brought me back to reality. The idea was so appealing I almost said yes, *please stay with me*, because I needed a friend more than anything else right now.

Almost. I put my hand on his shoulder. "It's a lovely suggestion. And I would love nothing more than to share my space with you, but I have a better idea."

He laid his glossy greens on me.

"Go to Paris."

"What do you mean, go to Paris? That's a nonsensical idea."

"If I've learned nothing else in my life, it's that it's unpredictable. And short. You and Rog love each other. You have something special. He asked you to go, for Pete's sake. When are you going to get another chance to do something so remarkably irresponsible? It's almost poetic."

Philippe stared at me long and hard. On cue, the cat reappeared and rubbed himself against his leg, mewing and staring up at him until finally my skinny human friend spoke.

"What about you? I feel as if we just got started on something wonderful here."

"We did. We do. It's not going to change. You'll be home at some point. Or I'll visit. I've never been anywhere outside of the country. I've never been anywhere. Think about it."

I wrapped my arms around him and he coughed out a laugh. "Who are you and what did you do with my friend?"

I squeezed the tears from my eyes over his shoulder so he wouldn't see. "She's right here. Getting stronger."

CHAPTER 48

There's no better pick-me-up than time with my sister and her children. When I called Charlie, offering to bring dinner, she told me she'd already started cooking and they'd set a place for me. Charlie's welcoming committee did not let me down, and I dropped to the foyer floor to gather my niece and nephew up in my arms, squeezing their joy and innocence from them as if I could somehow ingest them by osmosis.

While Charlie added the finishing touches to her meal, I played dolls with Maddie and Myles sat on my lap. With each visit, he changes and grows and learns more words, his personality coming through, and I fall in love more deeply. If I can't have my own children, I feel fulfilled right here.

After eating, I bathed Myles and borrowed a shirt from my sister after helping him into his feetie pajamas. I hung up my own soaked blouse over the shower, checked in on the children, who were relaxed and zoning in front of the television, and went to find Charlie.

She was in the den with Lance, who must have come home while I was in the bathroom with Myles. I paused at the door and watched them. They faced each other on the couch, heads close, whispering. Lance reached up and gently circled her ear, touching the soft, downy hair close to her scalp. She gazed down. They held hands and talked softly until finally he kissed her and stood. I retreated so he wouldn't see me and waited until he was across the room before I walked in.

"Sir Lance-A-Lot."

"Hey." He gave me a full hug, and kissed my cheek. Then he left me with Charlie.

My sister seemed more like her old self, and I felt better than I had in days.

"What are the kids doing?"

I sat down next to her. "Watching *Bluey*."

She tugged at the shirt I wore, and I gave her a sheepish grin. "I hope you don't mind. Your son is a beast in the bath. Who taught him to kick like that? Soaked me through."

"His sister."

"Hmmph. Big sisters can be trouble."

She rested on the couch. "I hate that *Bluey*. Makes me feel inadequate. What parent can play with their children all day? It's unrealistic."

"That's why you made Myles. So, she'd have a playmate."

"It's why Mom made you."

"And aren't you the lucky one?"

"I miss *Dawson's Creek*," she said. "James Van Der Beek."

"I preferred John Stamos."

My sister turned toward me. "Weren't you supposed to marry him?"

I nodded. "It wouldn't have worked out. Too old."

She started to giggle, which made me giggle, and for several minutes, we were back to where we began, me and her, before everything. After a while, Charlie calmed down. "It's been a long year."

"Oh yeah? How so?"

We broke into another giggle fit. I reached over and touched the dark, soft hair barely covering her scalp. "You did good."

"*You* did good, sister. Fill me in on what's going on with you."

I updated her on the status of the shop, the offer from Gina, and my advice to Philippe while Charlie sat quietly, eyes fixed ahead.

"You're going to be fine," she said. "I know it." Then she reached for my hand and held it. "Thank you, Stella. You kept me up. I don't know what you told him, but you kicked Lance's ass, metaphorically speaking. You're strong, for a little thing. Stronger than you know."

"Lance told you?" My little outburst at the bar felt as if it happened in another lifetime. I really thought he'd keep our conversation between us.

"He tells me everything, Es."

That was the thing about marriage. Relationships. They were a mystery to me.

"Have you spoken to Theo?" Charlie said.

"Since the hospital?"

"You didn't see him at the hospital."

"I did," I said.

Charlie sat up. Shifted to face me and tucked her leg beneath her. "How do I not know that?"

"He showed up in my room. Yelled at me. Left." I shrugged like it was no big deal.

She waited, but I had no more to say.

"So, what next?"

"What do you mean? That's it. End of story," I said.

"He didn't try to convince you he's the one for you?" Charlie said.

"What are we? Two characters in a book? Expecting some happy ending? Life doesn't work that way."

"Says who?"

I gripped her hand. She was right. Her life was a love story. A tale of strength and hope, trials, and victories. What will my story be, I wondered? And how will it end? "I'm not you."

"No. You're you. Stella Michelle Duprey, a woman worth fighting for."

"He came to his senses and realized I'm a lost cause. He shouldn't have to fight for me. I should know he's perfect. But you know what? I couldn't see perfect if there was a neon sign pointing to him, saying, *Stupid— this guy's the one.* The fact that I walked away and the fact that he walked away, speaks volumes."

She sighed. "Strange. I'm usually pretty good at this. I thought for sure he'd come back. Maybe the chemo dulled my gifted intuition."

"It's for the best. I need to focus on rebuilding my life. That's my priority."

Charlie stared at me until I felt uncomfortable. I sighed. "Okay, *Mom*! Let's talk about you. What size boobs are you getting? D? Double D? You know, if you get double D's, you can say 'I double-D dare you' whenever you want and mean it."

"You're sick."

"This is news?"

"And don't change the subject. It's time to face your life. You've done enough for me. Do for you."

"I face my life every day. It's rubbed into my reality with every breath I take. I'm trying to survive."

Charlie squeezed my hand. "Do more than that. You owe it to yourself."

"I'll try."

"There is no try. There is only do."

I saluted her. "Yes, Yoda."

She chuckled. "I'm going for C cup. Perfect size. Lance is on board. He doesn't care. He told me he doesn't care if I don't get any at all."

A few moments passed and we both burst out laughing.

"He's lying," I said, wiping away the tears.

"I know."

CHAPTER 49

My conversation with Charlie weighed on my mind the next morning. So, after walking the streets of Brooklyn for a few hours, contemplating the changes to my life, I made a decision.

I waited on the stoop of Theo's apartment shortly before I thought he'd be getting off work. When he didn't answer his apartment door, I figured I had a fifty-fifty chance of catching him home soon, either getting ready for the evening shift, or ending the afternoon shift.

The weather was mild, so I sat on the middle step and thought of the past weeks since we had last seen each other, how much I'd changed, how the conversation with my mother lifted a burden I didn't realize I'd been carrying, and it opened my eyes at long last to why my father left us. I'll never stop missing him. Knowing that he was coming back for us when he died is something I'll have to work through, the pain and solace balancing precariously in my heart.

The setting sun cast a golden glow on the street when I remembered Theo told me the guys stayed at work after their shifts to talk about the day and wait for their relief.

Two subway stops later, I didn't have to wait long in front of the fire station.

He walked out, running his hand through his hair, a habit I've come to love. My heart sang a thumping song as he neared. He stopped when he saw me. I swallowed my nerves.

"Hi," he said. No smile. Guarded.

"Hi."

His jaw tightened and awkward silence fell between us. Theo was fine with it, waiting for me.

"How are you?"

He shrugged. "I'm here."

Now that I was in front of him, all that I wanted to say flew from my mind. I'd had a speech prepared and an hour to perfect it. His face, those eyes, his whole being, prevented me from all logical thought.

"I had a long day. If there's something you came to tell me…" He glanced up the street and then to me. "Otherwise, I'm going to head home." He took a step to pass me, and I pressed my hand to his chest to stop him.

"I came to say I'm sorry. For everything. For pushing you away and for making you risk your life for me. I'm sorry for all of it."

He seemed disappointed. I know I was. This was not what I wanted to say.

"Apology accepted." Silence. "Is that all?" he said. He glanced past me, down the block again, impatient.

"No. I've learned a lot about my past recently, and it's taken me some time to come to terms with this new information." I inhaled deeply. "I've never been in love. I thought I was, but I was wrong. When I'm with you, or think about you, my body has a visceral reaction I can't control. My heart seems to do what it wants. It's jarring and exciting and wonderful and I hate it."

He tried to cover a smile.

"I've been doing a lot of self-reflecting. It's not easy, believe me. I pushed you away because I wasn't ready for all that I feel when I'm with you. I'm scared. But the thought of life without you scares me more." I cleared my throat and looked around. "Well, that's what I came here to tell you."

His eyes held mine. I know what I'd admitted might not make a difference anymore, though I hoped it would, but I was happy I said it. He should know he did nothing wrong. He deserved to know.

He blinked, breaking our connection, and turned to a woman approaching us. She slowed, pulling her waving hand down as she saw us facing each other. Then she paused, as if not wanting to interrupt us. She was stunning. Dark brown hair, rosy blush against her pale complexion. She was a perfect complement to the fireman standing in front of me.

I went to leave and realized who the woman was. I relaxed and smiled. "Is this Denise?"

Theo made eye contact with the woman and gave a small wave. "Hey, Angelica." Then he turned to me. "No."

I nodded. He'd moved on. Right. Of course. If it were his sister, Sam would be with her.

I took a step away. "Bye, Theo. Take care of yourself."

Walking down the street, my heart shattered, sending shards of pain through my body as I realized that I'd blown whatever chance we had to repair the damage I'd caused. I waited until I'd turned onto the next block before wiping my eyes, leaving behind the first man who filled my heart.

Philippe was at my door when I got to the apartment. We walked in together.

"How are you?"

I nodded, not willing to repeat what happened right yet.

"I have news," Philippe said.

"Oh, thank God. Tell me something."

He pulled me to my couch and sat us down. "I thought about what you said." I scrunched my nose, trying to remember. Lately, I've been saying so many things. Philippe sighed. "You know, life's short. Take chances. Blah, blah, blah."

"I'm sure I sounded more eloquent."

"You know what I mean. Rog and I had a long talk last night."

"And?"

"I decided to go to Paris with him."

My stomach dropped to my feet. He's going. I do remember saying something so stupid. I threw my arms around him. "That's amazing!"

He pulled away to see my face. "Are you sure? Do you think I'm making a crazy mistake?"

"Definitely not! How does Rog feel?"

Philippe's cheeks turned rosy. He was doing the right thing. "Oh, my friend. I'm so happy for you."

"I bought a ticket and I'm going to help him move and to see if I can do it. I'm still going forward with the salon. Tommy's going to be my liaison with the G.C. and keep me apprised of progress. For all I know, I might not want to stay. But I love him so much I can't let him go without trying."

I put my hands on his flawless cheeks.

He leaned his forehead to mine. "You'll be okay, you know," he said.

I nodded, which forced his head to nod, too. "I will. I don't know what I'll do without our talks, or your cooking, or cleaning, but I'll be okay."

CHAPTER 50

Hello Friends,

I'd like to take this opportunity to express my sincere gratitude to you all for believing in the shop and in me, for your unparalleled generosity, for your love and patronage, kind words and visits as Gina and I work diligently to reopen Back Between the Covers in time for the summer. After all, summer is for reading!

We promise the new store will offer a diverse selection of gently used independent and traditionally published works.

And don't forget, if you want it, we will find it.

That's a promise.

Until then, I wish you happy reading!

Stella

Gina and I focused on getting the shop open. As promised, our landlord covered the structural expenses and cleanup. We hired professional cleaners to wash the walls and floors. We spent nights at my apartment drawing diagrams and discussed the logistics of where we'd put the various genres and where we would set up book discussion groups.

We made lists of the types of books we wanted to sell, prioritizing diversity to reflect the neighborhood clientele. We talked about selling book accompaniments as well: bookmarks, colorful book protectors, greeting cards, and anything else that the opportunity would present. We'd decided to repeat the 3D book wall since it had been so popular.

We worked well together, and I felt optimistic about our combined endeavor. Gina's boyfriend and his friends helped us to set up our new bookshelves I'd purchased from a bookstore that was going out of business on Long Island.

"That won't be us," Gina said when I told her where I'd found the wooden shelves.

"Right."

Mom and I had taken Charlie out to celebrate the end of her chemo. While on Long Island, I'd stopped into the bookstore near Charlie's house and noted a few indie authors and poets who'd donated their books. I emailed one poet who was receptive to doing a reading our opening week and two authors immediately responded, agreeing to do signings.

Amidst the chaos of painters and the plumber (to install our brand-new toilet and sink) Gina brought me to the office, surprising me with a fire-proof safe. "For your book," she said, "and other important papers we shouldn't lose."

She still wouldn't accept a hug. We were up to fist bumps. Baby steps.

I bought Hemingway a new bed, so he'd have a soft place to rest, knowing he belonged to the streets of the city and amid the tomes of time and not in my tiny apartment. I'd passed the dry cleaners each day, waiting for Ms. Roselli to return and re-open, but the space remained closed and boarded. I knew my dress was ruined, but I hoped her business could be salvaged.

Two weeks before our opening, a For Rent sign hung in the dry cleaner's window. Perhaps she returned home to be closer to her children. I hoped so. I passed The Closet, expecting a similar For Rent sign, but saw Jeffrey inside. He was hanging new dresses on a rack. I waved and he gave me a thumbs up.

One week before our grand opening, we were ready. Gina brought in a bottle of champagne to celebrate.

"Shouldn't we wait for the opening?" I said.

The cork was freed from the bottle, emitting a pluck and sizzle as airy bubbles frothed over the lip. "We'll have a bottle then, too." She poured the bubbly into two paper cups. "You know what I noticed?"

I stared out to the street, distracted. "What's that?"

"You haven't been on your phone in a while."

I turned to her. "What do you mean? I use it every day."

"You haven't gone on that godforsaken site. You know, to stalk your ex."

"I unfollowed him."

She raised her thick, black eyebrows and nodded in approval. Then she shook her head.

"What?"

"You still seem sad."

"Sad? Are you kidding? I'm thrilled." I gestured around our new place. "Look at what we did!"

She watched me until I turned from her, pretending to take in the shop. It was more beautiful than before. We'll succeed. I felt it in my bones. Gina and me. A team. As happy as I was to be in a partnership—something I'd stopped believing I'd be a part of—I was scared shitless. People are unreliable. I was putting my faith in this young woman, and she knew it.

I was sad for unrelated reasons. But I was hopeful.

Gina lifted her glass. "To us." She looked around. "To living our best life."

"To us."

As we sipped, a fire truck roared past, its siren screaming, horn blaring. I went to the newly decorated window, craning my neck to watch the taillights down the street, the uniformed figures holding onto the rear until they were out of view.

CHAPTER 51

While planning the opening of our new store, Gina and I learned from my past mistakes and made some changes. We enlarged the children's section and added more small chairs for our Saturday reading hour. We added a full section dedicated to independently published authors and poets and unrepresented genres. We agreed to shelve single copies of most titles to avoid excess inventory, at least for the first year. After that, we'd reassess.

We repeated the seating area in the corner of the store for book group meetings and for respite from the outside. Gina brought in an old sectional that we split to fit the corner, and I found colorful pillows and another coffee table at Goodwill that fit well.

Shabby chic all over again. It was the perfect reading hideaway.

Gina used her social media prowess to spread the word about our reopening, and I updated the website, telling our story and sharing our gratitude for this amazing community who pulled together to save a bookshop.

The grand opening of Back Between the Covers occurred on a rainy Saturday in August. I insisted to Gina that this was a good sign. Readers love the rain. Who stays in to read on a gorgeous day? Sunny days are for hiking or day-tripping or lunch.

"Or shopping," Gina added, as we walked through the store one last time before I turned the *Come In! We're Open!* sign.

My chalkboard announced:

Welcome Back Between the Covers!
Come in, cozy up, and read

My mom showed up, of course, as well as Charlie, Lance, and the kids. Charlie brought trays of pastries and cookies for guests. I poured thirty mimosas and positioned them on a tray near the register.

Gina's boyfriend came in late morning with a new tattoo along his neck of a quote from a poet I didn't immediately recognize:

> *The past shouldn't be feared*
> *for it guides our future.*

Wise words from the cartoon, Moana.

He was pierced but not to the extent of his girlfriend, and he had an infectious laugh. Her book group also showed up. I was surprised to note the members seemed very much like me: various ages, very few tattoos between them, khaki-clad, button-down blouse-wearing, light makeup-faced women. And two men. My business partner continued to keep me on my toes.

Gina presented me with a gift at the opening, an extravagant coffee machine that she swore made better coffee than the deli I'd so adored. She was upset when I suggested we leave the machine in the store for customers who might want to make a cup while browsing. At her insistence, I reluctantly agreed to put it in our newly decorated office, where I kept her gift.

She unwrapped her new black backpack and turned it over in her hands, assessing the various pockets and zippers. I'd searched for the perfect replacement to her beloved but scrappy one and found it at an Army/Navy thrift shop, nearly new.

"When I saw this, I could only see you wearing it."

She nodded and her face broke into a beautiful smile. It was the best gift I'd ever bought.

In addition to the wall over the reading nook, we'd picked a perfect spot for her to paint, directly across from the cash register, so passersby would be able to see her creation through the large picture window from the street. She'd finished it only a few days ago. A near replica of the masterpiece she'd painted before the fire, only this time there was a minor difference; a fireman's hat was hidden in the leaves of the Giving Tree which ran up the side of the wall. An homage to the person who saved my life. I'd gasped when I caught it, surprised, but left it alone, which I knew she appreciated. My eye was drawn to it every time I looked at that wall.

Like her, it was extraordinary.

I still felt pangs of sorrow that she and her father didn't speak, that he couldn't see how talented his daughter was, how she might regret the time that passed without contact until it was too late. It was her life, her choice. But, as a friend, I could still offer suggestions based on experience.

Gina's enthusiasm grew as we discussed plans for the shop. Moments of joy shined through her tough exterior and knew I'd made the right decision.

At one point during late morning, the shop was filled with customers, sipping from flutes, noshing on miniature *petit fours*, and most importantly, perusing the shelves. Gorgeous spines lined the faux mahogany, made possible by the onslaught of contributions. I still had money left over for a rainy day. And there would be rainy days.

My sister sat on the floor of the children's section, reading *Babar* to her children, who sat on either side of her, enraptured, and I realized there are so many layers of bravery. I was stronger than I thought I could be. Charlie and Marion, too. I followed proudly in a line of brave women.

"Hey." Gina frowned at me. "Are you going to stand here like a statue all day, or would you like to take these people's money?"

Joan showed up midday, and I pulled her aside from the purchase line.

"Thank you for your contribution. It was too generous."

She hugged me. "A mere pittance for your help and support, Stella. You were here when I needed someone most. There's no price for that."

I tightened my hold on her. "The person who started the fund is anonymous."

Joan pulled away. "It wasn't me. I wish I could take the credit. Anyway, this place is even more perfect than it was." She returned to the line to pay for the pile of books in her arms.

"Gina, special friend's discount for our friend."

Gina nodded. "Got it."

I was restocking books when two hands covered my eyes from behind me. My heart thumped violently in my chest until I registered the fingers over my face were thin, soft, and smelled like Gruyere cheese. I yelped and spun around, right into Philippe's arms.

"What are you doing here! When did you get in?" He looked oh so suave in his dark blue linen suit and cream T-shirt, his dark hair slicked smooth from his forehead. "God, Paris looks good on you."

"I know, right? I'm a beast." He fluttered his long lashes and smiled.

I peeked over his shoulder. "Where's Rog?"

"Still in France." He shot me a dry glance. "Always working."

"Always?" My phone was filled with photos of Philippe and Rog's weekend travels. In all our texting and emails, my friend had not let on that he'd be returning.

A grin. "Okay, not *always*. I had to come home to see my girl in her new digs." He made a full circle, looking around the shop and then returned to me. "Fab. Like you."

I leaned into him. "It means so much that you're here."

"I know."

I laughed. "How long are you staying?"

"I'm not sure. I'm going next door after I leave you. I have a little business to discuss over there."

"Business?"

"I'm going to sell the salon, stay with my boy in the city of lights. I don't care what anyone says, those Parisians need *moi.* I'm applying for a work visa and plan to beautify the city. When I'm done, we're going to come back together."

"And then?"

He shrugged. "Who knows? You know what? I love that I don't know. It's so damn exciting."

I barely recalled the hours that passed. What I did remember was we had a steady influx of customers, which was incredible. Even Gina thought business was too good to be true, but I assured her we would do even better. After my family and Philippe left, I took my late lunch to the office where Hemingway kept vigil. As he and I dined on my liverwurst sandwich, I thought about how far I'd come since last year and how far I had yet to go.

It was the best tasting liverwurst sandwich I'd ever eaten.

Gina poked her head into the office. "Someone is here to see you."

Butterflies took flight in my belly. Up front, a woman around my age waited for me. I disguised my disappointment with a smile.

"Can I help you?"

"Are you Stella?"

"I am."

Her face broke open and she held out her hand. "Olivia Connelly."

It took a second for me to recognize the name and put it into context. When I did, I inhaled sharply, and her smile grew wider. "I'm so thrilled to meet you!" She was the author of the indie book I'd been recommending for the past several months. "I'm a huge fan!"

Olivia put a hand to her chest, clearly moved. "I'm a fan of yours as well. A reader contacted me after she'd read my book. She told me it was on your Top Picks table for weeks and wouldn't have found me if not for you."

I preened. "It's a treasure. I can't wait to read your next one."

"The woman who contacted me is an influencer and posted about it on her sites. I'm selling more in a day than I sold over three years. I was picked up by a New York publisher and they contracted me for two more books. I've never allowed myself to dream this would happen. And I have you to thank."

My eyes welled. "You earned it. Would you be interested in doing a book signing here with your next release?"

"I'd be honored. But first, I want to warn you of a future influx of business. I'm being interviewed on the *Today Show* and I'm going to promote your shop."

Gina and I couldn't stop talking about Olivia's visit as we cleaned after closing. We were giddy. Falling into our well-rehearsed routine, we had the shop in top shape in no time. Gina put away her new carpet sweeper (another gift from me) and returned up front.

"The author started the GoFundMe for you," she said.

"How do you know?"

"I asked."

"She admitted to it?"

"She didn't deny it. She put her finger to her lips asking me not to tell."

"But you're telling me."

She locked her eyes on mine. "My loyalty is to you, Stella."

Gina went home with her boyfriend, who'd returned to meet her. I watched them walk down the street, hand in hand, and thought of Theo, wondering what he was doing, if he was dating that woman I'd seen in front of the fire station, hoping he was happy. Hoping he was safe.

Philippe texted me.

Well?

Me: Success!

Philippe: As I knew it would be. ☺

I let out a happy sigh as I typed.

> Me: I don't know how to thank you for coming home for me.

> Philippe: You can start by taking me to dinner.

> Me: Free tonight?

> Philippe: No. Visiting my mom. How about tomorrow night?

I smiled.

> Me: I'd love nothing more.

> Philippe: I know. Are you home?

I took several moments scanning our shop. Warm volumes, waiting to be read. The book wall. Gina's paintings. Yes. I am home.

> Philippe: Heh lo?

Laughing, I replied:

> Me: Still at the shop. ☺

> Philippe: Perfect. xoxo

In no rush to leave, I folded onto the couch and put my feet up, hugging myself. I was doing this again. I couldn't believe I was doing this again. This time I had a partner. A friend. Money. The cat sidled onto the cushion next to me, his purring the only music playing. I scratched under his chin.

Never give up, girl.

I closed my eyes. Charlie looked good today. Almost like herself. She and Mom took the children home, Mom mentioning her dance class tonight. Her skin had a glow about her. She really was a beautiful woman. I wondered how I'd missed that.

A blaring horn outside startled me into movement. Hemingway jumped to the floor, gave me an extra purring circle of gratitude, and waited by the office door. I let him out and he sauntered down the alley, his tail aloft.

"Make good choices, buddy. See you tomorrow."

Rear door secured and locked, lights and music turned off, I walked through the shop, pausing at my father's book, nestled beautifully in a shadow box above the register. I was thankful to Gina for the gift, but it wouldn't be there long. I was going to want to touch it, read the inscription on the inside cover, smell the memory of my youth. Maybe one day soon, I would do it without accompanying pain and regret.

I was a few feet from the window and shrieked in surprise, pressing my hand over my heart.

CHAPTER 52

Outside, framed by the picture window, Theo frowned. He mouthed, *Sorry.*

I unlocked the door and let him in. He wore faded jeans and a navy T-shirt, his chestnut hair finger-combed, and his eyes were on mine. He was a sight, there was no denying it. But what was he doing here?

"I didn't expect to see you." Though I had hoped all day.

He put his hands in his pockets and turned a full three-sixty. "How'd it go?"

"We did well."

"Good for you, Stella."

He held onto that frown as he walked near the shelves, touching spines, and moving on. My whole body thrummed. My heart lurched in my chest. It'd been three months and twelve days since I'd seen him.

He circled the store, pausing a long time at the 3D book wall, and returned to me. "I've been thinking a lot about what you said that day." I opened my mouth to speak, and he held his hand up, stopping me. "Stella, I love my job. I'm not going to change who I am or what I do. I'd never ask that of you." His eyes held mine. "Is that something you can accept?"

"But, that woman..."

He looked confused until he understood I was asking about the beautiful woman who had met him at the fire station when I was there last.

"That was Frankie's wife."

"Oh." He'd let me believe she was there for him.

"I was still angry. Now, please answer me. Is that something you can accept?"

The thought of knowing what he was running into every

time he'd leave me made my stomach physically ache, but not being with him hurt more. "I'll always be afraid. I don't know if that feeling will ever go away."

Theo seemed to consider this. "I never thought love was possible for me again. Never thought I'd find someone who made me feel better about life." He leaned toward me, as if sharing a secret. "I've wanted to be with you from the first moment I saw you. I'm enamored with your compassion, the way you treat everyone around you, the depth of love you have for your family." He paused. "I'm slightly horrified by the way you can eat a pizza slice in three bites or slurp the dirty milk at the bottom of your cereal bowl, but these add to the mystery that is Stella."

I dropped my gaze to the floor as warmth bloomed beneath my skin.

He rubbed his chin. "You said you didn't know what genes you inherited. I do. Empathy. Kindness. Resilience. In the months I've known you, it's clear."

He put his hands on my face forcing my eyes up to his. "You'll never be compared to anyone else. You are brave and silly and awkward, and I want to be with you. I'm not going to walk away. Besides, you're a bit reckless. You need watching over."

The words, foreign to my heart, drifted down, settling into me.

"I've missed talking to you, Lucky Girl," he whispered as he leaned in to kiss me. I wrapped my arms around his neck, my fingers gloriously sifting through his hair. He pulled me close, hugging me so tightly, my entire body relaxed, unraveling the taut coil of disquietude that had been wrapped around me for years.

We parted. I wiped my eyes and laughed.

"What's so funny?"

"I was thinking this would be the perfect time for music to play us out, like in a movie."

He glanced out the window. "There's no sunset today, so that plan is shot."

I'd stopped believing in a happy ending, but Lord if this didn't feel like it would rival any book on my shelves.

His face took on a serious look. His hands held my arms. "There are going to be tough times, Stella. But trust that I'll stay and fight for you. For us."

I leaned into him and rested my cheek against his chest. I felt his heartbeat, solid and consistent, and squeezed my eyes. "I'll try. I promise I'll try."

Outside on the sidewalk, Theo said, "Do you have to go right home?"

"What do you have in mind?"

"I need to show you something."

I raised my eyebrows. "I've seen it already."

"I'm serious." The determination in his voice and his humorless expression made me uneasy. What could he want to show me that would cause him to be so somber?

He was parked down the street and we drove the few blocks to his fire station.

"Dinner?" I asked. I glanced at my watch, noting the time. Too late for dinner.

"No." Theo parked and jumped out of the car. He was at my door, taking my hand before I stepped from my seat. "I'll take you to dinner after, okay?"

He brought me directly into the garage and turned on the lights illuminating the resting trucks and shelves. Light shone from behind the doors to the living area.

"Are we going in?" I asked, confused as Theo pulled my tote off my shoulder and hung it on a hanger.

"No," he said. "Stay here."

He walked to a nearby closet, and I decided to keep my mouth shut until I understood our purpose or figured out why Theo was acting peculiar. For the life of me, I had no idea what we were doing here, but he seemed to be on a mission.

He came to me, carrying huge pants with attached suspenders, a mesh thing, and a fireman's jacket, black with reflective safety strips around the wrists, waist, and across the middle, which he laid at my feet. "Wha…?" He held up his hand, went back to the closet and returned this time with boots, a helmet, and an oxygen canister, placing them all down beside the other stuff already on the ground.

"What are you doing?"

He ran his hands through his hair before positioning the pants over the boots, directly in front of me.

"Step into these. Please," he added when he saw my reluctance.

I looked down into two large, gaping holes and bit my lip, peering at him. He nodded and waited. I did as instructed. He pulled the pants up my body, gently putting the suspenders on my shoulders. He stepped back in thought and then reconfigured the suspenders, so they crossed my torso.

"Better," he said to himself.

"If this is some strange sex fetish thing you firemen are into, I should warn you, I don't think I'm into it." I felt foolish, feeling like an emaciated Santa in his suit. The pants billowed around me. The boots reached to my knees and the toe cavity was cavernous, even with my shoes on.

"Lift your leg," he said, ignoring what I said.

I tried to pick up one leg but struggled against the weight of the pants and boot. "They're heavy."

"That's because they have three layers: the outer shell, a moisture barrier, and a thermal barrier. The boots are rubber with a steel toe." He lifted the coat and put it on me from behind. He held my shoulders when I swayed under its weight. It must weigh over ten pounds.

"You okay?"

I nodded, beginning to understand our purpose here. My eyes filled, but I didn't attempt to stop them. No more holding my emotions in check. Let him see me. All of me. He faced me directly, looking into my eyes, then to the ground as if considering acknowledging my reaction.

But he didn't.

"Good." He let go, and I struggled under the clothes. He

grabbed my arms again and cracked a smile for the first time all evening.

"It's so heavy," I said. I pulled my arms up a few inches to see the tips of my fingers peeking out from the sleeves.

"You're the tiniest person ever to wear this. At least, in my presence."

"Are these yours?"

He shook his head. "I'm going to let go now, okay?" He placed a thick, netted covering over my head and adjusted it so my face was open, and I could breathe.

"Theo," I said, but he put a finger over his lips, and I stopped.

"I'm going to put something over your face, but only for a minute. Do you trust me?" he said softly.

"Yes." I closed my eyes and felt him place straps on my head, shimmying them down until my face was covered with some sort of mask. It was uncomfortable and I felt claustrophobic, breathing in my own exhaled breath. When I thought I couldn't withstand anymore, he strapped something heavy onto my back so that I had to widen my legs to keep balanced. Finally, he slid gloves onto my hands and over my forearms.

"Open your eyes."

I did and he put the black helmet on top of my head. I felt completely trapped in this outfit, weighed down by the cumbersome uniform as I tried to look around through the mask which covered my entire face. My breath sounded deep and coarse and not like my own. Darth Vader came to mind.

"Stella, you are completely covered. The pants and jacket you're wearing are made of a flame-retardant material called Nomex. The netting, also made of Nomex fabric, called a hood, protects your head and neck from flame and heat. The mask allows you to breathe in a burning building. You're carrying a tank of oxygen, giving you four hours of time. The helmet protects your head from falling debris and high heat."

I felt foolish, barely able to keep myself upright under the weight of what had been added to my body. But Theo's face held no humor. This was not a joke or his idea of fun. This was his life, and he was trying to explain it to me.

"When I go to work, this is what I wear. This is what will allow me to return to you. But keep in mind, that even with all this protection, with all the training and experience I've accrued, things can happen out of my control, just as it can to anyone else, anywhere else. Do you understand?"

I nodded as tears trailed down my cheeks, which felt weird beneath the netting.

"Do you trust me when I tell you I'll do everything I can for you? Because I need to make sure you understand. I need you to be okay with this."

I nodded again.

"Say it."

I sniffed. "Luke, I am your fathe…"

He crossed his arms.

"Yes. I understand."

His eyes sought mine through the mask. "Okay," he said. "All right." He pulled the helmet from my head and placed it down on the ground. Then he started to pull the straps over my head but paused. "Close your eyes."

I felt him lift the heavy netting from my neck and face, left moist with heat and tears, freeing me to breathe in deeply. It felt good to be out from the confines of the mask and wrap. I don't know how these people do it. I can understand why, I think. It takes a special soul to go through all of this to save strangers. A special soul. And he loves me.

I opened my eyes to find him watching me carefully.

"You good?"

"I'm more than good."

Theo pulled the tank off, the jacket, boots, and finally, lifted me easily from the holes in the pants.

"I'll take you to dinner now," he said.

"Maybe I'll be a firefighter. What do you think?"

"You can do anything you want."

And then he kissed me.

CHAPTER 53

Eighteen months Later

I passed the Macintosh apples and went for the Honeycrisp, rummaging through the bin, humming to *Do You Hear What I Hear?* My scarf was held out of my way. Honeycrisp were on sale this week, still more expensive than the Macintosh, but sometimes we had to splurge. Right? I picked a dozen. I lifted my head searching for the navel oranges.

"They're over there," Theo said, dropping my scarf so he could grab the apples I'd picked and put them in the cart.

"Perfect."

We piled several oranges into our cart, and he pushed it further into the produce department, pulling cucumbers, onions, and peppers as I picked up a bushel of potatoes. Tonight, we were going to try a new meal. Theo's goal: to get more vegetables into my body.

He started to pass the cereal aisle, when I pulled him to turn, the cart's wheels squeaking in mild protest.

"Stella…"

"This is non-negotiable." I tossed a large box of Lucky Charms into the cart.

He put his hand on the back of my neck, exposed now with my new, chic haircut, and pulled my face close to his. "Bran, at least?" he whispered. "You're eating for more than yourself, you know."

I laughed and leaned in for a kiss. "Oh, I know. He loves Lucky Charms."

"He?"

"She?"

I rested my hand on my growing belly. Theo kissed me again. When we parted, I caught a woman watching us, a look of disgust I'd once worn myself.

Believe me, I wanted to tell her, *it's better than it looks.*

Instead, I offered my warmest smile and let Theo lead me out of the aisle.

At the checkout stand, Rhonda began to scan the food while we loaded the belt. Theo helped to bag while I dug out my coupons. You couldn't be too frugal. And it was free money. She lifted the large container of yogurt and handed it to Theo. He didn't notice the small smile on her face as she finished our order.

But I did.

ACKNOWLEDGEMENTS

I am deeply appreciative to each of the people listed below, who never fail to offer help, advice, opinions, support, and friendship.

My editors, Veronica Jordan and Kyra Wojdyla–Thank you for your insight and thoughtful suggestions on how to strengthen Stella's story.

Gina Ardito, editor, author, and friend, thank you for your unwavering support of *Lucky Girl* from the beginning and for always being available to me.

My writing partner and friend, Suzanne McKenna Link–I'm grateful for your input, line editing, and too many re-reads of Lucky Girl. I cherish our conversations and still thank my lucky stars for meeting you at the East Meadow Public Library all those years ago.

Suzanne Fyhrie Parrott, of First Steps Publishing–publisher, cover designer, beta reader, author, and friend—Thank you for your uncensored feedback, your inimitable book covers, formatting expertise, advice, humor, friendship, and long, meaningful conversations.

My beta readers help to make every story a little better. I can't adequately express my gratitude for the time you give me, your thoughtful, honest feedback, and your friendship: Valerie Dietrich, Theresa Buonocore, Cristina Tagliaferri, Eileen Nieves, Elaine Trumbull, Cathy Schembri, *Booked For Drinks*, of course: Sue Moran, Liz Tompkins, Mara Kelly, Patty Maletta, Kerri Messina, Eva Rizzi, and Deb Luoni, and my lovely cousin, Sandra Hogan.

Monica Carlsen, Suzanne Guacci, and Katie Mittelman–who knew me before I knew myself and have been supporting me since.

Nora Katz, old friend and survivor, who shared her story and patiently answered all my questions over Harvest Grain and Nut pancakes at IHOP all those years ago–I know it took me a while to get back to this, but I never forgot what you told me. Thank you for making sure I got it right, and for your generous feedback. Any mistakes are mine. You're my hero.

Janice McQuaid, survivor and friend, who generously shared her own story over wine. Your strength and openness are truly inspiring.

To my husband and sons–who are my world, and a constant source of love, kindness, and compassion (all with a dash of humor).

A note: *Where I've Been and Where I'm Going* does not exist, nor does the author, Olivia Connelly. The logline Stella used when describing it was borrowed from my own debut novel, *Both Sides of Love*.

This is the first book released into the world without my favorite reader. Mom, I know you're proud of me. You've said it enough to last my lifetime, and I thank you. I'll love you forever.

And Uncle Jimmy, who left us this year, too, I will miss you and our book conversations.

To you, dear reader—thank you for spending time with me. My gratitude knows no bounds.

I hope we meet again.

Kimberly

ABOUT THE AUTHOR

Kimberly Wenzler is the award-winning author of *Seasons Out of Time*, *The Fabric of Us*, *Letting Go*, and *Both Sides of Love*, as well as dozens of very short stories about life, love, and family on her blog. Kimberly's quest to explore complex family relationships and love continues to fuel her passion for writing Women's Fiction and Contemporary Romance. She lives on Long Island, New York, with her husband, two sons, and their charming, goofy pup, Archie.

Lucky Girl is her fifth novel.

Connect with Kimberly:

www.KimberlyWenzler.com

www.facebook.com/kimberlywenzler

Both Sides of Love

2022 Readers' Favorite
Silver medal winner in Women's
Fiction

2019 IAN Book of the Year Awards
for Women's Fiction Finalist

Beth has just come face to face with a secret past that could tear her life apart.

Every day, Beth Butler is reminded of the accident that left her emotionally and physically scarred. Uncomfortable in public, she devotes her time and energy to caring for her husband and child. To help her out of her isolation, her husband convinces Beth to attend a meeting at her daughter's school.

Secluded at the back of the room, Beth is surprised when gorgeous and outgoing Noreen White extends a hand in friendship. The two form a close bond and Beth starts to feel a sense of happiness and solace long missing from her life. As their relationship blossoms, Beth comes face to face with her past and is torn between maintaining her secret or confiding a truth that could tear both her friendship and family apart.

Both Sides of Love explores the power of friendship, the beauty of true love, and one woman's struggle to choose. Candid, humorous at times, and full of surprises, it is **a must-read for anyone who has ever loved, lost, and loved again**.

Letting Go

The Buchanans are living an idyllic life on Long Island. Max is a successful author, Lucy is his supportive stay-at-home wife, and their only child, Sammy, is the center of their world.

On February 1, 2007, their lives change forever.

A year later, Max is hiding behind writer's block—shuffling through daily life with minimal effort while eight-year-old Sammy devises his own process of dealing with his upturned world. His secret conversations with his mother give him the strength to adjust to his new life and new family dynamic.When trouble at school brings Max and Sammy's teacher together, Max is torn between awakened feelings of need and desire and the love he still harbors for his wife. Sammy forms a closer bond with Benjamin, the troubled teen across the street, who suffers from the pain of his past and plays a dangerous, illegal game. And Lucy, watching as her family unravels, is helpless. Or is she?

In Wenzler's second novel, *Letting Go* tells the heartwarming story about a mother who refuses to leave her child, and as she watches her husband begin a new life, must figure out how to hold on and when to let go.

The Fabric of Us

On the eve of Olivia Bennet's fiftieth birthday, she and her husband, Chris, toast to the next stage of their lives. Their children are settled; Ella is married and planning a family and Nick is starting his senior year at college.

After thirty years of sacrifices and struggles for their family, it is finally time to do all the things they've dreamed to do as a couple.

Always unpredictable, life has other plans for the Bennets when Olivia gets shocking news that threatens all that she and Chris have built together

Alternating between the past and present, *The Fabric of Us* beautifully unfolds the layers of a devoted marriage, exposing an interwoven thread of secrets and consequences that threaten to unravel a relationship once believed to be built on love, trust and faith.

Seasons Out of Time

Newly separated empty-nester Heather Harrison knows how to answer difficult everyday life questions. After all, being an advice columnist is a job she's excelled at for fifteen years. **But what would Dear Abby say about Heather's romantic interest in a younger man?**

After years of a lonely, failing marriage, a man nearly two decades younger challenges Heather to live. But along with the excitement of the unconventional romance comes the negative backlash of others. And a secret that may shatter her.

A journey of self-discovery awaits. Will Heather be brave enough endure it?

Seaplace Publishing
Northport, New York

www.KimberlyWenzler.com

**BY
KIMBERLY WENZLER**

Both Sides of Love

Letting Go
Love Story for Sammy

The Fabric of Us

Seasons Out of Time

Lucky Girl
Shelf-Life of a Single Woman

*Available everywhere
books are sold*

www.ingramcontent.com/pod-product-compliance
Lightning Source LLC
Chambersburg PA
CBHW050007120726
47903CB00006B/1669